M16

The Veiled Wolf

Maria Johnson

The Veiled Wolf

Olympia Publishers
London

www.olympiapublishers.com
OLYMPIA PAPERBACK EDITION

A CIP catalogue record for this title is
available from the British Library.

ISBN: 978-1-78830-390-3

First Published in 2019

Olympia Publishers
60 Cannon Street
London
EC4N 6NP

Printed in Great Britain

Dedication

"For my Nana, whose love of reading inspired me to read and to write"

"Praise my soul the King of Heaven,
To His feet thy tribute bring,
Ransomed, healed, restored, forgiven,
Who like me His praise should sing?"

Part One

Chapter One

I could perceive from the shadows around me, without needing to look up at the sun, that the hour was growing late. The grass, once vivid in the daylight, had softened and developed into a darker shade. The rocks either side of me grew ever more imposing in the strange, obscuring half-light. I kept having to refrain from pacing as my hand ever clutched the hilt of my blade.

We were at the bottom of a narrow valley, the shape of which I always distrusted. I became all the more frustrated as the blazing golden orb descended, all but fading from view. I knew it would scarce be twilight before night came. Soon all daylight would disappear completely, its absence further transforming the landscape around us into more twisted, gloomy versions.

I surveyed again the band of soldiers that were with me, numbering two hundred or so. Their countenances were impassive, as was mine. Many years of serving in Gaeson's army had taught me that discipline. I raised my arm to run a hand through my auburn hair and as I did so, one of the remnant rays of the sun glimmered on my armour, as if reminding me once again of my station and rank.

My horse, Epos seemed once again to grow agitated, for it seemed she cared for our present location no more than I did. I took the few steps to be beside my faithful companion and leant my arm down to stroke her neck; as usual this seemed to calm her.

"It won't be long now, girl," I murmured gently. As soon as I uttered this, I heard footsteps. I turned rapidly, my hand drawing slightly my sword as my heart rate quickened. I longed for it to be friend rather than foe and relaxed a little as John and Aife rounded the corner and came into view. I was pleased to see two of my oldest friends well, but not all tension had dissipated at being left in such a vulnerable state.

"Apologies, Your Highness." John bowed swiftly as he spoke. "There were two Bernician guards who blocked our path. They did not discover us, but we had to wait for them to leave." His breathing was a little heavy, I guessed they must have run back most of the way in order to travel back in what little of the day survived.

"For the moment, we are undetected, my lord," Aife said now, her breath also fractionally shorter. "They seem unaware of our presence. It would be safe to move forward."

"That is good news," I answered, my heart lightening further. "Let us make haste to leave this place and make camp before we march for Klumeck. Lead the way," I ordered. They both bowed and turned to mount their horses. Swiftly I set off, spurring Epos on a little so that I might ride with them.

"Sorry, brother," John whispered, as I came alongside them. "We had intended on coming back sooner, but—"

"Don't worry," I replied, as we rode quietly along the valley, "you were not that late returning." In truth, they had only left our company for an hour or two. It was just the wait had seemed far longer than that. I raised my head, finding I had to squint to see anything. In the wake of the sun, the twilight was fading even quicker than I had estimated. Two or three lanterns were lit to guide our path. I prayed they would not make us an obvious target, but there was nothing else for it unless we wished to travel blindly, which could be treacherous.

"How did my uncle's kingdom look?" I questioned, turning my head to my friends. In the near darkness, I could barely make out their features, so I could not tell whether the news would be good or ill.

"Much the same as when we last saw it, my lord," Aife answered. The image of that blazing wall of fire now blurred past in my mind's eye. Though most had managed to flee, I could still see the corpses of Klumeck citizens strewn around. "It does seem as though the Bernicians have left it deserted," Aife continued, pulling me back to the present.

"Do you think the reports from His Majesty King Cedric could be true, sire?" John asked as I clutched Epos' reins tighter. "Do you think it really will be unguarded?" I frowned ahead as I thought. All around me was now complete blackness, the few lanterns our only guide. I could not perceive the terrain around me, but I could tell from the way my horse rode that the ground was beginning to level out.

"I don't know," I pondered ere long. "One can only hope." My uncle's kingdom fortress, based just before a range of high hills, marked the beginning of Bernician lands. The rumours were that the Bernicians had retreated back into their own territory, to gather numbers and strength. My uncle had recently heard that Klumeck had been left for some time, therefore it was an ideal opportunity to take back Klumeck and strengthen our own position with minimal loss of life. We had lately been corresponding much in secret, with only those we most trusted passing the messages between Gaeson and Caer Ligualid, the capital city of Rheged, where King Cedric and our displaced people currently dwelt. Through this stealthy discourse, we had arranged to attack whichever Bernicians remained tonight, only a mile from our position.

"Your Highness." I heard a voice and recognised it immediately as belonging to the captain of the guard. I slowed Epos slightly as he came alongside me. "The soldiers say that the ground has gone soft. There seems to be a stretch of grass to our east," he reported. I nodded, for this seemed as good a place as any to make camp. Our strategy was to sleep for a few hours and attack before dawn.

"Very well, we shall make camp as swiftly as possible," I commanded him. It had taken a while, but I was now used to the regal, authoritative tone I often had to speak, for I had spent nine years in the army following the orders of the captain, before I discovered my true identity as a Royal of Rheged and King Cedric's nephew and heir. As such, it had taken time to adapt to give orders, rather than the one obeying them.

A few minutes later, the camp was established and some of the soldiers began the rota to keep watch. I entered my tent, thankfully beginning to strip off some of my armour. The day had been long, the metal grown heavy on me. I climbed into the uncomfortable bed — little more than a sheet of fabric on the floor — and began to think of home to distract me.

Home was Gaeson, where my wife would probably be asleep by now. A small smile grew on my face as I pictured her beautiful countenance, her good heart and her wisdom. We had been married now for a little over a year. I had long loved Evelyn, Queen of Gaeson, from afar, ever since the day we had met as children. She had escaped to be out in the snow and had come upon me crying, for my favourite horse had died. She had offered me a cloth to wipe my foolish tears away. After she had heard a guard approaching, I had helped her climb through the library window. That day, my nine-year-old self had vowed to love her, to serve and protect her.

Throughout my career as a soldier, I had therefore remained unmarried and devoted every moment I could not only to serving her late father King Reghan, but also to ensure her protection and welfare. That was before I had discovered the king was a tyrannical ruler, who wished to defy the Supreme Ruler of Rheged, King Urien, for his own glory and gain. King Cedric had marched upon Gaeson, back when I thought he was my enemy. I had been ordered by Captain Bredon to escape with Evelyn. The two of us had travelled through the forest, heading for Caer Ligualid. It was then King Cedric had arrived. I had believed he wished to capture her. Presently, I recalled vividly the way Evelyn and I had fallen off the cliff, holding on only to my horse's reins.

The rope had at once strained, unable to sustain both our weights. I remembered clearly drawing my sword, looking at Evelyn one last time and confessing my love for her, before cutting the rope to send me to my doom. Unexpectedly, however, I had not died. King Cedric had found me, brought me to Caer Ligualid and it was there I had learned the truth about my identity. I had discovered that I was King Cedric's nephew and therefore a Royal of Rheged and the long-lost heir of Klumeck. I discovered too that my oldest friend, Sarah, was actually my sister. I had also learnt King Reghan was the one who had ordered the deaths of my parents.

It was difficult to believe it was only a year and two months since Evelyn and I had married, having learned who I really was only two months before that. In the time following these revelations of my identity, the nightmares that had plagued me as a child had stopped. I'd suffered from these dark dreams all my life and it transpired they had been subconscious glimpses of my past, hinting that my life was not all it had seemed.

It was a cruel tragedy, therefore, that no sooner than I had discovered my new identity, we had received word Klumeck had been set ablaze. By the time we had come to her aid, the fortress was already burnt to the ground in front of our very eyes. Though thanks to God's grace most had been able to flee, my inheritance had been devastated. The displaced citizens had been welcomed at Caer Ligualid whilst Klumeck had been left in Bernician hands.

The reports that the Bernicians had withdrawn their forces from Klumeck, seeking to consolidate their troops, gave us hope that possibly their numbers were dwindling. Perhaps our victory a year ago had indeed helped to secure our lands. It barely seemed any time at all since that last battle at the island of Ynys Metcaut, deep in Bernician territory. Despite us winning the day, these lands had remained in their occupation.

We had in the year hence been attempting to drive any Bernicians further out of Rheged and to consolidate with our allies. We now knew that us who lived in Briton would have to fight together, or we would soon be defeated. This truth had become especially prevalent since King Urien's death, who had been assassinated during the battle of Ynys Metcaut through the betrayal of our former ally King Morgant.

Gaeson's army and I had then returned home, only to find that Queen Evelyn had been kidnapped. We had pursued the Bernicians who had taken her and rescued her, but not before an enemy soldier had sliced his blade against my love's throat. This wicked deed had been done by our former chief interrogator of the dungeon at Gaeson, who had really been a Bernician spy. A painful image of me at her bedside flashed through my mind, her features pale and weak. I had wept in fear and grief, believing her about to die.

I still found it a wondrous dream that she had returned from the break of death. More wondrous still, during her recovery she told me she returned the depth of my feelings. I had offered her the proposal of marriage and Evelyn had accepted. We were wed shortly after that and we had since found ourselves extremely content. Indeed, she believed that soon our love and joy would grow even further.

My heart quickened to think of it; the possibility that there could be new life already growing inside her, that in subsequent months that life would develop and form. She had been mistaken in her belief at carrying a child before, but in the few words I had spoken to her the morning I departed for Klumeck she had seemed so certain, affirming all the signs were there. I tried not to get my hopes up, but the task of calming my expectations seemed impossible.

After a few hours of fitful slumber John came into my tent to rouse me, but I was already awake and putting my armour on. The army was hastily taking down the camp and preparing to depart. I glanced up at the skies and was relieved to see the clouds had shifted during the night and now the canvas above was clear. The position of the stars told me it was another three hours before dawn; therefore, we could assume most of the Bernicians, apart from those keeping watch, would be asleep. We mounted our horses and stealthily made our way towards Klumeck. As we moved along, using only a few lanterns to avoid detection, I was reminded of the time King Cedric marched on our own lands, waging war against King Reghan. It was the same night that only my thirst had led us to see them, for our own watchmen had been drugged to sleep. This time, however, we were the ones leading charge against Klumeck: not against my uncle, but against the Bernicians who had captured it.

"It is just there, sire," Aife whispered, pointing to the edge of the small woods we had been creeping through several feet away, where a pile of rocks sat. This was the strategic position she and John had come to earlier.

"Very well," I answered, as we dismounted our horses once more. "Captain," I said, turning to my right to speak to him, "have we heard from King Cedric?"

"Yes, Your Highness," the captain replied. "A scout has just returned from them. His Majesty's soldiers say they are in there, ready and waiting," he reported.

"Good," I replied; this meant my uncle and his troops were in place at the other side of the treeline, facing the fortress itself. "Then give the order to douse the flames and form ranks. Await our signal," I instructed.

"Aye, my lord," Captain Bredon answered, immediately departing to carry out my commands.

"God be with you, John," I murmured to my friend before he left also, ready to lead the march alongside the captain.

"Also, with both of you," John responded to Aife and me, before following in his master's footsteps. I turned to view the fortress as he left, still in complete darkness apart from the beacons lit on each of the four walls that led into the fortress. Klumeck had long been established as a border kingdom, protecting Rheged from the Bernicians that were beyond. If we could reclaim these lands, it could be instrumental in the war.

There was a swift, barely audible shuffling as the other archers came to take their positions. Aife explained in hushed tones that there were twenty guards taking watch overall, five that walked along and back down each of the four walls. If we were very quick, we could shoot most of them before one of them sounded the alarms that would wake up the rest. The obvious advantage to taking Klumeck was that the fortress was so close to a treeline, so it was easy to hide in the woods and avoid detection, ready to jump out, as we were doing now.

"Remember what we said: we'll have to wait for them to be near a beacon," I said quietly. For a minute or two we watched the Bernician guards intently, trying to see their patterns. Their uniform pace meant that every few seconds, several of them had stood near a nearby lantern. There were ten of us ready to fire, which meant that we could eliminate half of them if our aim was true. In a hurried voice I instructed the archers which guard to shoot for along each wall. I also told them to aim for their heads, as in their arrogance they were not wearing helmets; this would be their downfall.

"Prepare to fire at my command," I breathed presently. The archers all placed arrows on their bowstrings; I did so too as I spoke. We waited in tense silence as the soldiers continued their patrol, ignorant of the imminent danger. As if with the same mind, the other archers and I all drew our arrows backwards.

"Fire!" I whispered loudly, just as the guards neared their beacons. We let our arrows fly and they soared towards their targets. In the next moment all ten arrows had impaled skulls and the guards fell where they were, instantly dead.

"Fire when ready, at all you can see," I commanded, as the Bernician soldiers at once raised their voices in alarm. My recent order was slightly unnecessary, as we were all placing more arrows and pulling strings taut once more. My eyes scanned the darkness and soon found their next target. Much to his misfortune and folly, he was standing next to the beacon, looking around him wildly. I could only make out his dim outline, but I could well imagine his terror.

I shook my head mentally, for it did not do to dwell on such thoughts in a battle; already this hesitation could have cost me the lives of my brothers and sisters in arms. I pushed any thoughts of his humanity aside and released the arrow. The moment I did, however, I saw another arrow pierce his skull before mine could. The soldier toppled to the floor and my arrow hit the wall directly behind where he had been standing.

"Sorry, brother," Aife whispered beside me. I sensed, rather than saw, her smirk and my own mouth curled in response. As chief archer, Aife was by far the fastest and the whole army knew none could outshoot her; she had taken advantage of my momentary hesitation.

"I would not apologise for such a shot, if I were you," I murmured back as I placed another arrow quickly on my bow and it found its home inside another guard's head.

The Bernician archers had by now begun to fire back, but we were still hidden behind the pile of rocks and the surrounding trees. The arrows landed for the most part harmlessly upon the ground, except for one that buried itself in another archer's leg, who immediately cried out.

"Surgeon!" I shouted and a few moments later I heard him reply that he was there; I smiled at his swift speed. It was the same physician who had treated my arm after it got wounded in a battle, nearly a year and a half ago. "Keep on firing!" I shouted, as we continued to shoot our flurry of arrows into the night. A few minutes later, I judged we had eliminated almost all of the enemy archers.

"Aife, it is time for the signal," I addressed her, after I had let my arrow fly into another foe who was stood near a beacon.

"Aye, my lord," Aife replied and lowered her bow a moment to retrieve the small horn she had been carrying around her neck. Immediately she lifted it to her mouth and blew, the sound of horn at once filling the night air. It seemed to suspend all other noise, even the cries of the fallen. In the instant after the horn had sounded, there was a loud cry as the troops of Gaeson, Klumeck and Caer Ligualid all rose as one.

"Cover them!" I shouted, though there were not many foes left. The plan of attack we had formed was going better than we could have hoped for: surely Klumeck would now be reclaimed. Not since the battle at Ynys Metcaut had the kingdoms of Rheged been so united.

The rest of our small army ran out into the open, carrying between them the long ladders and the large battering ram the combined troops from Caer Ligualid and Klumeck had brought with them. They advanced towards the large door, the only way in or out of the fortress. The other archers and I were kept occupied in trying to protect our comrades from enemy arrows above as more enemy archers appeared on the ramparts. Our party by the door struck the battering ram against the entrance repeatedly with intense strength and soon parts of the door were beginning to give way against the constant strain.

"Prepare to march," I said loudly, placing my bow on my back and drawing my sword. "This is when we retake Klumeck!" I shouted and the other archers chorused back in agreement. I smiled to myself. We were about to reclaim my uncle's kingdom, having attacked them with complete surprise, leaving ourselves with minimal injury and hardly any loss of life. I opened my mouth to give the order to charge, but before I spoke, suddenly a horn resounded.

"Aife," I said, glancing to her automatically, even knowing that the horn was too far away to be her, that her horn was nowhere near her mouth and that the instrument was a completely different tone to Gaeson's horn. Aife opened her mouth to reply when the horn blasted again. The noise seemed to be coming from over the tops of the high hills. I immediately raised my eyes to above the fortress, to the treacherous paths above.

"Wait," I muttered, for if they were coming from the mountains, that left few other possibilities. The horn sounded again, louder and nearer and I recognised it this time, confirming what I already knew. The powerful echoing blast filled me with dread.

"The Bernicians," Aife whispered, coming to the same conclusion I had. Then she looked to me. "Your orders, sire?" she asked. I frowned, however, watching in silence as the first of them emerged over the top of the high hills. "My Prince?" Aife prompted and I glanced at her.

"We fight, for now," I declared loudly, looking up and down my line of archers, though their faces remained in darkness. "Use your remaining arrows!"

The archers chorused in obedience as immediately we began firing. The battering ram had begun again in its force. I wondered whether, if we were able to take the fortress, we could then defend ourselves; but we were just about to break into it, leaving us extremely vulnerable. The best we could hope for was that there were not that many, but even as I thought this I knew it was folly. More and more Bernicians were spilling over the top of the hills, bearing down on us faster than any archers could shoot them down. Many of them bore lanterns, making them look like a sea of fire imposing on us with an unquenchable flame. All at once, I knew there were far too many of them for us to possibly be victorious.

"Cover me," I shouted to Aife and I jumped free of the treeline, racing to where my uncle King Cedric stood. He was beside King Owain, the Supreme Ruler of Rheged, next to the battering ram. I knew I had precious minutes — possibly not even that — before the Bernicians would be upon us. I therefore sprinted as quickly as my legs would allow. By the time I reached them they were standing in the shelter of the fortress doorway, attempting to both open Klumeck and defend themselves from the Bernicians clambering down from above them.

"Your Majesties," I shouted, coming to a halt beside them, "look!" I pointed up and I saw these two great kings raise their heads to behold the Bernician scourge. "There are far too many of them, we have to flee," I implored simply.

"Indeed," King Owain agreed immediately. "I was about to give the order myself, but your uncle seems determined," he added, sheathing his sword. "Retreat!" he bellowed. All at once the Caer Ligualid soldiers began running. A moment later and Aife had blown the Gaeson horn again, but this time the notes she sounded was the signal to flee. I glanced back at King Cedric, but he had not moved. He was transfixed, staring at the kingdom that used to be his.

"Uncle," I began, roughly taking his arm. He turned to looked at me. "I know this is not what we wanted, but what is the good is taking Klumeck now, only for us all to die? We are perhaps seventy in number and they have hundreds!" I pointed out. "We will take back Klumeck, uncle, but not this day. This day we have to run," I told him. For a moment the king looked back at his castle, with the door nearly open.

"Very well," my uncle yielded ere long, eyes swinging back to hold mine with a sad fury. "Retreat!" he bellowed. I gave him a quick nod, before racing back across the field towards the treeline. The Bernicians were nearly upon us, but when I returned to the rocks I saw Aife was still there.

"We were covering the others, my lord," Aife reported, guessing correctly at my unspoken question as she released another arrow into the night.

"All right, we will bring up the rear and cover those in front of us," I agreed. "Mount your horses, quickly!" I added and hurriedly climbed up on Epos, using my sword to cut the rope that bound her from a nearby tree. I reached back into my quiver and felt only four arrows left. All of us by now had quickly climbed on to our horses. I saw the one with the wounded knee was gritting his teeth, bracing himself for the pain that was about to get much worse.

Most of the Bernicians had now half scrambled, half fallen to the ground. To come down the hill this way seemed almost suicidal, but most of their force seemed to be surviving their treacherous paths. We carried on firing, to allow as many foot-soldiers as possible to delve into the thick forest that surrounded the castle and make their own escape.

"Now!" I shouted, when the last of them seemed to disappear into the woodland. I kicked Epos into a canter, holding onto the reins tightly. I heard the whistling of arrows flying past my ears as I weaved Epos erratically to avoid the trees. I could hear the thundering of hooves in the distance and automatically guided my horse nearer to them. I sensed Aife behind me had turned in her saddle and was beginning to shoot at our pursuers. I knew her skill enough to know each one would be hitting its target, despite our cantering. I reached for my bow and did the same, unleashing the last four arrows into the night to whichever of my foes was holding a beacon, hoping that each one found its target and sent a foe into oblivion.

"I have no arrows left, sire," Aife reported to me in warning after a minute or two. My quiver was also empty and soon we would be out of forest. I needed to think fast.

"I need to speak to King Cedric and King Owain," I stated, having an idea. I gathered the reins tighter again, spurring Epos into a gallop to catch up to them.

A little further on I perceived there were beacons sparsely lit, so I could roughly see where the front of our party was. Hurriedly I drew up alongside

King Owain, who was leading our conjoined troops in their retreat. As I neared him, I was beginning to glimpse the stars above from where the trees were getting sparser. Imminently we would be out of the forest altogether.

"Your Majesty," I greeted him hastily, moving the reins to slow down again, "I think I have a way we can escape undetected, but it will require much bravery and sacrifice," I explained. "We need a diversion," I continued. "If a small number of us were to light our beacons and ride straight west, the rest of us could travel south and escape," I explained. "If they rode hard at a gallop, hopefully by the time the Bernicians came upon them, they might be able to escape."

"That might work," King Owain nodded in agreement. "If they rode at a small distance from each other, it would look like our own torches," he continued. "They would pursue the decoy, rather than us. Do it," he ordered roughly. "I'll lead the main troops onwards. You spread the word and organise the diversion."

"At once, sire," I obeyed with a quick bow. Immediately I turned Epos back round and rode through the crowd, conveying the strategy to a few of the soldiers and telling them to spread the word amongst themselves. Soon, I had reached the end of the lines where the last riders were a little ahead of the foot-soldiers.

For these at the rear, it was far more dangerous; they were so close to the Bernicians I could almost smell them. The decoy soldiers would naturally be amongst the riders nearest to our enemies. There was a large chance that once they lit their lamps, they would not be able to gallop away in time to be out of shooting range. As soon as I had thought of this, nine brave men and women suddenly diverted their horses off course, holding their lanterns currently darkened that were about to be lit.

"God be with you all, my brothers and sisters," I said, as the they rode fast away from us. "I hope this works, Aife," I told her, as she appeared beside me. I looked behind us to see the Bernician beacons growing ever closer.

"It is a good plan, sire, it might work yet," Aife muttered. We delayed but a moment longer, watching the Bernicians get closer still, before I turned Epos round again on our new course of south, diverting off to our left.

"Keep going, boy," Aife encouraged to our her horse. Our faithful companions were beginning to tire with the galloping.

A minute or so later and Aife and I had reached the front of the lines again. I gave a swift report to King Owain and my uncle, confirming the strategy. The front of our force then abruptly changed our direction to south. I led the archers to the end of the treeline and swiftly we dismounted. I quickly tied Epos behind some shrubbery, hoping that in the darkness we would escape unseen. In the few seconds we had to spare, I hurriedly gave Epos some water.

"Your Highness, it is good to see you alive," the captain greeted from beside me. I turned to see him and John standing there. I gave a little smile at them, despite the dark circumstances.

"I'm sorry, sire," was all John whispered. In those three simple words, he had conveyed all the pain I felt at our doomed expedition.

"They're coming," was all I replied. "Prepare yourselves." I got back into position behind a tree and took a moment to peer across the plain.

As I watched, abruptly I saw nine brightly lit lamps break from the trees. The diversion had begun. These heroic soldiers broke into a gallop as soon as they were clear. The rest of us kept silent, so that I could hear every breath. Then a moment later, I heard the Bernician legion shouting as they pursued, saw the whistling of their arrows as they sought to attack the decoy riders. We pressed ourselves ever tighter against the leaves and branches and I was sure we were all making the same desperate plea to God that we would not be caught.

Then, it was over. The Bernicians had passed all of us to go across the field and we all let out our breath. However, I knew we were not out of danger yet. Swiftly I untied Epos and climbed atop her again. I felt her tense as I sat in the saddle.

"Easy, girl," I murmured, patting her neck, "we'll go slower this time." I walked her back towards King Owain and my uncle.

"We shall continue south, for now," said King Owain. "We'll travel at a trot, without beacons. Hopefully, by the time the Bernicians realise, it will be far too late for them to know where we went."

"Aye, my lord," I replied. "What about those diverting us, sire?" I asked him, but he was already ordering the captain to prepare the men.

"If they survive, we shall see our people again," King Cedric then told me grimly. "We depart," my uncle added to the Klumeck soldiers.

Within a few seconds, I had gently spurred Epos on into a trot and all of us rode in silence. Although we were now quite far away from the Bernician Army, we all travelled as if we were still in earshot. We travelled across the plain, going deeper into the very edge between Rheged and Bernicia. Though I could hardly see them, I knew the towering hills that separated us from the lands of our foes would be on our left. That was why I was so astonished that the Bernicians suddenly appeared above Klumeck, for to descend to us from those heights was extremely risky. I reflected they must have had cause to take such a gamble and realised all the more that this must have been planned; the Bernicians had known exactly of our schemes.

It was a strange paradox of emotion, to be fleeing away in the dark. It was a relief to be in relative safety from the scourge we had just survived, but every step we moved further away from Klumeck pained me. The ache of having come so close and yet not taking her back was palpable. Plus, not all of us had escaped so easily. I glanced across the plains in the direction of the decoy soldiers, but any trace of them and their Bernician pursuers were long gone. This was partly comforting, as it showed our enemy was nowhere near us, but I could not help but wonder how many of the decoy party were now sacrificed. Would we ever see them again, or even know their fate?

"They acted with great courage, sire," Aife muttered quietly beside me, for under the dim, sparse illumination of the stars, she must have seen the turn of my head and perceived well my thoughts. I nodded but gave no reply as our band continued sombrely into the night. Ere long I steered the reins gently, so that I drew closer alongside my friend.

"It should have been me, Aife," I murmured quietly to her. "I should have been among them," I stated, for I was filled with a deep bitterness that I had suggested putting their lives in danger but had not gone with them. Was that not cowardice, to propose death but not take part?

"No, sire," came Aife's immediate reply. "It is not your place to do so, Daniel," she whispered, her voice gentler now. "You are the Prince of

Klumeck and King Cedric's heir." I knew her meaning: she thought my life too valuable to risk. I swallowed my rising anger.

"I am not more important than they are," I whispered back, a little harsher than I'd meant. All I felt at being spared whilst they risked and perhaps gave their lives, was that it was wrong. I glanced back once more into the darkened fields, praying earnestly that the soldiers orchestrating the diversion would survive.

We were by now several miles away from the forest and we continued to ride into the night alongside the foot-soldiers. Epos was far more relaxed, going at a much slower pace. I could sense the tension beginning to dissipate from others also. Presently, the ground grew much steeper and soon we reached the top of a hill. We stopped for a moment and immediately I glanced once more across the plain, but there was still nothing but darkness. This meant the diversion soldiers had done well at staying ahead and gave me hope that most of them had survived. I knew the darkness would not remain so for long, however, soon the torches would be back, lighting up the anger of our foes for how they had been fooled.

"Our tracks will remain hidden till dawn." It was my uncle who spoke. I heard keenly the heaviness in his voice and knew well why. Our failure for him would be all the more wearying, for whilst I had lost my future inheritance, he had lost his home.

"Then we must keep moving," King Owain said impassively and spurred his horse into a trot. The rest of our band of soldiers followed and I fell in line beside my uncle.

"I'm so sorry, Uncle," was all I could think of to say, which seemed woefully inadequate. It was in essence the same thing John had said to me, yet whilst his speech had brought me comfort, my own rendition tasted of nothing but weakness.

"We would have succeeded, if not for the reinforcements," King Cedric replied, bitterness clear in his voice. "How did they know we were there, Daniel?" he asked now.

"I know not," I replied, having already thought of the same question. "It seems too ridiculous for it to be a coincidence," I added, vocalising my previous thoughts. "They must have been informed of our schemes."

"Indeed," my uncle agreed, "it does seem likely." I grew uneasy at the thought of a spy within our ranks. The interrogator had used such subterfuge, but since King Reghan's abdication we had thoroughly scrutinised our people for any other signs of deception.

"The rumours that the Bernicians had retreated, that Klumeck was near-deserted," I began presently, "where did those originate, sire?"

"From someone I trust," King Cedric replied gravely, "but this counsel was true. By all the reports, it should have been." I took from his tone he did not wish our conversation to continue. We therefore carried on at a trot in silence, each step taking us further away from the kingdom we had so nearly retaken.

Eventually, after heading so far south, we began to make our way west and at last we reached the road that would take us to Gaeson. It was then time to separate from my uncle, who with the other Klumeck soldiers would be heading back to Caer Ligualid with King Owain and Caer Ligualid's troops. We did a brief survey of our conjoined legion. It seemed only twenty-three were dead. Although this was a great loss of life, I was relieved it had not been greater, given the ambush. Of course, this number did not include the decoy soldiers, for we had no way of knowing how many of those might have met their demise also.

"We will discover what has happened here," King Cedric vowed, the rage clear in his tone. "There has to have been a spy. We will find him."

"Aye, we will," I replied. I clasped arms with my uncle in a brief embrace and I saw him nod at me in the near darkness. Then King Owain gave the order to move for Caer Ligualid and with nothing more said between us, my uncle steered his horse and I watched him leave. Then I turned and could just about make out the twenty or so riders from Gaeson. They had gathered round waiting for my orders, with Captain Bredon, John and Aife at the forefront.

"To Gaeson," I commanded and to my relief we set off for home, but even that comforting instruction could not eradicate how much we had dismally lost this night. We had not been able to reclaim Klumeck, the kingdom of which I was the heir, where my parents had lived and died. Instead, we had been forced to flee. Anger rose up alongside sadness and with it I made again the vow my uncle and I had spoken to each other. We would find out how the Bernicians knew of our plan. If there were indeed spies among us, they would not remain hidden. We would discover them and there would be nowhere left for them to run.

Chapter Two

The people of Gaeson were waiting for us as we arrived, lining the streets and waving small flags bearing Gaeson's banner. I smiled and waved, hiding the heavy, resigned emotion I truly felt. As I walked Epos up towards the castle itself, I tried to remember the positives. By God's grace most lives had been spared, but many had given their lives. I could see the worry begin to take form in some of the citizens' faces, of those that noticed the nine who had not returned. Their dismay compounded our recent failed mission and it made the possible treachery all the more bitter. My constant questions pressed harder. How had the Bernicians known? Who had informed them? Could the spies even be amongst Gaeson?

I was distracted by these heavy wonderings as we went through the castle gates and approached the castle beyond, where I saw my beloved wife and queen waiting for us. My heart rate quickened slightly as I smiled. Our troops came to stop before her and I quickly dismounted. I removed my helmet and gave a swift bow before her; she in turn gave a quick curtsey. As I straightened, I longed to take her in my arms, but had to suffice with the custom of quickly kissing her hand.

"Your Majesty," I greeted, thrilled to see my wife after over a week away, for my troops and I had travelled to Caer Ligualid first to discuss battle strategy.

"My Lord Prince Bryce," Evelyn replied in turn. I saw joy sparkle in her eyes as we beheld each other. Presently, however, I then saw concern come into her countenance as her gaze flickered over the state of the brothers and sisters behind me. Before she could ask what had happened Sarah came up beside me.

"Dear sister," I greeted her warmly, moving to kiss her hand also. As I did, a soldier came to take Epos to the stables. "I am sorry to report that we were not able to retake Klumeck, my lady," I told my queen. "The Bernicians seemed to know we were coming," I added heavily. I saw Evelyn's eyes darken at this.

"This way," was all she said, gesturing towards the palace doors. Clearly, she wanted to continue the report away from the watching eyes of the city. We therefore walked across the courtyard and entered the palace. The captain, John and Aife came with us: Bredon to report on the soldiers generally and Aife and John to report on their scout.

"Leave us," Evelyn commanded simply. The rest of the soldiers who always stood in the palace unless dismissed also departed. I thought perhaps my wife had already come to the same conclusion I had, that perhaps someone in Gaeson had informed the Bernicians of our strategy.

"It is good to see you alive and well, Daniel," my wife told me, as the doors shut. At once I took her in my arms and kissed her quickly, whilst Sarah also embraced Aife and John. "How has this happened? You worked on the battle strategy for weeks," Evelyn then enquired.

"I know not, Your Majesty," the captain replied. "The plan we had devised seemed to be working. His Highness and the other archers took out most of the guards keeping watch, then John and I advanced our regiment, followed by their Majesties King Cedric and King Owain leading their troops. We had the ladders and the battering ram, ready to break down the door."

"John and I had led a small force to scout out the enemy, my lady," Aife continued, giving a swift bow. "There seemed to be very few Bernicians there, as we had hoped."

"Bernician reinforcements suddenly arrived," I told Evelyn wearily. "They came running over the top of the hills, above Klumeck." Her eyes widened in surprise. "I think someone must have informed them," I continued. "How else did they know to come at that precise time?" I paused to rub my face wearily with my hands.

"That plan was devised in secret among the soldiers and officials, all of whom we trust," Evelyn stated. "You think there may still be Bernician spies in our ranks?"

"There are almost certainly still operatives from Bernicia in Rheged," I answered, repeating again the worry I had briefly discussed with my uncle. "Whether the spies are in Caer Ligualid, or here, or perhaps both... I know not," I concluded heavily.

"We were only able to escape because of the strategy His Highness had devised, Your Majesty," John spoke now. "A lot of lives were spared," he added. His speech was intended to encourage me, but all I could think of was the lives of those who had been slaughtered in the ambush and the unknown fate of the decoy soldiers.

Abruptly, the doors of the palace hall opened, admitting two of Evelyn's foremost advisors. I had met one of them before but had only seen the second at a distance. He was a tall, lean man, with cropped thick black hair and an amiable face that was cleanly shaved. From his build, I guessed he had himself once been a soldier.

"I called for my advisors, to explain the situation to them," Evelyn stated. "Prince Bryce, this is Lord Aldred," Evelyn introduced us, gesturing to one of the advisors. "You have seen him before, I think, in court. He has long been loyal to me and to my father also," she explained.

"A pleasure to meet you at last, Your Royal Highness," Aldred greeted formally, bowing low as he spoke. He smiled then and I noted how familiar his features were.

"Lord Aldred," I returned, clasping his arm briefly after he had straightened. "Tell me, have we ever met before? Your face seems very familiar," I stated and Aldred smiled.

"Yes, Your Highness has a good memory," Aldred answered, "I did once briefly know your father while I was serving under King Reghan. I even met your mother once, but our meeting lasted only moments. I came to the house when you were a child," he explained.

"I only knew him a little, my lord," he elaborated, seeing the surprise in my features. "I did not know him long before his unfortunate passing but in my brief acquaintance, I saw he was a very good man indeed." I gave a little smile at this, despite the events of the day.

"Thank you, he was," I agreed. I then turned to another of Evelyn's foremost advisors. "Lord Melvyn," I greeted, clasping his hand briefly. Lord Melvyn was shorter and a little thinner than Aldred and sported a curled moustache. Melvyn had recently been elected as the hand of the queen, meaning that if Evelyn, Sarah and I were away on royal duty, he would be the steward of the throne of Gaeson and rule in her stead. With the more formal pleasantries done, my queen then rose grandly to begin the official report of what had happened at Klumeck.

After we had finished our accounts, I then went directly to the armoury to discard all my armour to be cleaned, apart from my sword, which I carried with me at all times. Next, I retired to Evelyn's and my chambers, the grand room in which I had resided since our marriage. I took a long bath and lay there, soaking in the water and letting battle images flood through my mind. In particular, I kept visualising the man who I had nearly killed, the soldier Aife's arrow had claimed first. The way he had looked around wildly led me to think that perhaps he had not been fully trained in the army. As I continued to reflect, I remembered lowering the angle of my bow ever so slightly. Although I could not be sure, his head had been lower than that of his comrades, so possibly he had not been a full-grown man.

Strangely now, Joshua entered my thoughts. Or maybe it was not so strange after all. Joshua had been a boy of Gaeson not yet fourteen, who had died in battle. He had conscripted young so that he could help provide for his mother and two sisters, as his father himself had died some years before. Joshua had been terrified but had fought bravely. I had tried to keep him from harm, but found him after the battle, struck down by an enemy blade.

An old ache of sadness filled me as I thought of him, so I shook the thought of him away as I scrubbed the mire from my body. Then back in the main chamber, I was just pulling a fresh tunic over my head when Evelyn came in, much to my pleasant surprise. I had not expected to see her till the evening.

"I had a few minutes between duties," she explained simply, as I immediately crossed the room and took her in my arms. I kissed her deeply, as I had longed to do as soon as I had arrived. "How was your bath?" she asked presently, when we stepped apart again.

"Refreshing," I replied, still a little haunted by the image of Joshua, his blond hair covered in filth, his eyes wide in horror, the crimson stains of blood covering his ashen skin. I raised a hand to her cheek, choosing to dwell instead on how well she looked.

"How do you fare, my love?" I enquired of her casually. I longed to have our deepest desire confirmed, but I did not want to betray the hope in my tone.

"I am well, husband," Evelyn replied. Her sentence started bright enough, but as she spoke I caught the fading in her tone and the slight sadness enter in her eyes before she looked away. At once, I knew the answer to my unspoken question. Longing to comfort her, I placed my hands on her shoulders and placed a kiss on her forehead.

"All is still well," I tried to reassure her. "There is plenty of time for that yet." At this, my queen gave a sardonic smile and crossed our chamber. She opened the window and the warm, summer breeze filtered through.

"Tell that to our people," she muttered, with more than a hint of bitterness in her voice. Evelyn turned back to me then, arms folded. "We're royals, Daniel," she said flatly. "Everyone will be wondering about our heir. They will be expecting an announcement any day. From when I was very small," my queen continued, "I knew I would be the one to take the throne and royal succession would come from me. I have always known this pressure, but I always prayed the ability to bear children would never be an issue," she concluded.

I frowned as I took in her speech. Having been raised in a simple soldier's household, I had not quite realised the pressure there would be to produce an heir. I myself had never really considered the idea of children, having decided long ago I would probably never marry, before I knew the truth about who I really was. Since my marriage to Evelyn, however, I knew it was something I desired.

"We have only been married just over a year," I tried to point out. "We have not given it very long yet. I have heard that even when there are no issues, it still takes time to have children. Perhaps if, later on, it still hasn't happened... perhaps a year from now, when we have been married two years," I suggested, "then we could consider talking to the physician." Evelyn turned to regard me and gave a nod, a little of the tension dissipating from her.

"You speak wisely. I believe you are right," she sighed. "I shall just have to not care about the idle gossip that will undoubtedly come our way," she added, only a remnant of bitterness remaining. "What shall we do, though?" she asked now, her voice slightly worrying with doubt. "What if it is not to be?"

"If that is God's will," I replied, coming to stand before her and putting my hands on her shoulders again, "then we shall mourn together, but the kingdom will not be lost. I suppose Sarah would be the closest heir," I added, remembering that Evelyn's father, too, had been an only child. Evelyn had once had older siblings, but they had both died of fever when Evelyn was barely able to talk, long before she knew who she had lost. I knew she felt a similar kind of mourning to Sarah, the ache of missing those you could never remember.

"How, then, would we produce an heir, for the safety and security of Gaeson?" Evelyn challenged, sighing. "Since my siblings died, my mother was an only child and my father's one brother died as a child... there is no other to carry on the bloodline," she concluded despairingly.

"We could adopt," I reflected, thinking that in essence this was what my mother and father in Gaeson had done and I had never once questioned their love or care. I was also filled with momentary sadness, for all of Evelyn's relatives that were no more. Evelyn nodded, but said nothing further. I moved to sit back upon the bed, at once very tired. Evelyn saw this and gave me a sad smile, her hand running once affectionately through my damp, washed hair.

"Get some rest, my love," she advised, kissing me briefly on the forehead. "Alas, duties will not wait, even for a queen," she said wryly. The corner of my own mouth turned up slightly. I moved my head back against the pillow as she departed my company, only for more images of the battle to be replayed in my mind's eye.

In truth, exhausted though I was, I did not get much more sleep the rest of the day. I tossed and turned in fitful slumber, only to wake again. In the end, I abandoned the idea of rest and rose from the bed, pausing to rub my tired face with my heavy hands. I then took a moment to again mentally check my body, but it seemed I had escaped the battle unscathed.

I soon discovered however that although I was uninjured, I was moving at a much slower pace due to the stiffness of my muscles. It had been difficult terrain riding, both for the soldiers and the horses, with little chance of rest. Indeed, it seemed to take much longer than usual to take the normal route from the castle through the town to my old house. My thoughts were wearying, too, for I was still thinking of our failed mission, wondering whether there could be spies in Gaeson. Also, I could not easily put out of my mind the conversation with Evelyn, for not only was she not pregnant, but it was the first time she had ever expressed a doubt at being able to have children and though I had tried to encourage her, this thought was indeed troubling.

As I walked I tried to push such fears aside, reassuring myself that in all likelihood she would be bearing our child before long. Instead I lifted my head, so my face could be warmed by the sun. Such a contrast this was, to go for a summer stroll when the night before last there had been such horror of battle. I lowered my head again to see townspeople bowing or curtseying as they saw me. I gave them a short bend of my head in response.

Presently I came to the narrow street near the top of town where my mother lived, in the house that used to be mine. It now belonged to the seamstress Rachel, Joshua's mother, where she resided with her two daughters. Rachel had been ill and on the brink of bankruptcy when Joshua had died and in my fleeting encounter with him, I had promised to provide for his family should he die in battle.

The day I left for Ynys Metcaut, I gave Rachel the deeds to my house, having no further need of it. Encouragingly, since this transaction, Rachel's business had prospered and she herself had fully recovered. It turned out Rachel's condition had been simply a lack of food, since she had given every scrap to her daughters. Indeed, when I first met her, she had probably been on the brink of starvation. Her predicament had given me a renewed sense of conviction to help the poor. Indeed, since taking the throne Evelyn had discovered how much her late father had been content to accumulate his riches whilst poverty grew. Evelyn and I had therefore been working hard to try to resolve this.

As I neared my old home, I reflected it was still slightly strange to visit the house where I had spent my childhood but was no longer mine. I had gone from a soldier to a prince overnight, in a rapid transformation. In truth, it was still a little unsettling to give orders with confidence rather than to follow them, or to have everyone look my way when I walked through Gaeson's streets.

Presently I came to the front door and used a spare key Rachel had cut and returned to me so that I could easily visit my mother. I had the strange sense of familiarity and yet distance, as I crossed the threshold.

"Mother, I am home," I announced as I walked past the living chamber, where I had carried Rachel to warm herself by the fire the day they had moved to my home.

"Is that you, my son?" I heard her voice call and smiled. My mother had been bedridden for years, but even though she had not recovered enough to leave her bed she had improved a little more of late. "Daniel," she greeted warmly as I opened the chamber door, "how wonderful to see you."

"Mother," I returned and kissed her cheek warmly. I then sat down on the chair next to the bed, taking her hands in mine. "How fare you?"

"I feel well, my son. Rachel and her daughters left this morning to trade," she told me, "before the news of your return. I heard it did not go well," she added more gently.

"All was well until the Bernician reinforcements appeared," I leant back into the chair and rubbed eyes that were still somewhat deprived of sleep. "They came out of nowhere, Mother," I relayed wearily, "when we had prepared the element of surprise for weeks. It could not have been a coincidence," I confirmed grimly. Each time I thought it over, I was all the more certain. My mother raised her eyebrows at my conclusion.

"You suspect someone told the Bernicians of your plans to recapture Klumeck?" she deduced, folding her arms. I nodded. She had always been perceptive. My mouth set in a firm line as I thought of the lives that had been lost and at the unknown fate of the messengers. "If there are further spies, then it is likely they are the same spies involved at Gaeson a year and a half ago," she suggested, taking the same steps in logic I had done earlier.

"Aye," I affirmed heavily. "They must have a leader. I thought this was the interrogator who kidnapped Evelyn, but perhaps not," I reflected now, leaning forwards as I spoke. "They have covered their tracks well to not be discovered, until now, if they are here. I know not how to find them," I admitted.

"You could do what your father did, in the initial weeks after we brought you home," my mother reasoned. "After Bridget and I had found you and Sarah," Enid went on to explain, seeing my frown, "your father was concerned that there might be King Reghan's spies watching our every move. He feared that what we had done would be discovered and you would be lost."

"Aye, that makes sense," I agreed, for she had told me before how keen King Reghan had been to discover King Cedric's heirs, once he knew they were in his kingdom. "So, what did he do, to prevent me being discovered?" My mother smiled, as if this was obvious.

"He became a spy himself," she said patiently. "He and three others he trusted listened in on conversations, eavesdropped council meetings where the heirs were being discussed, followed the man who was then the captain to learn all he could." I nodded. This did seem obvious, once my mother had said it. "He was increasingly encouraged that King Reghan could not find you, nor Sarah. I think it was because you were separated from your sister," she added. "It broke our hearts to do it, my son, but I do not think you would have survived together. Because you had nothing to do with the other, everyone assumed you were simply relatives of those who died in the war. Then, as life moved on, most people simply thought you were our natural child."

"I understand," I replied, knowing once more how much I owed this woman my life. If not for her and Bridget's bravery, I knew Sarah and I would have been lost in the snow forever. "My father's actions were wise. This, I think, is the path to take," I pondered.

"I am glad your father can help you, even to this day. It has been a decade to the day since his passing," she added here. I saw the smile fade from her face as she thought of this. "It is nearly the same time as when I was struck with this illness," she added, gesturing to her bed. Not a day goes by where I do not miss him still," she declared sadly, with a small, sad sigh. I moved to take the hand nearest to me in both of mine.

"It is the same with me," I murmured back. Indeed, in all the months since I had discovered I was King Cedric's heir and my birth parents had lived and died in Klumeck, I had not forgotten the man who had raised me, who had taught me right from wrong and had given me knowledge of God since my birth.

As I later left my mother's company and headed back to the castle, I found myself thinking of him more deeply than I had of late, no doubt brought on by my conversation with my mother. I found my father's features were increasingly hard to remember, but if I closed my eyes and concentrated, his tall figure came before me. My father had possessed a warrior's strength and yet a heart of such gentleness it made others smile just to think of him. I found the same expression now coming, however faintly, upon my own features.

The glimpse of it vanished, though, as my mind turned once more to the spies that could be here, in my home. Could they be amongst these streets, these people I had always known and adored? Could they be amongst the soldiers I had trained with? There was such a bond among my brothers and sisters, forged through oft risking our lives for one another, that surely such a concept was nigh unthinkable. Yet I had once thought that about King Reghan, I reminded myself as I entered the castle. Was I too naïve, to think that betrayal was impossible for anyone else? I therefore resolved to implement my mother's advice. The spies needed to be spied upon.

***

"Your Highness!" It was five days later since I had returned from Klumeck and I was in the middle of a council meeting with Aldred and Melvyn, when John suddenly entered the chamber. A row of the advisors and officials turned as one to fix their eyes upon him. "Sorry to interrupt you, sire, my lords…" he added, bowing swiftly to all round him.

"Think nothing of it," I replied swiftly. "What's happened?" I added, seeing the urgency on my friend's face as he straightened once more.

"Her Majesty has sent word, my lord. The decoy soldiers from Gaeson have returned," he stated simply, a faint smile upon his features.

"Excellent," I said in immediate relief. "I wish to see them right away. The meeting is adjourned," I declared. The advisors around me bowed as I took my leave. "Do we know yet what happened to them?" I enquired as I followed John from the council chamber.

"No, my lord," John answered. "I was told they had entered Gaeson only a few minutes ago. I immediately ordered them to go to the palace hall and went to find you." I gave a single nod at this as we went to the palace to meet them.

As we arrived I perceived my wife was already there before me, sat upon her throne and dealing with another matter of civil business. I saw a small wooden table had been moved in at the side of the hall. It encouraged me greatly that all of the decoy soldiers from Gaeson sat around it, gulping bread and water as though they had not eaten for days. I was relieved all of them were alive and seemed well, for we had begun to lose hope we would never see them again. As the soldiers saw me, they at once stood to bow, with one still chewing a mouthful of bread.

"Please, carry on," I instructed them, as John brought another chair over for me to sit down. Captain Bredon was also stood behind the table and presently John stood beside him. "It lightens my heart to see you alive," I told them. "What happened?"

"We were kidnapped, Your Highness," one of the soldiers replied, wiping the breadcrumbs from his mouth with the back of his hand, "we were all caught by the Bernician Army who were pursuing us."

"They took us into Bernician land, my Lord Prince," said another, after taking a drink of water. "They said they wanted to take us to their commanders. But then one night, one of us managed to cut our bonds and we escaped. The other decoy soldiers returned to Caer Ligualid. We kept looking behind us to see if any had followed, but we could see no one," he concluded.

"Well done, men," I responded, smiling. "Your bravery and sacrifice will indeed be honoured. It's thanks to you the rest of us were able to escape." I then frowned, sitting forwards in my chair. "Did you overhear anything, about the attack? Perhaps how they knew of our plans?" I asked quietly.

"Aye, Your Highness," a third guard answered. "On the second night, they were discussing their strategy. I think they thought they were whispering, but we heard every word," he added as I glanced at him.

"They spoke of a man, sire, very indirectly," he continued. "He seems to be the one who informed them in every detail about retaking Klumeck.

What's more, my lord..." he seemed to hesitate. "They said the man comes from Gaeson," he admitted.

"Then it is as we feared," I murmured, sitting back again. This meant we had not rooted out all the traitors in our midst. It did indeed make sense that if there was a Bernician amongst us, he would have been in league with the interrogator, possibly even be the real villain. "Did you find out anything else about this man?" I pressed, leaning forwards again.

"No, my lord," the first guard who had spoken said as he finished another mouthful of bread, "except his name, which was not his true title, sire. They referred to him only by the name 'Wolf'." I frowned, for with this title, the identity of this man seemed to be veiled indeed. "They talked of him fearfully, as if he could have been in earshot," the guard continued presently. "I believe he must wield great power."

"Very well," I said, nodding as he ended his account. "You must be exhausted," I added, seeing they had finished their meal. "Does anyone else have anything of significance to say?" I waited a moment, but it seemed they had told me all they knew. "You are dismissed. Well done, all of you. Go and get some rest," I instructed.

"Thank you, sire," the same guard replied and as I stood, so did they. They gave me a quick bow and then swiftly departed the palace hall. A group of servants immediately came to remove the plates and goblets. Still more then appeared to take away the chairs and finally the table, but I almost paid them no heed. I went back to the middle of the hall, to further digest this terrible truth.

"I am thankful that all of the decoy soldiers have returned safely." I turned to see Evelyn descend the steps to come and stand next to me. "There is indeed a spy in Gaeson, then," she said at length with a sigh, vocalising what I had just been processing.

"Aye," I returned. "We must discover him, at all costs," I concluded rather needlessly, for how could Gaeson be safe, when there was a Bernician inside our very walls? "My mother had a thought," I said presently, relating to her my mother's notion to employ a soldier to spy on our own troops.

"That action may be needed, though I pray it is not," she affirmed. "In a few weeks the new recruits will enrol and be assessed," she commented. I nodded, for I could guess what she was about to suggest.

"You think a recruit would be the best for this task," I predicted. "I thought this would be the best way forward also," I said, for it certainly had logic on its side. If we employed a new recruit, they would be able to join many conversations with the honest view of getting to know their new comrades. Since they would have just joined our ranks, we would also have a far greater chance of their loyalty.

"I need to discuss this with the captain," I added abruptly. Evelyn nodded, as I strode to the far side of the palace hall, where John and the captain were waiting.

"Your Highness," Bredon greeted. "My study chamber, sire?" he guessed, as my wife sat down again upon her throne and resumed her business.

"Aye," I agreed, for even though there were only the palace guards and the people who were bringing their business to Evelyn, I wanted as few people to overhear us as possible. We made our way to his study chamber quickly and I turned to them as soon as the door shut.

"Have either of you ever had reason to suspect anyone in the army could be spies?" I asked immediately, as the captain came to stand by his desk.

"No, my lord," John and Bredon answered, almost at the same time. "I have always tested and trained every one of our brothers and sisters as they come through the recruitment process," my former master continued, "as I once did with you yourself, sire. All swear allegiance to you and to Her Majesty," he concluded at length.

"What do you wish us to do, sire?" John now asked quietly. "We will do whatever you ask." I glanced between them, wondering if they would obey me if they knew it to be wrong.

"I think we have no other choice than to watch those who may be watching us," I replied. "This was my mother's idea," I expounded, momentarily rubbing my neck. "Her Majesty also had the suggestion of employing one of the new recruits for such a task," I informed them.

"With respect," John spoke up presently and I turned to him. "Why do you suspect your army? All we know is that there is this spy known as the Wolf and that he was the one who told Bernicia of our plans to recapture Klumeck," John pointed out reasonably.

"I agree with your sentiments, John," the captain replied levelly, "but the fact remains the retaking of Klumeck was a military operation. We kept our strategy confidential to hardly any outside of the army, so it is likely it is one of our own."

"Who else, sire?" John asked the captain. "Her Majesty said some nobles and officials knew of the operation also, such as Lord Melvyn. I agree with you it was a military operation, but the Wolf could easily be an advisor," he added with folded arms.

"Aye, again good logic," I returned. "You're right that Lord Melvyn and the members of the council were in full knowledge of the scheme. The unfortunate reality is, it could be almost anyone," I pointed out presently with a sigh. "This Wolf figure could easily not be in a position of influence; he may have gotten the plans from someone else. However," I concluded thoughtfully, "I shall also watch the other council members closely and any other officials not on the council."

"Very well, sire," Bredon said after a pause. I could tell he and John were as saddened by the lengths we would have to go to as I was. "We shall have to be extremely careful about which recruit we select for this honour," he stated drily.

"Aye," I agreed. "Until then, we shall have to leave it to ourselves to be as vigilant as we can. Tell Aife about this, so she may be on her guard, but no one else," I instructed. "I think that is all for now."

"Very good, Your Highness," my captain concluded with a short bow of his head. "When the recruits are assessed, we shall see what new talents may be discovered." I gave a short nod at both of them and with that, my brothers departed my company. I folded my arms and gave a sigh. These were worrying times indeed and I knew my heart would not rest until this Veiled Wolf was discovered. With that resolve, I sat down at my desk and fetched a clean bit of parchment to write to Lord Melvyn, so that he could give me a list of all the officials who had known of the operation and anyone else at court. The list would be extremely large, I knew, but one would have to start somewhere. I dipped my quill into the ink and began to write. Whatever may come of it, I would discover the truth.

***

Two months after we had returned from Klumeck, the time had come for the new recruits to be initially trained and assessed. I was heading to the inner courtyard to observe them, to ascertain if one of them could be assigned to report on our soldiers to see if any were Bernician spies. Not much in Gaeson had changed since the decoy soldiers had returned, but all that had happened remained as fresh as though it had happened yesterday.

I had tried to resume life as normally as I could, which meant attending court and having several more meetings about the Bernician threat. My main emotion at these meetings was frustration, for the Wolf was still veiled to us. One thing I noticed however was that Melvyn, Evelyn's steward, seemed to be everywhere. Obviously, it was his duty to be at court, but there was something about his character I couldn't quite define.

The other prominent official was Lord Aldred, who claimed to have known my father briefly. His character seemed amiable and good, however. Both of them had served in King Reghan's time, so I could not help wondering if one of them (Melvyn in particular) could have been in league with the late king's corrupt advisors and the interrogator. All of the advisors had been examined, however and Evelyn certainly seemed confident in them.

I entered the large inner courtyard where the soldiers practised and trained, at the base of one of the towers where the soldiers resided. I already felt comfort in my surroundings, for it always felt like coming home be back here among my brothers and sisters. At once I saw Captain Bredon and John standing facing a line of men and women that I recognised instantly as the new recruits. Bredon folded his arms as he talked sternly, his clipped tone reaching my ears.

Presently his speech ended and as the recruits bowed, they bent down to pick up several long sticks at their feet and began to pair off, turning to one another. They then became still once more until, at the captain's order, they began combat with one another. Soon the air was filled with the thuds of wood hitting wood, the sound somehow muffled yet sharp. Bredon and John watched them, unmoving, to assess what their skills were. Most of the young warriors had chosen the smaller beams and wielded them like swords, but one or two had opted for the larger beams, instead holding them as spears. I smiled to myself as the recruits parried as they hit the other, remembering the time John and I had done the same activity. I took a few steps forward to observe them more closely. It became increasingly clear some were more skilled than others.

"Your Highness," Captain Bredon greeted, as he suddenly saw me. Instantly I wished I had remained hidden from view, for automatically the recruits stopped, turned to me and bowed.

"Please, carry on," I said with a wave of my hand, hoping that my presence would not interfere with their abilities. However, I reminded myself they would need to know how to fight alongside or even against monarchs, should they pass the assessments and be in a real battle.

"My lord," John greeted as I came to stand beside them, his arms casually folding once more as we observed them. "What do we think of them?"

"Looks like we have some good fighters here," I answered positively, "with some having a few things to learn," I added diplomatically as one soldier in particular suddenly dropped his wooden beam, caused by his assailant bringing down her weapon upon his hand.

"You have just lost your only weapon!" the captain shouted next to me. "Surely you have just given away your life!" As Bredon spoke, I had been expecting his partner to hit him with the stick, but the young lad surprised me by darting backwards with agility. To his credit, the recruit remained realistic by keeping one hand behind his back. I began to watch him with interest as he dodged again the weapon about to strike him. His features were young and ruddy and there was a sheen of sweat across his forehead. His eyebrows were creased with concentration and effort as the two partners waged the parody of war between them. The boy made several attempts to reclaim his blunt weapon, but each time his opponent cut him off.

"I wonder if he'll get the beam back," John muttered aloud to no one in particular as the lad leapt backwards yet again. Even some of the other recruits, who had mostly by now had a victor among them, had paused.

Soon a small crowd had formed around the two new soldiers in question, each determined to defeat the other and so prove their worth. The female warrior's countenance presently registered frustration as she attempted to hit him again and again. Each time he was just outside her grasp, but neither seemed to be tiring. Bredon was on the other side of John and I glanced at them as the captain seemed to whisper something in John's ear. John nodded and began to move into and through the crowd.

I was about to ask the captain what he had said, but this then became evident. In a move that was cruel but realistic, John silently took one of the beams from another recruit. He waited until the young boy's back was turned and then expertly leapt forward, hitting the boy's shoulder hard. The boy gave a grunt as he turned, shocked, towards John. In confusion, his opponent drove her beam forward to land squarely in his back the force of which made the lad collapse to his knees.

"You have just been greatly wounded. You would surely die from such a blow," John stated, a gleam of humour in his eyes as he lowered his beam.

"That was unfair!" the lad cried out in frustration, and I perceived the captain's eyes harden. "Sire, another attacked me from behind," he protested in a quieter tone.

"Indeed, as is realistic in battle," the captain answered him. "You should never be so immersed in combat with one that you allow yourself to be open to the attack of others. A valiant effort to the pair of you, but you need to be on guard against others and you," he added to his partner, "need to pick up on your speed, for he was able to evade your every attempt." She bent her head in a quick bow of agreement and the captain turned to comment on another pair.

"My Lord Captain," the young man said formally. The captain turned back, clearly surprised the recruit had more to say. "Sire, you yourself set up the rules for one-on-one combat. Had you stated a battle situation, I would have been on guard against others," he continued. I was surprised here also, for his speech to Bredon was both bold and reckless.

"Also, are there not many soldiers here? Would some not also be my allies, who would have seen my other opponent?" he questioned brazenly. I glanced at the captain's features, thin in his anger. I suppressed a smile, thoroughly enjoying the spectacle.

"You dare to speak with such arrogance to me, on our first day of training?" the captain barked. "It was done to teach you a lesson in humility, which you clearly also need training in," he continued loudly. Here, the young man had the grace to look downwards. "Since you raised the question, there might be circumstances where you are surrounded by the enemy and you have no friends to help you. As you claimed, however, you would have been on your guard against a battle situation...." he paused. I could guess the scenario the captain was planning. "Let us see how long you will do. Pick up your weapon!" he ordered abruptly.

"Sire." The recruit obeyed, picking up the beam immediately, his face flushed with frustration and determination.

"The rest of you are the surrounding enemy and our Lord Prince, John and I shall watch as this young hero attacks all of you and emerges the single victor. Prepare yourselves and await my command," Bredon instructed. Those still circling him, numbering about twenty, widened their eyes in realisation and adopted a combative stance. The young recruit hid any fluster well and simply wielded his wooden weapon, silently waiting.

"Charge!" the captain shouted and immediately the circle of twenty recruits leapt forward. I had expected the recruit to fall down immediately, but again to his credit he blocked the first few deftly, his feet leaping from left to right. He even managed to land his beam into one or two who clearly lacked ability before they were on him, but then one beam hit hard on his leg, another on his shoulder. A third beam darted towards him but was misjudged as the young recruit staggered downwards with the blows. Rather than his shoulder, the blunt weapon bashed his nose with a sudden, sickening crunch.

"Well, you lasted about ten more seconds than I anticipated," Bredon remarked almost lazily, "but you are still not quite the hero that we all hoped for. Can someone get him a cloth?" he added sarcastically, as the blood spurted from his face. "Go to the surgeon, boy, your nose appears to be broken."

"Sire," the recruit said in obedience, his voice muffled as one hand attempted to stem the crimson stream. He hurried off to the physician's chamber, clutching a cloth to his nose. We watched him hurry off the courtyard, the eyes of others widening as they witnessed him.

"Carry on with your exercises," Bredon announced, again sounding almost bored. As they resumed their fighting, I turned to my former commander, unsure of the ethics of what had just happened. "It is unfortunate that his nose was broken, my lord," he stated as if reading my mind, "but he did need to be lowered in his own sights somewhat."

"Granted," I agreed, "but you also put him in the middle of not trained experts but new recruits like himself. It is not surprising he ended up going to see the surgeon. The next time you wish to make a point," I added with somewhat of a rebuke, which was strange to do to my former master, "perhaps you could do so with those you can trust to not enact harm."

"Point taken, Your Highness," the captain replied with a nod. "It is not as though the wound will not heal, it will mend in a few days," he added with a sardonic smile. "John, perhaps you can finish off the training?" he added and then the captain had taken his leave, the bottom of his cloak swishing as it trailed behind him. John had come over to me and I glanced at him as he let out a low, quiet whistle, an incredulous smile on his own features.

"Terrified is the one who dares to question the captain," John reflected with a grin. I gave a wry smile at this. "He always picks one each year, to make an example of, does he not?" John mused, "so that all others will fear him."

"Aye," I answered, "I remember the boy the year we joined, who looked like he'd never held a beam before in his life. The captain ordered that he and another should combat. It was more than his nose that needed fixing," I reflected. John chortled. "His methods are cruel, but are certainly effective," I concluded presently. "I think I shall check on the lad's welfare," I added.

"Your Highness," John bowed as I departed his company. As I left him, I saw again the scuffle in my mind's eye. There was no debating that the lad had skill. For him to speak to the captain like that, though obviously foolish, showed great courage and resilience in his own convictions. It showed strength of character, too, that the recruit, rather than apologising and backing out of his claims, had indeed attempted to take on twenty single-handed. I could not help but wonder, in time, whether he could be the best recruit for the task we had in mind.

Presently I came to the surgeon's chamber, to find the door was ajar. The surgeon, Leigh, had been in post now almost ten years. It was the same man who had bandaged my arm after I had raised the alarm for battle and who had saved the captain from death after the injury to his chest. Leigh was also the gifted medic who had healed Aife of her fever and saved Evelyn when she had been pierced through the neck after her kidnapping. For all of Leigh's talents, I knew I and the rest of Gaeson would be eternally grateful. He had brought many of his patients back from the brink of death, more times than any of us could count.

"Your Highness," the recruit said as soon as he saw me, jumping up from the bed just as the physician had been about to finish with the bandages.

"Stay still," Leigh snapped and then glanced back at me. "Apologies, my lord, but the patient does need to stay in one place," he added a little sheepishly.

"Not at all," I replied with a smile. "I need to remember that for future visits, that people will suddenly leap up. A hazard of my role, I'm afraid," I added sardonically to Leigh, causing the corner of his mouth to turn, for how often had I wished I could simply go somewhere without heads turning and constant bowing?

"How is the patient?" I added as the surgeon finished bandaging the wound and began washing the blood from his hands.

"His nose will heal in a few days, sire," Leigh stated, confirming the captain's diagnosis. "You aren't the first recruit to be harmed in practice by order of the captain, nor shall you be the last. Do try to avoid any more broken bones," the surgeon added lightly as the boy stood.

"Aye, thank you," the recruit added, his voice taking on a sudden nasal quality that I struggled not to find comical. "Your Highness," he added, bowing less clumsily this time.

"What's your name, lad?" I asked him as I stepped back from the doorway and we stood together in the corridor.

"Ewan, my lord," he replied and bowed and stood back up again. "I apologise for my earlier behaviour, sire," Ewan added. I gave him a nod in acknowledgement.

"You have courage and spirit, I will give you that," I admitted, as I regarded him. "But that is not all what a soldier is. It all takes great discipline and following orders, even if the orders seem unfair or unjust to you," I reminded him.

"Yes, Your Highness. My lord," he added tentatively, "may I pose an enquiry?" I nodded, thus giving permission. "What if someone commands you to do something that you know to be wrong, morally? What is more important then, to obey the order, or to do what you know to be right?"

"A good question," I said with approval, for it showed discernment on his part. "It depends what is being asked of you and the motivation for it." As I spoke, I was thinking back to when I had defied King Urien and risked the whole might of Rheged to warn Gaeson of impending attack, risking my life in the process. This decision I had made had not been a secret by any means. Ewan might well have it in mind.

"It is a tricky situation to be in and you would have to think it through carefully. Above all, even kings are subservient under God's law," I concluded. "If you truly believe you cannot carry out the command, then you would have to tell the captain and accept the consequences for your actions. Mind you always try to obey your superiors in everything, however, as much as you are able. You are dismissed," I added. "I suggest you go and rest a while."

"Thank you, Your Highness," Ewan replied with another bow of his head. With that we parted company and I watched him leave. The other, female recruit now came to mind. Whilst she had not been able to hit him, I was suitably impressed at her agility and skill with a blade. It gave me further encouragement to consider that the pool of recruits was of a high calibre. In previous years people had joined hardly able to wield a wooden blade.

"Your Highness," said a voice and I turned towards it to see the female recruit who had fought Ewan, as if thoughts had conjured her before me. Immediately I perceived concern was evident in her features. "Is Ewan all right, my lord?" she asked, after bowing quickly.

"Yes, he is fine. It is only a broken nose. I sent him home," I informed her. At once her face relaxed. "What is your name?" I asked her.

"Cara, my Lord Prince, at your service," she responded as she bent her head in a bow again, revealing the small neat bob at the back of her head where she had tied her hair back.

"You had some skill out there," I told her presently, "you just need to work on actually hitting your target. You'd better get back to your training," I added, thinking that the captain would be waiting for her to return.

"Yes, Your Highness. Thank you, sire," she added and with that she was off, dashing down the corridor before the captain's wrath was further inflamed. I gave a quick smile at her hasty departure and then, still curious about how the recruits were doing, I walked back in the direction Cara had run. I entered the training courtyard to see it was deserted, but I could guess where they had gone. I took the path from it round to the outside of the castle and reached the stables, to see the recruits were all standing in the field beyond it.

They were positioned a little apart from one another along one horizontal line, bows and arrows in their hands and pointing at their individual targets in front of them. I came to stand beside John at the fence behind the stables, bordering on the field.

"My lord," John greeted again, as my hands came to casually lean on the highest wooden panel in front of me. "Is Ewan all right?"

"Aye, only a broken nose, as we thought," I replied. I was about to ask him how our new soldiers were faring at archery, but a quick observation told me this was obvious. The captain was gesturing in frustration, trying to help them. Indeed, it seemed many were not able to tell which end of the arrow was sharp.

"They'll add to the archers nicely," I attempted to encourage John, as I nodded to one or two down the end who were actually managing to hit their target. As I watched them, I was reminded keenly of a similar archery scene, many years ago, where John and I had first met Aife.

***

I noticed the archer at the end immediately, her oak-coloured hair tied up high behind her as her eyes focused on the task in hand. I watched in admiration as she stretched her bow perfectly taut and unleashed each arrow to flawlessly hit the target. Upon closer inspection of her countenance, I perceived beneath her concentration there was a glimmer of something that almost looked bored, as if the archery was as simple and effortless to her as blinking.

"Focus on your own target, Daniel, before the captain sees you!" John hissed next to me. Immediately I snapped my attention back to the circular target before me, placing another arrow upon my bow. I quickly fired it, watching a little triumphantly as it sailed in the air to land on one of the outer rings. This was an achievement in itself, as many seemed not to be able to hit the wooden target at all. I then glanced at the archer again, as yet another arrow landed perfectly in the middle of the smallest circle. I needed much more training if I was to be an effective archer in the army, but hitting a target perfectly each time seemed to be as natural to her as breathing.

"Lower your bows," the captain instructed, just as I reached behind to my quiver to discover it was empty. "It looks as though we have a range of skill amongst us," he told us drily. I suppressed a smile as I perceived John had only managed to hit his target twice, once on the outermost circle and once even beyond that, just hitting the edge of the target board. "Very well, collect your arrows," he concluded.

"Sire!" we chorused and swiftly hurried along the field to pick them up. Most of mine, bar two, had all landed in the circles. The other two were near, having just missed the target board. I had some sympathy with John and a few of the others, who would have to spend several minutes combing the fields beyond for their arrows.

Having collected all of mine, I turned and walked back to the starting point and found myself beside the archer who had hit the target perfectly every time. I frowned slightly as I caught sight of a strange mark on one of the arrows she carried, but then I realised the mark was identical on all of them.

"I inscribe them myself, it's so I don't mix them up," she explained, having seen me look. I glanced up at her. "These are my personal arrows," she added. "The captain let me use them today." We had now reached our targets and whilst I deposited the arrows into the crate next to the empty bow I had used, she kept hold of hers.

"Your own bow, too?" I guessed. She nodded. "I suspect this was not your first try at archery," I speculated. She smirked as she slung her bow casually behind her.

"I have known how to shoot since I was four," she told me. My eyes widened in surprise, for this was young indeed to begin learning the skill.

"My mother taught me, when we used to hunt," the strong young woman continued. "We used to live in one of the villages on the lake hills before we moved to Gaeson. She was very skilled," she added. There was a slight sadness that came upon her face then, that told me her mother was dead.

"I'm sorry," I told her meaningfully. She tilted her head a little in thanks. "I lost my father a few months ago," I informed her presently. "He was a soldier and he died in battle."

"Then I am sorry too," she told me. "I'm Aife," she added, as we reached the courtyard and I saw John walking over towards us.

"I'm Daniel," I replied, "this is John. John, this is Aife," I introduced, as he came to a stop beside us. John proceeded to also compliment her on her shooting and Aife gave a small smile in return. "Are you fifteen years also?" I added as we stood with the pool of other recruits, awaiting further instructions from the captain. "We turned fifteen a few months ago," I added. Aife gave a smile. "Actually, it is six months until I come of age, but I was permitted to join early because of my experience of hunting," she informed me. My eyes widened, for it was possible to join the army a little before age, but certainly not customary practice. I reasoned my new friend must possess extraordinary talent: indeed, I had already begun to witness it. John opened his mouth to comment but was cut off, as new orders came from the captain and we hurriedly formed ranks.

***

That had been just the start of our friendship. It did not matter that Aife and I were placed among the archers and John was not, nor that John and I were friends for years by the time we met her. It quickly became known among the recruits and in the general army that the three of us had formed a close bond. It was only a few days later that Aife also met Sarah and they also bonded instantly. The four of us had ever remained close. I then took a sidelong glance at John and found myself smiling a little, thankful that our close bonds of friendship had remained, despite my sudden change in identity a year ago.

Presently I surveyed the scene and frowned. There had been some talent displayed at the combat earlier and here at the archery. Already I suspected most would be enlisted into my queen's army, although some would not pass the initial assessments. Indeed, as I continued to view their progress, I realised I had already made the decision, having been convinced from my conversation with him outside Leigh's medical chambers. I would not ask Ewan yet, though; I would wait to see if the situation with the Wolf worsened. Little did I know I would only have to wait until the following day.

Chapter Three

"Your Highness," said a rough voice the next evening. I looked up to see Lord Aldred, one of Evelyn's chief advisors, standing in the doorway of my study chamber the next evening. Aldred's features were of an older man, but most of his hair was still dark. I then perceived there was some sweat on his forehead and that his countenance had a pained intensity about it.

"May I speak with you, sire?" he enquired, between pants, urgency clear in his tone. I noticed then that his breathing was heavy, as if he had run all the way here.

"Aye, of course." I had already gotten to my feet upon his entering my office. "Be seated, if you wish," I invited. He slumped into the smaller seat on the other side of the desk to mine, without his usual pomp and grace. "What has happened?" I asked, much concerned. It was not usual for him come to my study, as I had most dealings with him in the council chamber.

"I am afraid we do rather have a situation," he informed me, as he caught his breath. "Since I learned John and Aife would be listening in to the soldiers' conversations," he began hastily, "I too, have tried to be vigilant and listen in the shadows. I have overheard something this night, something most terrible," he continued and paused here to wipe his forehead with the back of his hand. I longed the man to hurry and tell me whatever horrors he knew, but in sympathy for his present state I bit my tongue.

"I heard a plot, to kill Her Majesty," he disclosed at last and here my eyes widened in shock. "I have arrested three, but I fear it is not enough to thwart their plans," he elaborated. He stood up, then, clearly in distress at the news he had been obliged to bear. He shook his head, pained; he half turned away.

"Is she safe?" I asked instantly, having come from my desk to the middle of the chamber. "I must go to her—"

"She is safe and well in your chamber, my Lord Prince," Aldred told me, his tone less heavy now his breathing had returned. "There are ten guards standing guard outside your door; I swear no harm will come to her. I bid you delay a little, so that I can relate the plot to you," he requested. I hesitated, but then nodded, for if there was no immediate danger, I wished to know all I could.

"What a terrible thought, that someone would want to kill Her Majesty!" he then exclaimed and as his harsh tone emitted this speech, his hand struck the stone of the wall.

"Forgive me, my lord," he said wearily, his passion dissipating as quickly as it had arisen. "Sire, do you mind if I..." he trailed off this next discourse, but his hand gestured at the wine on the table in the corner, rendering his speech clear enough.

"Be my guest, by all means," I replied heavily, sinking back into my chair as the news of what could have happened to Evelyn fully registered. "In fact, pour one for me, also."

"Of course, my lord," Aldred murmured and poured generous goblets for both of us. He sat down again, only a little more grandly as he handed one to me. He took a large sip whilst I did the same. "They are being interrogated as we speak," he said, taking another large gulp.

"Good man," I replied, taking another sip before putting the goblet down firmly back on the table, so that the red tonic sloshed a little in its vessel. "What did you hear? Tell me all."

"Aye, sire," he said. "I was in the inn off the square, sat on my own enjoying my dinner. I often eat there," he added unnecessarily, "when suddenly I began to hear their alarming conversation. They were at a table not far from mine. We were in an area of the inn that was relatively empty," he informed me. He closed his eyes now and leaned back in his chair a little as he thought. "They believed themselves to be whispering," he stated, "but they had taken so much drink that what they thought was hushed speech was louder than most people talk."

"I understand," I answered him rapidly, "but what did they actually speak of? What plot had they? When was this treason to take place?" I asked him impatiently.

"Of course, sire, forgive my preamble. The plot to kill her was this very night," he revealed. At this, I cursed under my breath. "In fact, I am convinced they were to carry out this abomination as soon as they had finished their refreshment," he continued. I gave a short nod at this but spoke no further, not wanting to delay him in his account.

"They were speaking of the Wolf, who was not present," he informed me quickly. "From what I could hear, they were speaking of replacing the usual guards outside your chamber door. One of them would have then knocked on the door and given you a false reason to quit your rooms. Without the protection, that same individual would have killed your wife as she slept, whilst the rest stood guard outside," he concluded sombrely.

"Sadly, I heard no more." Here he paused to take another gulp of wine before setting it back empty; he had drained it in a few mouthfuls. "They moved on to talk about women, in not the most respectful terms," he added wryly. "When I was convinced their plot would be discussed no longer, I implored a couple of off-duty soldiers in another area off the inn to help me arrest them and escort them to the dungeon. They seemed sober enough for the task," he concluded with a smirk.

"Then you have saved Her Majesty's life this day," I exhaled, relieved indeed she was safe. "This Veiled Wolf again," I repeated slowly. "You heard nothing more about him?" I asked presently, after tasting the wine again.

"It appears they were foolish about themselves, but clever about him, sire," Aldred returned, giving a little shake of his head as he spoke.

"You have done well in setting so many guards to protect her," I murmured, trying to think. "You say the guilty soldiers are already being interrogated. Do you think they will talk?" I asked him. At this, the corner of Aldred's mouth turned.

"I believe so, Your Highness. They did not seem to be all that resilient," he advised, moving his clasped hands so he stretched his fingers back as he spoke.

"That should make this quicker, at least," I stated, giving a quick nod. "Thank you, Aldred, sincerely. We shall have to speak to them immediately, to confirm there is no more threat. "We will only delay to ensure she is safe and taken to a place of hiding. I bid you accompany," I added, as I finished my own wine and stood.

"Of course, my lord," Aldred bowed a little more grandly. "It is my honour to serve." Swiftly both of us quit my study at once and I perceived much of his pomp seemed restored. We scarcely spoke until we reached my chamber, where I hoped and prayed Evelyn still safely resided. The only speech I did give was when I saw three soldiers passing by on their watch and summoned them; I would use them to take her to a place of safety. When Aldred, the other soldiers and I arrived on the corridor, I was relieved indeed to see all ten guards still in post.

"I bid you wait here a moment," I murmured and entered through the door quickly. I went through to the bedchamber where my heart was lightened considerably to seeing her safe. She stood in our chamber, fully dressed and with her sword buckled about her waist.

"Evelyn," I greeted with relief, "are you all right?" I asked nonetheless as I went immediately to her side, even though I saw she was in no danger.

"Aye, husband," a grim determination was upon her features, "I am well. Aldred has thwarted the plot," she added. "I am ready to depart," she said, "lest a greater number attack."

"Good," I returned quietly, moving to clutch her hand tightly for a moment. Then, abruptly I went to the door and listened carefully. Evelyn was holding the hilt of her blade and I gave a small smile at this. I knew my queen was not one who would relinquish her life easily.

"Escort Her Majesty to the loft in the stables and then remain on guard there," I instructed to the guards outside the chamber. I had named the first place that came into my mind. Was I being too sentimental, believing that the place I had spent so much time with my father, where I had first met my wife as a child, would be safe?

"Your Highness," the soldiers reiterated. If they were surprised at the order, their countenances, illuminated by the torch one of them bore, did not show it. I resolved it was a place that could be protected as any other. Besides, the order had already been given.

"Extinguish your lamps when you get there, so that your lights will not give you away," I commanded then. "I bid you keep hidden, my lady," I turned to say to my wife, "until I come for you." I brought Evelyn's hand to my mouth and kissed it briefly.

"Come, let us delay no longer." Evelyn spoke quickly to the guards as our hands broke contact. A moment later and they had gone, leaving Aldred and me alone in the corridor, along with the ten soldiers who had been posted outside my chambers. Having not been addressed, they had remained silent and still, as if none of the tense scene had occurred.

"It is possible that this chamber may be invaded tonight," I addressed the guards hastily. "You must be vigilant against all these attacks." The guards answered rapidly, confirming their obedience. "Lord Aldred, to the dungeon," I added and at once we set off to our destination.

As we neared it, we met two more soldiers, whom I also instructed to join us. The four of us made our way through the interconnecting stone walls of the castle, descending spiral staircases until at last we reached the dungeon entrance. I tensed slightly, the way I always did coming here, for it always brought to my mind the time I had been tortured here. Also, I recalled when I had almost killed King Reghan in my fury, after his abdication. I ignored this feeling however, determinedly pushing it aside as we entered the long, dank aisle, with cells either side.

Presently we came to a larger cell and I could already see the four soldiers, clapped in irons with their hands raised high above them, but their faces downcast to the floor. I perceived their eyes were hazed full with wine. My immediate wondering was how on earth, if Aldred had not caught them, they would have been able to complete their mission in such a state. Still, I was only too acquainted with soldiers who would muddy their heads with alcohol before battle or dangerous task. Many believed it replaced fear with notions of false confidence, when all it did was increase folly. Not only were they intoxicated, but as I stepped closer, I saw all of them looked as though they had been beaten to a pulp.

"Who has done this to them?" I demanded of Aldred, before we opened the cell doors. It had been quick work, for the advisor and I had been delayed only a few minutes, whilst he told me of the plot and we ensured Evelyn was safe.

"I assure you, my lord, this torture was not on my command," Aldred responded quickly, as I opened the cell door. Immediately the strong scents of blood, alcohol and dirt reached my nostrils. It seemed they had been kicked about in the mud before being brought here. It reminded me of when I had been harshly beaten by the interrogator, without being asked a single question. I therefore loathed to ever see such a display of injustice to a prisoner again.

"It may have been the prison guards, sire, after I had left them in their custody," Aldred remarked, presently confirming my suspicions. "I believe betraying one's fellow soldiers does make one rather unpopular," he pointed out diplomatically. I shook my head in response.

"These men are far from innocent, but that does not excuse needless brutality," I retorted hotly. "I wish to know who was responsible for this." We came to the metal bars in the cell, that separated us from the prisoners. "Now, open the door," I added in swift command to one of the soldiers. He immediately leapt forwards.

"Of course, Your Highness, I will look into the matter personally," Aldred assured as the soldier completed this task. "My lord is gracious indeed," he added, but I barely paid this last speech heed as I strode through it and came to crouch before them.

"Lord Aldred claims he overheard some of your conversation this night," I informed them at once. A quick scan with my eyes made me recognise them all, but since they had resided in one of the other army chambers to me, I did not know them well.

"What must it be like to be you, Daniel?" one of the soldiers now murmured, raising his head to look at me. He then abruptly coughed a little and I moved quickly back. "To be following orders one moment and then give them out the next. Such power, such privilege—" he broke off to cough again.

"How dare you speak to His Highness in such a way!" Aldred broke in loudly. The soldier in question jumped and his head lolled back against the wall.

"Listen to me," I persisted calmly, ignoring the councillor for the moment. "Why were you plotting to do this to your queen?" He did not answer, to my irritation. "Who is this Wolf working for?" I asked, louder and sterner.

"You will answer His Highness!" Aldred reinforced me, his voice rising to a shout. "Or you will face further consequences for your disobedience. Speak and you may be spared," he added warningly. The soldier's eyes flickered past me to Aldred and back to me again.

"We know not who he is," the soldier replied wearily. As he spoke, I noticed the thickness of his mouth where he had been hit in the face and a thin red welt where his lip had been cut open. "Is he a soldier? Is he in the council? Speak more, man," I pressed. He met my eyes, but then said nothing and looked down again.

"We only know him by that name," he said, then flinched slightly, faltering as he looked down once more. I reflected it must be sore for him to talk.

"What about the rest of you?" I questioned, turning to the others. "Tell me, who else was planning to attack Her Majesty? Were there any others?" I enquired harshly.

"No, sire, there were only us four," another rebel stated wearily. "The queen is safe, there will be no further attacks." I turned to stare at him hard for a moment, before glancing to the other two soldiers who so far had said nothing. One of them had a trail of drool, slowly suspending beneath his chin. I saw that none of them were in a state to say anything further.

"Does anyone have anything else to say? This may be the last chance for you to be of use," I cautioned. The men barely moved; they simply stayed with their heads slumped down to the stone-cold floor. "Very well," I murmured and stood, resigning myself to their stubbornness. The soldier on duty in the dungeon who had opened the gate for us stepped forwards again to close the metal bars behind us. Abruptly, I turned and grabbed him.

"Sire!" Aldred objected as I pushed the guard against the prison wall, my hand going to his neck in warning.

"Were you one of the ones who beat those men?" I asked, ignoring the councillor once again. My eyes were fixed only on the guard in front of me.

"No, Your Highness," the guard croaked back, throat slightly constricted from where I held him in place. "I only recently came onto duty, my lord," he added quickly and swallowed.

"Good," I answered him. "I pray you are telling the truth," I told him, searching his gaze, "for it will not take me long to find the culprits. Even guilty citizens are still members of this kingdom," I reminded him pointedly, "at Her Majesty's pleasure. I will not tolerate needless torture. Is that understood?" I challenged loudly. The guard nodded, though the movement was small, because my hand still restrained his throat.

"Here is your order," I continued, my speech soft now. "Remain outside the cell door and protect them from any further brutality. If any other soldier tells you otherwise, you are to inform them that you are following a direct command from your prince. If they are not safe when I return at dawn, then I will hold you directly responsible. Am I in any way unclear?"

"No, sire," he answered at once. I held his gaze for a moment longer and then I released him as abruptly as I had seized him. As we left the main door of the dungeon, I heard the advisor take a breath as though about to object and turned to him. At once his mouth closed.

"I thank you, Lord Aldred, for your actions tonight," I told him formally. "I bid you speak of this to no one. You are dismissed," I added quickly, "go and get some sleep."

"Thank you, Your Highness," he replied, with a final, grand bow. With that I left his company, still shaking with anger because of the way those prisoners had been attacked. They had plotted to kill my wife and though this filled me with rage also, I would not allow Gaeson to be a kingdom where prisoners were beaten to within an inch of survival. Immediately I longed to go to the stables to see that my wife was safe, but I trusted her skill and those of her guards. Besides, if there were any further perpetrators, they would have no reason to go to the stables.

Instead, then, I went immediately to one of the higher ramparts of the castle, where I knew Captain Bredon was on duty, overseeing the other guards on their night watch. Indeed, there he was, currently conversing with another guard. Whilst I waited for him to finish, I glanced through the night in the direction of the stables, but I could see nothing but darkness. After the guard had departed, I strode towards him. With the perception of a warrior who had been active for decades, the captain sensed the presence of another and turned around.

"Your Highness," he greeted me with a bow of his head as he came to face me, surprise already prevalent in his features. As he straightened again a moment later, his brows knitted together in a deep frown at my expression. "What is it, sire?" he enquired instantly.

"Not here," was all my reply, as I glanced at the soldiers. The seed of doubt, already planted, was now beginning to sprout. Bredon understood my hesitance and gave a curt nod. Therefore, neither of us spoke again until we had descended the spiral steps away from the rampart and had reached the safe confines of my study. Once there, I did not hesitate but directly related to him all that had happened in this last hour.

"It pains me to believe any of our comrades could be capable of such treachery, sire," my former master murmured in conclusion. We both stood by the fireplace, still lit from when I had been working in my study earlier. I outstretched my hands to the hearth, but the flames did not offer much consolation to the idea of betrayal.

"It pains me also, brother," I returned, sighing. "As much as I hate to say it, this confirms our suspicions that the Wolf is gathering soldiers from our own army as he sees fit," I concluded wearily. My arms dropped back to my sides as I looked up at him. "We have to implement our plan with one of our recruits. I know which one," I added meaningfully.

"Ewan," Bredon guessed immediately. He slowly let out his breath, as if struck anew by the awful reality of having to spy on those we trusted with our lives. "Are you sure, Daniel?" he asked, dropping my title in our earnest, frank discourse.

"No," I answered him honestly, leaning against my desk and folding my arms, "but I see no other course available to us. We must discover who else is working for the Wolf, for there may not be rowdy talk in an inn next time," I added pointedly.

"Can you give me any other option since we last spoke of this?" I then asked, wishing he could give me another course of action, but he remained silent. "Then there it is," I concluded heavily. "I trust Ewan's character more than any others," I informed him presently. "We must ask him now. Arrange a meeting and bring John. Ensure no one else sees you. That is all," I ended. The captain bowed at the orders I had given him.

"It will be done, Your Highness," Bredon responded and immediately left the room. Left alone, my hands rose to rub my tired eyes. A moment later and I heard the clinking of a guard's footsteps outside the door. I immediately tensed, but relaxed again as he made his way past. For our strategy to work, this meeting must not be discovered by anyone. It truly was difficult, to have served alongside these brothers and sisters for so long, yet to no longer know who to trust. In truth, I was finding the corruption of the late King Reghan easier to stomach than this. I sat down wearily at my desk and settled down to wait.

I was not reposed long, however, before there was a tap on the door. A moment later and the captain had entered my study, followed by John and Ewan, looking more than a little confused.

"Your Royal Highness," Ewan said. His greeting was louder than necessary and he nearly knocked a shelf as he bowed clumsily.

"Quiet, lad," Captain Bredon ordered in a whisper as John shut the door behind them, "do not be so hasty. Go, stand over there," he added with a clear gesture of irritation.

"Sorry, sire," Ewan replied, looking to the captain, John and me, as if applying the apology to all of us. He was quick to obey the captain's command and his expression was now carefully impassive, awaiting further instruction and clarification as to why he was here.

"I know our meeting is strange, Ewan," I began, "but we have to be certain that nobody can overhear this conversation. I have a task for you to do," I informed him, "the details of which must stay within these walls."

"Of course, my lord," Ewan answered swiftly, his voice now matching the volume of my own low tone. "I am ready to do whatever you command," he added, bowing his head.

"Good," I replied quietly, smiling a little at his enthusiasm. "It pains me to say this, but I am no longer sure I can trust all of our brothers and sisters in arms," I explained. Ewan's eyes widened at the thought. "The captain said you excelled in the trials, even with your stunt of combating all the other recruits."

"Aye, sire. My thirst to prove myself turned to folly," he admitted into the darkness the few hairs of stubble on his chin flickered in the soft lamplight as he spoke. I regarded him, inwardly a little impressed at his perceptive comment, despite his youth.

"It is a good strength, to be aware of your own shortcomings," I told him. "This is why we have asked you, because you are new to the army and therefore we trust you have not been corrupted. Though you are headstrong and a little rash," I admitted, "I believe you are not deceitful. You are earnest in your good nature," I told him.

"Thank you, sire," Ewan answered quietly. Just after he said this, we heard the tell-tale clinking footsteps of a guard on patrol. The three of us waited until there was silence again.

"We have little time," I cautioned him. "The guards patrol four times in the hour and this conversation must remain undetected. I know you have only been in the army a few weeks," I added, referring to the recruitment process. "We can take advantage of your new status, for you were only enlisted a few days ago.

"Your task is this," I continued quickly. "You must report any unusual activity, especially in conversations you might overhear. You can use your position of being new to gain trust, as you are welcomed into their ranks," I concluded.

"I know this is difficult," the captain began quietly, before Ewan could say anything. "We do not want you to be deceitful or to break trust any more than necessary, especially given the bonds of close friendship that are formed."

"The truth is…" John presently spoke and looked to me. I nodded directly, giving him permission to tell the lad about the foiled plot to murder Evelyn. "Only an hour ago, Lord Aldred overheard the talk of four soldiers, discussing a plot to kill Her Majesty," John continued.

"I am sorry indeed to hear that, Your Highness," Ewan instantly responded to me. His sombre face, reflecting in the dim light of the lantern and the deliberate carefulness of the way he spoke, suddenly made him appear well advanced of his sixteen years. Indeed, it was a complete contrast to the seemingly clumsy and undignified way in which he had entered my study.

"Our priority is to find these culprits," Captain Bredon then instructed him, with his arms still folded. "We must ensure the safety of Gaeson, at all costs." Ewan had glanced down to the floor and even in the dim light I could make out his frown. A moment later, however, he looked up, his countenance clear.

"I will strive to do all that you ask of me, Your Highness," he whispered. I looked into his eyes and saw his honesty and loyalty were clear. There was indeed a resilience to his character.

"Your dedication to your people and to the crown are commendable," I encouraged him. "You are passionate and forthright, Ewan. These are good traits indeed," I continued. "However, this task will require discipline, sensitivity and much forethought. You must work on these disciplines and not let your haste overtake your sense," I advised him.

"If I might speak boldly for a moment, my lord," Ewan replied, "the day you met me, I was foolhardy with the other recruits," he reiterated. "I thank you for the chance to prove my worth. I give you my word, sire, I will not let you down."

"Good lad," I answered him with a small smile. "John, I bid you take him back to the regimental chambers. We must be quick," I whispered.

"Your Highness," John and Ewan whispered, bowing before they quit my study. I remained there a moment, reflecting that the meeting with Ewan had been encouraging, even though it made the task before the young lad no less pleasant to think of.

"Very well," I concluded to no one in particular, though the captain was still present. "I ask you to remain vigilant also, as always. I need to go and find my wife," I added abruptly, ever anxious to ensure she was safe even though the danger seemed to have passed.

"Of course, sire," Captain Bredon replied. For the final time I left this room and headed directly to the stables, at once wishing to ensure Evelyn was safe.

It was with great relief that I arrived to see my wife standing outside the stables with several guards who had escorted her, looking as though no force on earth could move them from her protection. I smiled to myself, for I was equally amused and frustrated at her refusal to actually hide in the stables themselves. A quick word with the soldiers outside confirmed that all was at peace, but my heart did not truly ease until I saw her coming over to stand beside me.

"Prince Bryce," Evelyn greeted me formally. "Is all well?" she asked me quickly. "Did you discover any more about who plotted this foul plot?"

"Aye, my queen," I assured her at once. "I bid we go some distance away, I have much to tell you. Stay here and remain on guard," I added to the soldier, who sounded his obedience. At my instruction, he lit his torch that we would find our way back to the stable. I then picked up another lamp as my own beacon. Thus, able to see our way across the field, I led Evelyn away. Together we walked for about a mile and at this safe distance I set the lamp down on a wooden stump, the remnant of a sawn tree. We moved a little away until we blended in the darkness, for whilst we were being well protected from afar, I knew we were even safer not so illuminated.

"I thought you were going to hide in the stables," I muttered in jest annoyance, as we sat down on the grass. It was near where the recruits' arrows had landed a few days ago, when they had tried their hands at archery. The green blades still retained some lingering warmth, for the sun had shone with unexpected heat today, despite it being mid-autumn.

"You know me, Daniel. I'm not the hiding type," she replied with a smirk and I conceded this with a nod.

"Aye, even when the battle horn sounds you are oft reluctant to go to the caves," I murmured in agreement and then proceeded to give her a fuller account of all that had happened this night. "I am just so pleased you are safe," I ended, moving my wife's hand to my mouth to kiss it briefly. "Hopefully Ewan will infiltrate the spies, discover the Wolf's identity and all will be revealed," I concluded with feeling.

"We owe Aldred a great debt," she agreed. She spoke nothing further on the matter but instead turned to rest her head on my shoulder. The gravity of what had nearly occurred left us weary and neither one of us wished for a prolonged discussion. "Do you remember the night you told me about the stars?" my wife asked, her voice suddenly small and soft. "The night we hid in the forest." My free hand brushed the nearby green but invisible reeds as she spoke.

"Aye, like it was yesterday," I replied. "I had no idea who I really was," I then reflected and at this Evelyn turned her face towards me, but I could only perceive her outline.

"I disagree, my husband," she spoke and even in the dark, I sensed the smile in her voice. "You becoming a prince changed your outer surface, but not who you were underneath. You showed me everything I needed to know about your character the day you cut that rope."

"Thank you," I returned with a smile of my own. Together the two of us turned to look back at the stars. "It was not I who saved your life this day," I told her now. "I owe your safety to Aldred," I repeated, for it was not I who had rescued her this night. "It is good to have Aldred as a friend, you were right to keep him on when you took the throne from your father."

My wife said nothing to this and in the brief pause, I sensed some semblance of sadness. "Evelyn?" I prompted, my arm going to wrap around hers.

"Hmm? Yes," she agreed. "Sorry, I was thinking about my father." At this she shuffled a little closer, turning to her side so her head rested on my shoulder again. My free hand now went to rest behind my head. "Tell me about the stars again," she implored.

"Aye," I assented turning briefly to kiss her forehead. I lifted a finger above me and as I did that night in the forest, so many moons ago, I traced their patterns across the sky, explaining the constellations the way my father had taught me.

"Do you still have it, my boy from the snow?" she asked softly, halfway through my narration, her hand affectionally moving to my chest pocket. I smiled as one hand reached within the tunic, to retrieve the lace cloth she had given me, when we had met in the snow as children.

"Always," I told her simply, handing the lace cloth to her for a moment. She turned it over in her hands, a little smile on her face.

"Do you think we will have children, Daniel?" she asked me with a sigh as she handed it back. I glanced at her with some surprise at the sudden choice of topic, but then I knew the subject was ever at the forefront of my mind and I paused a moment before answering. I wished to comfort her, but I knew well not all who wished to have children were able to. My mother who had raised me in Gaeson was an example of this.

"I know not, love," I answered ere long. "I hope so, by God's will. It is in his hands," I reassured her and kissed her forehead once more. "Now, do you wish to hear more?" I teased lightly. Her head nodded mutely against my shoulder. I continued my tales of the sky, as her chin rested against the nape of my neck. I wound an arm around her comfortably and soon became all the more aware of her warm body against mine. The relief of her safety and the nearness of her to me abruptly made me long for her.

"Well, my queen," I teased, as I ended the account of the stars and abruptly rolled on top of her, "how about we attempt to make a child now?"

"What, here?" Evelyn giggled, sounding positively scandalised. "What about the guard?" she asked doubtfully, realising I was serious as my hands went to the bottom of her dress.

"He is a mile away, we can see their lantern from here." I felt my wife's head turn to gaze at the aforementioned orb of light, seeming like a small, floating ball at this distance. "He will not move until we tell him too," I added and as she giggled lightly, I bent my head to kiss her soundly. She offered no more doubt but only returned my passion, as my hands reached down to untie the sash still about her waist. I knew the guard would notice if we turned the light off altogether, so instead I took my wife's hand and led her a little away, further into the darkness.

A while later, we came back to the tree stump where I had left the light on. Soon, dim light shone around us once more. I glanced back to the nature all around me, the only witness to what we had just done. I looked again at my lovely wife and could not help but laugh at her normally neat curls, now in complete disarray.

"Your hair," I explained at her raised eyebrows, in question of my gentle mockery. She gave a wry smile as her hands came upon her tousled curls, some of which had come loose. There was also the occasional twig and grass blade now stuck within her raven locks.

"Well, whose doing is that?" she enquired accusingly, making me chuckle. "I'll have to do it again," my wife then tutted as she freed her hair from the circular cords that bound it.

"I'll have to rest first," I joked. My wife pulled a face as her hand came to punch my shoulder lightly, her features bearing the contradiction of being unimpressed when really her eyes sparkled with humour. Both hands then came to pull her hair loose and I watched with some awe as they expertly ran through her curls swiftly, clearing them of twigs and the like before brushing it smooth and flat again with her fingers. I then watched as with a final flourish, she swept up and twisted her curls effortlessly back into a neat bun and fastened it into place. "Better?" she asked.

"Perfect," I replied with a smile. My hands quickly ran through my own hair then and I stood, brushing the worst of the grass from my arms and legs whist she did the same. I then took a step towards my wife, one hand resting round her waist and the other at the rounded flatness of her stomach.

"Just think, my wife," I murmured, pausing to kiss the nape of her neck, "there might be new life in you, even now." The danger we had avoided seemed distant history in the light of this new hope. She gave a contented smile at the thought as our temples touched briefly.

"One can only hope," she replied wistfully. "Let's retire," she added, her hands coming to straighten her hair a final time. "Our chamber is surely safe by now."

"Aye," I agreed as I bent to pick up the torch and the two of us walked back together, hand in hand. We dismissed the guard as we passed him. As we walked back to the castle, the previous tension came back again I wondered who this Veiled Wolf might be. "We will discover him, Evelyn," I declared finally. "He will not destroy our home."

"Yes," was all she replied for now, as we came to our chamber. "However, we shall not accomplish anything whilst I am this tired," she added as we came to bed. I chuckled and kissed the top of her head as I lay down beside her.

"Goodnight, my love," I murmured tenderly. We came together in a brief, final kiss before she turned away, leaving me once more with my own thoughts, reaching again for the lace cloth Evelyn had given me that day in the snow.

I knew I had been so passionate with her because I was so relieved she was safe, the adrenaline of desire replacing the despair when she could have been harmed. I realised now too I had been a little ashamed it was not me that had saved her, but Lord Aldred. Danger for the present had been averted, but my heart ached to ponder what could have happened if the councillor had not overheard those drunken soldiers in the tavern.

I wondered now what could have happened, if all had gone to their plan. If they had knocked on the door with some pretence, would I have gone away from her so quickly, unaware it could have been the last time I ever beheld her? I rolled over in bed to gaze at the silhouette of my wife and with my grip still tight on the lace cloth, I promised anew I would solve this. I would indeed protect her from all harm, as I had once vowed that day in the snow.

Chapter Four

I raced out of the door of my old house at the cry of the battle horn, my footsteps crunching onto fresh snow as I ran. I had been visiting my mother when the alarm had sounded, piercing the previous stillness of the day. It was about three months since the night of the plot to kill Evelyn and the current chaotic scene was a sharp contrast with the tranquillity I had known with her under the stars, despite the danger of the Veiled Wolf. I murmured a swift prayer that Evelyn was already at the caves where our citizens evacuated to, not only for her own safety but so that she would be ready to defend our people in refuge there.

"Go, Daniel," Sarah instructed quickly, running out into the street after me and I turned to her. "I'll make sure your mother gets to the cave." I hesitated a moment, but she had already turned away from me.

"You two, help me, quickly!" she shouted to two soldiers also running towards the castle. They came towards us immediately and quickly bowed.

"Go and get my mother from upstairs, she is bedridden," I explained to them rapidly. Instantly they ran inside to follow my order.

"What is happening? Is it Bernicia?" Rachel asked as she and her two daughters ran outside, her face creased with worry.

"I believe so," I answered her swiftly, "but we will defend you to the end," I added defiantly. As I ended this the two guards appeared back outside, holding a chair between them with my mother sitting precariously upon it.

"Yes, of course," my mother said, "but you will not provide protection for us standing here. Get to the castle. I pray you will remain safe, my son," she added, softly.

"Aye," I returned, swiftly kissing her hand. "I'll see you all soon," I added determinedly and paused to briefly touch my sister's shoulder, before sprinting through the narrow streets towards the castle. Presently I came to the courtyard and abruptly raced across it. By now it was largely deserted, apart from the last few soldiers running into position.

I hoped by now all of Gaeson not fighting were safely in the caves, where we would protect them until our last breath. I entered the base of the tower where all of the soldiers had amassed, ready for the dance of war to begin. Epos and another horse stood there, ready for us to ride out to speak with those intent on destroying us before the battle began. We waited a few more minutes whilst the last remaining soldiers came into position and then all was quiet. Even the horses did not move very much but as always, seemed to sense what was about to happen.

"My lord," Bredon uttered quietly in my ear after a few more moments. I hid my surprise that he was waiting for me. It was the first time any enemy had come to Gaeson after my change in identity and I was unused to taking the lead in battle.

"Let us see whether any negotiation is possible," I instructed. I was already readying Epos as I spoke.

"Aye, sire," Bredon said. He gestured to a soldier above him, who raised the portcullis. As he did this, he too mounted this horse. The sharp gate disappeared into the archway above it, leaving only the metal tips visible. This time I knew they were waiting for me and without any further delay, I spurred Epos into a gallop and we sped out into the morning. Beside me was my former master and bringing up the rear was another rider bearing Gaeson's banner. The sunshine beat splendidly down on us, further reflecting onto the snow. There was a tragic irony about the weather being so fine when there was so much blood about to be shed.

We descended the hill from the castle over the wet ground, our horses' hooves trudging through the frozen slush as they went. A contingent from Bernicia was already fast on its way to meet us and we met them halfway down the hill. As I slowed Epos down, she began to nudge her head anxiously.

"Steady, girl," I whispered, reaching to stroke her pale, rich coat. The Bernician party stopped a few feet away and then I raised my head. "I am Prince Bryce of Rheged, heir to the throne of Klumeck," I greeted them formally. "I speak for Queen Evelyn of Gaeson and bring you greetings of peace. However, I warn you this castle is ready to defend itself," I continued evenly.

"I speak in the stead of King Hussa of Bernicia," the soldier opposite me said. "I can assure you, Your Highness, that we come to conquer your kingdom and its lands. I suggest you prepare for your immediate surrender, otherwise you will face the pain of death."

"Very well. It seems talking is short indeed," I answered his cold speech. Allow me to warn you that you will not find Gaeson as easy to take as you imagine," I informed him. "We return to the castle," I added in command to the captain.

"Your Royal Highness," Bredon formally assented. The three of us rode swiftly back up the hill across the courtyard. The portcullis thundered down after us promptly after we had passed through.

"Take the horses back to the stables and return here as soon as you can," I added to a nearby soldier as I swung down again from Epos and gave her mane a final pat. The soldier muttered his obedience quickly, as he took the reins from us, leaving a trail of frost in his wake.

"Captain," I murmured turning to my former commander, "I bid you speak to our army, with the wisdom you have always done. I will go to my position atop the balcony."

"Aye, sire," Bredon replied swiftly. This done, at last I ascended the spiral staircase and came to a halt beside Aife, who was giving instructions to the other archers.

"Where have they come from?" I ground out in frustration. By the look on Aife's face, she was wondering the same thing. Indeed, they had amassed so quickly that I suspected those who had chased us from Klumeck may have had other comrades camped nearby. Perhaps those Bernicians had joined ranks with the rest of their forces. We were far smaller and easier to take than Caer Ligualid, so this had been their first move.

"It has been a while since any enemy came to our gates." Captain Bredon's voice, clear and crisp, rang out below, distracting me from further pondering. Indeed, a silent suspense had descended as he paused. In this brief silence, I thought quickly. The last time we had been marched against was nigh a year and a half ago, by King Urien himself. He had appeared at dawn along with King Cedric to deal with the corrupt King Reghan, Evelyn's late father.

I had just discovered my identity and learned that Gaeson, not Klumeck, was the rogue kingdom that stood against Rheged. I had risked everything to tell Gaeson the truth and after Evelyn had forced King Reghan to abdicate, we were able to avoid bloodshed. I feared, however, that we would not have such an outcome today. I reflected now that since joining Gaeson's army a decade ago, we had never before had Bernicia themselves invade our home. All conflicts had been when we were at war with Klumeck.

"We will prevail, however," my captain presently stated, in avid determination. I nodded firmly to his speech, as if we could keep our enemies at bay through sheer will. "Trust in God and do not lose heart, for even if we lose our lives in defence of our home, there is a far better home waiting for us. For Gaeson!" he added in conclusion, raising his sword high.

"For Gaeson!" the army responded. High up on the ramparts, I plucked my first arrow from my quiver.

"Prepare to fire," I commanded in a low voice, placing the arrow upon my bow and stretching it taut. We waited in the deathly quiet and it was so silent I could hear the collective twang of strings from other archers.

The Bernicians emitted the almighty roar of a battle cry. Suddenly, they were rushing towards us. It was rather unsettling to see them racing in the broad daylight and I had to fight the urge to crouch down, for both sides were all the more vulnerable in the almost dazzling sunshine.

"Fire!" I shouted, releasing my fingers. The arrow shot forward, racing through the sky before descending in its arc and finding its way home into the advancing enemy.

"Fire at will!" I cried, as we released yet more arrows into the early morning. Despite our archers' great skill, soon the Bernicians were hounding against the walls of my home. I knew we were outnumbered with them not even at full force. Even as we pierced them the multitude was already at our walls, spattering the white ground with crimson.

"Reinforcements at this wall!" I shouted, but it was of little use, for it looked as though each one was already overrun. As I observed the Bernicians below, I saw them now move a long, heavy structure and recognised instantly what it was.

"The ram!" I cried, giving my last command hurriedly, as we aimed towards the Bernicians threatening to break the portcullis. The metal was vast and strong, but could it withstand such repeated blows? I released another arrow into the air, reaching behind me to my quiver for another, but grasped at nothing. I realised instantly in frustration that I was out of arrows. Glancing quickly, I saw Aife had only two left. I slung my bow onto my back decisively, instead drawing my sword.

"We must go to where they will breach," I instructed, for there was nothing else we could do here with no arrows left to fire.

"Aye, my lord," Aife agreed, grasping at the spear beside her and turning to me. "Where you lead, we will follow to the end, sire," she added as the other archers wielded their other weapons. I gave her a brief smile in thanks, which quickly disappeared at further sounds of war.

"To battle, then," I stated, raising my sword high. "Charge!" I shouted. The twenty of us ran downstairs through the castle, as yet untouched by the enemy. We sprinted as fast as our armour would allow down the spiral staircases, pounding along the corridors. A few seconds later, we entered the courtyard which was already starting to overrun. The scene gave me a swift reminder of the time Captain Bredon and I had fought the Bernician spies here, the night Evelyn was almost kidnapped.

As we broke into the courtyard, Aife launched her spear and I watched it sail into the head of an enemy soldier, taking him down instantly. In the next moment, hardly slowing, she stooped to grab an enemy blade and took down the first few she came across, before she retrieved her spear from the man's head, flicking off the gore as she flourished it.

"Drive them back!" I shouted loudly as I ploughed into the enemy, wielding my sword high before slicing it down into them. The Bernicians fought back, parrying me as I made the blows. The first man I strategically hit with my sword, making him stagger. I then angled my sword to kiss his neck and his warm blood spattered across my face as he fell. I ducked as my next opponent swung his sword high and I pirouetted whilst low. My sword contacted his side, but it was deflected by his armour.

I then darted back as his blade came down towards me, bringing my own up to block it. Abruptly metal clashed towards metal and as we both pushed forward with our swords, I clearly saw his face. His countenance was fiery and determined, but as I had expected, there was nothing particularly evil in his expression. He was simply a soldier following the orders of his king. Our blades pressed further together, neither of us giving in to the other. The resolve in his features confirmed the already obvious truth that he meant to kill me. As with every other battle I had fought, I knew that it was him or me. With extreme effort, I swiped his sword away, bent and slashed my sword against his leg.

My opponent immediately fell to the floor, clutching his bleeding leg. I saw his form tense, preparing for my final blow. I perceived, however, that my injury to him would prevent his further fighting but gave him a good chance of a survival. Therefore, I left him where he was sprawled across the snowy, stone floor and made my way further across the courtyard, fighting off each opponent that came my way.

Abruptly, a man suddenly lashed out with the hilt of his blade, knocking it hard into my temple. My head bled at once as I fell to the floor, over my left eye so that I had to swipe the crimson fluid away to be able to see. As soon as my vision was clear from this red stream, I saw the man who had hit me with his sword raised high. I instantly rolled to my right through the snow and groaned aloud as the force of the blow hit the armour on my leg. I groaned aloud at the painful impact, but it had not pierced my skin.

To my horror, as my enemy advanced upon me I saw my sword was out of reach. Instead I lunged to him, my hand retrieved my dagger from my boot. Just before we made contact my arm flew up, so my small blade pierced his side where there was a gap in his armour.

"Don't let any of them through!" I shouted as I seized my sword, sat up and angrily wiped more of my blood from my face. However, the enemy was pressing ever closer against us. The combat became quicker and more intense as we attempted to stop the Bernicians from intruding our lives and homes. As with every other battle, after the first few individuals my opponents blurred into one. At one point, the hilt of another sword smashed into my jaw. I fell onto the floor once again, but as I landed in the frost I thrashed my sword against my enemy and felt my blade slice across the softness of flesh at his arm.

As he fell I pulled myself to my feet, mentally assessing my injuries. My jaw ached, but my mouth had not filled with blood. The Bernician soldier in question must have hit my cheek at an awkward angle, or else it would surely be broken. I rose up quickly, half turning to block the next blow, but even as I parried him I already knew my own disadvantage. Instantly, I knew this could well be my last fight, for as I made to block him again, his position meant he could easily knock the sword from my hand.

I leapt backwards, but then felt the stone wall of the courtyard behind me. My opponent sneered in victory, already knowing he had won. There was no time to reach my dagger and I glanced about me, but it was too late. My foe's smirk grew as I prepared for my immediate death, my last thought of Evelyn's smile.

"Your Highness!" came a familiar shout, as a sword thrust into the man's side. As my foe fell to his death, I saw it was Ewan. "He was too immersed into the combat of one, sire," the lad sniggered, repeating what John had told him during the recruits' assessment. I smiled back in relief to still be alive.

"Are you injured, my lord?" Ewan asked more seriously, obviously seeing the blood on my face as I bent to pick up my sword.

"I shall live, thanks to you," I panted, clapping my hand on his shoulder in gratitude. I used the brief respite to survey the scene, as I removed blood and snow from my eyes. "It looks like the battle is turning," I said, to my encouragement and surprise, for there had been such a swarm. Possibly I had overestimated their numbers, or perhaps underestimated our own force.

"For Gaeson?" I asked him as I took a firmer grip on my own blade. Ewan gave a nod as he wielded his own sword in front of him.

"For Gaeson, sire," he replied bravely. With that, the two of us ran forwards, back into the scourge. As I did, I uttered a quick prayer for the rash but kind young soldier who had saved my life. Metal clashed against metal once more as I brought my sword down upon the Bernician soldiers. The outside world again receded so that it was only me and the ones I fought. It was the age-old, simple calculation of my life, or the life I had to take.

Presently, I looked to my left and suddenly saw my captain was surrounded. At once I changed direction, beginning to fight my way over.

As I raced towards my friend, abruptly I ducked to miss a blow from another foe. I rolled to my side and slashed my blade across his knee. The enemy groaned, falling to the ground. He was immobilised for the moment and that was enough. I leapt up and ran around him, determined to reach Bredon in time.

"Captain!" I shouted, as I ran across Gaeson's courtyard. The image of him fighting in the courtyard once before came again to my mind. Captain Bredon was skilfully warding off his attackers, blocking one and then another, fighting off six of them at once. I did not slow down as I reached him but used all my strength to slam into the first assailant, knocking him clean to the ground. One of the others immediately turned to me, but not before I pulled my dagger back out from my boot. As I leapt to my feet, the small point of my blade found its home in his side.

"Thank you, my lord," the captain called, panting a little. I gave him a quick smile as I drew another away from him. Then, to my horror, three more enemies appeared behind him. He had sensed them, however, immediately twirling round to parry the swinging of a spear. Two more Bernicians then appeared to the left of me and I was embroiled in yet more combat. I tried to fight my way back to the captain, but there were too many of them. I had a sense of impending doom that I alone could not save my old mentor's life.

Abruptly, a spear flew past me to land in the shoulder of one of the soldiers attacking Bredon. I smiled in hope, instantly recognising it as Aife's. As I cut down another foe she ran past, not even slowing as she drew her sword, but not before one of the captain's remaining attackers had sliced his sword against my friend's neck.

"No!" I roared in anger and despair as I struck my latest foe down and sprinted the final few steps to his side. Gaeson reinforcements appeared around me, but they were too late. "Surgeon!" I cried, as I attempted to stem the bleeding.

"It is too late, sire," the captain rasped out, his hand waving away my pitiful attempts. To my terror, as his warm blood ran over my futile hands, I feared he might be right.

"Please hold on," I whispered back. The last time he had lain in the courtyard like this, blood had been spurting from his chest. I had thought him dead then, but his death might well be now, at this very moment.

"It has been an honour to serve you, Your Highness," Bredon replied. I longed for him to not talk like this. "You have been a fine soldier and an even greater prince. I believe you will be an even finer king, when the time comes," he rasped.

"Do not speak, save your strength," I told him urgently. "Surgeon!" I shouted again, but to no avail. Rather than following my instructions, he slowly moved his hand to grasp mine, taking it away from his wound. "I have to stop the bleeding," I pleaded desperately.

"You have already seen my injury is fatal," he told me calmly, breathing heavily in between each word. "All is well, my friend. I go to a place where there is no more sorrow or pain," he reminded me with a small smile. In his eyes saw the hope of heaven, rather than the fear of death in his gaze, but that could not fully remove the sting of grief at his parting.

"I have to tell you something, sire," he continued haggardly, "whilst I still draw breath. There's something you must know… something I have kept from you." I frowned but let him speak, distracted by what he was about to tell me. "I had hoped to spare you this pain, but…" he coughed a little, flecks of blood forming on his lips.

"The man… who murdered your parents," he began, "the assassin that King Reghan ordered. He's still alive," he declared, "here in this kingdom." My eyes widened in shock at his words. "I am sorry for this deception, my friend. It is someone you know. He is… the Wolf," he concluded heavily. He spoke no further, but I could think of no words to say. I was stunned into silence for a few moments, before another bought of coughing overtook him.

"Please don't leave me," I told him selfishly, numb with shock about what he had just revealed to me. "I need your counsel." He was ever struggling for breath. "Who is he, Bredon?"

"It has been an honour to call you a friend, Daniel, my brother in arms," he told me now weakly. "I couldn't tell you who it was, because… he trailed off and I saw he was making a final, strained effort at speech. "He is…" he groaned and then his head rolled back as death took him.

"Bredon," I pleaded again. My hands, slick with his blood, moved to shake his shoulders. "No, please—"

"My lord." John was beside me, his hand on my shoulder. He stopped abruptly as I bowed my head down towards my fallen captain. "Sire, is he...?"

"Aye, he's dead," I confirmed sadly, still holding his head in my hands. "He has gone to be with God." Presently, Aife came beside us also. Gently I laid his head back upon the snowy floor, picked up my sword and straightened slowly. I turned to survey the rest of the battle; the enemy was still at large.

"We fight on," I said heavily as Aife bent to pick up her sword, "otherwise our great captain died for nothing."

"Aye, sire," John affirmed. "For the captain," he added and Aife raised her spear in agreement. In the next moment, the three of us raced towards the enemy once more, knowing we were fighting for Gaeson's very survival. I was fuelled by my rage and grief for my captain and friend. I did not know which individual had killed Bredon, so my hatred was upon all foes I came across. I unleashed my fury onto them, as though each one of them had been the one who had slain Bredon.

Eventually, as I twirled out of the way of yet another foe and brought my sword down upon him, I looked around me and saw that there were no other attackers in my vicinity. The large battalion looked as though it was defeated: any survivors were now retreating. I knew that though they probably had outnumbered us, this was by no means the whole Bernician Army. This then confirmed my suspicions, that this was the same force that had ambushed us at Klumeck. Knowing we had made our escape, they had therefore marched against us at Gaeson.

As the adrenaline drained, I sighed as I lowered my shield and sheathed my sword. At last, then, I removed my helmet and felt my head gingerly, gritting my teeth against the soreness. The blood was no longer flowing but had instead begun to congeal, so possibly I could escape stitches. I glanced down and glimpsed the afternoon sunlight as it glinted off the courtyard stone, touching both the wounded and the dead. Leigh the physician was making his way among the bodies, tending to those he could, but most were already being piled up to later be burned.

"Ewan," I abruptly remarked, as I recognised the young soldier's face as he lay upon the ground. He had a large smear of blood upon his head. I ran over to him, dropped to my knees beside him, checking his pulse. "Leigh, over here!" I called, seeing that he was still alive. The surgeon came beside me moments later with fresh bandages. "Will he live?"

"I think so, Your Highness," Leigh replied, at my urgent request. He frowned in concentration as he began wrapping clean, white cloth around Ewan's head. "This is the recruit who had his noise broken," the surgeon commented absently. "You two, move him to the medical chambers," he now ordered two Gaeson soldiers walking past. "Sire, your head—"

"It is a small injury, already healing," I cut him off with a dismissive wave of my hand. "Treat those at death's door first, my friend," I ordered him. With a nod of obedience, Leigh was off. As I straightened once more, I saw Evelyn coming out onto the courtyard from the cave.

"We were informed the battle was over," Evelyn informed me, a little breathlessly. "I have given the order that the people can return to their homes. You are injured," she added, gesturing to my cheek and my head.

"The freshest blood is not mine," I muttered. I rubbed my hands roughly on my armour, for my hands were wet with the remnants of the captain's injury. The blood from the wound at my temple had long dried. "It's from the captain. He is dead," I declared sadly. My wife's eyes widened; sorrow at once filled her countenance.

"I am sorry," Evelyn replied. As I thought of him, it sank anew what my late mentor had declared to me with his final breath. The Wolf was the man who had killed my parents... the thought of it actually made me stagger backwards.

"What is it?" my wife asked, her eyes searching mine, as my head was filled with Bredon's revelation.

"I shall tell you later, my lady," I returned swiftly. I wished to tell her this very moment, but more soldiers were walking past, attending the wounded and the dead. This was neither the time nor the place. "For now, we must secure the kingdom," I concluded at length with a sigh.

"Aye, of course," she responded. I touched her briefly, then watched her as she walked quickly to John to hear from him the report of the battle. I then gazed around at the soldiers occupied in the aftermath of the combat and realised I was regarding them with no small amount of suspicion, striking my heart with further heaviness. The seed of doubt of traitors in our midst had been planted at the ambush at Klumeck, watered at the plot to kill my queen and now was fully blossoming in my mind at the thought that this Wolf was also my parents' assassin.

For I knew I had no reason to doubt Bredon's last confession. The dreadful deeds of the Wolf were still a secret that no one else had been burdened with, for no one else had been in audience.

Who was this Veiled Wolf? The question burned round my insides again and again. Not only did I suspect he had been behind every act of Bernician espionage last year, but he had also killed many of my forces, without mentioning my own family. Rage grew and built deep within me even with just the thought of it. Presently I clenched my fists to keep calm, so tight that the tips of my knuckles turned white. My fingernails embedded into my palms, so that they left tiny crescent indents in my hands when I removed them.

I resolved to repeat the conversation to nobody, except those I trusted most. First to Evelyn and Sarah, then to John and Aife. I knew my uncle would have to be told also and could well imagine his pain at hearing that his wife's and sister's murderer was still alive.

"Your Highness," John's voice suddenly addressed me presently. I opened my eyes slowly to look at him. "The courtyard is almost clear," he reported, as I had already observed. I glanced back at the place where Bredon had fallen. His body was gone, but I knew he would not be burned. His body would be buried in the fresh, green grass near the tomb of Gaeson's monarchs, away from his blood and gore.

"This never gets any easier," I replied heavily. Indeed, I had surveyed this scene countless times, where warriors began to clear away the aftermath of a battle, and never was this cleansing work more difficult to swallow.

"No, my lord," John agreed quietly. "Usually the courtyard is spared such a massacre," he commented. I nodded grimly, for later, when this was cleared away, the castle servants would appear to scrub the stones clean. How much hot water would it take, I wondered, to make everything clean again? To deny this travesty had ever taken place?

"Aye, it was too close this time," I reflected, knowing how near to the palace the enemy had come. "How are our defences?"

"They are being rebuilt as we speak, sire," he answered. "We will ensure as much as possible that no one breaks through again. Such unexpected force," he commented, running a hand through his dark hair, as matted together with sweat as mine was. He seemed to pause a moment. "I suspect this is the same troops that attacked us at Klumeck," he ventured now.

"Aye," I affirmed. "They then chased us back here, knowing Caer Ligualid would be too fortified," I stated, reiterating the theory. The two of us halted our conversation for another moment, simply watching as the dead continued to be gathered. "I want to make you captain, John," I then informed him quietly. He immediately turned to me.

"It would be an honour to serve, Your Highness," John assented with a bow of his head. "I am ready to do whatever you ask of me, sire," my friend added sincerely.

"I know. You have my thanks." I paused here and glanced around, but there were too many soldiers passing by us. "I have something else to tell you, but not here. I need to speak with Sarah and Evelyn first. I must speak with Ewan, also, if it is possible," I added. "Can you enquire from Leigh how he is doing? Perhaps we can meet him in the infirmary."

"Of course, Your Highness, I shall speak with Leigh directly," John replied. "Have you any further orders, sire?"

"Aye," I replied tiredly, rubbing my eyes with the hands that I knew were still stained with Bredon's blood. "Tell my wife and my sister to meet me in my office chamber at sunset. Other than that, continue your duties as normal, brother," I informed him.

"It will be done, my lord," John replied quietly. He gave a final short bow of his head and then left my company. I glanced round once more to my people, seeing my kin, the women and men who were my people, wearing the weariness of battle, still in their armour and aiding where they could. I saw then that the Wolf sought to divide us, to make me question every single person in Gaeson. I defied him, then, as my fists again closed of their own accord. I told myself I would not let myself view each citizen with suspicion. I would not let him tear us apart, on today of all days. So, I

81

let out the breath I had been holding. Instead, I dug into the work of emptying Gaeson of her dead.

About halfway through this gruesome task, I lifted my head after laying the body of a fallen comrade on the pile of soldiers. I saw both Lord Aldred and Lord Melvyn had come to join us in the courtyard. Whilst Aldred had gotten alongside us, however, with his sleeves folded back and his countenance showing horror and concern, Melvyn stood apart, near one of the courtyard walls. His arms were folded, with his expression unreadable.

Abruptly Melvyn met my eye, then a moment later left, departing the scene altogether. I frowned as I stared after him. Perhaps I was right to be so suspicious of this official who did not wish to dirty his hands in blood. Had I just locked my gaze with the Wolf, the man who had killed my kin? I knew not. With a frustrated sigh, I instead got back to the work.

It was three hours later when I at last left the battlefield, headed back to the castle. Though I was reluctant, I first reported to the surgical chambers. Leigh confirmed I did indeed need stitches. After this uncomfortable appointment, I then retired to my chamber. A bath had been filled, but the clear contents of the large basin were lukewarm. I paused a moment, gazing at my reflection in the water. I perceived the thin red line across my forehead, accompanied by five neat lines where Leigh had applied the stitches. There was also the swollen patch on my cheek, an angry red ball that was sore to the touch.

I ignored this injury and plunged my arms into the water, scooping it onto my arms and chest. I took the wash cloth, let it soak up all it could carry and applied it to my cheek. The pain in my face faded somewhat. I pressed the cloth a little firmer and the tepid liquid gushed down in rivulets, mingling with my gruff stubble and coming to drip down onto my shoulders. I could only just about remember the bash to my head from where a sword hilt had slammed into me, for so much of the battle had been a blur.

I also had a large bruise beginning to show on my arm, but I paid this no heed. My injuries were nothing compared to what Bredon had endured. I closed my eyes, then, as sadness rose up in me once again. I had followed him as my captain for nine years, ever since I first enlisted in the army. Then there was this past year, when he had been under my command.

Despite his initial doubts, when I first discovered my true identity, Bredon had then seamlessly changed to pledge his loyalty to me the night Gaeson discovered I was the Prince of Klumeck. Always, I had counted him as a friend.

I longed for nothing more but to crawl into bed and will this awful day to be over, but I had the meeting with Evelyn and Sarah. As weary as though my legs were made of lead, I dressed in a fresh tunic and trudged back through the corridors of the castle. Ere long, I entered my study to see Sarah and Evelyn already waiting for me.

"I'm so sorry about Bredon, Daniel," my sister murmured gently, coming forward to embrace me. I held on to her for a moment, taking strength in her compassion. As we pulled apart, I closed my eyes again a moment, under the weight of all that had happened.

"What is it, Daniel?" Evelyn asked as Sarah shut the door behind us. I found I still did not have the heart to tell them the heavy burden my former commander had imparted.

"Bredon told me something, before he died," I said at length, coming to my desk. I slumped into the chair, reaching for the jug of wine. I knew they were waiting for me to continue, but I took a long gulp of the fortifying drink first, before placing the goblet back down hard. At last I looked up to meet their eyes again, to see my wife and sister gazing back expectantly.

"In his final words," I related eventually, "he revealed more about the Wolf. He told me that not only is he the spy ringleader we have been searching for," I continued, taking a breath here with my eyes flickering to Sarah, "he is also the assassin King Reghan ordered to kill our parents."

"What?" My sister objected immediately, standing up abruptly from where she had been sitting by the fireplace. Evelyn's countenance was also a picture of shock. Sarah paused a moment, staring into the dying embers of the fireplace, before her gaze snapped back to mine. "Tell me you know who he is," she pleaded urgently.

"I know not," I sighed, my hands coming to rest under my chin. "Bredon died before he could tell me. He definitely knew who it was, though," I added, "of that I am certain. He told me that I knew him, as well," I finished in gritted teeth.

"What are we to do?" my wife interjected, but I barely heard her. My head was again fully preoccupied with the thought that the assassin was still alive and was in Gaeson.

"We must take even greater care in who we trust," I warned, sitting forward and clasping my hands together as I spoke. Sarah sat back down in her chair again, the conflicting emotions prevalent in her features. I said nothing further and Evelyn picked up a poker by the fire and prodded idly, trying to get a little more warmth to enter the room. I suspected the chill was not only due to deepest winter, but at the loss of our friend. I felt as though all the fires in all the world could not displace this persistent cold.

"We must discover who this is, at once," Sarah stated quietly, abruptly breaking the silence that had descended on us for a few moments.

"But how?" Evelyn asked doubtfully, replacing the poker back in its stand and sitting in the other chair opposite my sister. "We know it could be almost anyone in Gaeson, including any of the soldiers that you have worked with. Has Ewan discovered anything?" my wife enquired.

"He is due to report to me soon," I replied with a sigh. "John and Aife are coming here so we can discuss the matter," I told them heavily. I so longed for the Wolf not to be a soldier, for I had served Gaeson so long with my brothers and sisters, depending on them for survival. I frowned then, wondering if I should tell them about Melvyn... but all I had seen was a strange expression. I would have to be sure, before accusing such a noble figure.

"I prayed that the time of spies was done, once we had caught the interrogator," I uttered vaguely instead. Just for a moment, then, I saw the villain again, slitting Evelyn's throat, crimson blood spurting from her neck as his blade sliced across it.

"One can only hope Ewan sheds further light," Sarah said. She then went to poke the fire as Evelyn had done, but I sensed this was only for want of something to do. "What will you do next?" my sister added as she turned back to me once again.

"I have already made John captain," I informed them, for this was an obvious move. "He will be on his guard all the more. We will resolve this, I promise you both. Other than that, it is more important than ever that no one else know about this," I added.

"Agreed," my wife replied. "I won't even tell our advisors. You never know who might be listening." Abruptly I thought of Melvyn again, but said nothing. Evelyn stood here, stretching. "There will not be anything else to decide until after you have spoken with Ewan," she said, with a finality to her speech.

"Aye," I affirmed. "John will be here momentarily to tell me of his condition," I added. "I am glad to see both of you safe," I concluded. They both gave me a smile at this. After they departed I reclined back into my chair. I felt as weak after warfare as I had when Joshua died. I reached to refill the goblet of wine before bringing it to my lips. The tonic's strong flavour filled my mouth before sliding gratefully down my throat, warming my insides gently. I leant my head back, hoping that a few moments slumber would find me.

When there came a knock on my door a few minutes later, however, I was still awake. I had passed the seconds simply staring at the concave stone of the ceiling, with the cracks littered across it. It was as though my mind was simply refusing to allow my body the rest it needed.

"Enter," I uttered briefly. My eyes did not immediately move as the door opened, for I already knew who it would be. By the time I looked at John, he was already at my desk.

"Your Highness," he greeted, "I have just come from the infirmary. Leigh told me that Ewan has stopped bleeding, but he is currently slumbering deeply. He expects he will wake up in a few hours, however," he added in reassurance.

"Good," I murmured in return. I secretly wished for the world of dreaming also. I frowned then as I thought. "I think we have to meet Ewan, to see what he's been up to the last few months," I said.

"I understand, sire, but Ewan might need a few days to recover," my friend answered cautiously. "He has not long been out of surgery; he is bound to be disoriented still."

"I know, but I do not think this can wait. John... the captain told me something before he died, brother," I informed him presently, "something I couldn't tell you before." I gestured for him to sit down opposite as I spoke. Rapidly, I related to him what Bredon had said about the Wolf being my parents' assassin.

"I'm sorry, my lord," he answered when I had finished, a deep frown on his countenance. He knew how this latest information about the Wolf had made things far more personal. "I will inform you the moment Ewan is awake," John told me quietly. "Until then, I will be more vigilant about the soldiers than ever."

"Very well. That is all for now, brother," I added, dismissing him. I remained at my desk, however, frowning again as I thought. I already knew from John almost half of our army was either wounded or dead. With the numbers we had fought against, it was a miracle it had not been more. I reflected upon this with a heavy heart, knowing that we had secured victory and security for our kingdom, but at a great cost.

How long would it take, I wondered, for Ewan to discover the traitors in our midst? How long before we caught the Wolf, this veiled assassin who kept so silent and yet caused so much harm? Could it be Melvyn, or was it a soldier? I turned to gaze through the partially open window, seeing the day was nearly over. Despite the remnant light from the sunset, I knew this was the darkest day Gaeson had faced for many years. I could only pray such a day would never reach our home again.

Part Two

Chapter Five
Six months later

"Your Majesty, Your Royal Highness." A soldier dressed in Caer Ligualid armour burst into the palace hall. I did not recognise him as he sank to his knees before us. At once his countenance told us the matter was urgent.

"I bear a message from His Majesty King Owain," he greeted me, placing a clasped arm upon his chest in allegiance to his king. Automatically I stood, whilst Evelyn remained in her seat. Yet another council meeting had been under way for some time, but it looked like it would have to be immediately adjourned.

"Your Majesty, we have received word that the Bernicians are again on the move," the guard reported. We believe they have amassed as one and they may well be already marching for Caer Ligualid as we speak." At this, my queen stood also.

"Very well," she replied swiftly. "Send for the captain of the guard at once!" she called to the Gaeson soldiers standing guard near the back of the hall. "Receive some rest and nourishment and then ride straight back to His Majesty King Owain," she directed to the messenger. "Inform him we will come to his aid. We will set off as soon as we are prepared."

"Yes, my queen," replied the Caer Ligualid soldier gratefully, relief emanating from him. "Thank you, Your Majesty. Your Highness," he added. He quickly departed backwards, his back still leant forwards towards us. I turned to my wife, whose countenance held grim determination as she stared at the hall doors.

It was six months since the Bernician Army had come within in an inch of taking our home, but alas, we were no closer to discovering the identity of the assassin. Ewan had recovered well and had in the first instance informed John of all he had found. The young soldier had confirmed our theory that several soldiers worked for the Wolf, leading to the arrest of several soldiers. I still knew Gaeson's army fairly well, so each revelation of betrayal had sent a stab to my heart.

The seasons had changed considerably, with the rains washing the snow away. We were now in the heart of the summer, but the blazing sunshine did not dispel the uneasiness of betrayal. Rather, from Ewan's work, it had been a further dismay to glimpse at how vast the network might be and how closely the Wolf protected himself. Evelyn and I kept a close watch over the council. I still had told no one of my doubts about Melvyn, who had seemed this past half-year the perfect example of a loyal noble. Indeed, I was beginning to wonder whether the shroud of mystery surrounding this villain would ever be solved.

"The meeting is adjourned," Evelyn presently called in a loud voice. "Pray say nothing about this until the captain can inform the army. Please have us in your prayers as we prepare to depart for Caer Ligualid. That is all," she concluded in a grim, clipped tone.

We?" I echoed quietly, as the councillors departed from their seats and made their way out of the grand chamber. "I will not be marching for Caer Ligualid alone?" I asked quietly, in the wake of their departure. A faint smile glimpsed at her features.

"No, my husband, this time we shall ride together. I need to lead this army as well, Daniel," she added softly. "Besides, I have things to discuss with King Owain, the latest details of the Wolf who is still working among us. Caer Ligualid also need to be on their guard."

"Yes," I agreed quietly in turn, "but surely, I could bring the matters before him myself. There is no need for you to—"

"There is every need," Evelyn interrupted a little hotly. "You need to remember that I am queen, Daniel," she said at my frown. "It is my decision and there are times when it is I that need to lead upon the throne. Melvyn can rule in my stead," she added. "There are some duties I need to perform myself," she concluded with a wry smile.

"Quite right, sister." I turned at the other voice I knew so well, to see Sarah standing across the council chamber, partially leaning against one of the pillars. "What's more," she continued as she straightened and strode forward towards us, "I'm coming too."

"Yes, I am," she repeated decidedly as she came to a stop, before I could voice the objection already springing to my lips. "You know this mystery affects me as much as you, Daniel, let alone the rest of Rheged. I will guard those in the innermost part of the city if I must, brother," she concluded, "but I am coming."

I said nothing for a moment, holding her gaze as I weighed her speech carefully. Of course, I longed for her to stay here in Gaeson where it was safer, where the enemy was not marching on our gates. I knew, however, that she had every right to discover this mystery. This Veiled Wolf did not assassinate only my parents, but hers as well. How could it be right, then, to try to prevent her coming with us?

"Very well," I relented at last. Immediately Sarah's features lightened, the corner of her mouth turning. "Mind that you do go to the sanctuary should the horn sound," I added, wishing her as far away from danger as possible.

"Aye, of course," Sarah replied happily. She stepped forward to kiss my cheek, a smooth contrast of skin to my stubble. "I'll be careful," she whispered softly, her hand touching mine briefly.

"That is settled, then," Evelyn said, as though it were purely a matter of academic business. "I will be glad of your company on the road," my wife added to my sister.

"Here is John," I declared, as my queen and my sister now turned to see him running into the vast throne chamber.

"Your Majesty, Your Highnesses," he said, sinking into a bow the way the soldier from Caer Ligualid had done. "What are your orders, my lady?" he asked, standing once more.

"Captain," she greeted, formally and swiftly. "We have just received word from Caer Ligualid," she explained. "Go, prepare the army. We need to be ready to march as soon as we are able," she commanded grimly.

"Very good, Your Majesty." John bowed, then at once departed to obey her orders. In the wake of her speech I glanced up to the large open window, where I could see the sun at its peak: it was about noon. We could be ready to leave within the hour, therefore, we would almost be passing the lake by the time it was nightfall.

I glanced at my wife and sister to perceive they were both looking towards me. I kept my face impassive as my thoughts turned to them. I hoped they would be unaware of my warring emotions. I knew they were both strong and very able fighters, but I could not help the uneasy thought that I might lose them both. They had both promised to head to the refuge within the city once the Angles arrived, but even then, they would not be totally safe. I knew how fierce the Bernicians were, this invading power that was as brutal as the Saxons who attempted to conquer the south of our island. Evelyn and Sarah then both walked out of the hall, talking with one another, no doubt preparing. I watched them leave a moment before leaving to begin the preparations myself, but I still couldn't help the little tightness in my heart.

I then headed directly for the armoury. John's order had been enforced swiftly, as I had known it would be, for there were already soldiers here. It was bustling full of brothers and sisters by the time I left once more, fully arrayed in the pure gleam of royal armour. I made my way back out to the courtyard and within moments Evelyn also arrived, fully dressed in her own battle dress.

Even though my wife and I had come here early, I saw a few soldiers already lined in their ranks. As well as that there were even a few citizens waiting at the other side of the courtyard, their faces grim and voices almost muted in sparse conversation. I glanced towards my queen, resisting the temptation to persuade her to stay here at Gaeson. I knew, however, that she needed to find out, first hand, all she could. I was certain she hoped, as much as I did, that King Owain and King Cedric might shed further light on the mystery, that remained as veiled as the day Bredon had died in this very place.

Presently I crossed the short distance to Epos, already prepared for the ride ahead. She grunted softly as I greeted her, stroking the teardrop shaped splash of white in the middle of her head, only gently contrasting with the parchment ash of her coat. My father used to joke it was the part of her that was purest of all. As I stroked my mare gently, I lingered on this memory, for since I had discovered my identity as a Royal of Rheged, I found I did not think as often of the man who had raised me in Gaeson. Never could I forget him, though, who had instilled in me the ideals of bravery, integrity and sacrifice.

"Your Highness," a stable boy came out, walking over to me with two more horses and snapping my mind back to the present. "She is fed, watered and ready to go, my lord," he added.

"Aye, lad, that I can see," I agreed. "You have my thanks," I told him. The boy smiled and bent his head at my praise. The boy could not be more than twelve and as he hurried back in the direction of the stable, I smiled to myself, remembering how I had been a stable boy myself at that age. I wondered if he too, was aiding the work of his father. My mind turned to Kellen of Gaeson again, as I watched the lad hasten back to the stables. He had been a good father, I reflected. The notion brought me much comfort, as a small smile touched my face.

The smile quickly disappeared from my face, however, as I glanced around the square. There was an incessant clinking of metal as soldiers filed out of their regimental chambers and joined their ranks. In truth, it was still strange at times to not be in the regimental tower, to not be among them, to take my place in the lines as I had done for so many years, for I was Prince Bryce now, a Rheged royal and heir to Klumeck's throne. I was glad of the change in identity for many reasons, not least because I had rediscovered my sister and been able to marry the love of my life. No amount of repeating that to myself, however, could fully eradicate the eeriness of leading this army, preparing to give orders rather than follow them.

Many more of Gaeson's citizens now filled the courtyard, the atmosphere a tense quietness. It was far too silent for such a throng to be gathered in one place, particularly in the middle of the day. The townspeople should be bustling with trade, not gathered here to bid farewell to their kin. As I looked about, I could see friends and lovers embracing. Soldiers were passed extra rations of water, bread and cheese, as well as a few hidden skins of wine being placed in their grasp that were quickly concealed. The city was brave indeed, but it did not take long to see past the veneer to the underlying anxiety. It was the communal, unspoken fear that those they were waving off may never come back again.

Presently, Evelyn and Sarah had taken their places beside me and I knew the time to set off had come. I glanced around at our party once more, to see Aldred and Melvyn mount their horses as part of our number.

"I thought Lord Melvyn would remain in Gaeson, to act as steward in your stead," I muttered with surprise to my queen, for that was what she had articulated not an hour ago.

"Aye, but I thought it would be good to have them with us. They were loyal to Gaeson during my father's reign... I thought King Cedric might well want their advice. Who knows, with their wisdom the Wolf might be unveiled. Another advisor is acting as steward," she added. "Why, is there an issue?"

"I—" I paused here. I had not been happy indeed at the thought of Melvyn ruling Gaeson, not whilst I suspected he could possibly be the Wolf. "It is nothing," I stated, for out of him coming to Caer Ligualid or ruling Gaeson whilst we were away, surely this was the lesser of two evils. Him joining our party might well be a blessing in disguise. At least we would have Lord Aldred in our company also, who had long gained my trust when his swift action had saved Evelyn's life.

"We are ready to depart, Your Majesty, Your Highnesses," John presently said from beside me. I dragged my thoughts away from Melvyn as Aife then came into position on the other side of Sarah. I nodded and swung up onto Epos.

"Then give the order, captain," I returned formally to him. "You need not be too hasty though, John," I added more quietly, "let them tarry awhile." John bent his head in agreement and turned to face the army, my brothers and sisters in arms. I gripped my reins a little tighter, waiting for the five of us to take the lead at his order.

"Prepare to march," John commanded, a couple of minutes later. We began to depart, as I nudged Epos into a slow walk. As we manoeuvred across the courtyard, I prayed that all who were leaving now would return home again safely. The people clamoured after us as we neared the portcullis, which had been rebuilt after the last battle. Indeed, just before it, it was so crowded that our horses had to travel in one protracted line. Eventually, however, we reached the barbed gate which had been raised for us. I swung around in my saddle to behold my people, who were forced to tearfully come to a stop. Then I steered Epos to the front and before my courage could fail, began the descent.

We soon reached the bottom of the hill and followed the trail of the quickest route through the forest. As we trotted our horses through the tightly knit trees, with the thick scent of pine in the air, I was mindful of another time in this woodland. We were even retracing the same steps Evelyn and I had made when fleeing to Caer Ligualid so many moons ago, long before I had known who I really was.

I looked to my queen to see if she had any signs of the memory, but her impassive countenance was fixed on the scene ahead of her. A moment later, however, she glanced my way. Her face softened, the corner of her mouth lifting only for an instant. Then she looked away again, wearing the neutral expression she had been trained to wear all of her life. The subtle smile was enough, though, to tell me she remembered the event as clearly as I did. I wasn't sure why, but this silent communication brought me some comfort.

By late afternoon, we had cleared the forest and had made substantial progress along the well-worn road to Caer Ligualid. Our trail had gradually taken us higher and soon we reached the crest of the high ground. We traversed it as the sun sank lower still, with the great lake set below us to our left. The burning gaze of the orb, a vivid orange, set everything around us ablaze. This colour then doubled as the lake, so pure and clear, reflected back everything it touched. At this altitude, at one point we glimpsed the mountains to our right. Though the sun was not directly touching them, they appeared a soft, faded blue against the vibrant turquoise air.

"Have you ever seen the great lake look so beautiful?" my wife asked quietly beside me, clearly having the same thought.

"Aye, once," I murmured softly, as we surveyed it. "We had this view when we left for Bernicia," I explained to her and she nodded silently beside me. "I sense the same magic has descended on us again." Such splendid scenery almost made me forget the apprehension of what lay ahead, as it had done the last time we were on the road to war. Not only was there the imminent threat of the Angles knocking on Caer Ligualid's gates, but I also did not much relish the prospect of informing my uncle of the Wolf in fuller detail.

"To camp in such a peaceful place would surely soothe our hearts," Evelyn suggested presently. "Captain," she called to John, urging her steed on a few more paces, "we shall stay here for the night. Give the order to camp," she instructed.

"Yes, Your Majesty," John bowed a little atop his horse. As he began ordering the vast majority of our army, I could see the news pleased him and our troops. If the terrible storm of war was to come to us again, then it would be good to dwell a little longer in the daylight.

By the time the tents were swiftly constructed, the sun had almost disappeared. We all sat down where we were, to watch the last of the golden orb sink below the horizon. Stretched above it appeared brilliant streaks of coral, gold and lilac, against the turquoise sheen of the sky. All of these magnificent hues were again doubled in extension, as the lake reflected further this combining of light and shadow. As I stood observing it next to Evelyn, it was easy to push aside the demons awaiting us before such beauty. Here, with such a stunning sunset and with the warmth of a summer's evening lazily heating us, it was possible to forget the danger we were in.

After a moment I noticed again that there was an eerie quietness, but nothing like the tense, sombre mood of when we left this afternoon. Instead it was the kind of silence a child might have when believing to have seen magic. It was the kind that made one not speak, lest the spell might be broken and turn all back to normality. It had been like this the time before on the road to Ynys Metcaut, when the beauty had stilled our hearts, lessening the doom of death threatening to engulf us. On impulse, Evelyn reached out and took my hand, her fingers intertwining with mine. A small smile glimpsed my face as I returned the contact, though we both continued staring ahead.

"The cliff you fell from will be not far from here," Evelyn murmured. I merely nodded at her speech, for coming to such a place had made me a little reticent. My queen seemed to sense this, for she said nothing further, only rested her ahead against my shoulder. Abruptly I wished this piece of time, just the two of us and this sunset, could pause forever. I knew this could be the last time I held her in peace, the last time together before the war.

The spell lasted until nightfall, as the soldiers talked easily with one another. John, Sarah, Aife, Evelyn and I ate together with general levity, as twilight turned to darker blue and clouds began to stretch across the sky. By the time night truly came, most stars were well hidden. The sombre mood grew almost tangibly as the sky blackened. My brothers and sisters in arms organised the watch and prepared for bed in the same tense air as when we had left Gaeson that morning.

I perceived well the reason for this quietness, for when dawn came, we would be that much closer to war. Even my wife and I did not speak much as we entered our tent, removing our heavy pieces of armour with relief. We climbed into the makeshift bed and bade each other a swift goodnight. My mixed emotions were still deciding whether I was pleased she was here. Part of me was pleased we had not been forced to part company, for she was still the one my heart loved most. I also knew she was my queen, an independent monarch who would do as she willed. Yet, also, I could not help but wish she was far away from here, safe away from war.

As was often the case on the way to battle, I had little sleep. Some slumber found me, however, for ere long my eyes opened to see a small light filtering through the gap in the tent. The light was really a looming grey shade, only somewhat brighter than darkness, preceding the first glimpse of dawn. This told me it was not yet dawn, but it was near. Though it was summer, the thick steel canopy above me seemed to have brought a chill to the air. I glanced to wake my queen, but saw she was already stirring.

We spoke little, as we had done the previous night, whilst we dressed and pulled on our armour in the early morning. By the time we left our tents and ate a hurried breakfast of boiled wheat, the darker slate of the canopy above me had gone, with a lighter, softer hue stretched in its stead. This was just as dull as the darker hue before it, however, still seeming to envelop all of us in its shroud, exacerbating our dreariness.

By the time we had taken down our camp and set off once more for Caer Ligualid, the day had warmed considerably, but with none of the sun that had shone so vividly the day before. The air was incredibly warm and muggy with little air to cool us. My forehead was soon slick with sweat, despite having wiped my forehead with a cool cloth numerous times.

It was a relief, then, to see King Owain's realm on the horizon, knowing the stuffy march was almost over. It was more encouraging, still, to see Rheged's capital kingdom and its lands looked untouched by the enemy. Others seemed to feel it too, as we entered Caer Ligualid's gates, for I felt trepidation lift easily off us, like we had all cast down some invisible burden. Presently we entered the main courtyard, far larger and grander than the one in Gaeson.

"Your Supreme Majesty King Owain, Your Majesty King Cedric," we chorused, for both rulers were waiting for us as we had expected. We had dismounted our horses and Evelyn and Sarah curtseyed whilst the rest of us bowed low.

"Your Majesty Queen Evelyn, Your Royal Highness Prince Bryce, Your Royal Highness Princess Lynette," King Owain declared in response as we straightened. "Thank you for coming to us so swiftly. Please know you are most welcome here."

"Indeed," my uncle said, smiling broadly as he stepped forward. He clasped my arm in a warm greeting, then turned to embrace my wife and sister, also. "I sense our day is already far brighter," he commented, as we began to walk together towards the castle. King Owain and his captain had remained outside, to give John instructions about the strategy for when the Bernicians came. I hesitated at King Cedric's speech. For how long would he hold that opinion?

"What is it, Daniel?" my uncle asked, frowning. He had obviously seen my smile fade slightly. I reflected again that perhaps I was not as good at impassiveness as I believed. Or maybe, it was only with those closest to me that my heart seemed all too visible. "Nephew? What is going on?" King Cedric prompted.

"This is something I have longed to tell you, but I did not know I could trust such a message arrive to you safely," I began, before hesitating again. I was unsure if 'longing' reflected my true feelings, for I also dreaded having to tell him of the Wolf. My uncle's eyebrows rose.

"We have spies among us once more," I informed him, ere long, as we paused in one of Caer Ligualid's external corridors. "I was hoping we could find whoever was responsible, but—"

"Spies in Rheged again," King Cedric interjected with a heavy sigh, his arms folding. "Well, what is it? I sense that is not all," King Cedric added, his perception serving him well.

"You may remember that six months ago, Bernicia came to Gaeson. We were barely able to hold them off," I said, the memory of that dreadful day as fresh as ever in my mind. My uncle nodded shortly, for I had sent him a brief note to inform him that therefore Caer Ligualid should be all the more on its guard.

"What I could not tell you in my letter," I explained, "was that my former captain of the guard died that day. In his last words, he disclosed something to me that he must have kept hidden the entire time I knew him."

"Yes?" he asked impatiently. I took a breath here, for I sorely wished I did not have to tell him. I knew the pain it would inflict, how it would resurface the wounds that may still haunt his dreams. "Tell me, my boy," he implored, as if he knew the reason for my reluctance. I swallowed, my gaze flickering across his countenance.

"There is one spy in particular who seems to be orchestrating all the deception," I admitted at length, "known as the Wolf. My captain told me… this man is also the assassin," I at last revealed quietly.

I knew I need say no more, for it was evident my uncle understood. Shock entered his features as he took a step back, almost staggering under the weight of these deep and terrible words. He reached out to grasp a nearby wall, leaning against it. Almost all of the ruddy complexion had gone, leaving his skin pale underneath his beard.

"He died before I could find out anything more, or why he had never told me," I continued, a little inanely, for what speech could improve such dreadful news? My uncle still did not speak. In this moment, this mighty king had never looked so weak.

"I see," King Cedric ere long uttered, his tone heavy. He raised a hand to wipe it across his face. "You truly do not know anything more?" he asked slowly. The colour was still drained from him. I shook my head, wishing I could give him the answer to this mystery, that which I desperately longed for myself. I perceived my uncle's brow creased to no small amount of anger.

"You knew this for six months?" King Cedric voiced, in a hoarse whisper. "Why did you not tell me this beforehand? Even if you suspected you could not get a letter to me safely, why did you not travel here in person, or send another in your stead?" he challenged.

"I did not mean to hide it from you, Uncle," I replied, feeling a little ashamed. "It has taken this long to rebuild Gaeson's defences. Three months before Gaeson was attacked, there was a plot to kill Evelyn," I added quietly. My uncle's face took on more shock at this news. "I did not want to leave Gaeson in case she was attacked. We have discovered that the Wolf's network is vast, involving many soldiers and citizens. We could have both come to see you, but in the light of the battle, she could not be spared her duties," I continued, feeling that all of these, though true, were poor excuses. "I did not know who I could trust to take the letter to you and I could not guarantee it would not be intercepted along the way. I'm sorry, sire," I concluded a little thinly.

"I see," he murmured again. I could tell he thought my reasons were as feeble as I did. "So, this Wolf murdered Angharad, Imogen and Adair," he repeated roughly, speaking the names of my aunt and my parents.

"Yes." My voice was as sombre as his, for I desperately did not wish to confirm this terrible truth. In his mind, too, must be the child he would never know, for Angharad had been pregnant when they had been so brutally murdered in their beds. In my weakness, I could think of nothing further to say and a brief silence descended over us.

A castle guard here appeared with a goblet of wine from somewhere. I watched as my uncle tilted this to his mouth and drained it with two swift gulps before handing the empty vessel back. The little crimson trail left on his beard only seemed to further contrast with his unusually pale features. I looked away from King Cedric's telling gaze. For the first time, then, I perceived that whilst Evelyn was also looking at my uncle, Sarah was looking at her. Her expression was a little strange; indeed, I found I could not fathom my sister's countenance. As I watched her, however, a moment later she caught my eye and her face quickly changed.

"We were able to interrogate some that work for the Wolf," Evelyn said presently. I lingered over Sarah a moment longer, for her countenance, changing so rapidly, was stranger still, before I turned back to my wife.

"We learnt that the spy is of a high rank within the Bernician Army. He seems to have quite a network of Gaeson soldiers," she added with a little bitterness.

"Very well," my uncle said heavily. "I thank you, my lady, that you have come with such speed. Our scout has assured us that the Bernicians are on their way: we are awaiting the horn to sound at any moment," he added, at last straightening.

"We are thankful for the troops you have brought, especially so soon since your last fight," he continued. "My captain will take them to the banquet hall to rest. We must report these findings to King Owain," he concluded formally, as resolve took shape in his features.

"Aye, Uncle," I affirmed. As we resumed the walk, King Cedric strode off ahead. "Sarah, wait a moment," I implored. Evelyn glanced to me but continued walking, soon falling in beside my uncle. I saw her slip her hand on his arm in compassion.

"Is everything all right? I saw the way you were looking at Evelyn," I told my sister. She frowned, a look of surprise on her face.

"I bid you go on without us," I called to King Cedric, who had turned back. His eyebrows rose again, but he and Evelyn then left our company, as my eyes moved back to Sarah.

"I do not know what you mean," Sarah replied, casually and simply. She turned to follow the others, but I took her arm.

"Aye, you do," I affirmed, "for in all of this I would have expected you to be occupied with the news about our parents, or the threat from the Bernicians. Instead I find you looking at my wife. Why?" I persisted.

"Very well," Sarah relented after a pause. She now moved to lean against the stone of the wall the way our uncle had done. "I wondered…" She hesitated. I waited, a frown creasing my features. "I think Evelyn could be hiding something," she admitted at last.

"What?" I questioned, hearing my voice rise in defensiveness. "What could she be hiding?" I asked immediately. "For what purpose?"

"I know not," Sarah admitted with a sigh. "However, she seems not herself lately. Ever since we found out the assassin was still alive and Captain Bredon died, she seems to have been more agitated," she explained.

"Haven't we all?" I responded. My sister conceded this with a nod of her head but said nothing further. I moved to sit beside Sarah for a moment. Together we looked through an archway of stone to the sun behind it, for at last the skies had cleared. The sunshine glistened as though all was right with the world. I tried not to think how much more pain could be in our midst before the golden orb rose once more.

"What are you trying to say, Sarah?" I asked quietly ere long. "You think that Evelyn might know more about the assassin than she is saying?"

"I am only saying that the logic of things makes it a possibility," my sister answered cautiously. "The captain was a loyal friend who gave his life to serve Gaeson. Therefore, I believe he must have had a reason for not telling you about the Wolf." I nodded in agreement. "Daniel, perhaps he was following orders. Perhaps he was protecting your love for her."

"Protecting it?" I echoed in confusion. "Why should it need protecting?" Sarah did not answer immediately and abruptly there seemed to be sadness in her countenance. "Well?" I persisted, bordering on rudeness.

"To protect you from the truth, that Evelyn could know who the assassin is," she answered softly. My eyebrows shot up, ready to ridicule this suggestion as folly and nonsense. "I'm sorry," she went on quickly as my mouth opened to object. "I sincerely long not to think ill of her. But it was my parents also that died," she pointed out. "Since you agree Bredon would have been following orders—"

"This is absurd," I snapped with a wave of my hand. "How dare you accuse my wife of such things? To think she could be capable of such deceit!" I exclaimed, shaking my head.

"I'm sorry, brother," Sarah repeated. I could see the pain my heated words had caused her, but I could hardly understand her speech. "I just want this mystery to be solved as much as you do and thought it seemed odd—"

"Well, you are looking at the wrong person," I interrupted hotly. "He simply could have been following Reghan's orders, without Evelyn having any knowledge," I suggested, attempting to calm my temper and offer a more reasonable suggestion.

"I know," Sarah replied. I detected some sadness in her speech. "I wondered this, but Bredon knew well King Reghan's corruption. Why would he persist in therefore following his orders? I thought it was a possibility, that is all. I sincerely hope I am wrong," she added. I opened my mouth to reply but stopped as I saw John approaching.

"Your Highnesses," John said with a short bow of his head, "King Owain states that you are both required in the palace hall." There was a brief pause, as he looked between us. "I apologise for the interruption—"

"Not at all, John," Sarah replied quickly, her tone at once almost forcefully bright. "Lead the way," she added.

"My lady," he bowed once more and before I could speak to Sarah, she was off, following swiftly in his footsteps. I began to follow as well, already regretting the harsh way I had spoken. I found myself wishing with all my heart that Sarah was wrong.

Swiftly we entered the grand palace hall at Caer Ligualid. Though I had expected it, it still looked a little strange to see King Owain sitting on his father's throne. My next thought, however, as I walked across the hall and bowed, was that he seemed as regal as King Urien had ever done.

"King Cedric, Queen Evelyn, Prince Bryce, Princess Lynette," King Owain greeted us formally again as we bowed to him, using the name my parents had given Sarah and me. "I am pleased to welcome you into my hall," he added as we straightened. He stood now from his throne, scratching his beard with a large hand as he descended the steps to us.

"King Cedric told me you had something you wished to discuss," King Owain added abruptly, turning back to me.

"Aye, Your Majesty," King Cedric agreed with another bow of his head. "Prince Bryce has just revealed to me the most troubling news. It seems, sire, that this Wolf who is the Bernician spy is also the assassin who murdered half my family, on the orders of King Reghan."

King Owain breathed in sharply through his nostrils and his gaze hardened, but he did not immediately speak. Here, I observe a noted difference between him and his father. Whilst King Urien had looked cold in his cruelty, King Owain's countenance seemed to be passionate; I would not be surprised if he was prone to furious outbursts of rage.

"I see," King Owain said at last and I perceived his tone seemed almost forcibly even. "We have no idea who this Wolf might be?"

"No, Your Majesty," I returned, as my uncle turned to me. "This was told to me by my former captain as he died. He took his last breath before he could make the spy known."

"A pity," King Owain remarked a little listlessly. I swallowed my irritation that Bredon's death could be referred to so trivially.

"We also believe this Wolf could also be the head of the spies who had infiltrated Gaeson almost eighteen months ago, my lord," I continued, when the great king said nothing further. "This person might even be the one who orchestrated such events, nearly leading to Queen Evelyn's death."

"I remember," King Owain replied, then still did not speak further. I swallowed more annoyance, wondering how King Owain led his people effectively if everything was done with such slowness.

"I propose the Wolf must be revealed as quickly as possible, as well as all those who might be working with him, sire," I said to him, when I could bear his silence no longer. At my speech, King Owain turned to me, fixing upon me his passionate gaze.

"I thought King Owain, not Prince Bryce, was King of Caer Ligualid," he said angrily. I made myself swallow any kind of retort, but instead to bow my head and wait in acquiescence.

"I see you are determined to solve this mystery, Daniel," he continued more evenly. "Perhaps this would be for the good of Gaeson and Rheged. However, there is wisdom in the old adage, to be prudent about what you desire. For when the full truth of things is known, you may not have wished to speed its coming." He sighed. "Very well, I thank you for your report, you are dismissed," he abruptly concluded and gave a single nod to us. It took all my military training to humbly bow and leave his palace and not implore him harshly to speak plainly. We had travelled all the way here, I thought angrily, just to endure his riddles?

"What on earth was he speaking of?" I snapped to King Cedric, as soon as Sarah closed the door behind us. Sarah, Evelyn, my uncle and I were in his main reception chamber at the palace. My uncle did not immediately answer me but went to his jug of wine and poured himself a large goblet. "That was the shortest briefing I have ever had with a king. What did he even mean?" I challenged loudly.

"Calm yourself," King Cedric instructed me simply. "Wine?" He offered, but I shook my head. I knew the tonic would only swell my anger and muddy my thoughts. I needed a clear head to understand King Owain's opacity.

"I believe His Majesty meant we should be careful in how much we want to solve this mystery," my uncle said after he had tasted the wine himself. "The truth may not be what we expect and when it does come to light, we may wish we did not know."

"His thinking is preposterous," I challenged hotly. "Truth is always preferable to deceit, surely," I pointed out, attempting to be calm.

"Yes, but at what cost, Daniel?" Evelyn asked quietly and we all turned to her. "It may bring other things to the surface that you wish you did not know. I think that is what King Owain meant," she suggested.

"This is likely the man that ordered the interrogator to kidnap you, Evelyn," I reminded her, my tone still a little harsh. "I nearly lost you," I said, a little gentler. "Are you now saying we shouldn't try to solve this mystery? It is not only because of my parents," I continued. "The Wolf poses a great threat to Gaeson and to Rheged as a whole. It was probably this man who informed the Bernicians we were to try to retake Klumeck," I explained.

"Of course, I'm not saying we should not try to stop him. Of course, we should," she clarified, nodding. "I'm simply saying I think I understand what King Owain meant."

"Aye," King Cedric nodded, clearly agreeing with my wife. "You need to grow a little more in patience, my boy," my uncle told me wisely. "Nobody wants your parents and my wife retributed more than I, but there is more occupying King Owain's thoughts than our family," he explained. "Remember that a large contingent of the Bernician Army is marching against us, as we speak. Their troops are still thoroughly depleted since the last great battle where King Urien fell and from their recent fight in Gaeson, but we will not have the same allies as before."

"The Coalition Kings," I guessed. These were the three kings of different regions who had come to fight alongside us in the great battle last year.

"We already know that King Morgant's treachery runs deep," King Cedric confirmed. This we already knew, for he was the one who had orchestrated King Urien's assassination upon the battlefield. "We believe he may well be in league with the Bernicians in order to regain some of his lost power," he said. My uncle then leant back, his arms folding as he paused and fixed his gaze on each one of us in turn. It seemed he was deliberating something.

"What I tell you now, must stay in this chamber," he instructed ere long. Immediately the three of us nodded at this request. "Three weeks ago, King Owain's brother Elffin was attacked and killed by King Morgant." King Cedric revealed heavily.

"It did not take long for that snake to strike again," I returned angrily, my eyes widening. It seemed my family was not the only kin to be murdered.

"Indeed," my uncle returned drily. "We are keeping that knowledge quiet for as long as possible, for His Majesty knows it will weaken him and his throne if all the kingdom should know," my uncle explained. "That is also not his only problem with the allies, however," he resumed. "King Owain's alliance with King Rhydderch, King Urien's cousin who also helped us in that battle, is also breaking down. It would not surprise me if King Rhydderch was soon to become our enemy. These are troublesome times," my uncle sighed. "It seems the more King Owain tries to hold onto his kingdom, the more it begins to crack with outside pressures. That is why he does not seem to give your parents and my wife much thought."

"In essence, then, if we are to solve this mystery, it is up to us," Sarah surmised now. My sister had accepted my uncle's offer of wine: I wondered if it was because of our heated exchange. Presently she took another drink. "It seems we must also do it quickly, if we want to know the truth before the Bernicians arrive," she continued. I nodded at this. "Has Ewan found out anything of note recently?" she asked next, her first speech to me since our conversation.

"He has only discovered a few of the soldiers the spy has working for him," I replied, shaking my head, "but nothing of the magnitude that will reveal the assassin to us. Ewan had overheard Caer Ligualid mentioned a few times," I added to my uncle, "so we were hoping that something more may be discovered about him here. That is also why I delayed in coming to you," I explained. "If I suddenly decided to visit, the Wolf may think we had discovered more about him."

"Very well, though you could have found a way still, nephew. Six months is a long time," he replied wearily. I nodded, knowing he was right. Had it been my pride? Had I wanted to tell my uncle the awful news only when the veiled villain was discovered?

"We'll say no more about it," he said a little curtly, taking another drink of wine. "Let us all be vigilant and hope that we find something. In the meantime, you should all rest," he added, looking round at the three of us. "You have had a harsh journey to get here so speedily and you will need your strength for when the enemy arrives."

***

"This is a strange place for us to meet, Your Highness," came a direct, slightly mocking voice, matching up exactly with my memory of the speaker.

"Aye, well, these are strange times of late," I replied evasively. I watched then as a moment later Taliesin, the late King Urien's former bard, stepped out of the shadows. He now served King Owain. It was three hours after our arrival and I had arranged to meet up with the poet in one of the city's alleys, not wishing to be overheard. I knew he had spent years in the great king's company. I suspected that if King Urien knew about the spy, then this man standing opposite me would also. "These days it is difficult to know who to trust," I admitted at length.

"I see, my lord," Taliesin said, his eyes squinting up at me from his short stature. "Do you trust me, then, sire?" he asked, a little sarcastically.

"No, bard, I do not," I replied honestly. I saw his mouth turn to a further smirk. "You were one of King Urien's closest associates, however. I need to know—"

"Who this Veiled Wolf is, that you are seeking," he interrupted as he folded his arms. My eyes widened. "King Owain still keeps me in the palace hall. I am often not easily noticed if I do not wish to be," he explained. "It is easy to hear kingdoms rife with talk of such matters," he continued. "One only needs to take the time to learn how to listen."

"That is what I am hoping, so further light can be shed on his identity," I agreed. "Well, do you know who he is?" I prompted.

"I do not," Taliesin replied after a moment, much to my frustration. "I have heard of dealings with this Anglian spy in Gaeson's kingdom, for it seemed to serve Rheged to keep him alive. I knew of him only as the Wolf, but I believe King Urien knew his identity. The great king had records of his dealings with the spy, perhaps you can learn more about him from them."

"That would be progress indeed," I affirmed to his suggestion. "Where are the records?" I enquired immediately, making Taliesin smirk again. I hid a sigh, remembering he had been this trying in our last encounter. "Well?" I pressed him.

"Alas," the bard replied at length, just as my patience was beginning to give out, "they are secrets he has taken with him to the grave."

"Speak sense, Taliesin! I do have not time for your riddles!" I ground out in frustration. "Many have died, including my own parents, because of him," I continued more calmly. "Tell me plainly, man, does that mean they are lost forever?" I asked quickly.

"That is not what I said," Taliesin returned, a little of the smile still on his face. "I must take my leave, before the castle speaks of our meeting. Unless you want your spy to discover we had this conversation? Farewell, Your Highness," he abruptly said and suddenly he had stepped back into the shadows again.

"Taliesin! Wait!" I shouted, sprinting into the darkness after him. There were many interconnected streets, however: I had already lost sight of him. There was no telling which one of them he had gone down. I knew therefore I would only get lost and cursed in frustration. I resigned to head back to the main street, taking a deep breath and pushing the annoyance from my mind. Instead, I tried concentrate on what the bard had said. He had specifically said the documents he had spoken of were not destroyed. What did this then mean?

"Taliesin said the secrets were taken with King Urien to the grave," I murmured aloud. "If they are not lost, then…" I snapped my fingers in realisation. "Of course!" I said, for it left one other option. With that conclusion in my mind, I broke into a run back to the castle.

"Move aside," I ordered, as I came to the guard keeping watch outside my uncle's chambers. "I must speak with His Majesty at once, on an urgent matter," I informed him, as the guard appeared to hesitate. He glanced down at my hand, which held two large cloaks, with a frown on his face. "You would do well to listen to your future king," I informed him flatly.

"Yes, Your Highness." The guard bowed rapidly as his expression cleared. "Of course, my lord." He moved quickly down the corridor until he was out of earshot, but where he could still view us. I waited until he had stopped, then raised my hand and knocked on the door loudly.

"Your Majesty, wake up," I called. "I must speak with you. I bid you get up, Uncle." As I finished saying this, the door opened. King Cedric looked at me in frustration.

"What are you doing, nephew? Do you not know what hour it is?" he asked in irritation, then his eyes widened as he took in my urgent expression. "What is it?"

"I bid to come inside, Uncle," I replied quickly. At once he opened the door further to admit me. "I have just spoken to Taliesin, King Urien's former bard," I told him rapidly, as soon as I closed the door behind me.

"He alluded to secret documents, recording conversations between King Urien and the Wolf," I continued. "Taliesin told me that the secrets had gone with him to the grave, but not destroyed. If they are not lost—"

"Then they are buried with him," King Cedric interjected, leaning against a table as he came to the same conclusion I had. "This is excellent news indeed. We must go to King Urien's tomb as soon as possible, for we know not when the Bernicians will arrive," he said in earnest.

"Aye, that is why I came to you now," I agreed. "Taliesin also said the whole castle is alive with talk and one only needs to listen," I added. "Someone could have even been listening and has already gone to remove the documents."

"We must depart," King Cedric replied, "for we cannot risk anyone else having knowledge of this. However," he hesitated now, "are we sure the bard is telling the truth? What if he is deliberately leading us on a fool's errand to risk breaking the law of not respecting the bodies of fallen monarchs?" he asked.

"I suppose we do not know," I admitted evenly, folding my arms, "but if King Urien does have something buried with him, sire, then there is only one way to find out." My uncle frowned as he seemed to consider this.

"Very well," he said, "let us go tonight. Let this stay only between us and the guard posted outside," he concluded. "We will need a third to help us open the tomb door."

"Yes." I was relieved the time of discussion was over, as swiftly we stepped back out into the corridor. "You," I said, donning one of the cloaks I had brought with us. "You're coming with us," I informed him as I turned up the hood on my cloak, "you must be silent as the night."

"I am ready to serve, Your Majesty, Your Highness," the guard whispered back at once, bowing his head as my uncle put on his own cloak.

"Good," King Cedric said. "You are to go in front of us, walking normally. Your prince and I will stay behind, clinging to the shadows. There is to be no communication between us. We are heading for the royal tomb," he added. The guard's eyes widened, but he did not object.

"Aye, my lords," he whispered. King Cedric gave a nod back and with that the guard started off. My uncle and I waited a few moments as he headed off. Then, making our footsteps as soundless as possible, we followed next to the wall at a slower pace. With each step, I prayed that the identity of the Wolf might at last be unveiled with these documents. Already, I wondered if it might confirm it was Melvyn after all.

Thankfully, the journey to the royal tomb was uneventful enough. Once or twice a Caer Ligualid patrol came past, but we clung to the wall and held our breath whilst we waited. The night remained silent, however, as we remained undiscovered. Ere long, we arrived at the tomb entrance. There was no guard posted, for the final resting place of the mighty King Urien was so revered that no one dared come near. Besides us, no one else knew of the secrets within (or so we prayed, given Taliesin's warning), so why should it need protecting? My heart lightened that our arrival could remain undetected. The guard who had come before us came to a stop outside the sealed door and stood at his soldier's stance, awaiting instructions.

"Open the tomb," King Cedric commanded now to the guard. The soldier's eyes widened as he faltered, looking between us. I knew well why, for this would go against all his instincts of leaving King Urien's grave untouched.

"Do you dare disobey a direct order from your king?" The question from my uncle was soft, but to my ears he had never sounded more powerful. It was clear King Cedric had no cause to shout, for the merest whisper of the threat of treason was enough to quell his hesitation.

"Of course not, Your Majesty. I beg your forgiveness, my lords," the guard returned immediately, bowing as low as humanly possible. He uttered his obedience so swiftly, he almost tripped over his words. The soldier seemed young in his service, for the fear in his voice was palpable. Though, I wondered, perhaps even the most seasoned warriors would tremble so in the presence of a king's ire.

Hastily, the soldier went right to the door. It was clear the cover had not been opened since King Urien had been laid here. Ordinarily, the tomb would not be opened until any other royals joined his resting place. The guard exerted all his strength, but it seemed the door would not give. After a moment, then, King Cedric and I came to press all our weight against it.

Abruptly, then, after a few moments of shifting movement, the door gave away and flew open. The three of us were propelled inside, but we managed to regain our footing. We were standing then in a long, dark corridor I had only once before glimpsed from a distance, when King Urien had been carried inside on the day of his funeral.

"Your oil lamp," my uncle said simply to the soldier. At once, the guard picked it up and handed it to him. "This way," King Cedric instructed. This time he led us, with me following and the guard at our rear. The guard was clearly cautious we would be discovered, for in the dim light I kept seeming him turn around, to see if anyone was hidden in the shadows behind us.

The air was dank and moist, only exacerbating the foul stench of death that seemed to cling to the damp, cold walls. I was sure, too, that my head kept brushing against things. I imagined dirty, vast cobwebs with sticky threads, laden with ancient dust. It made me run my hands through my hair every other moment, as I tried to remove the horrible stuff from my head. We kept up this unpleasant journey until at last, we came to the open chamber where King Urien was buried. As my uncle stepped closer to the stone coffin, I saw by his lamp it was just as ornate as I remembered.

"King Urien has been buried in here for over nigh two years," King Ceric said gruffly. "As such…" he paused here, "this will not be a pleasant sight," he warned both of us. I nodded, moving forwards to grip the edge of the coffin firmly. "Guard," my uncle muttered.

"Aye, my lord." The warrior hastened to obey, for he would not dare try his king's patience a second time. The guard and I heaved against the stone slab, pushing with all our might. Slowly, the coffin roof slid off and a far stronger odour of death reached my nostrils. We stepped back as King Cedric held up the lamp and I took in the gruesome sight.

The great king's body had transformed dramatically since he had been shut up in his coffin. His body had to me the appearance of rotten wood. His corpse had developed brown scales, with cracks of darker brown revealing further decay underneath. I had only ever seen the freshly dead, in the aftermath of a battle. I was therefore simultaneously revolted and riveted at the sight of this legendary ruler who looked as if his body had eaten itself slowly from the inside.

"Prince Bryce," my uncle presently reminded me. His tone was a little impatient, snapping me out of my morbid curiosity.

"Of course, apologies, sire," I replied, stepping ever closer. "Sorry, Your Majesty," I murmured to the corpse, before I plunged my hands into the coffin, focusing in the spare gaps around him rather than the body itself. I rummaged for a few moments, trying as much as possible trying not to touch the decaying monarch.

"I think—" I began, as my fingers touched what felt like leather. "Yes, I've found something," I said, as I pulled the case free. My uncle brought the lamp yet nearer as I flipped the leather lid of the case and pulled out several sheets of paper.

"This must be it," my uncle murmured. "Check if there's anything else," he ordered. Swiftly I plunged my hands back inside, feeling all around, but there was nothing else there apart from the corpse itself.

"That is all there is, my lord," I added, removing my hands once more. "Taliesin looks as though he was telling the truth."

"We shall analyse this when we get back to the castle," my uncle declared. "Let us be hasty, before we are discovered." As quickly as we could, the guard and I heaved the stone lid of the coffin back into place. I was grateful our dreadful task was done, as each step took us away from death and back towards the ancient city, still full of life. We walked back through the tombs with haste, for we knew not how much longer life would remain in the Rheged's capital. Every moment was surely bringing the Bernicians that much closer to us.

Chapter Six

I felt I could finally breathe again as we emerged into the warm, summer evening, alive with the throng of buzzing insects. I stood there a moment, rubbing my hair clean again and again. I revelled in the fresh, gentle breeze wafting in my face, cleansing me greatly from the aroma of death.

"It looks as though we remained undetected," King Cedric murmured gravely, as he handed the oil lamp back to the guard.

"Aye," I murmured, for as I looked around, there seemed no one in sight. My uncle and I donned the cloaks once more, for we had removed them in the catacomb. There had been no need to be in disguise. Besides, although the damp corridors had been cool, there had also been an uncomfortable humidity.

"We will follow you back the way we came," I instructed the guard, if only to distract myself from the fresh memory of King Urien's tomb.

"Very good, my lords," the guard said quickly. As I spoke I pulled the hood up on my cloak, hiding the case of documents within. Relief had been all too evident in his voice to be ordered back to Caer Ligualid. King Cedric and I walked again a little behind him, staying close to the shadows. We were as fortunate in returning as we had been visiting the tomb, for soon we were back at the castle, with seemingly no one being any the wiser. Presently, then, we arrived outside my uncle's chambers.

"You may resume your normal duties," King Cedric ordered the guard rather grandly. "Know that you have performed a great service for your king this night. It is a service, however, that you must keep silent about for the rest of your days," he added threateningly. My uncle's thick, rugged auburn beard seemed aglow in the light of the oil lamp.

"If you speak," my king whispered severely, so quiet I had to strain to hear him, "it will cost you your life. Do you understand?" He breathed softly, in such menace I doubted even his worst enemies would struggle to disobey.

"Yes, my lord," the guard bent his head low at once. "It is my honour to serve Your Majesty," he concluded.

"Very well, then. You are dismissed," my uncle concluded in his normal voice. The guard bowed again and hence departed our company. Though it was his soldier's tread, I perceived he was walking away a little faster. Clearly, he could not wait to escape our company. "Bryce, I bid you come in," my uncle then invited me. "I doubt either of us can wait until morning."

"Aye, Uncle," I answered heavily. I followed him inside his chamber, taking off my cloak as I did so. I removed the leather case, hopefully the best clue to uncover the Veiled Wolf. King Cedric placed the oil lamp carefully down near it. By its dim light, we made out the slanted scrawl of writing.

"Taliesin was right," I whispered ere long, as I took in the words on the page. "It does seem to be a conversation between King Urien and the Wolf. Why did King Urien have it buried with him?" I asked with a frown.

"That I do not know, my nephew," King Cedric murmured, as he too read quickly. "Perhaps he wished for no one to come across it. I suppose he could have simply destroyed it, but maybe he couldn't dispose what could be the only evidence we have of such a wicked man."

"Here looks to be the beginning," I said presently, as I found another page. My uncle swiftly moved a chair to sit at the table beside me and I pushed the pages between us. Together, then, we began to read.

Wolf: I do not know why you wish to have these conversations recorded, Your Majesty. What if someone were to discover them?

King Urien: That is my business alone. Perhaps in case one day, not far from now, the truth about you may need to be disclosed. You have betrayed other kings, why not me?

Wolf: You would not dare reveal me, my lord king. You know I am not some piece in a game. I alone have kept you aware of King Reghan's movements. Who else warned you of his betrayal? Who else informed you Prince Bryce dared disobey you to run back to Gaeson?

King Urien: Aye, you have had your uses. Let us not forget, however, that it was you who poisoned King Reghan against me and the rest of

Rheged. It was you who made him so loathe and fear King Cedric, that he sent you to destroy his heirs. I know you truly serve Bernicia, you rat!

Wolf: Careful, O great lord. You think I come here with no contingency in place? You dare threaten me, when you know the damage I could cause to Gaeson and the rest of Rheged? You want me to be your friend, Your Majesty, not your enemy.

King Urien: Then tell me something of use to me. Make it worth my while to have you in my counsel.

Wolf: Very well, my liege. It looks as though my people are retreating within their lands, to the island of Ynys Metcaut. If you strike them whilst you are consolidating their forces, you might well achieve victory for Rheged.

King Urien: What a farce! Bernicia still has far too much power for me to lead a war against them. Even when they are depleted, they are still a fierce beast.

Wolf: I was not suggesting you wage war against them alone, my lord. There are other kingdoms you could align yourself with. Your cousin King Gwollag perhaps, or King Rhydderch. There is also King Morgant, for do not forget he himself once ruled Bernician lands, before they were stripped away from him by my people.

King Urien: Everyone knows that King Morgant is a traitor. I would not trust him with a single blade of grass, let alone any soldier in my army.

Wolf: Of course not, sire, but he has more cause to war with Bernicia than any other king. If you do not take this chance whilst they are weakened, they will only consolidate their forces all the more. Unless you do not dare take this chance?

King Urien: How dare you! Only a fool would dare speak to me in such a way. You are fortunate I do not behead you this instant, consequences be damned! Very well, if this is the best opportunity to strike, then so be it.

Wolf: Very good, my king. I am sure that you will win the day.

King Urien: Tell me, then, if you are so assured of my victory, why do you tell me of this plot at all? Who do you truly serve, that you should betray so many of your own people?

Wolf: As I have told you before, Your Majesty, I am most loyal to myself. I will freely look to Rheged and my own people. Whoever will best allow me to advance my power are my allies.

King Urien: What lofty morals you have! So, it benefits you the most to allow me to slaughter your own people?

Wolf: Aye, Your Majesty, in ways that you cannot imagine. One day, sire, perhaps you will understand.

My uncle and I looked up at each other slowly after we had read this particular page. My mind was racing; I felt like my heart was stuck in my throat.

"The Wolf seems to be powerful indeed," my uncle presently reflected. "I would never have fathomed one could speak that way to King Urien and survive."

"Aye," I murmured back. I rifled through the rest of the documents, scanning them quickly. My eyes widened, then, as I came upon another revelation. "Look, here," I pointed.

King Urien: I am beginning to lose sight of your usefulness, so perhaps your schemes should finally come to an end. Do not think it would be difficult for me to slay you here, on the spot.

Wolf: King Reghan was a fool to think that he could defy me, for that is why I had him killed. I think he had finally begun to see me for who I was, but for so long he was oblivious! It was all too easy to use the interrogator to put the watchmen to sleep. How easy it was, also, to put King Cedric's small spying force to the sword and steal their armour. How opportune that was for my men to attack Gaeson with that fool's own colours! So, do not be deceived you could be rid of me so easily, my lord king.

King Urien: You are right, King Reghan was a fool. Do not, however, make the mistake of thinking I am also. You'd best still your threats and continue to be useful, or I will make you wish that you had never been born.

Wolf: Careful, sire, for even now, even though Queen Evelyn has the crown upon her head, even though King Cedric's heir still lives, I am the one who is truly king in Gaeson, for they do not even know I exist. Do you really want to know what I will do to you, should you try to make good with your threats?

"It was this man, all along," I whispered slowly, as the realisation sank in. It was what we had already suspected, but it was another thing entirely to see it written down in front of me. Every event that had happened in those three months, when my entire world changed, from the night my thirst had woken me, to the battle at Ynys Metcaut, had been orchestrated by the Wolf. With each line I read of his foul deeds, my hatred of him grew deeper. Bitterness turned stronger in my stomach and further pierced my heart. Who could he be, this veiled monster who spoke to King Urien like this? Could Lord Melvyn really be at the root of such evil?

"We still do not know his identity," I sighed at last, sitting back. Much to my frustration, none of the rest of the pages had anything equal in significance. "However, more light is shed on a few things," I reflected. "We know now why King Urien was so confident in attacking Ynys Metcaut two years ago and why he wished to join forces with the other kings. It gives a window indeed into the Wolf's character."

"The Wolf deceived King Urien indeed, to persuade him to wage war against Bernicia that day," King Cedric muttered. "It was probably him who orchestrated the plot to assassinate King Urien. If our great king had lived, we would not be so depleted. The whole war with the Angles itself might be over by now."

"Then he truly might be loyal to Bernicia," I agreed. "Or, he could be playing both sides for his own ends, as he said so himself. What are we to do, Uncle?"

Just as this question escaped my lips, the horns blasted throughout the castle and I leapt up. The noise was different to the one in Gaeson, but I could easily guess its meaning.

"The Bernicians are here," King Cedric confirmed, quickly slipping the documents into his case. He rushed to hide the documents in one of his cupboards. He stood up slowly and turned to face me, with a quiet, wise anger in his countenance, his auburn curls of his hair and beard again almost crackling in the oil lamp's light. "We prepare for war, Daniel," he stated. "These records must not be found, at any cost."

"Aye, Uncle." Together, we departed his chambers. We were already equipped with swords, but we were not yet prepared for battle. Therefore, we swiftly headed to the Caer Ligualid armoury, which was divided into our respective kingdoms. I sped to Gaeson's section and hastily donned my armour and picked up my helmet and shield. Lastly, I slung my bow and quiver onto my back. I followed the soldiers who had done the same, following the steps of the soldiers from Gaeson, Klumeck and Caer Ligualid. One again, the warriors of Rheged were united, as we marched as one towards the royal courtyard.

"I am to be with the archers, my lord," I informed him as we reached a particular set of stairs. King Cedric gave a quick nod, then pulled me into a quick embrace.

"Keep silent about the documents for now, nephew," he whispered in my ear. "Stay safe, my lad," he then said louder as we pulled apart, our arms still clasped.

"You as well, Uncle. I shall see you soon," I added quickly, as we broke apart again. With that, he was gone, calmly descending the spiral steps as if the hell of battle was not about to knock on our door. I lingered a moment, watching him turn the corner and disappear, before I too was gone. I hastened up the steps instead, hurrying to the higher ramparts to join the archers. As I did, I prayed there would not be too much blood spilled this night.

"Aife," I called urgently, spotting her immediately after the archers bowed, chorusing their greeting to me. At once, my friend ran over.

"Her Majesty and Her Royal Highness are both already in the refuge within the city, my lord," she said quietly, anticipating my question well. My heart lightened with relief to know that for the moment, they were safe.

"Good, thank you," I murmured back. It eased me greatly that my wife and sister had both kept their word.

"Your archers are ready and awaiting your command, sire," she added, slightly louder. I nodded to this, as I turned to look out from the rampart. Far too palpable was the rhythmic clunking of the armour as the Bernician scourge marched towards us, growing louder and louder with each passing moment. It was still the dead of night, but our enemy were lit by a thousand beacons. It reminded me keenly of that first battle when thirst had stopped my slumber.

My eyes narrowed, as I realised anew this too had been at the hand of the Veiled Wolf. It was he who had caused King Reghan to attack my uncle and thus provoke King Cedric's reaction of war: it was he who had caused the watchmen to sleep. That scene, though, terrifying as it had been almost a year and a half ago, was nowhere near as vast as the one before us now. I made myself remember, though, that this was not just Gaeson.

Indeed, we were on Caer Ligualid's legendary walls, with all the might of Rheged gathered here. I was used to defending our small castle, but these walls were far higher, the ramparts seeming far more fortified. I hoped and prayed we would defend ourselves all the better against the Bernician scourge. United as we were, we might just emerge victorious.

All of Rheged had not been all assembled for a battle since that fateful day we had besieged Ynys Metcaut, with the aid of the Coalition Kings. All had gone well, until King Morgant had ordered King Urien assassinated. I shook my head, recalling that this, too, had probably been at the instigation of the Wolf. I could only pray there would be no similar betrayals this time, for I knew how frail alliances could be. King Cedric had told me several times I was the tangible link between the alliance of Klumeck and Gaeson, having been born in one kingdom and raised in the other: also, for having married Gaeson's queen.

I could only hope the peace was irrevocable, for if Klumeck and Gaeson were to separate again, what would I do? I would be the husband of one monarch and heir to the other. Indeed, if God did bless us with children, then the child would be heir to both kingdoms. This thought raised again the unhappy prospect of being unable to bear children, for as far as we knew Evelyn had not become with child the last six months. I pushed this unhappy thought away, however, for I did not want to dwell on such a thing with a battle about to start.

My thoughts once again returned to the thought of the Wolf and the dark notions of betrayal. Despite my recent reflections upon our strong concord as brothers and sisters of Rheged, I automatically turned to scan the row of archers under my command. Their countenances were set and determined, appearing ready to risk their lives. Yet how did I know one of them was not working for the Wolf? Which friends were really our foes? Could one of them be the veiled monster himself, who wielded such wicked power?

"All will be well, my lord," she presently murmured from beside me. "They will not break through." I nodded once in reply, as I watched the sea of lights grow ever closer.

As the tense silence continued to surround us like a fog, in my peripheral vision I perceived some of the other archers shift on their feet nervously. I shook my head to clear my thoughts, swallowing my foolish suspicions. Now was the time for unity, not to ponder betrayal and subterfuge. None of us could afford to mistrust one another, for our very lives depended upon it. Therefore, I forced the assassin away from my mind.

"Take heart, brothers and sisters," I instead said quietly, seeking to encourage them. Joshua appeared before my mind, as he often did before a battle. Was it any wonder that young lad had been so afraid? Who could prevent terror from consuming these men and women, given the dreadful horrors that awaited us?

My gaze flickered down slightly, imagining the rest of the soldiers stood together in the lower ramparts and within the castle, all waiting King Owain's orders, as we were. I knew among them would be Conall, the Klumeck soldier whose brother I had indirectly killed in that first battle when I could not slumber. His brother had been named Glyn and had charged towards me. I had leapt out of the way and he had therefore toppled from the rampart, descending to his death. In the next battle I had been confronted by Conall himself, seeking vengeance for his brother. God's grace had granted me the chance to spare his life, but he had been captured by our forces.

The next time I saw him was after I had discovered my true identity as a Royal of Rheged and King Cedric's heir. All Klumeck soldiers had been officially pardoned, released as a symbol of the new-found unity between Gaeson and Klumeck. It was then I had learned his name and the name of his brother. The last time I had seen him was at a distance, as the Klumeck soldiers separated from us to return to Caer Ligualid, on the march home from Ynys Metcaut. Would he be somewhere here now, for this battle to start? I assumed so, unless he had died or been injured in previous battles. I uttered a quick prayer he would be safe.

Ere long the Bernicians finally stopped in their lines. Only moments later, lit by a single beacon, their leaders broke forth from their assembly to gallop into the night. An instant later I saw King Cedric gallop out to meet them. A third soldier rode beside them with a lantern of his own, with a fourth bringing up the rear, bearing Caer Ligualid's banner.

The two leading parties came to a stop, mere feet away from each other. It was far too dark to perceive what was going on, but it was obvious a battle was inevitable. The Bernicians would hardly have marched their army all this way to make peace. As we watched the scene and the tension continued to mount, I distractedly wiped my brow, where a thick sheen of sweat formed.

After only a minute, King Owain's party suddenly turned, swiftly riding back to the safety of Caer Ligualid's castle. By the torchlight I saw my uncle's face. It bore an expression I had seen many times before, on royals and soldiers alike, for it was the countenance of war. I tightened my grip on my bow, raising it high as I took my aim.

"Prepare to fire," I said levelly. It was an almost unnecessary order, as we were all ready for the immediacy of battle regardless. By the flickering torchlight of our foes in the distance, I could just about make out the faces of the enemy. My conscience was pricked, just as it normally was. How many soldiers was I about to kill? I wondered, before I could stop it. How many had spouses or children, hoping their loved ones in return? How many lives was I about to ruin?

"We are to defend our people at all costs," I said, reminding myself as well as others. It was their decision to march and make war against us: we could not abandon those we loved. Indeed, it was the thought of Evelyn and Sarah, who were both in the innermost refuge of the city ready to protect the unarmed citizens there, that kept my arm steady. I resolved to have those two women I loved in my mind.

Abruptly, a distant call came from the Bernicians to charge. At once the massed enemy began racing towards us.

"For Rheged," I declared loudly, "may God be with us all. Fire!" I roared my command. As one, we let our arrows fly into the night.

"Fire when ready!" I shouted my next command, already setting my next arrow upon the bow. A moment later and this one too sailed across the sky, with the hope it would find its home. The Bernicians advanced upon us fast, as we continued to rain our arrows down upon them. In the lower parts of the castle, the other soldiers were ready to protect Caer Ligualid from any that made it onto the castle walls.

After I cut down the first few of the enemy, the battle began to pass by in a blur. There was a threat in this, for when had I ceased feeling every soldier I killed? When had war begun numbing my conscience? They were too far away, these remote shapes of the enemy. I was beginning to forget each one could have a home, parents, spouse, or children. I was beginning to forget I was killing real people, each with flesh and blood, with bodies, minds and souls. I was starting to overlook their humanity.

"Defend at all costs!" I called, blinking hard. In this pondering I had not lost concentration, but it would not do to dwell on their souls now. As despicable as it was, my lack of humanity was a distinct advantage in war.

As the minutes of the battle ticked on, presently my quiver was nearly empty. By this point, the Bernicians had set their ladders against Caer Ligualid's walls. I fired the last two arrows at soldiers nearing the tops of the ladders, almost upon us at the highest ramparts. Then, I swiftly drew my sword, just in time to cut into the first man who came over the top.

My blade found its home in his neck, the force of impact severing his head clean off. His warm blood sprayed my chin as the soldier fell back down, his head following him. The encounter was as different as it could be from shooting the enemy from afar. Momentarily I staggered, lost in the face of the man I had just killed. That panic in his gaze, in those eyes which would forever judge me from his grave.

"My lord!" Aife put a man to her axe and hastily grabbed me. "Are you all right brother?" she asked me quickly, having seen me tarry, witnessing the blood on my face.

"Yes, I'm fine," I replied, roughly wiping my chin with the back of my hand, "the blood is not mine." My breastplate had also been spattered with it, but I did not pay it heed, not whilst Caer Ligualid was still in danger. "Onwards," I added and Aife nodded, the serious expression of war upon her own countenance also.

A moment later and she was gone, lost in the battle once more. The battle raged on and I tried to block the man's face from my vision as I twisted and turned, killing each enemy soldier that stood between myself and the citizens of Rheged.

There were all the usual sounds: the screaming, the grunts, the scraping of metal. A dodge to the left, a swing to the right. My nostrils filled with the acrid scent of blood that hung thick in the air, so close I could almost taste it. I pressed on, ignoring my senses. I relied on instinct alone, as I performed the horribly familiar movements in this ancient dance of war. My steps parried and blocked, as I evaded and leapt forward to strike the enemy.

It was much later in the battle when the ramparts finally seemed clear of the enemy. I put my latest foe to the sword and straightened, breathing heavily with the effort. I wiped more war stains that were not mine from my features and leant against a wall, exhausted. I looked towards the sky to see it had paled considerably. Dawn was near. My eyes lowered to survey the battle. To my relief, Bernicia had not yet invaded the kingdom. In fact, they seemed to be retreating. Then, as my gaze roved over the warfare, I caught sight of King Cedric. He was cut off from allies and looking to be fighting off several enemies at once.

Abruptly I turned, thundering down from the ramparts. My only thought was to save my uncle from what could be certain doom. I desperately did not want him to share the same fate as Bredon. I could not be too late this time. I leapt from the spiral staircase to the hall, where many Rheged soldiers had gathered before the battle began. The main door had been partially broken down, but quickly I perceived we had not been overrun; the gap in the barricade only had a handful of soldiers near it.

Determinedly, I ploughed into this warring huddle of both friend and foe. I dodged the blade of an enemy, breaking into a sprint as I did so. I soon raced across the courtyard, where only the day before Evelyn and I had been greeted by King Owain in a state of peace. It was such a contrast to the picture now. There was a Klumeck soldier near the field beyond and I had to half push past her as I ran.

The soldier raised her sword as she staggered, then I caught the confusion in her features at her prince as I rushed on. I paid her no heed, however, for I only had eyes for my king and the hope I could assist him. I sprinted through this epic arena where so much blood had been spilled, weaving my way past clusters of combat. To my relief, I perceived that several Gaeson and Klumeck soldiers had already come to his aid, but what I saw made my blood run cold.

Although many of the Bernicians were fleeing the battle, as their horn (presumably, the order to retreat) blasted, a few were remaining in combat with my uncle. There was a soldier in particular whose face was set in determination. As I neared, my steps taking me as fast as my body could possibly allow, my eyes were on his countenance. There was something far too convicted in his stare to be simply an enemy soldier. An unpleasantly familiar memory tugged...

"No!" I shouted, as I realised this soldier bore the same expression as Llofan Llaf Difo, the man in the last battle who had assassinated King Urien. The man, we now suspected, who had been executing the orders of the Wolf... literally.

"King Cedric!" I roared, as this foe cut down another Briton soldier and turned back to my uncle. I was a few steps away from him still: saw the small smile of satisfaction and triumph on my enemy's countenance.

My uncle turned in warning towards the assassin, sword raised, but it was too late. The sword of the enemy soldier came crashing in at my uncle's side, slicing through a gap underneath the chainmail.

"No! Uncle!" I bellowed. I charged forwards, but a Klumeck soldier had got there before me. As the warrior twirled to cut the assassin down, I caught a glimpse of whirling chestnut hair. With a jolt, I realised the soldier was Sarah.

Where had she come from? Had she discovered Bernicia was retreating and come to aid in the final push? Or had she broken her word and never actually gone to the city's refuge in the first place? I pushed this from my mind, however, as Sarah wielded her blade, for now was hardly the time to wonder where she had been.

As I rushed the last few steps to the bloody scene, my sister struck the enemy first in his leg. Then, as he fell to the floor, she impaled his stomach and the tip came clean out the other side. Sarah left her sword where it was still in our foe and collapsed to her knees next to King Cedric. Gently, she pulled our uncle's head onto her lap. I rushed forwards, coming to my knees beside her also.

"Uncle," she whispered passionately, hurriedly removing her helmet with one hand, "I have you." A smile flashed across his features, despite his obvious pain. I took one glance at his wound and despair hit me in the stomach, for I had seen enough battle wounds to know it was fatal. I would be unable to save him, just as I had been helpless to save my captain.

"Lynette—" this great king murmured, as the life ebbed away from him. He exerted his remaining strength to outstretch his hand to his niece. Sarah moved to grasp his hand and his blood smeared their connecting palms.

"Bryce—" he said next. He turned his head towards me with a grunt, reaching out with his free hand. I took his warm hand in mine and my heart contracted. For how long would it remain warm? How many moments of life did he have? I reflected on his use of our birth names and hoped that in his last seconds of life, his thoughts were of his happiest times. I imagined him picturing his wife, or his sister and her husband.

Tears threatened to blind my sight, but I obstinately blinked them away. I was unwilling to let anything cloud my final view of him, this king I had come to have such affection for. It had never felt more absurd to remember how I had once hated him, believing him to be my enemy.

"Please don't die, Uncle," Sarah whispered, already weeping. If King Cedric could be kept alive by sheer will, then he would surely have had a full recovery. Alas, I knew this was not to be, no matter how much I hoped and prayed. Our uncle's eyes kept switching between us, gazing at us with such tenderness that my tears could be held back no longer and I felt the first, fresh pools of wetness travel down my cheeks.

"I wish I could stay with you, my love," he said sadly, "but know what joy I have had in knowing you both. Take care of each other and our people," he added, his eyes glancing between us. "You will make a fine king," he added to me. With another shock I realised that I was about to become a king. I had not processed this reality yet, for currently I was just a young boy, grieving the loss of my uncle. At this moment I was not a prince about to inherit a throne, but abruptly I felt I was a young lad of fifteen again, weeping in the stable loft about the death of my father. Surely, then, I was nowhere near ready to take on the title of king.

"Rule with care, seek God's counsel," my uncle wheezed, his breathing even more laboured. Suddenly I was a prince on the battlefield again and my ears strained to take every attention I could to my king's final orders. "You still need to govern them, though they are displaced. I have a final command, for both of you," he then said. His eyes became frantic, piercing our souls as they flew between us.

"You said your old captain spoke of the Wolf, that he knew him." King Cedric spoke fiercely, intently. "Solve the mystery, Bryce," he now whispered. "Find out who…" he trailed off here, his speech breaking to take another breath. "Find out why they had to die."

"Aye, Your Majesty," I answered quietly. My eyes closed momentarily, to clear the tears that were now flowing fast. "I promise, Uncle, I promise. Please," I muttered desperately. I did not know what the rest of my sentence would be, for there was nothing to keep him from dying. My uncle was no longer looking at us, instead stared into the distance. Presently he smiled, as though with all the strength he had left.

"Angharad," he breathed weakly. I blinked fresh tears, for I knew God was taking him. He had spoken of his wife, so cruelly snatched from him, bearing the child none of us could know. "It's far too long, my darling…"

"She is waiting for you, Uncle," Sarah muttered brokenly, as his head still rested on her lap. "So is your child. Go and be with God; see them at last," she instructed gently.

"My love…" our Uncle murmured. Then he gave a loud breath that cut halfway in his throat; his hands were limp in our hands. King Cedric was dead, with his eyes still fixed somewhere far away, beyond this world, the ghost of his smile still upon his face.

For a moment, Sarah and I remained quiet as we watched him. I imagined him seeing our God at last, reunited with his wife and the child he had never met. Slowly, I lifted my free hand and it came to rest on the red mass of his hair, matted with dirt, sweat and the blood of warfare.

"Long live the king," I managed ere long, when I could at last trust my voice enough to speak. Sarah glanced up at me in her weeping, the sobs racking through the heart of her.

"Oh, Daniel," she whispered. The pain of my sister moved me even more. My throat tightened, again rendering me unable to speak. I leant forward to embrace her and we clung to each other hard, her head resting on the metal armour on my shoulder. Thus positioned we mourned, grieving for our uncle. He had been the only family member we'd had left, save each other. I had never been more thankful that this woman in my arms was my sister.

"I have you, Lynny," I whispered, using the nickname I had used for her as a child. Sarah said nothing in reply: we simply held each other in silence. After a minute or so we moved apart. All seemed eerily quiet now, as it oft was after war. I was glad we had been given this privacy to grieve. I lifted my heavy arms, to attempt to remove the signs of my weeping.

Indeed, the initial wave of grief seemed to have ebbed a little. Presently Sarah bent forward, swept the auburn locks of hair from our uncle's forehead and bent down to kiss it. Once she had straightened, she looked to me, taking my hand.

"Long live the king," she whispered and bowed her head. A mix of shock radiated through the gnawing despair, as I realised she was speaking to me. I dropped her hand quicker than intended in reflex. I saw Sarah's countenance take on sympathy for my position, of taking on this title I was nowhere near prepared for.

"Sarah," I said after a pause and swallowed. In my mind was the expression of the soldier who had killed King Cedric. "Did you see the man's face?" I asked urgently.

"Aye," Sarah replied quietly. "It was almost as if—" suddenly, she broke off. "We shall talk of this later," she concluded, as I frowned.

"Your Highnesses!" It was John who spoke from behind me, rendering it obvious why Sarah had ceased her speech. If King Cedric had indeed been assassinated, we would do well to keep it to ourselves. Not even John should know, until we were sure.

"The battle is over," our friend began his report a little needlessly, for the sounds of combat had long been replaced with the groans of the wounded and grieving alike. My captain then stopped short as he saw Sarah and me crouched down beside the dead body of our uncle. I took a moment to wipe my hands over my face once again. I desperately wished to remove all traces of tears, but I imagined all I had done was smudge the blood and grime on my face.

"Is His Majesty—?" John began, running the last few steps to stand beside me. He stilled his speech, the answer to his question obvious.

"Yes," I interrupted, anticipating his question. "The king is dead," I declared woodenly, thankfully able to utter that dreadful sentence without grief making my voice crack. John came to stand beside where I was kneeling. His hand went directly to my shoulder.

"I'm so deeply sorry, Daniel, Sarah," he murmured, "for your loss." I was so thankful he had addressed me as a friend rather than a king. I moved my hand to clasp where his hand remained on my shoulder, letting him comfort me. I knew I had never loved my friend more than at this moment. I had never been more grateful our brotherhood transcended title and rank.

A moment later, I reluctantly rose from the ground and John took his hand away. In the next instant John took four paces back, drew his sword and sank to bended knee upon the ground. He pointed his blade down so that it struck the earth, softened by mud and blood alike. One hand rested on the hilt of his sword, the other clenched into a fist at his chest.

"Long live the king," he said, his face bowed to the ground. "May my sword and my heart live to serve you always, Your Majesty," he declared.

As he spoke, I caught sight of Aife running over to us. I caught the shock and then sadness in her face, as she at once registered what had happened. In the next moment, she too had bent to one knee beside John. She struck the earth with her spear, as John had done with his blade.

"Long live the king," Aife repeated the phrase. I knew I was going to hear those four words many times more. Neither of them spoke further. I realised they were waiting for me. I walked over to them, putting one hand on John's shoulder and the other on Aife's.

"Rise, both of you," I ordered and they both straightened. Looking at them both, I found I was able to smile a little. "I am glad to have such friends in my counsel," I affirmed. John and Aife smiled faintly also, as they inclined their heads. Then the pain of my uncle's parting hit me again and the smile vanished from my face as I glanced back at his bloodied body. I sniffed loudly as if to clear my thoughts, then turned back to John.

"Captain," I addressed him, for formality seemed the most appropriate. John instantly straightened, awaiting orders. "I bid you get soldiers, to carry my uncle back to the castle."

"At once, Your Majesty," John replied, giving a bow of his head before departing to carry out my command. After he left, I raised my head up to the skies to see the morning had dawned grey and bleak, with none of the light of the sun in sight. This seemed most fitting and for a few moments I stared dully up to the canvas above me. All sounds still seemed muted and I shifted my gaze to the field around me, taking in the sombre scene.

Already John was heading back towards me with four soldiers, obeying my first order as king to take my uncle's body away. My gaze then went to the countless Rheged soldiers, all traipsing back to that ancient city. Some were carrying wounded, others carrying the dead. It was as if with every thud of their boots upon the naked earth, rucked and covered in blood from the fallen, they were taking the essence of a soul with them.

"Your Majesty," the quiet greeting came. My eyes moved slowly back to John as his greeting reached my ears. The four men he had gathered stood beside him, two of them carrying a makeshift stretcher between them. As they laid it down on the ground, I sensed Sarah was holding back a sob. I reached out to take her hand, as she choked the noise off in her throat. My sister took a step closer to me and I moved to wind an arm round her. Thus positioned, we watched the soldiers treat our uncle with great dignity and care, for which I was thankful indeed.

One of them had brought a large square of cloth with him, drenched in water from somewhere. He began dabbing away most of the blood and grime on King Cedric's face and hands. Another had retrieved my uncle's sword, wiping it upon the grass to clean it. When they had finished, King Cedric almost looked as if he was simply reclining on his bed, in the midst of a happy daydream. Then, they bent his arms at the elbows, clasping them together upon his breastplate.

Their finishing touch was placing my uncle's sword upon his breastplate, lying flat with the hilt underneath his joined hands. This had all been done wordlessly, with a silent respect. Just as mutely, they now moved around the stretcher and lifted my kin effortlessly, as if his weight had been lighter than air. John glanced at me and at my nod, they began walking back to the city. I rubbed a hand yet again over my face, setting my countenance resolutely as I walked behind the stretcher. Sarah fell into step beside me, keeping the body of our uncle in our sights.

I reflected now upon the man who had been my king, my uncle and my friend. He had always kept a wise counsel and a kind heart. From the moment he had first discovered I was his nephew, he had treated me with affection and love. His joy had been abundant, too, at finding his niece also alive and well. It was only in this hour of passing, I realised just how much I had loved my uncle also.

Intermingled with the grief was the ever-increasing apprehension that I was now the King of Klumeck. I would have to have a coronation, presumably here in Caer Ligualid. It marvelled me anew that I had ever regarded this people and the king as my enemies, with great bitterness. It was strange to reflect how I had once battled with the soldiers I had now inherited as my army. They were my people, I reflected, though most of the displaced Klumeck citizens resided in Caer Ligualid. Would I have to be a king without a people, or could they move to Gaeson?

I was pulled away from these thoughts, as those slowly carrying my uncle stopped and Sarah and I came to a halt behind them. We were back in the grand courtyard once more, now mostly clear. I was relieved to see for the most part, we had kept the Bernician scourge at bay. The rest of the citizens were coming out of the inner refuge where they had been protected. They looked unharmed, but distress and anxiety were written plain upon their features as they began searching for the wounded and the dead that would belong to many of them.

Abruptly, I became aware that people had stopped in their distressing movements. I perceived people taking in King Cedric on the stretcher and turning to look at me in grieving recognition. Before I could try to utter that I wished they would not, people from Gaeson, Klumeck and Caer Ligualid alike began dropping to their knees. The party carrying my uncle gently lowered him to the ground, so that they too could kneel. Even Sarah took a step back from me to bow low.

"Long live the king!" John shouted from beside me. As one, from their bended knees, they chorused back this refrain. Then they were silent again and a warm breeze whistled past my face in the interlude. Were they waiting for me to speak? I was too busy swallowing my grief to speak. Surely, if I opened my mouth, despair would stream forth rather than words. Besides, what could I say? Any speech that came to mind seemed so trite and foolish.

Instead of talking, trying to not let my arm shake, I brought my hand in a closed fist to my mouth, pressing my knuckles against my lips. Then, I stretched my hand out, away from me, in the direction of the battlefield. It was the symbol Gaeson always performed after battle, as a sign of remembrance to those who had fallen. At the siege of Ynys Metcaut, the soldiers of Caer Ligualid and Klumeck had also learnt this simple, poignant action. Presently, I beheld all of Rheged's warriors and citizens copy this action, whichever kingdom they hailed from.

"Your Majesty," said a voice I knew and loved. I turned to look at my wife. I noticed instantly a vivid line of red across her left eyebrow. Thankfully the mark was thin and looked as though it did not need stitches. Apart from this my queen appeared uninjured, for which I was immensely grateful and relieved. Evelyn walked slowly over to me and curtseyed low, bowing her head. Then, she took my hand and kissed it gently. It was our first contact since the battle began.

"Long live the king," my queen whispered, her breath catching in her throat in her sadness. Her grieved tone almost undid me, but somehow, I managed to stem the cascade of my emotions. Rather than speaking, my gaze went to her eyebrow.

"I am fine, it is only a scratch," she responded, rightly anticipating my next question. "Only a few managed to get to the heart of the city, the vast majority were held off here in the courtyard," Evelyn added in explanation, a little breathlessly. "We put to the sword those that did. The civilians were unharmed."

"Good," I managed hoarsely, swallowing. "Captain," I said, turning to look at him. I heard the first tremor in my voice and swallowed hard again, using all the military training I could muster to maintain my impassivity. John straightened again, as one waiting for orders.

"Take King Cedric inside, his body must be prepared for burial," I continued, my speech stronger. Yet it sounded foreign to my ears, as if my voice was not quite my own.

"Your Majesties, Your Royal Highness," John bowed, before the party carrying my uncle headed towards the castle. I began to follow them and as I did, the suspenseful silence seemed to end. Soon the combined voices of Rheged rose up, with the calls of people searching for their dead. In a perverse way part of me was glad to hear their distressed calls, for the sooner attention was away from me, the better.

Dimly, I wondered where King Owain was and his brothers who would have been fighting in the war, whom I had only met briefly. Then I caught sight of him at the edge of the crowd. Slowly, he inclined his head to me before leaving the courtyard also. At first, I wondered at his lack of speech, but then I had understood. As Caer Ligualid's king, he was the Supreme Ruler of Rheged and a superior monarch to me. Had he spoken, he would have immediately taken all attention.

As much as I wished he had made people look to him, I realised his silence was the greatest respect of all. He had allowed all honour to be given to my late uncle without any distraction from him. It showed the greatest honour, for a king not to seek such glory for himself, though it was within his rights. I stared at the spot where King Owain had stood for a moment, before also making my way towards the entrance of the castle.

Instead of following the party of soldiers who had taken my uncle, however, I turned down a different corridor. I longed, just for a few moments, to be as far away from other people as possible. I was hardly aware of where my feet took me, until I reached my uncle's chambers. Nobody was guarding it, but why would they? My king was dead. I ran inside, swallowing at the fresh heartache the sight of his empty chambers gave me. All of his possessions were around, all looking so lived-in still. In truth, I was barely able to sink into the nearest chair as at last the dam on my heart broke.

Abruptly I remained there as my emotions at last poured forth, arms clutched about my chest tightly and head bowed towards the floor as I sobbed. Ere long, the fresh wave of grief receded, as I rubbed my weary countenance. I imagined it to be still congealed with the mixture of tears, sweat and blood. I stood, spent from such depth of feeling. I could hardly believe less than twelve hours ago, I had stood in this chamber with him, reading the documents we had found in King Urien's tomb.

At this thought, I trudged to the cupboard King Cedric had hidden the documents in, for it was the main reason I came here. To my horror, however, as I looked through it, the leather case was gone. I searched the wooden compartment again and again, but it was no use. The sheets detailing King Urien's dealings with the Wolf were gone, vanished into thin air.

How could someone have known about them? I wondered, thinking quickly. The only other person was the guard, but such was his fear in the face of my uncle I sincerely doubted he would have broken his silence. He had also left when we entered the chamber, so when would he have had the opportunity?

It must have been someone who had snuck back here after the battle horn sounded, I realised. Who could it have been? I deduced it must have been someone in league with the Wolf, if not the veiled monster himself. In frustration I slammed the cupboard door shut with a loud bang. There was little else to do here now the chamber was devoid of its secrets, so I presently I departed my uncle's chambers.

My pace seemed unusually heavy as I walked the little way to the chamber reserved for Evelyn and myself. As I entered the rooms I realised my pace was not only slow due to emotion, for I still wore my armour. In my haste to secure the documents I had gone straight to King Cedric's chambers. Clearly, though, I had not been fast enough, for the documents were already missing by the time I got there.

Relieved to still be alone for the moment, I slowly pulled off each piece of armour and removed my battle-stained garments. I left them discarded about the floor, instead wearily heading to the bathroom. A steaming bath was waiting for me, with a small pile of clean clothes waiting beside it. I climbed into the bath, submerging my tired form up to my chin in the hot water, but made no move to cleanse myself. Instead I remained still, as the images from war washed over me, the way they always did. The harsh image of my uncle's corpse was ever before me. Though I did not weep fully, a few tears did well.

"Daniel?" Presently I heard my wife call my name quietly, as she came into the main chamber. I greeted her back, hoping my voice sounded even. I immediately rubbed water roughly onto my face. I winced slightly at the contact with my open cuts and bruises, but I was determined to wash away all remnants of weeping. I did not want to be seen weeping, even in front of my wife. At length, when I hoped any tears were gone, I began to wash the grime from my body.

As I did this, I heard the door open again and heard her talking. I heard her instruct a guard to remove my amour and the clothing I had left about the room. Evelyn then said nothing further to me and I was grateful for this. My wife knew me well enough: I currently wished to be alone. We were both similar in this respect, for both her royal upbringing and my identity as a soldier had trained us to hide our emotions, instead expressing weaknesses alone.

My identity as a king suddenly jolted through me again. I would have to become even better at being impassive, for sometimes I wondered whether I wasn't nearly as effective at hiding my heart as I thought. Was it only during extraordinary examples of grief and hardship, such as now, when I could not help my emotion from showing? Or was I simply far more transparent than I believed? Either way, it was very rare I showed raw emotion to another. Indeed, even doing so in front of Evelyn made me cringe.

Presently I clambered out of the large wooden tub, drying myself wearily. It had not just been my armour, for even undressed my limbs felt very heavy. I changed into the pristine garments, in complete contrast to my former clothes stained with war. I headed back to the main chamber and collapsed directly onto the bed. I rolled over to glance at Evelyn, who had just finished changing into her formal, regal robes.

"Was your bath refreshing?" Evelyn murmured as she sat on the bed next to me. I found I barely had the strength to nod. My queen reached her hand to run through my still damp hair.

"You have nothing to apologise for or feel ashamed of, husband," Evelyn whispered quietly. As I stared at the ceiling, the corner of my mouth turned ever so slightly that already, she knew I had wept, though I had washed the signs away. "It is always safe to be open with me," she reminded me. I glanced towards her at that, mindful of what Sarah had said only yesterday.

"The same with you, my love," I told her quietly. She smiled at me then, which somehow even in my grief I managed to return, albeit faintly. "I meant to ask you," I asked casually as I sat up, "did you find out anything further about the assassin from King Owain? Anything I need to know?" I asked, looking at her. Evelyn seemed to ponder this, before shaking her head.

"No, it is still a mystery," she sighed, shaking her head. Her answer was neutral, as she ran her hand through her loose, raven curls, not noticing the slight seed of doubt in my question. "Have you?" she asked back now. "You have not told me what you were doing last night. I woke when the horn sounded, but you were already gone," she murmured. "You did not retire to bed, did you?"

"No," I answered. "I had arranged to meet Taliesin, as I supposed he might have known something about the spy. I was right," I admitted. Swiftly, I told her how my uncle and I had gone to the tomb to find the missing documents and to take them back to King Cedric's chamber. I detailed that we had rapidly read through them, to be interrupted by the horn for battle. I then concluded with the further alarming mystery that the documents were missing.

"It did not reveal his identity, but it was enough to confirm everything we feared. They were his last words to me today, to ask me to solve this mystery," I murmured ere long, my uncle's final speech in my mind's eye. "I will discover the truth about who he is, even if it takes me to my last breath," I added resolutely, almost speaking more to myself than to her.

"I do not doubt it," she replied quietly, her gentle words bringing me back to the present as she pulled me slowly towards her. My head came to rest upon her shoulder, as her arm embraced me. "As for now, you need your rest." Her tone was nearly as low as a whisper. "Most of Caer Ligualid will be sleeping by now. I will wake you later for the banquet."

"The banquet," I repeated hoarsely, giving a hollow laugh into her shoulder in derision. The banquet was the very last thing I wished to do.

"I know it seems absurd," Evelyn agreed, "but it is precisely because we have lost the ones we love that we need to gather together. The feast is not only to celebrate the victory. Yes, it is a victory," she reinforced with a nod, "but a chance for us to grieve together."

"Aye, I know," I sighed, as I lay back upon the bed, unable to dwell on anything except my dead uncle and the people I was suddenly king over. This was my last thought, for I was just aware of my wife's kiss upon my cheek before I sank into slumber, deep and dreamless.

Chapter Seven

I woke with the same sensation I had when I slipped into slumber, as my wife pressed a gentle kiss to my forehead. As her head rose away from mine, my hands moved to rub my face and I flinched, feeling again the bruises I could not remember getting.

"Here," Evelyn murmured, pushing a small goblet into my hands as I sat up. It was hot tea, made with stewed bitter herbs and honey. "You'll need your strength," she told me, with that compassionate smile again on her face. She then left the bed to straighten her raven curls with her fingers, preparing herself anew for the banquet.

"I'll be fine tonight," I returned brusquely, for even though I knew her smile had been one of compassion and sympathy, my pride whispered to me there could be some semblance of pity, also. I knew this was ridiculous, but such was my disdain of vulnerability. I could not stand the notion that she thought I was weak.

"I'm sure you will," was all she replied. I wrapped my hands around the goblet as I sipped my tea, trying not to let the heat scald my mouth. Presently I stood, ignoring my aching body and crossing to the wardrobe to retrieve my formal robes.

This was to be my first public appearance as king, I realised, other than in that grand courtyard after the battle, with my dead uncle laid only a few feet away. How many more times would that awful phrase, 'Long live the king', be uttered? Those four words that reminded me again and again my king was dead? I wondered how King Owain had stood it, after the assassination of his father. Evelyn, too, had heard the refrain 'Long live the queen' after her father had been killed. I imagined all in the palace hall, chorusing it once more. As I pulled my regal tunic over my head, I further realised I would be expected to make a speech. It was the very last thing I felt like doing.

"It only needs to be short," Evelyn told me abruptly, as I buckled my belt. I glanced at her without much surprise, for my queen always seemed to read my mind. Perhaps I would never fully be able to hide my emotions from her. Perhaps, this was simply called marriage.

"You need have no fear, Daniel," she encouraged me now, stepping over to briefly touch my shoulder. "You are a fantastic orator." I wanted to thank her for her words, because I knew she meant to comfort me. Yet I stayed quiet, as for some reason I was resentful of her consolation. My wife seemed to sense even this, as she said nothing further until we were both ready to leave.

As we departed our chamber, dressed in our royal finery, my legs felt like lead. I had never felt quite as lethargic after battle. Was this some physical manifestation of grief? Evelyn had tucked her arm into mine, but in truth she seemed to support my steps as much as I did hers. We made our way together through the interweaving corridors, eventually coming to the large, grand staircase leading to the banquet hall. Nobles and soldiers turned to fix their gaze upon us as we descended the staircase rather grandly. In truth, I rather felt like a fool.

We entered the banquet hall, with still all eyes following our movements. A pregnant silence filled the ornate chamber, that was somehow loud, almost as if I could hear nothing itself. I told myself this quiet was simply the custom: they silenced for us as they would for any other royals. However, I could not but feel their collective gaze more keenly, as if they were piercing down into my very soul, seeing the very heart of me. Surely, they had penetrated through all perception of pomposity to see the frail stable boy inside, mourning the loss of another man he loved and yet was helpless to save.

I was thankful indeed when the attention switched from us to the floor, as they all either bowed or curtseyed low. Evelyn and I walked past them all, to take our places at the royal table. As soon as we arrived, my queen moved her hand to touch my elbow briefly before moving to sit down. It was a gentle reminder to give my speech, as if I could have forgotten. Everyone else sat down also, with a corporate creaking of chairs.

"We stand here," I began abruptly. At once my voice sounded foreign again to my ears, far higher pitched than intended. I broke off, hastily coughing to clear my throat. "We stand here today united," I tried again. To my relief my voice sounded much more normal. "United," I repeated, "against those who would seek to oppress and harm us. Never before have I witnessed the bonds of our respective lands. Never before have I been so proud to not only belong to Gaeson, but to be of Klumeck blood also." I paused here; a quiet, collective murmur of agreement resounded through the chamber.

"We are joined with Caer Ligualid, as one people under His Supreme Majesty, King Owain. Such a bond, under his rule, will never be easily torn apart." A slightly louder cheer echoed, at the mention of our resplendent monarch.

"It is strange to think His Majesty King Cedric is no longer with us," I went on. A lump of grief abruptly threatened to knot in my throat: swiftly I swallowed it. "He was a strong ruler, courageous and wise," I continued. "We will recall forever his honour and strength in battle. Ever since I came to know him, however, what struck me most was his heart.

"From the moment he found me and claimed me as his heir," I continued, "I was taken by the kindness and joy in his nature. He treated me like a son and was gracious whilst I wrestled with my identity. He was even more gracious and loving, also, to my sister, Her Royal Highness, Princess Lynette," I gestured to Sarah briefly. "In truth, it did not take long for either of us to view him like a father." I paused here again, surveying the audience before me.

"The father who had raised me died when I was fifteen," I revealed to the chamber. "Then, when Princess Lynette and I learnt of our identity and how our family had been murdered," I reflected, "I was in despair that I was without a father again. Yet, fatherless I was not," I declared presently, "for I had him as my father. Not only did he instruct me as his heir, but he loved me as his son. He loved Princess Lynette, too, as his own child. That is how my regard for him will remain," I told my audience. "For today, we have not only lost a king, but a father as well. His Majesty King Cedric was a father to us all," I concluded.

There was only a moment of quiet, before my audience exploded. They got to their feet, roaring their approval. I found it strange at first for my sombre words to be met with such rigorous cheer, but perhaps it was because Rheged viewed my uncle the way I had done.

I sat down, as the last of my strength left me. Underneath the table, Evelyn reached for my hand. Finding it, she rubbed her thumb over mine and I found I was grateful for her comfort. With my free hand, I took a large gulp from my goblet of mead. Presently, relief entered my emotions as well as grief, that the speech was over. As I replaced the goblet, I caught Sarah's eye from beside me, her eyes full of unshed tears. A small smile was on her face, that let me know she approved of my words. This pleased me greatly, for suddenly hers was the only opinion I cared about.

As the cheers died down, King Owain stood to give his own speech. Once again, I appreciated his respect for my uncle, that he had allowed my tribute to King Cedric before his own words. The Supreme King of Rheged now spoke grand words about courage and sacrifice, but in truth I hardly heard him. It was as if I could feel myself floating away, as if I was not really present. I stood when the other royals did, signalling the end of his speech. I joined automatically in the cheer, also, though my heart was not really in it.

At last the formalities seemed to be over, as I slumped back down to my seat and took another mouthful of mead. I was not really hungry, even though I had barely eaten in the last twenty-four hours. A servant brought forth a plate of food, decadent and smelling divine. I knew I could not just fill my stomach with drink, so I made myself eat. Partaking in the feast also meant I could be reserved from speaking. Rather I listened to the conversation between Evelyn and Sarah, who both seemed to understand I did not wish to talk. I did not really focus on what they were saying, rather I listened to the collective throng of words shared around the long banquet benches. I made out tones of laughter and cheer as comrades shared victories, but also clear was the grimness of those consoling each other in the deaths of their warriors, loved and cherished.

Presently a different sound filled my ears. Although it was in this chamber, it seemed as far away as I felt. I looked to see a minstrel in a corner near to me, playing a harp. The notes floated towards me, the sweet, delicate melody somehow reaching me despite so much rowdy talk. I felt a little of the awful tension begin to seep away, as I drank mead and listened.

"Are you well, Daniel?" Abruptly, my eyes opened fully as I glanced at my sister, who was frowning at me. I realised I had been squinting strangely, in attempt to listen to the music.

"Aye, Lynny," I returned, taking another mouthful of mead. Her mouth turned in a small smile at the nickname I had used of her as an infant, before we had been separated. I supposed it was because of King Cedric's death that my mind was in the past.

"I was listening to the music," I explained to her quietly, but she raised her eyebrows, unable to hear my speech, though she was next to me. "The harp," I explained, louder. Sarah's frown deepened and then her brows rose again.

"Oh, yes. How on earth can you hear that?" she asked in surprise. I smiled faintly, for I was not sure how I heard it, either. All I knew was that this music was the most beautiful, haunting tones I had ever heard. I knew they would forever be intermingled with this day, for they seemed to resonate with my very soul.

"Brother, we still need to discuss—" Sarah suddenly began, the smile fading from her countenance. "What we thought we saw today..." she hesitated again. I nodded, already guessing the meaning behind her words.

"I know," I answered meaningfully. Her gaze hardened slightly. In that moment, I knew no discussion was necessary: we understood each other well enough. Our uncle had indeed been assassinated, in almost the same way King Urien had been.

"Of what are you speaking?" Evelyn enquired here, looking between us. I considered telling her, but as I glanced around I suspected we could still be overheard, despite the noise.

"Not here," I murmured quietly. "I'll tell you later." Evelyn rose her eyebrows but said nothing further on the topic. Instead, she reached for another piece of bread. A moment later, Sarah struck up conversation again with my queen. I listened for the music again, but it seemed to have stopped. I glanced across to see the harpist had gone: the grand instrument was deserted. I lifted the mead once again to my mouth, feeling a little bereft in its absence.

My thoughts turned to what I would tell Evelyn tonight, about the true nature of my uncle's death. As I did so, my eyes furtively glanced around the ornate chamber. They scanned, until they settled upon one target; Lord Melvyn, sitting and talking with Lord Aldred and some of King Owain's advisors. I saw his countenance was almost too fitting: an expression of relief at victory, yet sadness for the fallen. Was he the Wolf, who had orchestrated King Cedric's death?

If King Cedric had been assassinated as Sarah and I suspected, then the Veiled Wolf was here, destroying the lives of my kin, piece by piece. How many royals would die, before we brought him to justice? How many lives would suffer before he was discovered? That was the terrible, unanswerable question I was faced with. At present the only solution I could reach for was my mead, as I re-filled the goblet generously. It was the simple consolation of oblivion.

***

Three days later, King Cedric's funeral dawned a particular monochrome grey. This seemed very apt, as the dark billowing clouds overhead seemed to utterly transform the city. It seemed devoid of its usual liveliness, as I stood in the courtyard in my royal robes, feeling again like a fool in all the pomp. Though the courtyard was full, the people were so silent that even the quiet summer breeze was almost tangible as it rifled past us.

Unlike at the banquet, the woman who grasped my arm was not Evelyn, but Sarah. As siblings we mourned our uncle, the man who had indeed been a third father for us, after the father who had sired us and the fathers who had raised us in Gaeson. I felt a rush of gratitude, at these four men who had loved us, either when we were together or when we were separated.

Presently, the memory of the banquet brought again to my mind that haunting harp melody, as clear in my mind now as it had been then. I had wondered whether I would be able to recall it, for my head had grown heavy with mead that night. It was much later still, with speech hushed and a little intoxicated with mead, that I was finally able to relate to Evelyn the terrible true nature of King Cedric's death.

As the image of how our uncle had died again shot through me, my right hand crossed to grasp the hand of Sarah, still tucked under my arm. In front of us stood King Owain, ready to lead the procession, with Evelyn standing beside him. Then, further ahead were the bearers of the coffin, each holding a corner of the large wooden box. I knew all too well whose remains were inside. I swallowed, trying to push the image of King Cedric's corpse away.

A cleric moved out from the crowds now, wearing black garments and with his head bent in respect. King Owain moved to stand to the side, his right hand holding casually the hilt of his sword. I witnessed him only in my peripheral vision, however, for my gaze was ever fixed on the coffin. I wished somehow, I could summon him from the dead. I knew I could do so, if this power could be done by pure volition. I knew he had gone to be with God and though this did give me comfort and hope, it did not ease the pain of his passing, nor make the ache less real. As the cleric began speaking, Sarah shifted slightly. In response, I tightened my grip on her hand.

In all probability, the cleric spoke with great wisdom. However, like with King Owain's speech at the banquet, I barely heard a word he said. Indeed, I felt like I was numb, yet paradoxically I also felt as though my insides were as heavy as lead. My gaze lifted a little to the canvas above and though the darkened sky had been apt it at once seemed apt it now grew tiresome, for the grey showed no sign of lifting.

Gradually some words from the cleric reached me, despite my distracted mind. The priest spoke of God's goodness and sovereignty; that one day we were certain to see King Cedric again, in the midst of the mighty throng of heaven. This truth was certain, for all who belonged to God who passed through the earth as all people had done before us. I clung to this line, this single thread of hope that was the only anchor in such turbulent, stormy seas.

Ere long the cleric finished his sermon. As he prayed for King Cedric's kin and people, the coffin was lowered into the ground. Presently a final prayer was said, then the ceremony was over. Slowly, we made our way back to the palace hall where there would be yet another feast, this time to celebrate King Cedric's life. I had long perceived that a funeral made people walk at half the normal speed and it was the case now. I found I was glad of this, however, for my legs still seemed to be as though they were weighed down with heavy metal. Sarah's hand had not moved from my arm. Thus positioned, we travelled together.

I perceived this second feast in the same serene slowness as the banquet after the battle, as though I was still not quite engaged with the reality around me. Though my grief at my uncle's death had ebbed somewhat, I felt I still could not participate fully in the delicacies before me nor join in with the conversation that King Owain, Sarah and Evelyn were having. The marked difference to the night three days previous was the lack of harp. Strangely, I found I missed those haunting notes. I heard only a cluttered talk, that sounded only unpleasant in comparison. It was a relief, then, when ere long the feast ended, the evening finally over.

***

Four days later, marking a week since King Cedric had died, I woke with the sombre knowledge that it was the day of my coronation. In truth, I had been dreading it. My kingship had arrived, without me having any great desire for it. The occasion took place in the palace hall. King Owain sat in his throne, by far the largest and most ornate.

Set a little apart from him, a few steps down, was the smaller chair. My uncle had sat here ever since he had come to Caer Ligualid. This throne was still grand, about as ornate as Evelyn's throne in Gaeson. It looked modest, almost humble, however, beside King Owain's throne.

Of course, this past week, the throne had sat empty and as the service began, I swallowed the conflicted emotions at the knowledge I would soon have to take my place there. It was the same cleric leading the ceremony who had taken King Cedric's funeral. I found myself going through the formalities, raising my hand at certain points to reiterate words I had hardly noticed myself learning. I repeated the same promises Evelyn had made at her coronation, still feeling so numb I wondered if my heart was really in them.

I did wish to lead my people rightly and with justice, though, as King Cedric had done. I prayed a quick prayer that God would help me in this daunting task, for if I was to be half the king my uncle had been, then hopefully Klumeck would thrive under His grace. Ere long the formal

144

service ended. I hid a sigh, then, as I made my way to another banquet. It was the third feast in a week, which seemed ridiculously excessive. After all, a week ago this fair city had come the closest it ever had done to utter devastation. Could such extravagance be justified, with the battle so fresh? How could we afford the luxury of feasting, as people sought to rebuild their lives?

My feelings were such that before I left the feast, I took a moment to raise the matter with King Owain. I was greatly encouraged, when he told me he shared my conviction and had already instructed that any food left over should be given to the rest of the kingdom, particularly to those in most need. Indeed, when later I departed the hall with Evelyn, I perceived the castle servants busily collecting the remnants of the banquet. The market stalls would be open the following morning, the food would be freely given out.

At last with the exhaustion of the day over and the still unwanted title of king now mine, I sat down wearily on the bed in our chambers. Evelyn closed the chamber door beside us and I watched my wife as she loosened her hair, saying nothing for a moment.

"Did you feel this strangeness after your coronation?" I asked ere long. She turned to me, a small smile of understanding upon her features. Presently I inhaled deeply and let out the air again slowly, almost as if I was relearning the vital process of breathing. Perhaps it was because I felt I was drowning, overwhelmed by the weight of my responsibility.

"You will become used to it," my wife murmured reassuringly, her hand stroking my cheek once in affection. I cursed my weak ignorance, here, for in my naivety I had expected King Cedric to live for a long time yet. Indeed, it had taken so long adjusting to be a prince, I had hardly considered what being a king would be like. The most pressing thought on my mind, however, was that I should try to obey my uncle's last wishes at all costs. I did not yet know the identity of the Wolf, but I could try to lead my people, as best I could.

"There is something which we must discuss," I told her abruptly. My words sounded rushed, as though they had escaped my lips before I could retrieve them.

"Oh?" Evelyn murmured, beginning to undo the lacing of her dress. She did not seem surprised. Possibly with her perception, she could already guess the conversation's theme.

"It will not be long before we return to Gaeson," I told her evenly. Why was I raising this matter now, if I wanted to minimalize any possibility of conflict, when we were both so fatigued? I knew, however, my passion for the subject could not be held back any longer,

"The people of Klumeck will want to know where they will reside," I said neutrally. Evelyn smoothed down the slightly crumpled form of her undergarments whilst I spoke.

"I see," she responded, just as calmly. I perceived that my wife did not look surprised in the slightest. "This does not have to be decided now," she ventured.

"Of course, you are right," I nodded, for I knew she spoke with sense. My wife looked a little relieved at this. For a few moments, silence filled the room again. In this brief respite, I could hear the low, indistinguishable murmurs of a conversation outside the open window. I wondered inanely if people were meeting in secret.

"I think all Klumeck citizens should come to live in Gaeson," I proposed quickly. So much for waiting, I rebuked myself. Evelyn gave a little sigh of resignation in response, as she came to sit beside me on the bed.

"Many will have rebuilt their lives here after they were forced to flee," Evelyn reminded me. I nodded again in agreement.

"Of course," I affirmed. "It is fine if they wish to stay, but I think as many as possible should move if they can. It would boost Gaeson's trade, further cement the bonds of peace—"

"But we do not have space for them, Daniel," she countered, cutting me short. Her tone was calm, objective, factual. "There is far more space for them here," she pointed out. "They have far more resources for the kingdom to extend, should they need to—"

"I care not," I interrupted hotly. My wife's face took on surprise and annoyance at my harsh speech. "I'm sorry, but I don't," I continued, softer and far more peaceably. "I became a king today, Evelyn," I emphasised, attempting to be more patient. "I became ruler of these people. My uncle's dying words were that I should care for them and lead them as far as God would allow." I swallowed here, but Evelyn did not interrupt. In the pause I perceived the familiar clunking of an armoured guard passing by the door.

"How can I lead these people if I do not live with them?" I surmised presently, voicing the question to myself as well as her. "How can I be a king without a kingdom?"

"I understand all that you say," Evelyn returned here, her tone slow and full of empathy. "I fear, however, that what you ask simply cannot be done."

"Why not?" I returned, sharper than I intended. "We housed the Klumeck soldiers among us without too much difficulty," I pointed out, again lowering my tone.

"That was only the soldiers, Daniel," Evelyn countered, her tone relatively gentle still but now a little firmer, "for only a brief time. You are talking about moving a whole people to Gaeson permanently."

"I cannot be a king without a kingdom, Evelyn," I restated my passionate refrain. "What else would you have us do? Separate so that I remain in Caer Ligualid with my people and you return to Gaeson to rule yours?"

"A ridiculous suggestion," Evelyn now sniped. "I have to look out for what is in the best interests of Gaeson, Daniel. I do not think there is enough room for both peoples."

"I thought we were all united?" I retorted, my voice rising. It seemed the time for calm was over. "I thought one of the reasons for marriage was to bring together our nations, or am I mistaken?" I challenged.

"You are not," my wife replied sharply. She paused here, attempting to calm our discourse. "The fact remains, husband, that I am not Queen of Klumeck, but of Gaeson. There is not enough housing, enough food. Gaeson may not want to have extra citizens. It is too soon. It is not that long ago we were enemies with them. Now you want us to all dwell together?"

"It is not 'them'," I informed her quietly. "Or have you forgotten I am among them also? I am of Klumeck blood. I am their king," I declared. "I made promises to them today, Evelyn, that I intend to keep. I will not abandon my people. The decision is made!" I ended loudly, as my wife glared. Abruptly, I knew both of our supplies of patience had run dry.

"Oh, is it?" she scorned, her voice rife with sarcasm. "You may be the King of Klumeck, Daniel, but you cannot make decisions on behalf of Gaeson. That is my domain! I say we cannot house both, lest you doom us all to poverty," she challenged.

"Dooming you to poverty, am I?" I demanded, in another shout. "Just because I want to do right by our people? Yes, wife, they are your people too, by marriage! I am not going to abandon them just because you are not willing!"

"I will not let you override my commands, because of your unnecessary conscience," Evelyn snapped back. "The Klumeck people seem content to dwell here. They may not even wish to be uprooted. I say, here they will remain," she concluded her speech. Her voice had gone much quieter than mine, yet she spoke with the cold resolve of steel.

"At least let us speak to the advisors about it," she attempted a more reconcilable tone, but I was still frowning at her previous speech. How could this woman of kindness and compassion currently be so without feeling?

"Very well," I growled, "although it seems my opinion is not necessary for your command, Your Majesty," I told her angrily. In my fury, I then abruptly departed the chamber, banging the door loudly behind me. I could hear her calls for me to return but I ignored her, instead allowing my footsteps to take me further away from her.

The next morning seemed to dawn cold, despite the summer heat. Perhaps it was only the atmosphere, for Evelyn and I had spoken little to each other since our altercation. I had returned to our Caer Ligualid chambers only an hour or so after leaving, but she was already in bed, asleep. I strongly suspected, however, she could have been feigning this slumber.

"Let us resolve this matter now," I said abruptly to my wife over breakfast. "The people of Klumeck could be wondering if we are to make such a decision."

"Very well," my queen replied, her tone heavy. "What do you propose we do?" she asked, after wiping her mouth delicately with a small cloth.

"You are perhaps right that we need counsel," I suggested, in an attempt to pacify her. "Aldred came with us to Caer Ligualid, he will be able to advise us," I answered her. "So long as it isn't Melvyn," I added under my breath.

"Why not Lord Melvyn?" Evelyn enquired, frowning as she leaned back in her chair. I hesitated, wondering whether I should relate my suspicions to her about him… but it was still all conjecture. I felt I had to have actual evidence before relating it to her.

"It's nothing," I evaded. My wife frowned, but as she opened her mouth to speak, a castle servant entered to take our plates and other breakfast things. "I bid you tell the guard outside to send for Lord Aldred," I ordered him. The servant bowed in obedience immediately. As he retreated, I turned back to Evelyn.

"It is what it is," I replied to her obviously. "We must make the best of it. Know this, however," I said, standing up from the table, "that as far as I can see it, I will not be a king without a people. Rather, I cannot," I emphasised.

"Therefore, my queen, you have a choice before you." I did not state this choice aloud, but I could see from the widened eyes that she knew my full meaning. I was threatening to stay here among my people, if she refused. It was probably empty, for I knew not how I could leave this woman I loved so, even in our present difficulties. I only hoped to persuade her.

"You ask of me an impossible thing, husband," Evelyn replied after a moment, as she stood with a sigh.

"Do I?" I challenged, frowning again. "You knew who I was when you agreed to marry me," I pointed out. "You also knew my uncle would not live forever. What did you expect would happen?" I asked her. At this, she regarded me.

"I suppose I believed that the Klumeck citizens would stay here, where their lives are," Evelyn answered, folding her arms. "At any rate, we both thought your uncle's death was a long way from now," she concluded sadly.

"Well, on that we are agreed," I conceded at length, feeling again the heaviness of losing him. My queen gave a brief smile of consolation and the tension in my heart eased slightly. I longed to have peace between us, but she could not seem to understand. How could I abandon the Klumeck citizens? I was sure my uncle's last wish was not for me to simply return to

Gaeson, as though nothing had changed. How could I be a king, without a people?

"Your Majesties," Aldred greeted presently, his amiable tone already setting me further at ease. We both turned to him, as he entered the dining chamber, bowing low. "I happened to be nearby, my lord, my lady," he added, in explanation for his speed. "You sent for me?"

"Aye," I answered him. "Please sit, we need your counsel." I gestured to an empty seat at the table. Aldred gave another grand bow of agreement and went directly to the table. Evelyn and I sat down in our seats also. Quickly, Evelyn and I explained to him our predicament, whilst our listener remained silent until we had finished the account.

"I can well perceive the difficulty this poses, Your Majesties," Aldred began most diplomatically, after a short pause. He frowned and then sat back, lacing his long fingers together. "Might I make the point, my lady," he directed to Evelyn, "that it would not be impossible, purely from a practical perspective, to move the Klumeck citizens to Gaeson."

"That is my wondering," I agreed, trying my best not to sound triumphant. "It was my uncle's last words to me that I lead our people well," I reiterated to our advisor. "How can I lead them, without physically being among them?" I repeated my refrain.

"You make me sound so very cold and harsh," Evelyn cut in here sharply, glaring at me quickly. "You know I would long for you to lead your people well and for you to obey King Cedric's last command. Do not forget, husband, how fond of him I also was," she ended. I did then feel a little remorse at my speech.

"I just fear having all Klumeck citizens residing with us could not be done without causing severe detriment to both peoples," she continued. "There is simply not enough housing or money to sustain them."

"Forgive me, Your Majesties," Aldred interrupted gently. We both looked to him. "With the greatest respect, I am not at all sure this is true. Consider that many soldiers fell when the Bernicians knocked at our doors. Further to that, Klumeck's own soldiers have been further depleted by the recent battle.

"However, I do agree with you, Your Majesty," he was swift to add to our queen, "that there might not be enough room for them all to reside at

Gaeson. May I offer a compromise?" he suggested wisely. We both nodded at him to continue.

"As you know, Your Majesties," he began courteously, "there are many villages of trade not too far away from Gaeson but still well within the realm of Gaeson itself. What if the Klumeck citizens moved to those places? They would not be within the castle walls, but they would still belong to the Gaeson kingdom and be only half a day's journey away," he concluded.

"I am not sure whether those villages will be able to sustain them," Evelyn said. "I am willing to try it, however," she added, glancing in my direction again. I frowned, for I longed to have Klumeck within the boundaries of the castle town itself. I wanted them to know they were welcome to Gaeson, not just cast off to the outside. However, I also knew that villages a few miles away was a lot better than being a king without a people at all.

"Very well," I relented at last. "I would like it to be known, though, that the Klumeck citizens are welcome to move closer as the opportunity arises. They are to be considered our equals in the kingdom," I emphasised.

"Well said, sire," Aldred bowed, "I shall draw up a document, outlining what we have discussed. It will detail the rights of Klumeck citizens to reside in Gaeson's villages and move to the castle town itself, should circumstances grant it." He paused here. "If you are both of one mind with this decision, Your Majesties... was there anything else?"

"No, that was all," Evelyn confirmed his dismissal. "Thank you, Lord Aldred." Our advisor gave a long bow with his usual pomp. He then departed, his scholarly robes trailing behind him as he quitted our chambers. "His solution seems so obvious," she remarked now. "I wonder why we did not come to it ourselves."

"We were probably not yet ready to think of other options," I replied to her quietly. "Both of us were convinced in our arguments. One cannot often see the solution when in the midst of anger," I reflected wryly. She gave a small smile in agreement. I felt tension lift from us, leaving me only feeling a little ashamed of my conduct towards her.

"I am glad there seems to be peace between us again," Evelyn said as the two of us joined hands. "I did not mean dishonour to your uncle,

Daniel," she spoke quietly, "I want you to follow his wishes as much as humanly possible. I just—"

"I know, my love," I assured her. "I am sorry I was so rash. You know I could never leave you," I emphasised, holding her hand tightly.

"I should hope so," Evelyn murmured back, eyes sparkling with a little humour. "I know you were just thinking of our people, all of them." At this, I smiled, leaning in to kiss her cheek.

"I have to meet Ewan," I told her presently, after I lingered a moment, inhaling her scent before I parted from her company. It seemed at last that blood was once more flowing through my muscles and limbs, after a week of listless lethargy, for at last my pace seemed swift again.

Caer Ligualid was still very quiet. Part of me was pleased at this, for the last thing I wanted was citizens bowing and heads turning in every direction. It was sombre and unsettling, however, to see the marketplace so muted still, the mournful air still prevalent after the recent battle. I walked through this almost tangible air, heading straight for the mystical pool where I had arranged to meet Ewan, via John's arrangements.

The pool itself was as deserted as the town had been. This was fortunate for our meeting, for often many citizens gathered here. I had not set foot in this place since I had first discovered my true identity. The meeting place seemed apt, as I stared into the same water as when I had pondered who I was and where I truly came from. Now, though, when I peered into the pool, I found myself gazing at the reflection of a king.

Presently I heard someone coming. I ducked into a corner of the cave, stepping closer into the shadows. Ewan then entered, however, looking about stealthily.

"Over here," I called quietly, for there was no one else currently present. The young lad saw me at once and as he walked over, I perceived his movements were a lot more precise. He seemed to have indeed gained some skill.

"Your Majesty," Ewan greeted, bowing low. It was the first time I had properly met with him, since the night he had been assigned his task of spying on our brothers and sisters. This close, I could see how he had changed further into manhood, in the last half a year. The now seventeen-year-old was slightly taller but was no longer gangly-looking. His muscles had grown, making his frame slightly stockier.

"The captain said you wished to see me, my lord," Ewan muttered. I perceived his voice was deeper, too. "I was not followed, sire," he added, glancing furtively behind him as he spoke.

"Aye, you have done well to keep hidden," I affirmed. "As you know, the captain updates me each time you report to him," I said. "You have been extremely successful these past six months, lad. Thanks to you, we have now captured at least four who have confessed to be either Bernicians or working for them."

"Thank you, my lord the king," Ewan answered here, bending his head. A slight smile of pride glimpsed his features. Though fairly soon into interrogations we had discovered none of these were the Wolf, further sowing seeds of despair into how vast the Wolf's network might be, Ewan was right to be proud of his efforts. They had been significant accomplishments.

"However," I began, folding my arms and adopting a less commending tone, "the captain has lately told me that you were hesitant in your last meeting with him."

"I do not know what he means, sire," Ewan said, far too quickly. He had also glanced away from me as he spoke. Could he tell how evident his deceit was, I wondered? On the one hand it showed the lad might still have some maturing to do. The fact he was unskilled in lying, though, also showed me it was in contrast to his usually honest nature.

"Do you remember when I first set this task before you, Ewan?" My tone had grown softer now. "I told you I trusted you, because I knew your honest nature. I can tell when you are lying, lad," I declared, articulating my previous thoughts. "I think you are hiding something, but you are reluctant to tell me. Do you not know the lives you could spare?" I challenged him.

"May I speak freely, my lord?" he returned quietly. I almost smiled, because it would surprise me if I ever had a meeting without his frankness. The pained conflict in his eyes, however, stilled any expression from reaching my mouth. Instead I simply nodded.

"I did not expect such difficulty in this task," Ewan declared, a little bitterly. "You are asking me to betray someone I know well, when I might be wrong."

"No injustice will be done to them if they are innocent," I replied. "If there is someone, you have an obligation to tell me," I told him, but still he hesitated. "There are lives at stake here," I reiterated, my voice rising slightly higher in frustration. "My uncle died, Ewan," I emphasised. "I'm not about to risk any more lives just because you are too timid."

"It's not cowardice," he cut across, a little loudly. I narrowed my eyes. "I'm sorry, Your Majesty," he added quickly, in worry of my potential wrath. "But it is more complicated—"

"Why?" I interjected hotly. "Who are you trying to protect?" I challenged. At this question he bowed his head, a flush filling his features. Suddenly I realised, my anger dissipating. "Cara," I said simply. His face hardened a fraction, proving me right. "I know you are close to her," I said, "I understand—"

"You were once a soldier like us, sire," Ewan interrupted. I folded my arms, for he still had to learn to not be so hasty. "You were good friends with the captain and with Aife before you discovered the truth," he continued. "How would you have felt, if you had been asked to spy on them? Just because you might have seen something unusual…" he trailed off.

"When I came back from here, to warn Gaeson, all of them thought I was a traitor to the throne," I reminded the young recruit. "I had to confront my own king, lad. I then had to convince the woman I loved that I did not despise her," I finished hotly. At this, Ewan looked away sharply.

"Oh," I said, folding my arms again. I suddenly understood his predicament more fully. "You're in love with Cara, aren't you?" I questioned simply. Ewan's gaze was on the floor, but his face became redder still.

"That is difficult indeed," I empathised, "but we warned you about attachments. We told you we did not know who they could be."

"I know, sire, but… Cara, my lord," he protested, a little feebly. "I am sure I know her almost as well as myself," he emphasised presently. "I am sure what she was doing was—"

"You said you saw her doing something unusual," I interrupted. "Tell me what it was," I implored him. "Gaeson, the whole of Rheged, could be at stake," I reminded him, seeing his reluctance. "If you truly love her, you will want to protect her, as well as everyone else. It could be she does not know what she is doing, in which case she needs to be made aware. We cannot help her, until you tell me," I concluded seriously.

In all honesty, it was not my intention to manipulate him, but it looked like Ewan had certainly seen something to make him suspicious. It was only because of who it was that he was hesitating. I sincerely hoped, too, that we would be able to help her.

"I saw…" he faltered, then sighed resignedly. "I was out on night patrol, three weeks ago." His tone was flat and weary, unlike his usual passion. I swallowed my frustration that Ewan had noticed something three weeks ago and done nothing, but I could understand his delay, if love was part of the equation.

"As I was walking along, out of the stables, I saw Cara. She was talking with another soldier," he continued, talking faster now. "I did not recognise him, my lord, but they seemed to be having a rather intense disagreement. He seemed to pass her some kind of envelope," he concluded his account.

"I see," I replied at length, after a few moments' pause. Ewan's face was still conflicted, love and loyalty battling in his countenance. It was a tension I remembered well. "Did she see you, that day?" I asked.

"No, my lord," he answered swiftly. "Nor have I spoken to her about it, for so I wished to believe there was nothing in it," he added. "What will you do, sire?" he asked abruptly.

"Nothing for the moment," I replied, thinking. "The captain will watch her closely," I cautioned him. "I pray, too, that this will come to nothing. You have done the right thing, lad," I added, as his gaze flickered to the floor again. "Is there anything else?"

"No, my lord," he repeated. This time, I could see the openness in his gaze. I nodded, satisfied that he was telling me the truth.

"Very well," I responded, a little weary myself. "You are dismissed," I added. The recruit bowed low, before turning to leave. "Ewan," I called quietly. He turned back. "I appreciate your position, your passion also," I told him. "However, I will not tolerate rudeness again, or you holding things back from me," I warned.

"Yes, Your Majesty. It will not happen again," he told me, bowing swiftly again. I sighed as he left, empathising greatly with his situation, for if I ever had cause to doubt Evelyn, if I ever thought she had deceived me, I would be utterly lost in how to resolve it.

It was only three days since my conversation with Ewan, a week after King Cedric's funeral, when we were given the opportunity to investigate Cara's secret actions. Ewan had overheard Cara discreetly talking with a Gaeson soldier about meeting later this night and to his credit, the lad had reported it to John in the first instance. Ewan believed it was the same individual he had seen her with three weeks earlier.

I pulled the hood of my cloak a little further down to further disguise my features, for I was to investigate the encounter myself. It was the same cloak I had donned the night of the battle, when I had gone with my uncle, in secret, to King Urien's tomb. I forced myself to push away the memories of that night, one of the last times I had seen King Cedric alive. I needed to focus on the task at hand. I was again trailing behind a soldier, but this time I was following Ewan.

I followed Ewan slowly, keeping my distance from him as he traversed the city's streets. We passed by an open tavern, the light from its oil lamps shining brightly. I glanced in its direction to see it was crowded with customers. I knew from my time of being a soldier this would be the ordinary citizens' feasts. Most people, including any soldiers off duty, would be gathering for the purposes of celebrating victory and commiserating over the dead.

Ewan went straight past this comforting, brightly lit place, therefore, so did I. I was impressed at his stealth, for the lad had not looked round to me once. His tread, too, was even and sure. Indeed, his pace showed no signs of the possible turmoil inside him, as he prepared to confront the woman he had come to love. All Ewan had told John was that she had again arranged to meet a soldier after dark. All of us knew, however, that her motive could well be betrayal.

Presently, Ewan came to a stop, near the wall of a small building. We were at the edge of one of Caer Ligualid's many market squares and the lad now leant casually against the wooden frame of a trade stall. Though I was already well concealed in the dark, I pressed myself further into one of the square's edges, further stepping into the shadows. I glanced around, but there seemed to be nobody else in sight. This was encouraging, for I did not wish the Wolf to know we were potentially pursuing one of his spies. I could hear the faint whisper of conversation; I sensed Cara and the other soldier were very near, perhaps hiding behind another stall.

Ewan did then look round casually. I smiled a little at his stealth. He then stood a little straighter, his form tensing. I heard it, then, too: it was the sound of footsteps. Ewan fixed his gaze to around the corner from him and stood motionless, waiting.

"A little late to be walking, isn't it?" Ewan's voice was measured, almost lazy, as at last Cara began walking past him. At once she spun on the spot, her hand already on the hilt of her sword. "It is only me," he added, stepping out from the stall.

"Oh, Ewan. You did startle me." Her tone was light, amiable. I perceived she looked about her, before her gaze returned to him. "What are you doing here?"

"I was about to enquire that of you," he replied evasively. "I just saw you, from around the corner. Who were you speaking with? What's that he gave you?" he asked evenly. Whilst he spoke, I glanced down to see a small package in her hand.

"This? It is nothing," she replied quickly. "He was a friend giving some money he owed me, that is all."

"What for?" He asked her, a sudden edge in his voice. Next, he laughed, but it sounded forced. "You can hardly blame me for wondering, can you?" he reasoned. "After all, why are you meeting him in the middle of the night? You must admit, it does look suspicious."

"You doubt me?" Cara bristled. "My friend is a blacksmith who has just finished his labour for the day. Since he knew I would be here, he requested I give the money to a blacksmith in Gaeson, on his behalf." I frowned, for the deceit in her tale was obvious, despite her steady tone. It would almost be comical, if not for the dire circumstances if she was indeed a traitor.

"How charitable of you," Ewan remarked, the sarcasm was clear in his tone as he took a step closer. Clearly, he thought the story as believable as I did.

"You're a poor liar, Cara," he breathed, a little menacingly. Despite his soft whisper, the voice reached me. "Why don't you tell me what you're actually doing? I saw that man you were talking to. He's no more a blacksmith than I am," he concluded.

"Well, he was. It's the truth," she protested her lie. Her tone was still mostly steady, with only the slightest fluster. "Come, Ewan," she murmured, her speech now strong, alluring, almost teasing. "Do you not trust me?" My eyebrows rose as she leaned forward towards him. He bent his head as she lifted her chin, meeting her in a brief kiss.

"You're right that the hour is late," she agreed abruptly, her tone light as she stepped back. "If you'll excuse me, I must get some rest."

"Very well," Ewan said. Weariness and conflict were prevalent in his voice. He watched her leave, his head turning to follow the direction she had taken back to the castle. Then he exhaled loudly as his shoulders slumped, a sigh of resignation and distrust, before his soldier's pose straightened again. Then he turned, pointing his face in my direction. I was impressed he knew exactly where I stood.

"Don't bow, don't speak," I muttered quietly to him, before he gave away my position. "Come over, but don't look at me." The lad walked casually over, leaning against a nearby pillar.

"I'm sorry this situation is so difficult," I murmured. Ewan looked down to the ground. Despite the dark, I got the impression he was blushing. "Did you believe her?" I asked directly.

"No, my lord," he answered. He lifted his head to the sky as he spoke. "I do not, as much as I want to. I think she could be one of the Wolf's spies, sire." I caught the sadness in his words, feeling another wave of sympathy.

"What would you have me do, Your Majesty?" he asked grimly. I glanced at his silhouette, but I still could not make out his countenance. I knew what I needed to ask of him, but I wished I could spare him the pain he was so obviously in. In time, he would learn how to better hide his heart.

"I'm sorry to put you in this situation, my friend," I reiterated, "but I want you to continue to report on her. Do not confront her again, for this conversation will have already made her on her guard towards you. We leave for Gaeson in the morning," I reminded him. "When we are back, seem to trust her. Report any information to the captain," I commanded.

"Yes, Your Majesty," he responded immediately, but without bowing, as per my instructions. "It will be done, my lord," he added. There was only loyal obedience in his tone.

"Very well, Ewan. Dismissed," I instructed. Without a word or another glance in my direction, Ewan then departed my company. With my arms folded, I watched his silhouette a few moments later, until it blended with the darkness beyond.

What would I do, if someone asked me to spy on Evelyn? I thought back to the conversation with Sarah, the day we arrived in Caer Ligualid. There would never be any need for that, I told myself. I trusted her wholeheartedly and knew her motives were pure. What if there was ever a seed of doubt, though? I wondered. I could well imagine one's pain, to doubt a loved one.

***

"I wish to speak with you, brother," Sarah's voice reached me. I looked up, to see her standing in the doorway of the study chamber I had been allocated in Caer Ligualid. It was the next morning and I was in the process of clearing the chamber out, ready for our later departure.

"Evelyn told me you are going to invite Klumeck citizens to go back with you, to live in the towns surrounding Gaeson," my sister said.

"Aye, that is true," I replied. Sarah smiled warmly, then, as she entered the chamber. "I see this pleases you," I suggested, as I straightened from leaning at my desk.

"Aye, but it will take a while for those in Klumeck to be ready to depart," my sister continued, tucking her usual stray hair behind her ear as she spoke. "After all, it will take many of them more than a few days to be ready to leave, most will be changing their entire livelihoods. Even then, many more may choose to stay here in Caer Ligualid."

"That is also true," I agreed. "What is it you are thinking?" I added, as she walked further into the chamber, her arms folded casually.

"I agree with you that whilst they are welcome in Caer Ligualid and King Owain is their high ruler, he will not be king over them in the same way our uncle was," Sarah said. "I know you must return to Gaeson, for you are married to Evelyn. However," she added, "I do not have to leave. I

159

propose that I stay here, to be among our people, for the time being. I have already spoken to King Owain about the idea." I smiled broadly as she ended her speech, wondering why I had not thought of this myself.

"Of course, a wonderful idea," I affirmed, coming around the desk to her. "I'm sure the people of Klumeck will be delighted. I am only sorry I did not think of it earlier. I think it right to leave at least one member of our family here." Sarah's smile widened at this as she nodded.

"I think it is what our uncle would have wanted." She spoke softly, her smile turning a little sad at the thought of him. At this, I stepped forward to embrace her.

"I agree," I told her hoarsely, as I held her. "I and all of Gaeson shall miss you, though. I shall have to visit my mother more, too, as you seem to see her more than me," I murmured in her ear. Sarah chuckled quietly before we stepped apart a little.

"Take care, my brother who is a king," she murmured back. "I suppose Evelyn will keep you from executing too many disagreeable subjects." It was my turn to laugh then, as I briefly tapped her nose in affection. Sarah left, then, a smile remaining on my face as I tidied away the last few papers, putting them in a leather case. Briefly my mind took me to a similar case, now missing, that had contained the evidence of King Urien's dealings with the Veiled Wolf.

My smile was replaced with a frown, as I vacated the study chamber. Was Cara working for him? He had as good as murdered my uncle: what further horrors did he have in store? Could he be Lord Melvyn, or could he be a soldier? As I headed to the grand courtyard where we were to soon take our leave, I vowed that if I could not solve the mystery of him here in Caer Ligualid, I would not rest in Gaeson until it was revealed.

Chapter Eight

As always, the first sight of the castle atop Gaeson's hill made me smile a little. Some of the tension that seemed constantly in my shoulders seeped away. I turned upon Epos, to see the same faint expression upon my queen's countenance also. I sensed the same relief filter throughout our troops, only slightly lessening the sombre mood common in the wake of the recent battle. Had it only been ten days since we had left at such speed, having heard the Bernicians were on their way? Was it only so recently, that my uncle had breathed his last?

I turned to look at the people journeying home with us. Alongside the Gaeson Army were around a hundred Klumeck people, who had chosen to pack in haste to come back with us. Many of them were soldiers, as well as citizens who were changing their whole lives. I had heard from King Owain that more intended to join us later, after they had settled their affairs in Caer Ligualid. The rest had decided to remain in Caer Ligualid for the time being.

"Aife," I called presently. My archer friend turned her horse to ride closer alongside me. "You are from one of these villages, can you escort them into these places?"

"Aye, Your Majesty," she returned, bending a swift bow of her head from atop her stallion. She gathered her reins and turned, riding towards the Klumeck captain to convey my orders. I had some sadness at the order, for ideally, I longed for them to live within Gaeson's walls. However, I knew this was not practical, for there was not enough room for them in the castle town itself.

"Klumeck people, listen to me," I called, after the Klumeck captain had issued orders to them. They all turned towards me, straightening to stand at attention. "You are welcome to come to the town whenever you like," I emphasised. "We also encourage any who can to join our army. Though you may live outside the castle walls, Gaeson is your home," I declared, hoping to encourage them.

"I bid you all get some rest," I added, knowing the journey may well have wearied them, especially given the recent fight and all they had lost. "Report back to the castle later," I called to Aife as they prepared to leave.

"My lord," she said simply, bending her head once more, before turning to lead the lines of Klumeck citizens away. Decisively, I turned Epos round again.

"Onwards, to home," my queen murmured. There was a chorus of obedience at her command, then, as together we began lead our people up the hill.

***

"What is it, my love?" It was but three days after our return to Gaeson. I had come to our chamber to find Evelyn in bed reading, but I could tell instantly she was not concentrating on a word. When I came closer, I saw her expression was troubled indeed.

"Evelyn?" I prompted gently, when she did not answer. Here, at last Evelyn put down her book. When she looked up, her countenance looked almost upon the point of weeping; already the tears were forming in her eyes. This shocked me, for both of us still found it hard even now to express such raw emotion. Immediately, I knew this spelt bad news.

"I..." she began slowly and swallowed. What was it, I wondered, that had produced such sadness? Then a seed of despair began to form, that perhaps I already knew. I had been so preoccupied with my uncle's death and seeking to discover the Wolf's identity, I had hardly noticed we had already passed the height of summer. With a jolt, I realised it was about a year since I had returned from Klumeck, after we failed to recapture it. It was about twelve months, then, since she had first confided to me her fears about not being able to bear children.

"I was examined by Leigh today," she admitted ere long. The despair blossomed, as though my suspicions were confirmed. I bit my lip, waiting for her to say more. "He was able to tell me the diagnosis right away." My wife hesitated here.

"What did the physician say?" I asked, when I could bear the pause no longer. A wave of sadness had already hit me, so why did I speed this along?

Alas, I could think of no way to prolong the inevitable. Besides, waiting seemed only worse.

"He said it was extremely unlikely that we should ever have children," Evelyn at last confided. I heard her voice catch as she looked away, saw her raise her hand to wipe the first tear or two that had already fallen. I felt my own heart breaking as I sat down upon the bed beside her, joining my hands with hers.

"In technical terms," she continued, a little resentment entering her voice here, "the surgeon told me my body was not strong. "I am too weak to have children, apparently," she concluded bitterly. She was not looking at me but staring into the middle of the chamber.

"That's ridiculous," I automatically protested. "You're the strongest person I know," I murmured honestly, "even with counting Sarah and Aife." There merest smirk turned at her mouth, but it was the faintest ghost of the expression.

"He meant my womb, specifically," Evelyn clarified quietly, eyes full of unshed tears. I observed she hardly seemed able to look at me: she continued staring into the middle distance. "Leigh said that some wombs God ordains will carry children, others not. He said it would be possible to conceive, but—" She paused here, swallowing, as her voice caught again.

"That even if I were to be with child," she resumed brokenly, "I might not be able to keep it until the child came to be born." She spoke hurriedly now, through short breaths, her gaze down at our joined hands. "I'm so sorry," she murmured.

"The fault is not yours," I told her instantly. "Evelyn, look at me," I requested now, but her eyes still did not meet mine. "Wife, I bid you look at me," I repeated, more firmly. At last her gaze shifted to me, unguarded. As I saw the pain and shame in her countenance, I understood why she had previously looked away.

"Evelyn," I began deliberately, "I tell you again, the fault is not yours. As Leigh said, this is God's will. You have nothing to be ashamed of," I muttered, desperate for her to know this. Another tear began to trail slowly down her face. I rose my hand to wipe it, my touch remaining there, underneath the grieving eyes that bore into mine.

"Do you hear me, my love?" I murmured, my thumb roving over her cheek. Her gaze searched mine, before at length she nodded. I took her in my arms, embracing her. "I'm so sorry," I muttered. My sympathy had never sounded so contrite, nor fallen so utterly short. Evelyn said nothing, only moved to rest her head on my shoulder. I held her tightly, longing to comfort her.

I too battled with the pain of this sad news. Fresh grief lodged deep in my soul, as I registered the agony of what she had told me. I had long been taught from the Scriptures that all good things in this world were gifts from God. It seemed all the more important for us to have this gift, in order to secure the heir for both Gaeson and Klumeck. Why, then, did it seem our good Lord had withheld it from us?

My free hand was placed upon her knee. She now pressed hers next to it, interweaving her fingers with mine. We sat there together on the bed for a good while, but without speaking. I found myself thinking of my mother, who when she admitted to finding Sarah and me wandering in the snow, had also revealed that she and my father had been unable to have children. At the time the news had made me a little sad, but to my shame I had treated the information rather academically. Had they been just as heartbroken? I wondered now.

Evelyn's head was buried in my neck and though her breathing was slightly rough, I could tell from the dryness of my skin that she was not weeping. Part of me longed for Evelyn to wail and sob, but she was as used to shutting her emotions down as I was. I sought to find the right words, but each time I attempted to comfort my lady, my speech felt like hollow platitudes. In the end, we simply held each other quietly in the dark. Perhaps, though, I reflected, one just had to sit alongside another with pain. Perhaps, sometimes, silence was the best consolation of all.

It was difficult to discern how long we had sat there, for soon we lost all sense of time. The closed window meant there was no moonlight, nor any stars to trace the passing of minutes or hours. Indeed, apart from a dimly flickering candle on her side of the bed, there was no source of light in the chamber at all. Eventually, I noticed Evelyn's change of breathing: she had fallen asleep. Gently, then, I laid her down upon the bed. Though my love stirred, she did not wake. I drew up the covers over her, then reached to snuff out the candle. Then my hand went again to hers, as I remained seated on the bed beside her.

How selfish had I been, over the last year? I wondered presently. My anxiety over childbearing had come to me from time to time, but most of my heart had seemed only to dwell on the Wolf. Then, in the last week, it seemed I'd had no room but for the grief of my uncle. I had not even realised the time had come for Evelyn to speak to the surgeon. Perhaps she had perceived my mind too preoccupied, or maybe she wished to spare me anxiety by telling me only once she knew. This was logical, of course, but I still felt a little remorse that she had not told me of her appointment with Leigh. Did I simply assume my wife would always be perfectly strong, because she was also my queen? In truth, I felt I had failed her, rather abysmally.

This shame intermingled with the increasing ache of what she had told me. I could almost feel it rising, like a flood filling the chamber. The tide of pain swelled and as I stared through the dark at the wife I could not see, the air felt so thick with grief I found I could hardly bear it. Decidedly, then, I leant forwards press a brief kiss to her forehead before leaving the room.

I travelled swiftly, down the corridor to one of the castle walls. Abruptly I emerged onto one of Gaeson's higher ramparts. I stopped still, breathing fresh air in thick gulps. I heard murmured voices, then I turned to see two see guards of the watch, two men I had known briefly from my time as a soldier. I could hear a thread of humour in their tones: the conversation seemed enjoyable. Their talk abruptly ceased as they stilled and bowed to me. I nodded to them and they resumed their patrol.

A few paces on, the conversation struck up again. A moment later, one of them laughed loudly, sounding so normal and jovial that my hands clenched in frustration. How dare they? I seethed. How dare others carry on, as though their king and queen had not received such dreadful news? There was part of me, however, that was encouraged. There was hope that outside my own grief, the world still turned.

I, too, then resumed walking, leaving the ramparts and descending several spiral staircases. My feet seemed to me moving almost of their own volition, for I hardly knew where I was going until I realised I was outside Leigh's chamber. I realised I sought consolation from him, since despite the fact he was the bearer of the terrible news, he was the only person in the world besides Evelyn and me who knew our troubles.

I came to a stop as I saw his closed door, hesitating a moment. It was the middle of the night, perhaps he was asleep? The door then opened, however, as a soldier began to leave the surgery. I heard Leigh's voice, giving instructions to the soldier to rest, so not to cause further harm to an injury. That seemed his most common advice, I reflected, as the guard departed down a different corridor to me. As the surgeon made to close his door, I stepped forwards. The doctor spotted me then and instantly he widened the door open again, bowing.

"Your Majesty," he said simply. His countenance was solemn, unsurprised. "Come in, my lord," he invited, as he straightened. At his request I entered his surgery, suddenly not at all sure why I was there. I observed Leigh was already pouring out two goblets of mead from a jug.

"Here, my king," he said, handing one to me. "Sometimes the oldest medicine works the best," he added, as the corner of his mouth turned a little.

"Aye," I murmured faintly. I tried to return the smile, but I knew at once how hollow it must have appeared. I took a large gulp of the honeyed tonic as I sat down.

"I'm so sorry, my friend," Leigh said, as he sat down in the chair behind his desk, taking a sip himself. "I wished with all my heart to give Her Majesty better news."

"Thank you," I replied, as I took another drink, unsure of what else to say. "Are you sure there is nothing that can be done?" I burst out in frustration. Leigh gave a sigh in response.

"As horrific as battle wounds are, most of them are bones that need setting, or cuts that need stitching," Leigh responded resignedly. "Either the wounds are mendable, or they are severe enough to kill. Time decides that, one way or another. As unpleasant as it is, it is at least usually clear. I wish that all of medicine was as simple, but some things are not.

"The process of child bearing has always been a mystery," Leigh contemplated presently, as he sat back in his chair. His gaze rose momentarily to the ceiling. "It works for so many so quickly and yet others cannot. Your own parents, for example, who raised you in Gaeson."

"They would have had this very conversation with you," I guessed, again reflecting anew what my parents must have gone through.

"Yes, my lord," Leigh confirmed with a nod. "It is a tragedy indeed the condition has struck the same family twice. Many citizens of Gaeson have lost a child," the physician continued, "either whilst carrying, or after the child has been born. These are devastating losses, intense in pain. Some never recover from their grief. This is a different kind of pain, however, sire," he then clarified. "This agony is silent, wearying, resigned. Rather than grieving what you have lost, you are at this point grieving what you may not be able to know."

"Aye," was all I could whisper, as the fullness of the grief cut through me again. As difficult as it was, I found Leigh's factual account extremely helpful. It was as if he was voicing everything I had not been able to recognise myself. I took another gulp of mead. "What do you advise, given our particular situation?" I enquired next.

"The pressures of being royal does make this more unfortunate, Your Majesty," he agreed with a nod. "I have thought it over and I can present two options to you, unless in time we also think of a third. The first," he added, pausing to taste the mead again, "is that you are simply honest with your people. Gaeson will no doubt grieve," he said, "but they shall recover. I am sure, when the time came to adopt, they would celebrate with you."

"What is the other option?" I asked. I perceived my doctor hesitated. He seemed to taste the mead again to evade answering. "Leigh?" I prompted.

"There is one possibility, although I cannot officially recommend it," he said at last, scratching the stubble on his chin as he thought. "It is not truly ethical," he warned.

"Go on," I said, desperate for any way for us to keep the sad truth to ourselves. I did not want Evelyn to have to bear the stares from others, the curious looks from her citizens.

"As timing would have it, there is a certain situation that could be helpful to you," he began vaguely. "About three months ago, sire, a young lady of seventeen came to see me, complaining of tiredness and nausea. A fairly quick examination confirmed the diagnosis. She was with child," he concluded. "She had begun carrying the child six weeks previously.

"She had herself also suspected her condition," Leigh continued, "which is why she came to me rather than another physician. I am, as it were, more sympathetic than other surgeons," Leigh said diplomatically, "for the child was conceived under illegitimate circumstances."

"I see," I replied inanely, for I did not see at all. In fact, I was swallowing a fresh pint of resentment that this woman, barely into adulthood, had come to bear a child, probably unwanted, so effortlessly. This had never seemed crueller, when Evelyn and I were unable to have what we most desired. "What does this have to do with our situation?" I asked bluntly.

"Her name is Morwenna and she works at the castle as a maid," Leigh replied, a hand coming to scratch his chin again. "The child is healthy, though it is small. Her frame is slight, so though she is over five months pregnant, her swelling is not much yet," he continued. "In two weeks, I believe people will start to notice. No doubt she would lose her position and bring dishonour upon her parents," he reflected.

"What of it?" I asked harshly. I still not understand the relevance of this. I was also so wrapped up in my own grief that I found myself caring very little for this woman's unfortunate situation. Leigh simply smiled a little.

"Here is my proposal, my lord king," he suggested at last. "In about a month's time, sire, you could announce to Gaeson that Her Majesty is with child," Leigh continued. At this, my eyebrows rose in great surprise.

"Soon, before Morwenna's pregnancy becomes obvious," he explained, "I would make the false diagnosis that she has contracted a disease and order she be moved to an isolated area of the castle, to prevent illness spreading. She would be kept away until the child is born. I would attend her and ensure she was comfortable," he added.

"Meanwhile," he continued outlining his proposal, "at the time Her Majesty's stomach should be full with child, we also retire our lady to her chamber. We then claim there is a complication with the pregnancy, that requires bed rest. Such circumstances are not unusual."

"So then when the child is born of this maid," I guessed, "we would take it, claiming it as the baby my wife was supposedly carrying."

Leigh gave a nod.

I sighed, taking another gulp of the honeyed tonic, for this seemed too much to take. "It would involve deceiving almost everyone," I pointed out, "as well as depriving the girl of her child."

"The young woman in question has already confided in me she is desperate to find a way out of her situation, as she put it," Leigh answered here. "Of course, if she were to change her mind, that would be a different question. However, as far as I know, she would welcome the proposal." The plan seemed to be too ridiculous for words, yet I knew I was considering it.

"The plan does contain unethical elements," Leigh reiterated, as I lifted up my goblet to drain it. "However, if you were interested, then it could well be an outcome that would please all persons involved. You will not have long to decide, my lord," he cautioned.

"Yes," I murmured and stood, running a hand through my auburn hair. "I shall speak to Evelyn," I muttered and turned to take my leave, placing my hand upon the door handle.

"Sire," Leigh said. I turned back. "Please know that whatever you decide—" he said and paused here to cross the chamber. "I am truly sorry, Daniel," he said, dropping titles for a moment as he put his arm on my shoulder. "My door is always open," he emphasised.

"Thank you, brother," I murmured, touching his arm briefly in gratitude. As I headed back down the corridors, I reflected his sympathy had not seemed trite at all. Perhaps, then, Evelyn had taken some comfort from my words after all.

When I returned to my queen, I saw she was awake again, reading once more by the candle she had relit. I suspected, though, that she still was not really taking in any words. As I closed the chamber door, she put down her book.

"I needed some fresh air," I explained simply, as she rubbed her hands wearily over her face. Evelyn nodded, then, as her hands dropped back to her sides. "I wasn't really thinking about my path, but I ended up at the surgery. I spoke to Leigh," I informed her.

"What did he say?" Evelyn asked a little tiredly, with no surprise in her voice at where I had gone. She wrapped her shawl a little closer around her, though in the warmth of the season, the chamber did not seem particularly cold. "Well?" she prompted.

Slowly I raised my eyes to hers, relating all of the conversation I'd had with Leigh and outlining his plan. Evelyn stayed quiet, giving no comment until the account was finished. When I was done, she sat back as a faint smile touched her features.

"I did not think we would be able to have a child so quickly," she said ere long. "The thought that we could do it, too, with the rest of Gaeson unaware—" at this I stood up from the chair, my emotions whirling at the thought that Evelyn, too, was considering it. "What?" my wife asked, having seen the expression on my face.

"We do not have to make a decision on this now," I began gently, "but can we honestly claim to love our people, with such a deception?" My wife frowned: already I saw the objections rising to her lips.

"I know it would make things so much easier to pretend the child was naturally ours," I continued swiftly, "but consider how I grew up, believing I was the natural child of my parents in Gaeson. When I discovered the truth about my parents, that I was the heir to the throne of Klumeck, my world fell apart." I slumped into one of the chairs by the empty fireplace, leaning forwards and resting my hands under my chin.

"My honest feelings are that I do not want to bring up the child with the same deception also," I admitted. "My parents had no choice, for they would have risked my life by revealing the truth. The child would not be in this position, for we can choose honesty without danger."

"I understand," Evelyn said quietly here, "but it would make us look so weak, Daniel. It would make the kingdom look so weak. I'm so ashamed," she declared passionately, lowering her gaze to the bedclothes, rather than me. "I'm so ashamed I cannot bear you a child, my husband," she concluded quietly, her voice rife with pain and bitterness.

Quietly I moved from the chair to sit on the bed beside her, for I was overcome with compassion for my wife. With one hand, I took one of hers that lay beside her, squeezing it tightly. The other came to rest upon the thick tresses of her beautiful raven hair. I pressed my head against those curls, too, that I might whisper comfort into her ear.

"Hear me, again, my wife," I whispered, the strands of hair near her ear blowing gently with my breath as I spoke. "There is no shame in this, as I said earlier. Yes, there is deep sadness and pain, but that does not mean you are to blame for it." I sat back from her now and gently pressed my hand underneath her chin. I lifted her countenance to meet mine and I saw her eyes shining with silent grief.

"I love you just as I ever did, my darling," I attempted to soothe her. "I have never for one moment, even now, thought you weak," I declared. I heard her breathing change, sensed the dam on her emotions was near its breaking point.

"You do not always have to be so strong, you know," I implored her. "I know you do with the rest of Rheged, but not with me. It is safe for you to let your grief go, otherwise it will consume you." At these whispers I saw the pools of wetness begin to appear on her cheeks. As sad as it was to witness her heartbreak, I knew it was better than having it all locked inside her.

"I think we both still need to learn," I whispered, a hair's breadth away from her, "that it is part of marriage to grieve together. Let your grief go, my love. I am here to wipe away your tears, just as you are here to wipe away mine," I ended quietly.

"Oh, Daniel," she uttered in reply, her voice choked and broken with her pain as her final defences broke. Her head moved to my shoulder as her grief began to undo her. My queen began to weep, quietly at first, then mourning much louder. Soon, her whole body shook with sobs, each one seeming to rock her very soul. In the two years and three months since we had wed, this was the first time I was truly seeing her cry like this. I moved to hold her all the tighter, closing my own eyes with the pain. I too began to weep a little, as the grief overwhelmed us.

Ere long we again lost track of time, but eventually her sobs quietened as her tears ceased their flow. Neither of us spoke yet as I lifted her face again to mine. As tenderly as I could, I then moved my thumbs over her eyes and cheeks, keeping my promise to wipe her tears away.

"Do not apologise for your tears," I murmured, for already I could see her beginning to cringe at her outburst of emotion. As if to still the feeling of shame in its tracks, I pressed my face to hers, kissing her cheeks, moist from where tears had fallen. "There is no shame in grief, just as you told me, the day my uncle died," I whispered. A moment later, she nodded.

"Very well," she muttered presently, as she sniffed and swallowed. "You're right, of course," she added abruptly, as her hands dropped limply in front of her. "It would be wrong to deceive our child, as well as the rest of Gaeson."

"Aye," I whispered softly in agreement, as I moved my hands to join hers again, interlacing our fingers together.

"Besides," she muttered, sniffing again, "the truth of the matter would come out in the end. Truth always does." She spoke with such sadness that my heart almost broke all over again.

"Perhaps this is not the time to say such a thing," I ventured quietly into this pause, "but I think we have to believe in the hope that all will be well." Her features stiffened, her eyes hardening as they met mine. I knew well why, for surely such speech seemed careless and cruel.

"By this I mean that we will have a child, Evelyn," I declared to her, squeezing her hands again. "It may not come from our bodies, but we will have a child to raise as our very own. It may not come from our bodies," I reiterated, "but that does not mean we will love it any less," I concluded. My wife had closed her eyes as I spoke. Presently fresh tears escaped under her lids.

"I believe you are right," she whispered eventually, her eyes opening again. "It does not make the pain any less, though," she added hoarsely, sighing.

"No, it doesn't," I agreed simply, as my arms enveloped her again. As I held her, I prayed my words had provided some comfort. Then I lifted my head, my gaze rising to the ceiling above us. As I watched the stone above me flicker in the soft light, I prayed silently that God would not abandon us in such difficult, painful times.

***

I lifted my eyes again to the stars, whilst I waited for Aife to join me. The thick, muggy clouds that had oft covered the sky of late had finally moved, leaving me to free to gaze upon the sentinels above. I was sitting on a low stone wall, that bordered one of the fields outside the castle. Some hundred feet to my left was the field where we practised archery. The stables where

I had worked and first met Evelyn as a child were behind me. A few feet ahead, going beyond the curve of the castle wall, was the short path that connected Gaeson's castle to the town.

It was but five days since Evelyn had told me of the painful discovery that we would not be able naturally have our own children. In recent days, I had confided in John and my mother. They had given me much comfort and wise council, which I had appreciated. In particular, my mother had encouraged me that parenting was still possible, as made evident by how she had always loved me. Despite this, however, telling them had still left me weary in my bones. I longed to tell Sarah, but she was still in Caer Ligualid, having remained with the rest of Klumeck's people. I had thought about writing, but knew not how to put such dreadful news in a letter.

Presently, I sensed movement in the distance. Instinctively, I knew it was my friend. We had chosen to meet here, as hopefully the Wolf would not be able to hear our scheme.

"Your Majesty," came her sure, quiet voice, as she sat down next to me on the stone wall. My eyes glanced round, but I knew her skill well enough. She had not been followed. "I glanced around the stables first, my lord," she murmured next. "All have retired."

"I perceived that also," I muttered in agreement. "Did John tell you what Ewan said?" My eyes scanned furtively round as I spoke, for the stars and moonlight gave us a little a light. It had never been more important for our talk to remain in darkness, for if all worked, in one month's time, the monster might be unveiled at last.

"Aye, sire," Aife whispered back. Ewan had reported to John earlier this day that he had once again overheard Cara speaking to a Gaeson soldier. We suspected it was the same guard, whom she had originally met in Gaeson and then again on the eve of leaving Caer Ligualid. What we hoped, however, was that a month from today, Cara would be meeting with the Wolf himself. We had chosen to meet this very night, as I believed the nearer the day of the meeting, the greater chance there might be of being overheard.

"You and I shall be in position on the rooftops," I began explaining my strategy. "Ewan will follow Cara through Gaeson and we shall do nothing until he arrives. Once we catch sight at him, you will then fire an arrow at him," I outlined in a rapid murmur.

"I would not mind at all if you killed him," I added, with a faint smirk tracing my features with the thought, "but it is probably necessary to keep him alive, at least until we know his plans." Indeed, I knew the whole of me would yearn to slay the villain on the spot, but I would have to resist such an urge.

"Very good, my lord," Aife muttered from beside me. I spoke nothing further to this and we descended into silence for a few moments. I had not seen much of my sister-in-arms of late, so she still did not know my sad news. Though part of me longed to tell her, I also did not wish to become wearier still.

"It is a beautiful night, is it not?" Aife commented presently. I glanced back up again, to see the skies had cleared further. The canopy was alight with a million diamonds. The night was as vivid as when I had lain with my wife under the stars, back when I was almost drunk with the relief that my queen was safe, after Aldred had foiled the plot to kill her. That, too, was when hope still bloomed that a child could be ours naturally.

"My lord?" Aife prompted from the near darkness. There was a tone of concern: she had noticed I had not replied to her. "What is it?" she asked again, her tone even gentler.

"I forget how well you know me, sister," I reflected in reply as I glanced at her. My friend rose her eyebrows slightly in reply, but still she said nothing. I noted how tactful she was being, for I needed to only say it was nothing and the subject would be dropped.

"Recently, we have come to know," I began ere long, knowing I wished to confide in her, "that the time may never come for us to bear children. In fact, it is almost impossible." I sighed in resignation. I was glad I had told her, but with each person we told, the certainty of it became more real and therefore, the knowledge was all the crueller.

"I'm so sorry, Daniel," Aife whispered. Her hand came to grip my arm in compassion, the shock and empathy clear in her tone. My hand went to the one that held my arm instantly, grateful she had dropped my title. I was thankful indeed, that the bonds of our friendship broke any division that rank or royalty could have formed between us.

"Aye," I replied simply, my voice thick and heavy. My sister spoke no more. Presently I took my hand away, instead running it through my hair. "Leigh examined her just after we returned from Caer Ligualid," I added here.

"Almost as soon as we were wed, Evelyn was keen to start a family," I began to explain. "The particular pressures of being royal, being King Reghan's only heir... she was anxious to produce a child. I was all too happy at the thought of fatherhood," I emphasised. My voice became all the hoarser, as I spoke quietly into the dark

"The idea of creating something together, that was half of me and half of her... a child I could hold in my arms and know was mine, whom I would love forever." I finished here, as my voice caught with emotion. I swallowed hard, pushing back down the grief that had begun once more to well inside me.

"Oh, my brother," was all she murmured in reply. The clear, intense feeling in her tone almost undid me. In compassion, she reached out again, this time to touch my shoulder. In response, I leant my head towards her so that our temples briefly touched.

"No decisions have to be made yet, but there is still a way to secure the throne," she suggested tentatively, her voice laced with the yet unspoken hope of adoption.

"I know," I replied quietly, as I pulled my head away from hers again. "Leigh did have a proposal, actually," I added, as I shifted to find a more comfortable position on the wall.

"He told me that there is a young maid at the castle, Morwenna, who is unmarried and with child," I said. I then related to her Leigh's idea about the maid, trying and probably failing to keep resentment out of my tone, for what had happened so easily for the young woman. "At one point he suggested we could deceive our people and claim the child as biologically ours. He did say he could not officially recommend the ethics of it," I pointed out quickly.

"I see," Aife replied at length. The neutrality in her voice made me smirk. If she had been outraged by the surgeon's scandalous suggestion, she gave no signs of showing it. "What will you do?" she enquired here. At this I sighed again.

"Evelyn was sorely tempted, as was I," I admitted, "but in my heart, I know the deception would be wrong. My parents in Gaeson raised me, without telling me who I was," I continued sombrely, articulating what I had previously said to Evelyn. "Though they did it to protect us from danger, it was still a deception. You know the shock it gave me, when the truth was discovered," I remembered with feeling.

"You and everyone else," Aife replied, nudging my shoulder a little in jest. I smirked again, conceding this with a single nod of my head. As I glanced down briefly with this movement, I noted the silver light of the moon had faded from the wall, casting us in further darkness. I looked up to see that a small cluster of clouds had partially covered the moon.

"It sounds as if you have made a decision already," she said, "but the fact remains, there is still a maid with child. Perhaps you could simply be honest with Gaeson and tell them you plan to adopt it," she suggested.

"Aye, that will probably be the way of things," I agreed with a nod. "Everyone will wonder where the child has come from, through," I pointed out.

"Ah, let them wonder," Aife responded, with a wave of her hand. "People will always gossip, no matter what you tell them, or whether it was true or false. You need only say it was a child of Rheged, without any parents willing to raise it.

"I cannot imagine the pain this must cause you," Aife reflected now, her hand touching my arm again, "but in God's providence, this child might be the way to have all you desire."

"Indeed," I replied heavily. "In all honesty, though, I do struggle that God has not given us a child naturally. It seems such a good gift, especially in our particular circumstances. So why would he withhold it from us?" I pondered a little resentfully, scuffing a loose stone with the tip of my boot as I spoke.

"I do not know," Aife replied quietly. "I suppose we are not God, we are only His creatures. We cannot know why He gives gifts to some and not to others. Consider how you have moved from a soldier to a king, whilst others know only poverty. I do not mean to belittle your hurt, brother," she added, for she must have noticed my features stiffen. "The fact God ordains us to walk down different roads does not make it any easier to travel among them. For example, consider—" she went on, but then abruptly she paused.

"Consider what?" I prompted from beside the wall, from where I had been listening sombrely. I knew how wise her counsel was, even if I did not want to hear it. I glanced at Aife in the darkness, then, just able to make out her countenance. There was a small frown upon her countenance. Presently, she sighed.

"Consider how long you have loved Her Majesty," Aife continued ere long. "You were able to marry her, due to your status. Yet God seems to will others unable to marry those they might love," she concluded, with a kind of emptiness to her final speech.

"What is your meaning?" I enquired, though I could guess. I had long seen the close friendship John and Aife shared. At times, I had wondered whether there was anything more.

"I think you know," was all her reply. The clouds parted, then, allowing me an even better glimpse at my friend's features. There was a smile upon her face, yet there was sadness in her eyes. In all my years of loving Evelyn from afar, I had sometimes wondered whether any other soldier had felt such unrequited love.

"In truth, I do not know my regard for him," Aife admitted now with a sigh. "Most of the time, I am fully content in my friendship with him, that we are brother and sister. We seem to be comrades so well, as if we were kin from the same blood. Yet, there are other times," she confided, "when I see him and wonder whether there could be anything more." She sighed again.

"You know the life of a soldier," she said pointedly. "Even if I was sure I wished to marry him, it would be tragedy enough, if I lost him to war as a friend. If he was my husband—"

"Aye, I understand," I said here, as she concluded. I too had felt this, before Evelyn and I were wed, even before I had known my true identity. I still felt keen despair, even now, at the thought of my lady going into battle and not returning. Even in the caves, there was always the dreadful possibility our walls could be breached. My love's life could still be lost for the sake of her people, just as my own life could disappear. It was the way of war.

"I made my peace with my situation with him, long ago," Aife presently remarked. "I think we have both decided we would rather remain as we are. He seems content to be Gaeson's captain, as I am as chief archer." Her own head lifted to also look at the stars.

"It took me a long time to see it is not a sin to remain unmarried," she murmured ere long. "Indeed, many times I think I serve Gaeson better unattached. I still need reminding of that, though, at times," she added, with another smirk. This then faded, though, as she looked at me.

"I'm sorry, my lord. I do not mean to trivialise your pain, by talking of my own griefs. I only meant that each of us have particular roads of hardship," she concluded. "The road may feel cruel, but that does not mean God has abandoned us, or that He is not still good."

"You speak with much wisdom, sister," I returned quietly, reaching for her hand again. "If one day you should ever tire of archery, I shall appoint you to the royal council." She sniggered at this. "I am sorry you do not have all that you wish for with John," I ventured.

"I do not even know if it is what I wish for," she admitted with a sigh. "Maybe it could have been, in another life, had we not both joined the army. It seems I was always destined for this, though," she added now, "from the first days my mother took me to hunt." Her other arm went to my shoulder. "I will pray for you and Her Majesty," she offered.

"You have my thanks," I returned with a smile, my free hand coming to join hers. "I am glad, sister, that we can speak freely, as we always have done."

"Of course, Daniel," she returned at once. "Know that you can always speak to me and to John also. You might be a great king now, but you are still our brother," she quipped. My smile broadened.

"I am glad of it," I told her, my heart lightening a little in gratitude of her counsel. I took her hand, kissing it briefly in affection, before I jumped from the wall. I stretched, a little stiff from where I had been sitting. "I should go back to Evelyn," I said, rubbing my face briefly.

"The power of grief might cause you to shut each other out," Aife said, a little bluntly, as she came to stand. I lowered my hands to look at her, to see concern anew in her eyes. "I bid you do not let it. Call out to God and take comfort in each other. Do not let this cause a division between you," she advised. My eyebrows rose a little, but I nodded.

"Your Majesty," she added more formally. I bade her farewell and watched her disappear into the night. I stood watching the spot where she had blended with the darkness, pondering how true her last words had seemed. Aife did not speak of it much, but she had once confided to us of the pain of when her brother, only eleven years old, had fallen from his horse and died.

Had the grief for her brother caused a rift in their family? I wondered now. Perhaps her parents had drawn apart from one another, in the wake of his passing? Or perhaps it was purely hypothetical. Either way, I knew how true her words had been. I resolved not to let this current pain, nor anything else, ever separate me from my wife. I vowed not even the Veiled Wolf and all his poison would tear us apart.

Part Three

Chapter Nine

"Are you ready, sister?" I asked Aife quietly, who stood beside me on the rooftop of one of the buildings in Gaeson.

"Aye, Your Majesty," she returned in equal stealth. It was one month since my conversation with Aife where we had planned the strategy of this night. In the four weeks since, Evelyn and I had confirmed to Leigh that we would adopt Morwenna's child.

The physician had confirmed to us that the maid's pregnancy was at last starting to show (since the child was small, the swelling had not begun sooner). As such, she had been moved to a solitary area of the castle, feigning a disease. Evelyn had yet to announce the news to Gaeson, but we planned to do so soon.

"Let us move," I whispered, focusing again on the task at hand. We were travelling to a rooftop which would give us an excellent vantage point to view the meeting between Cara and the Wolf. Once there, we could implement the plan we had discussed one month previously, where we hoped to both uncover Cara's betrayal and, hopefully, to capture the monster himself.

Silently and swiftly, then, we travelled through the night, soon coming to our position near Gaeson's church building. We had chosen the higher route, both to have a better vantage point for seeing him and because the assassin's spies might be all around, hidden around any street corner. For this to work, it was vital that we should not be detected until at the last possible moment, when the trap would be set.

John had climbed the church tower and stood in our line of sight, across the small square that lay between us. I could not make him out in the darkness, but I imagined him standing there, sword drawn, ready to shout to our comrades hidden in the building. If there were spies hidden around every corner, I was aware the capture of the Wolf might well lead to civil war. I had made the decision not to sound the horn unless absolutely necessary, for I believed since blood could be on our streets, the safest place for our citizens would be behind their own doors.

We prayed tonight would not come to such warfare, as tomorrow was Gaeson's annual parade. The timing could not be helped, however. Indeed, it was likely the assassin had chosen this night, believing Gaeson to be so busy with preparations that the meeting could slip past undiscovered. In truth it would have done so, without the work of Ewan.

"There she is," I whispered presently, as Cara came into view. She was made visible by the sparsely-lit lanterns hanging from buildings, or from the indoor glow of a tavern as she passed it. Her countenance was grimly determined, eyes furtively looking about her. Instinctively I shifted further back, though in the darkness I knew it was fairly impossible for her to see me.

As we watched Cara come to a stop near a bench on the east side of the courtyard, I held my breath. Now all we needed to do was to wait for the Wolf to appear. The monster that was normally the predator had become our prey. As I watched with as much patience as I could muster, I reflected again how glad I was I had come this night. Evelyn had pointed out that now I was a king I need not be present, given the soldiers already delegated for this task.

Whilst I agreed with her in principle, I knew my own heart too much not to know that I had to be here to confront the Wolf tonight. If the assassin was to be caught as we all hoped, then I sorely wished to be there for his unveiling.

"The Wolf, my lord," Aife whispered presently, just a moment before I also caught sight of him. A cloaked figure was walking grandly up the streets. Even with the tavern lights upon him, with him being literally so veiled it was impossible to discern his identity, my instincts told me it was him. I observed the Wolf was almost gliding towards the meeting point, in a way that seemed familiar. I frowned, stretching to peer at him closer. I had not forgotten my misgivings about Melvyn. Could it be him, under that cloak?

Whoever he was, he seemed very sure about the security of the meeting as he strode confidently forward. It made me wonder whether perhaps his spies really were all around, for it was a strange paradox that his pace seemed deliberate and yet also casual, almost lazy. I watched, in all suspense, as Cara saw him and stood a little straighter as she turned to him.

"She seems to be handing him something," my sister-in-arms murmured, as her hand outstretched a bag to him. The assassin reached out a hand from his cloak to take it.

"The money she got in Caer Ligualid," I guessed, my eyes trained on the darkened bench. Presently their heads began moving in the tell-tale signs of silent conversation.

"We knew it wouldn't be a blacksmith," Aife muttered, making me smirk . I sensed her moving her bow into position, as she set her arrow upon it. I placed an arrow upon my own bow, which I had brought just in case all did not go to plan. If battle did break out, we might need to support John's troops from above.

"On my order, on the count of three," I whispered, as we both stretched our bows taut. I sensed Aife nod beside me in the darkness. Abruptly, then, a loud guffaw sounded from the tavern, making my eyebrows rise a little. It was strange how this night could still seem so ordinary, given what was about to happen. "One," I began in a harsh murmur, "two—"

"Wait, sire," she whispered suddenly. Instantly, I slackened my bow, knowing she would have a good reason to delay. "There is movement, my lord, at the west side of the square." I frowned, as I looked in that direction, knowing how accurate her sharp eyes were. All seemed still, but then I caught a flurry of movement in the corner of my eye. A moment later, I then glimpsed a face I knew well, as he passed by the dim lantern of a building.

"Ewan!" I hissed in frustration. "What is he doing here?" I challenged, but immediately I already knew. He wished to confront Cara, just as I wished to confront the Wolf. Perhaps if battle did break out in this courtyard, he also wished to protect the woman he loved from harm, even if she was a traitor. John had given him very strict orders to stay away tonight, given his complicated position. It was a command that, evidently, Ewan had chosen to disobey.

"Your orders, sire?" Aife now whispered beside me. My eyes had already gone back to the bench, but thankfully there was no evidence they had seen him. Perhaps Ewan had indeed slipped past unnoticed. Then I frowned into the darkness, for although they seemed unalerted to his presence, there did seem a change in their body movements. Though I could only make out their outlines, I perceived Cara had stepped back, her hands outstretched in a placating gesture.

"My lord?" Aife prompted quietly from beside me, as I continued to watch them. The Wolf had taken a step closer to her; from what I could make out, their talk seemed to have become more animated. Perhaps he was even threatening her. "We must act now," she warned.

"Aye," I affirmed. "Ewan isn't doing anything. We proceed as planned," I decided in a swift whisper, for instinct also told me we had little time. "On my command," I repeated.

"One," I began again, tensely. I had the same adrenaline filling me as when a battle was about to start. In many ways, it could be. "Two," I murmured.

The moment before the word 'three' issued from my lips, suddenly Cara leapt back, as the Wolf's blade rose. Before either of us could do anything or even think, there was a flicker of movement from where Ewan had been hiding. We saw him fly out into plain view, just in time to parry the monster's blow.

Our arrows were still trained on the Wolf, as there was a brief scuffle between him and Ewan. It was obvious, however, that for all his enthusiasm, the young recruit did not have a chance. Ewan raised his sword to strike the spy, but the assassin easily sidestepped him to dodge and brought the hilt of his sword to bash painfully against Ewan's face.

As the lad collapsed to the floor, the spy turned to flee. I immediately unleashed the arrow, but instinct told me he had already moved. I sensed Aife beside me, her bow moving as she tracked his escape. Just before he melted into the darkness, she let fly her arrow. I uttered a quick prayer it had found its home. As he disappeared from view, we swiftly slung our bows onto our backs.

"After him," I ordered, but Aife was already running, flinging herself onto the next building in the direction of the Wolf and her arrow. John and his legion, having witnessed the event, had rushed out into the streets in the same direction, as they sought the spy's capture.

As they did this, I hurried down the ladder to confront Ewan and Cara. I was resolved that if the Wolf had escaped, at least we could interrogate her. I leapt free to the floor, drawing my sword as I turned. Ewan had his back to me, his blade already drawn. It was mostly lowered, but the tip of his sword was pointed towards Cara, who stared back towards him, stricken. Then, her eyes shifted, as suddenly she spotted me.

"Your Majesty," she gasped, sinking to her knees, knowing there was no chance to fight or escape. If Cara had been stricken before, there was pure fear in her gaze now. I had seen people cower before the wrath of a king before, but it was a new feeling for the king to be me. Cara's gaze then bent to the floor as I stepped forward. I guessed she probably believed her only chance of survival was to throw herself onto whatever semblance of mercy I might still have, and she was right.

"You will stay where you are, silent, if you mean to stay my sword," I hissed at her. It was then I noticed that the mutters of friendly chatter from the nearby tavern had ceased. I looked towards it, to see many people staring out of the open doorway of the inn.

"Go back to your mead!" I shouted. The people immediately drew back, away from the light. Broken, hushed talk soon began again in the tavern, but other than that all seemed still.

"Ewan," I rounded on him, to see he too had knelt down. I could see a thin, red welt extending from his lip down to his jaw from where the spy had struck him, his lower face covered in blood. It was fortunate the lad's jaw was still intact, but I had little sympathy. "We had him within our grasp, Ewan! What happened?" I roared at him in frustration.

"He moved to take her life, my lord," Ewan responded quietly, his head bent towards the floor as Cara's was. "I could not let him kill her," he muttered.

"That decision was not yours to make," I spat. "Did you at least see who he was?" I asked next, ignoring Cara for the moment.

"He was too far away to be recognised, sire," Ewan answered me, remorse all prevalent in his voice. "I only happened to catch the glint of his blade and then—it was too quick," he murmured. "I have failed you, sire," he added mournfully, as he looked down.

"Your Majesty," Aife called. I raised my head to look at her as she stepped out into the darkness. In her hands, she held both our arrows and the Wolf's cloak.

"I'm sorry, sire," she began apologetically, for I could already see the Wolf was not in her custody. "My arrow caught in his cloak, but he had simply removed it before I got there. Yours was nearby," she concluded. I swallowed hard, pushing back down a fresh bout of fury.

"Your aim was good, Aife. He was running in the darkness with next to no visibility," I replied heavily, as if all my strength had gone out of me.

"The captain is still in pursuit," my friend now pointed out. I simply nodded, knowing that in this darkness, with the Wolf as skilled as he was, there was little chance of him being caught. With this knowledge, at last my anger abruptly erupted.

With a loud curse and a roar of rage, I slammed my blade into the wood of a closed window. I was still for a moment in the wake of such raw anger, my eyes closed. Aife, Cara and Ewan were as motionless as stone. In the silence, I imagined I could hear the splinters of hacked wood fall softly to the ground. After a few seconds, with a little effort I pulled my sword free, opened my eyes and turned to the three of them, with my face still set in anger.

"You are a traitor," I spat as looked at Cara. "You deliberately disobeyed my order and cost me my spy," I added to Ewan. Both of them were silent, their eyes still on the stone of the courtyard. "You should both be glad I drove my blade into the wood and not into your skulls," I hissed at them. Eventually, then, I sheathed my sword.

"Aife," I spoke, my voice still heavy with ire, "take Cara to the dungeon. She is to be locked in a cell, under guard. Ewan, go home until the captain sends for you. You are fortunate not to be going to the dungeon as well," I added to him. I knew Ewan's incompetence could be enough to have him deprived of his head, given what was at stake.

"Right away, Your Majesty," Aife answered with a bow. "On your feet," she snapped at them in the next moment. They both rose with due shame. One went meekly to his home, the other was escorted by Aife to the dungeon. I would visit Cara in the morning, for I wished to make her sweat a little before we talked. It was only a small consolation, however, that we could speak with her. It was the Wolf himself we had sought to capture.

"Your Majesty." The sombre voice of John came to me, his voice breaking into the muffled quiet, for the tavern still only spoke hushed, strained talk. With nothing else to do, the customers had turned to gossip. No doubt they were wondering what had transpired, to cause Gaeson's soldiers to run through the streets and for their king's anger to erupt so visibly.

"Report, captain," I said inanely as I turned to my friend. From his grim countenance and the way his bushy eyebrows were burrowed, I already knew the Wolf had slipped away.

"The Wolf has escaped, sire," he answered at last. I gave a single nod, folding my arms. "The soldiers are in the process of securing the town, but it looks as though his spies were not waiting for us, sire."

"Indeed, otherwise we would be battling with them now," I affirmed. "The Wolf would have chosen to fight rather than flee."

"Yes, sire," John said. There was a moment of quiet, then. "Do you have any further orders, my lord?" I shook my head. There was little else to do until I spoke to Cara. She was now our only lead in discovering the assassin's identity.

"Very well, Your Majesty," John murmured. Then, in the next moment, he desisted with formality and he reached out to touch my shoulder. "I'm sorry, brother," he murmured. "Try to get some rest," he suggested gently.

"Aye," I nodded heavily. "I will interrogate Cara early next morn," I added. "She's our only chance to discover who he is. Try to get some rest yourself," I added to him. We clasped arms briefly, before he went in the direction of our small band to check on their progress.

After he left, I lingered only a moment before turning back towards the castle. My hand held the hilt of my blade lest I came upon the enemy, but as we had predicted, there seemed to be none of the Wolf's spies around, waiting to ambush me from the shadows as I walked. Though obviously it was best by far to have Gaeson in safety, part of me was rueful there were no foes present. It was wrong to wish for war, but in my current mood I would have relished the opportunity to put the enemy to the sword.

I took the uneventful route back through Gaeson, uncaring now who might see me in the middle of the night. I only took one stop at the armoury, before my footsteps took me to Evelyn's and my chamber. I swung the door open loudly, causing my wife to jump up in bed.

"Well?" she asked at once. My queen was alert, with anxiety in her features. No doubt she craved to solve this mystery as much as I did. I did not immediately respond, only moved to unbuckle my belt. "Did you catch him?" Evelyn prompted.

"No," I replied shortly. "He was there, Evelyn," I muttered in frustration, as my belt hit the floor. My blade clanged loudly as it landed. "He was there, but he slipped through our grasp yet again," I concluded, still seething.

"What happened?" she asked, sighing in resignation. I did not answer for a moment, pausing to pull my tunic over my head and reach for my nightshirt. My wife prompted me no further as I sat on the edge of the bed. Instead she shuffled closer, wrapping her warm arms around my bare chest. I was leant forward, my elbows upon my legs with my hands at my head.

"Aife and I were on the rooftops as planned, with John and his troops in the church," I began the account. "We witnessed Cara and then the Wolf enter the square and talk to each other. All seemed well, but then—Ewan was there," I concluded bitterly.

"I thought you ordered him to stay away," she said in surprise. I nodded, my hands moving slightly upon my forehead.

"Ewan seemed to just stand there, watching, so we went on as planned. A moment before Aife fired her arrow, the Wolf suddenly drew his blade to strike Cara—"

"So, he came to her rescue," Evelyn guessed immediately, for I had told her of Ewan's feelings for her. I nodded mutely. "The spy escaped?" she asked.

"Aye," I admitted heavily. "My arrow missed by quite a way," I mused regretfully. "Aife's shot was brilliant, but she hit his cloak. We came so close to catching him!" I declared angrily. In response, Evelyn shuffled even closer to me, laying her head on my shoulder.

"I'm sorry," she murmured into my neck. "I knew what it meant for you to catch him." As she spoke, I moved my hands to join hers. As our fingers interlaced, I finally felt some of the anger in me lessen. My queen shifted her head but kept it on my shoulder still.

"I think I know who he is, Evelyn," I ventured heavily. "Though I did not see him, I have had the suspicion for a while. I wanted to be sure first, but—" my wife lifted her head to look at me as I spoke, the question in her eyes.

"I think it might be Melvyn," I admitted ere long. Her eyes at once widened, stricken. "I have no proof, as I say," I added. "I just—sense it."

"I hope not," Evelyn muttered, her head once again on my shoulder. "He was one of my father's most loyal advisors." I said nothing else to this.

"Cara is in the dungeon, I take it," she murmured, angling her head away from my neck a little as she spoke. I felt the top of her hair rustle softly against my jaw as I nodded.

"I'll question her tomorrow. Currently she's the only lead on him, whether it's Melvyn or not," I said, repeating to what I had told John.

"Aye," she mused in agreement. My lady then sat back from me to sit up straighter. "What are you going to do with Ewan?"

"I'm not sure," I replied honestly, glancing at her. "I'm angry with Ewan, of course, but I understand," I relented ere long. I was voicing what until now, I had been too angry to admit. "To watch the one you love, about to be killed… it would be inhumane to do nothing. It must hurt him, too, knowing the one he loves is our betrayer." I sighed, stretching my arms above my head before they dropped listlessly back to my sides.

Presently I glanced at Evelyn, noticing she had not yet replied. She was looking away from me, with a sheen of pain upon her countenance. It was all too familiar these past few days. Remorse and shame filled me, for I had pushed the recent sad news to the back of my mind, in order to focus more on catching the Wolf.

"How are you faring today, my love?" I enquired quietly. I moved a hand to brush aside a few stray curls that had crawled forward on her face, as she met my gaze.

"I am well," Evelyn replied evenly. She said nothing else, so I let the subject drop. My eyes lowered to the bed, where our hands moved to clasp upon it.

"I know the times are sad, love," I began, "but it is only three months, perhaps even earlier, until Morwenna gives birth. Then the child can be ours," I reassured her. "We will need to announce it to Gaeson soon."

"Aye, I know," she responded quickly. Her tone had been a little dismissive. Perhaps she found the subject still too painful to discuss, which

I could well understand. On impulse as I sought to comfort her, I bent my head to kiss a bare patch of her shoulder. I lingered there a moment as my lips pressed against her soft skin, inhaling the scent of her.

"You should get some rest," she said quietly, "You will need it if you're going to interrogate Cara." Her tone seemed slightly strained. My wife pulled away then, shuffling back to her side of the bed and pulling the bedclothes around her.

"Aye, of course," I agreed. "I've had a trying day," I pointed out, a vast understatement. "I wasn't suggesting…" my voice trailed off, as my hand clumsily gestured between us.

"I know," she replied, with her smile tight. Then, her countenance faded to sadness. "I…" she began, then stilled. "Goodnight," she said instead, kissing my cheek briefly before turning away. She blew out the candle, casting us both into darkness.

"Goodnight," I replied, lying down beside her. I frowned a little, wondering at her behaviour. It was only a little over a month since Evelyn had told me the sad news of her infertility. Both of our emotions these last four weeks had been complicated, therefore, I had no great need to rush our coming together again.

Still, I remembered what Aife had said about the possibility of grief shutting one another out. It felt a little painful, then, that even a simple act of intimacy, like kissing her shoulder, would cause her to pull away. Since the night she had told me, I had sensed a distance between us, almost too subtle to mention but still tangible.

As if Evelyn could read my thoughts and wished to prove me wrong, abruptly her arm reached through the covers and her hand came to join the one of mine that was lying by my side.

"I love you, Daniel," she muttered rapidly, her voice thick. There was no change in her breathing, so I could not tell if she was weeping.

"I love you," I returned. I rolled towards her now, so that her back was against my chest. I tucked my legs a little under hers, our joined hands resting lightly against her stomach. "I always will," I murmured.

"I know," she replied, brokenly. I frowned through the darkness, for I was beginning to wonder if there was something else here, too, as well as her grief. "Forgive me, husband," she muttered, as though again she could read my mind, "I'm tired, that's all," she dismissed it.

"There's nothing to forgive," I told her quietly. I kissed her shoulder briefly again, before laying my head back down on the pillow. Neither of us spoke further and after a few moments, I sensed some of the tension start to lift from her. I frowned again, my eyes staring into what would be her head as we lay there in the dark. Could she be hiding something else from me? It was if she was building an invisible shield between us, that seemed to grow stronger and stronger. It was as if she was building an invisible wall around her, one brick at a time. As my eyelids grew heavy with the tiredness of the day worn out, my last thought before sleep took me was a hope that I would find a way to break the wall down.

***

I woke long before dawn the next morning, to be greeted by the familiar sounds of Evelyn's slumber. I too tried to get back to sleep, but my thoughts of the Wolf and Cara kept me awake. I had originally intended to visit her after sunrise, but it seemed my heart would give me no rest. Eventually I lit a candle on my side of the bed, glancing at my wife before I began to dress. A few of her raven curls had strayed across her face, but underneath, her countenance was relaxed. I hoped her dreams had given her some freedom from the burdens that seemed to surround her when she was conscious.

"Daniel," she murmured, just as I was pulling my boots on. I turned to see her blinking at me sleepily, her tousled hair loose about her shoulders as she lifted her head. "Is it dawn?"

"No, not for another few hours," I murmured, as I finished lacing my boots. "I couldn't go back to sleep," I informed her. "You should do so, though," I added.

"You're going to visit Cara," she stated then, the relaxed countenance of her dreaming fading as she woke fully.

"Aye," I nodded. "I'll be back before the night is over." I bent to kiss her forehead before quitting our chambers and making my way through the castle towards the dungeon. A guard opened the gate for me, admitting me into the castle prison. I strode down a dank corridor towards Cara's cell. As I reached it, I was surprised to see Ewan sitting there, as if waiting for me.

The lad was awake, staring glumly at the floor. He was slouched on a hard, wooden chair, looking as though he had not slept at all. A lantern, suspended on a nearby wall, gave enough light to dimly illuminate his conflicted countenance. As I neared him, he must have heard my footsteps, for his head jerked up, his eyes flickered wide.

"Your Majesty," he croaked, an instant later. His gaze moved back to the stone-cold floor of the dungeon, as he sank from his hard chair to a bow on bended knee.

"What are you doing here?" I hissed angrily. "I sent you home, Ewan. Are you incapable of following even the simplest order?" I challenged hotly. I wrestled with my emotions as I watched him, for I felt upon the fine line between compassion and anger.

"I pleaded with the guards to let me help watch her, my lord," Ewan returned swiftly, head still pointed towards the ground. "I believed the Wolf might come back, to slay her during the night, before she could give any answers. The last thing I wanted to do was fail you, my lord," he emphasised, now raising his head to look at me. I observed that the red welt on his cheek had expanded, now swollen large with dark bruising.

"I know my life may well be forfeit," Ewan continued passionately. "I will submit to whatever punishment seems best to you, my lord the king. Only—I had to be here, sire." He paused here. "I did not speak to her, sire," he ended, a little weakly now.

"I should hope not!" I returned angrily, almost before he could finish his speech. "Get up," I instructed immediately. Abruptly, he got to his feet. "Go home this time, Ewan, before I lock you in here also. I'll decide what to do with you later," I warned.

"Yes, Your Majesty. I—" he bent his head whilst he paused here, then raised his head to look at me square in the eyes again. "I beg you to let me stay, sire. She might co-operate if I am here," he added. I pondered this, knowing it could be effective.

"Very well, but you are to say nothing," I relented. He bent his head in obedience. I then abruptly walked past him, walking only a little further down the dank corridor. At once, I saw her through the bars, with chains clapped around her hands. It was with some irony that I noted this was the same cell I had been in, after I had come back to Gaeson after discovering my true identity. I had long ago resolved, however, never to treat a prisoner the way the interrogator had treated me: beating me to a pulp without asking me a single question.

"Your Majesty," Cara whispered hoarsely, as I opened the door to the cell. Ewan closed it behind us as I went right up to her, undoing the chains that held her wrists. At once she crumpled to the floor. Ewan moved a stool from the corner of the cell and I sat down on it. He then remained standing as Cara sat herself up again, rubbing the marks where her chains had been. Her eyes flickered to me, seeming to ignore Ewan entirely.

"Who is the spy, Cara?" I asked her quietly, seeing no reason to delay. "Why did you betray us and work for him?" There was no answer. "Speak, for it may yet mean redemption," I implored her. At this, she smiled ruefully.

"You think there is a chance to survive, my lord?" Cara spoke so softly, I had to strain my ears to hear her. "I am already dead," she declared a bitterly. "I was the day he first spoke to me. I have been living in death's shadow ever since," she concluded. I hid a sigh, in irritation at her dramatics.

"Tell us who he is, Cara," I repeated patiently. "This dungeon is safe. You are protected here," I assured her. At this she scoffed.

"I cannot be safe anywhere, my king," she retorted. Internally, I bristled slightly at her sarcasm. "There is no chain he cannot break," she continued. "He has such avarice for power and operates such evil, right under your nose."

"Then tell us who he is," I beseeched a third time. "If you do not, then he is not the only one to be afraid of," I pointed out. "You were caught dealing with the enemy, that makes you guilty of treason, too. You know what happens to traitors, Cara," I warned. "If you tell me all you know, I might yet be able to spare your life."

"You ask what I cannot do," she answered me now, a little sadness in her face as she held my gaze. "If I do not speak, then only I will die. If I do speak…" she trailed off.

"Well?" I asked, but Cara merely lowered her head. "Speak sense!" I shouted. "What will happen if you speak?" I asked, trying to be calmer. At this, Cara looked up at me.

"He said the day I told you anything, half of Gaeson would die before the sun set. Including you, Ewan," she added, her head turning to acknowledge him for the first time. "That is why I lied to you, because I did not want you to come to harm. You cannot stop him," she added, looking to me. "He is a monster."

"Don't you think I know that?" I retorted. "That man killed half my family," I added passionately. "Even as recently as the last battle. I believe it was the Wolf who killed my uncle," I emphasised. Cara nodded with no surprise on her features which angered me even further, as she confirmed this terrible truth she clearly already knew.

"Then you know how capable he is," Cara replied. "You have seen his devastation first hand. "He is high up in the Bernician Army and he—he orchestrates many things." She broke off and looked away. "I've said too much already."

"No, you haven't," I snarled in frustration. "You've barely said anything." Cara was still looking away and I drew my blade once more as my anger rose. "If you do not say more, then those words could well be your last," I ground out. I sensed Ewan shifting behind me, but in my rage, I cared not how he felt at such an ultimatum.

"Tell me the truth, Cara," I challenged her. "I believe it to be Lord Melvyn. Am I right?" I roared. Cara only smiled faintly, but this time there was no sarcasm in her features. There was no hint on her features, either, of whether my theory about Melvyn was correct. Only for a moment, it unnerved me how similar the expression was to the one Evelyn had worn recently.

"I already have seen my last of daylight, my lord," was all Cara said. My eyes narrowed again at her further dramatics. She must have seen my expression in the dark, for now she lifted her head higher. Her sad smile vanished, her face tensing a little in anger.

"You think I am exaggerating?" she enquired hotly. "Yes, he killed your family, but he has the capacity to kill hundreds, even thousands." She spoke rapidly, her words almost fumbling in her haste to speak them. "Whether by his blade or yours, sire, I will be dead by morning."

"I thought I would be terrified of death," she murmured, as the bitter smile came back. "But there's a kind of liberation in it, too. It doesn't matter, don't you see?" she said, raising her face so that her gaze could better examine mine. "It matters not what I say to you, or the madness you display. I am already dead, my king, whatever I do."

"Not if you tell me the truth," I implored her. I forced my tone to become gentler, calmer. I crossed the feet between us, the tip of my boot rustling one of the chains as I crouched down. Her countenance was again pointed towards the floor, but here I put my hand under my chin. I raised it, making our gazes meet again. "If you tell me all I need to know, then I will spare your life," I vowed. "I have a whole army that can protect you, if need be," I added.

"Do you, sire? A whole army?" she echoed faintly, her voice suddenly a whisper. "How many of your soldiers do you think truly belong to you, my lord? Do you imagine I'm the only one he has manipulated and trapped? Do you believe the whole legion are loyal to you?" She continued her questions, each one speaking doubt into me. "Do you really think you or anyone else can protect me from him? He is everywhere. He may be able to hear us, even now," she whispered. I frowned, unnerved. Could all of this be possible? Could it really be that this man would take Cara's life before the sun rose?

"Besides, my king, what of the rest of Gaeson?" she continued. "If I do not reveal his identity, then only I will die but if I tell you, then our people will be destroyed."

"What is his plan, Cara?" I asked her now, in quiet urgency. Cara had hung her head again; presently she shook it.

"There is no way of stopping him. I just—" she paused here, considering, a small frown across her brows. "Very well, Your Majesty, I shall make a deal with you," she said, raising her head to meet mine once more. "If by this time tomorrow I am still alive, I will tell you all I know. One day's grace, my king. If I am still breathing, all shall be revealed."

Her head lowered again, as I reflected on this woman who seemed a ghost of her former self. Where had that confident, spirited warrior gone, who had duelled with Ewan that day of recruits' training? Cara really did look like one preparing for death. Part of me was beginning to believe her, despite her recent actions. Or was I only being naïve?

"Very well," I said, deciding as I stood. "This time tomorrow, Cara. I give my word I will do all I can to keep you alive, and then I expect all questions answered."

"Thank you, my king," Cara bent her head in response. I gave her a final nod. "Ewan, with me," I said, glancing his way. The young man was staring at her intently, but his face was difficult to decipher. No doubt he was battling with many different emotions, also.

"Ewan," Cara called, as he dutifully turned to the cell door to follow my footsteps. In the dim light, I glimpsed the pain in his features as he turned back. "I am sorry," was all she said.

"As am I," Ewan returned, after a pause. There was a heaviness in his tone that was well beyond his years. "I pray you survive the day," he murmured presently. His sad gaze lingered upon her for a moment longer, before he turned to me decisively.

"Come," I said quietly. The two of us then walked down the dank corridor for some moments without speaking. I was a little ahead, whilst I pondered what to say to him.

"Your Majesty," Ewan said abruptly. I turned back, to see he had sank down to his knees once more. "I have not disobeyed your orders once, but twice." His tone was even heavier, disgust at himself prevalent. "I cost you the capture of the Wolf, whom I have been seeking to reveal in your service this past six months," he continued, remorse filling his speech.

"I wish to accept the consequence for these actions and to throw myself onto your wise judgement, my lord the king," he said abruptly, his gaze still fixed on the cobbled stone beneath us. "If you wish me to stay in one of these cells, or fall upon this sword I bear, then I shall. Your word is my law, sire," he finished eloquently.

"Noble words," I replied. That was what they were, whatever else I might now think of him. I folded my arms as I regarded him, deciding his fate. "You did cost me my spy, Ewan, even knowing he was the assassin of my kin." The young soldier remained as still and as silent as the stone beneath his feet, as he waited for his fate to be decided. I felt keenly my power, for I could end his life as easily as I could pardon him.

"However," I resumed, "I am not without sympathy for you. I can see you love Cara very deeply," I said. The tips of Ewan's ears turned a little red at this. "Had Her Majesty the Queen been in such danger I would not have hesitated to save her life, even at the risk of disobeying orders and losing the Wolf," I reflected.

"Therefore, your punishment is that you are relieved of duty for the next fortnight, without pay," I concluded at last. "I suggest you use this time to reflect on this matter. Mind you are very careful about the friendships you make in future," I said in a final reprimand. Ewan seemed to wait a moment longer, before drawing his blade to hold it flat against both his palms.

"Thank you, Your Majesty, for your benevolent mercy," he declared now with passion. "May you deal with me severely, my lord the king, should I ever fail you again. If I ever displease you again, sire, may you take my sword and drive it to my heart," he finished.

"I'm sure it won't come to that, lad," I informed him, "on your feet." At this quiet order he stood, sheathing his sword again. "Besides, I'd use my blade, anyway," I told him, as the corner of my mouth turned. "Mine is probably sharper."

"Aye, sire," Ewan murmured, a smile twitching upon his own countenance. "I could do with a visit to the blacksmith."

"Very well," I concluded with a final nod. "You are dismissed. Go home." At this, Ewan gave a frown, still from where he crouched.

"My lord, I beg that you let me guard in the dungeon this next day, being relieved of duty with tomorrow's dawn," he requested. I folded my arms, ready to rebuke him harshly for his impertinence, even now.

"Cara believes her life will be taken from her," Ewan implored. His conflicted face had been cast to the ground, but he lifted his gaze once more. "Even if you were to trust no others, you can trust I would never allow a hair on her head to be injured. Please, sire, allow me to watch over her," I considered his request with my arms still folded. His request seemed noble enough, but what if he was so devoted to her, he would help her escape?

"Very well," I said at length, "but I will send two other guards to aid you keep watch." I searched his expression carefully, but he seemed pleased rather than disappointed at this.

"Thank you, my lord the king," Ewan said as he stood and bent his head quickly once more. At this he took a step towards the dungeon, but then he turned back. "Your Majesty, you asked Cara if it could be Lord Melvyn," he said.

"Aye," I returned quietly. I noted the lack of surprise on his features. "You have seen something to suspect him?" I asked.

"Not as such, my lord king," Ewan replied, frowning again as he deliberated. "Yet, there is something about his countenance I do not trust. He does seem to be hiding something."

"Indeed," I nodded shortly at his conclusion. "I suppose we shall see. I'll send the guards to you. I expect you to keep her from escaping, also," I reminded him pointedly.

"Of course, Your Majesty." Ewan bowed low before finally departing back to Cara's cell. I watched him leave, this lad who had grown into a man these last few months, both daring and loyal. I prayed he would not so easily fall into future traps. I frowned as I remembered Cara's words. Would she be as safe as I hoped? Was someone to attempt to break into the dungeon?

In a few hours the dawn would come. It was the day of the parade, the festival celebrating Gaeson, her people and her home. All the regiment would march proudly through Gaeson's streets. Could the Veiled Wolf have planned some attack? I resolved to tell John once more to take every precaution, even with the soldiers he trusted most.

Ere long I returned to my bedchamber to find Evelyn sleeping. As I observed this and climbed back into bed beside her, I had a notion that brought me comfort, for whatever happened, even with the frustrations of this night, hopefully, by the deal I had made with Cara, all would be revealed by the dawn breaking tomorrow.

Chapter Ten

It was a few hours later when I awoke drowsily from slumber. I had not fully slipped back into sleep due to the eventful night, but I had been able to doze a little. Through the partially open window, I could already hear the murmured voices of citizens in the courtyard. They must have risen not long after I returned to bed, in order to begin the parade preparations. There was an air of excitement, which brought a smile to my face. I turned to see Evelyn was still asleep, then bent my head to kiss her forehead briefly. My wife's eyes remained shut, but the corner of her mouth turned. The general happiness about her countenance made me smile further.

This was a great relief, since the past week — nay, since my uncle died and long before that, possibly since the death of Bredon just over seven months ago — joy had seemed far from our hearts. Finally, the hope the maid Morwenna would give us her child seemed to be overcoming the sorrow that the child would not come from our own bodies. The sadness was still very prevalent, but the dream that we would soon be able to raise a child ourselves was beginning to blossom.

Presently, Evelyn rose from the bed. Even before she changed from her night-clothes, she had gone straight to the speech that she would read from later that day. I lingered in the comforting warmth of the covers for a moment, angling my head towards her whilst one hand reposed behind my head. My wife was frowning with a troubled expression.

"Your words will be fine," I said, to assure her. Evelyn's head jerked up to mine and my eyes widened a little. "Sorry, I didn't mean to startle you." It was surprising in itself that I had startled her. My queen's military training that came with a royal education meant she was as perceptive of others' movements as I was. It struck me then how apprehensive she really was.

"You have given hundreds of speeches like this," I said now as I sat up, running a hand through my unkempt auburn hair. I was a little confused about the depths of her anxiety. "Why should today be any different?"

"Oh, it is just that people are expecting remarkable things." I hid my frown, for her voice did not seem quite right. It was a little too high, a little too fast. Abruptly, she then let the papers drop from her hands with a sigh. "They want to be entertained," my wife said. "It is the one day of the year when I feel I am not myself. Never mind," she added suddenly, clearly dismissing the topic. She stood a little too quickly, then, as she turned away from me.

"I'm sure all will be well," was all I said, deciding to let the matter drop, though I frowned at her turned back. Perhaps, I reflected, it was because soon she knew she would have to tell the truth to Gaeson about our issues with having children. Maybe, somehow, it was affecting how she was with her people. I kept these notions to myself, however, as I went to the window to push it further open. The sun was newly risen, just beginning to glisten all it touched.

"It is not long since dawn," I told her, as I hastily dressed. "I must go to check on Cara—" Just then, as the words left my mouth, there was a knock on the chamber door.

"My lord, it's the dungeon." It was John's voice that reached me, as I fastened the buckle on my belt. I nodded briefly in farewell to Evelyn before I reached out to the corridor to join my captain.

"Let's go," I commanded, as we both already began to run. There were six other soldiers with him. Was she attacked already? I wondered, after only three hours or so since I had last seen her? "Have you sent for Leigh?" I directed urgently.

"Aye, my lord," my friend returned swiftly, "he will meet us there." I nodded and there was no further dialogue as we ran. What had happened? I cursed myself under my breath that I had not placed more guards in the dungeon, but there we had three just outside the cell, including Ewan. Then there were four that stood outside the main entrance. Seven had seemed plenty a few hours ago. Was I still being naïve to the assassin's power, even now? I rebuked myself. Had I not heeded Cara's warning strongly enough?

Minutes later, we reached the dungeon door, swords already drawn. It was immediately apparent, however, that all the violence had already been done. The four guards lay sprawled upon the stone floor, with pools beside them dark and slick with blood. Another soldier lay near them.

"Dead," John muttered beside me, after checking for signs of life. The other soldiers checked the remaining fallen guards, then nodded to confirm the same diagnosis. "I appointed all four guards personally, my lord," my captain added. "The fifth man must have been working for the Wolf. If there is only one dead spy here, sire, then—"

"Open the door," I ordered grimly, reaching the same conclusion that the others may well have made it to the cell. The dungeon door creaked slowly open, as I wielded my sword in front of me. We then sped down the dank corridor, my heart rate quickening. Would anyone be left alive? There was no sign in the passage of a battle, but as we approached the cell door, once again the acrid scent of blood that reached my nostrils was all too pervasive.

As the cell door was pushed open, a gruesome sight reached my eyes. Ewan was sprawled near the chain rungs, shifting a little in pain. His face was covered in blood, but my heart had lightened slightly to see that at least the lad was still alive. I glanced around me as Leigh rushed over to tend him. One of John's men confirmed another Gaeson soldier was still alive, slumped unconscious near the back wall of the cell.

Cara, though, seemed to be nowhere in sight. As more light entered the cell, I saw two other men in the far corner. A guard quickly checked them to confirm they were both dead, also.

"What happened, Ewan?" I asked, as at last this obvious question was able spring from my lips. "Where is Cara?" Ewan managed to raise his head a little.

"I... I don't know, sire," he admitted, the brokenness clear in his voice. "Three of them came in here," he continued weakly. "One of the guards who came to aid me, sire, was working for the Wolf." I cursed at this foul news. "I put one to the sword and the other guard who fought for Gaeson did too," he murmured, "but they knocked him to the ground. The two remaining spies cut her chains and took her," he concluded. "She's gone," he reiterated faintly, sounding as though the very heart of him was dead.

"We'll try to find her, Ewan," I tried to assure him. "Speak nothing more for now, lad. The most important thing now is for you to rest." At this, he only moved his head a little further back, so it rested against the cell wall.

"I brought stretchers with me," the surgeon said, after he had done what he could to stem the bleeding. He beckoned with his hand and more soldiers also came into the cell, carrying two stretchers. Gently, they lifted Ewan and the unconscious soldier onto the makeshift mats.

"Ewan should certainly recover," the physician said as he straightened, his hands stained crimson from his toils. "As for the other… I'm unsure. I'll do all I can," he added as we followed the party back outside. I inhaled the fresh air, but the scent of blood remained, mingled on Leigh's hands and the guards still lying dead outside the main dungeon door. "Cara is probably dead, sire," Leigh directed to me quietly.

"Aye," I murmured back with a sigh. "Either that, or with the enemy." I had a wave of compassion for Ewan, who surely knew that the woman he loved was either dead, a prisoner of the Wolf, or that she had betrayed us all once more.

"Go back and prepare for the parade," John directed the other men who had come with him. At once they bowed and headed away. My captain then turned and walked towards me. His countenance was unreadable, but for the set of his jaw. My friend was deeply angered at the loss of life here, as I was. My features also tightened at the thought of the second guard I had ordered to be posted with Ewan, whose treachery was all too obvious.

"You couldn't have known, brother," John told me, having accurately guessed my thoughts. His speech was intended to comfort me, but in truth it only distressed me further.

"That is exactly my worry, John," I told him. "It seems the Wolf has ensured we will never know who belongs to him until he acts. How many agents could he have?"

"Aye," John muttered, his voice pained as I glanced back to where the dead Gaeson soldiers were being removed from outside the dungeon door. "Do you wish the parade to go on, sire?" my captain enquired, as he glanced me. I frowned, thinking quickly.

"Cara told me all might be revealed today," I said. "Perhaps the Wolf will reveal himself at last. If we cancel the parade, that opportunity might be lost." I swallowed hard, for what if his scheme left half of Gaeson dead?

"I will not let that monster so fill us with fear that we cannot be together this day," I eventually decided. "Take every precaution you can, to ensure the safety of Gaeson," I ordered him.

"Your Majesty," John replied formally with a bow. With that, the two of us went our separate ways. I went to prepare for the parade, whilst John headed to the regimental chambers, no doubt to issue some last-minute instructions for the army.

"What happened?" Evelyn's immediate question reached my ears, as I again entered my chamber. Though my clothes had not been tainted with blood, I felt as though I was. The first thing I did, then, was to reach for a clean tunic.

"The dungeon was attacked," I told her heavily, after pulling the fresh article of clothing over my head. "The four guards to the dungeon entrance are dead. Out of the two guards I sent to aid Ewan," I said as I turned to her, "one of them was a spy who helped defeat Ewan and the other soldier loyal to us. Whoever they were took Cara with them," I concluded flatly.

"How awful," Evelyn said, her hand upon my arm. "I assume we are continuing," she added, as I reached for my formal robes. I only nodded. Evelyn then let go of my arm, seeing I did not want to discuss the matter further. I was thankful for her tact, remaining silent as I donned the rest of my full regalia.

Outside the dungeon it had seemed well for the day to go on, but currently the pomp of the parade had never seemed more ridiculous, given what had just happened. I turned back to my wife to see again the same troubled frown on her face. As she sensed me watching her, though, her expression quickly cleared, instead shooting me a brief smile. I found myself hiding yet another frown at her strange behaviour. Could she be hiding something?

"What is it, Evelyn?" I asked her at last, after she had just turned around. Evelyn turned back with nothing unusual in her countenance.

"I'm just tired and anxious about the day," she returned, in a voice that sounded so ordinary, I wondered if it was false. "I did not sleep well last night, thinking about Ewan and Cara and the Wolf, as well as this speech which is far more minor a matter," she sighed. "The hour grows late, husband," she added with a glance to the window. "The parade will start soon."

"Very well," I replied neutrally. A minute or so later, at last ready, we left our chamber. As we did, my queen tucked her hand underneath my arm. We both kept glancing around us and I guessed she was checking for any suspicious activity, as I was. I knew the Wolf could well have further horrors planned for this day. Yet, I could not shake the niggling doubt that the person who had been most suspicious was my wife, who still had hold of my arm.

"Daniel," she began in a rapid, urgent tone, after we had walked through the palace hall, just coming to the doors that would lead to the courtyard. I stilled as my hand touched the handle, turning towards her.

"I…" my wife opened her mouth, but then seemed to change her mind. "I love you," she said at last, repeating the declaration she had made last night.

"I love you also," I replied, surprised and pleased by her sudden affection uttered once more. My hand moved from the door to her cheek. "Are you sure everything is well?"

"Of course," she answered, far too quickly. All this did was confirm my suspicion that something definitely was not right. I wondered then whether Sarah was right about my wife hiding something. I resolved to enquire and to get to the truth of it, as soon as the day was done.

"We'll miss the parade," she continued abruptly. She then abruptly opened the palace door herself, opening the way to the sun-streamed square. I plastered a smile on my face, my external countenance one of cheer, but inside I was ever watchful. Would the Wolf execute some awful plan? Was that, too, why my queen was so anxious? As I glanced about, I was met with the faces of happy citizens; children and adults in anticipation of the day, waving small Gaeson flags in excitement.

Immediately before the parade was due to start, my wife gave her speech. They were words of wisdom, delivered with such confidence that it gave no credence to her apprehension. Indeed, she delivered the words so effortlessly, it confirmed in my mind that the speech had not been the source of her anxiety at all. Why had she been so apprehensive, then? Was it because of the Wolf? I had been checking every countenance all day, but nothing seemed out of place.

I had spotted Melvyn a few times in the crowd, but he seemed as innocent and happy as the next bystander. In a way I was pleased he was there, for I could keep an eye on him. As the day wore on, Evelyn relaxed, seemingly becoming increasingly relieved. As morning gave way to afternoon and the sun began its descend into the sky the tension in me too began to lift, for perhaps the Wolf had been bluffing. It was truly possible that maybe no doom was to befall us this day.

Amidst the celebrations, however, my mind continually questioned what had happened in the dungeon at daybreak. I had received a report saying that Ewan was recovering a little, but the other soldier was still unconscious. We still had no clue as to Cara's whereabouts. Was she even still alive? Was she the assassin's prisoner or accomplice? I could only imagine the anguish the young lad was going through, pondering these difficult thoughts.

Indeed, such was my mind on these themes, that when near the end of the festivities we went back to the palace hall, I almost missed Evelyn's expression. I glanced to my left, to see my queen was standing absolutely rigid, with all colour drained from her countenance. Frowning, I followed her gaze to see both Aldred and Melvyn stood there in the vast chamber.

"It is time," Aldred said quietly. Without warning he then suddenly drew his sword. His behaviour had changed so quickly, it was almost comical but for the earnest sincerity in his features. "The Veiled Wolf is in our midst, after all."

"Aye," I replied, my eyes on Melvyn. "I believe it is. What do you have planned, Wolf? You murdered my kin!" I drew my sword also. Aldred began to wave his sword wildly, as if it was only for practice. I frowned, wondering whether he intended to intimidate Melvyn. This seemed to work, for Melvyn had stepped back. He was unarmed, much to his ruin. There was surprise in his features, no doubt at being caught.

"What are you doing, Aldred?" Evelyn asked quietly ere long. Aldred only laughed, his eyes open wide with a wild expression upon his face. "Don't do this," she implored him now. I frowned at my wife in confusion.

"The Wolf is here, as he said," I told my queen. "Surely it is better we catch him in this moment?" Evelyn glanced at me, her expression stricken. It made me all the more confused.

"Do not pretend, Your Majesty," a voice used her title mockingly. "I warned you this day would come, did I not? You paid me no heed." However, the snake-like voice did not belong to Melvyn. I glanced to Aldred, my advisor and my friend.

"Aldred, what are you doing?" It was my time to ask this question. Melvyn took a step back, surprise and horror further filling his features. My friend took a step towards Evelyn, sword still drawn. "Get back from your queen," I said in instinct, stepping between them.

"Ah yes," he chuckled, his features now positively joyous. He would almost appear harmless, apart from the malice I perceived in his eyes. "What a man you married, my queen. The man who was taken so cruelly from his childhood. This man, who served your father faithfully, unknowing that he had so needlessly ordered their deaths."

"Take care of your words," I warned him instantly. Aldred smiled sinisterly and the cold expression sent a chill down my spine. I glanced again at Melvyn, still horrified. There was one conclusion that seemed to make sense of this scene, but surely it was impossible. I glanced back to my advisor, to see his amiable smile had vanished; far crueller stood in its place. I knew I had never seen this expression before, yet there was something horribly familiar about it. There was a tugging at my memory, like there had been the first time we had been properly introduced.

"You never told your precious husband, did you?" Aldred asked, glancing again at my wife. "Your loyal knight, your 'boy from the snow', as I have heard you term him." Then Aldred suddenly gave a mocking gasp, putting his hands over his mouth in false shock.

"But then, how could you have done?" he went on evenly as he moved his hands away, his voice suddenly cold. "For how could he ever trust you again? This man so pure of heart, who has saved your life. No wonder you kept the truth from him," he snarled.

"Speak no more, you treacherous snake!" Evelyn cut across him quickly, "or he will slay you where you stand. Your words are like a cruel serpent." Melvyn stepped back further, almost level with the pillars now. Apart from his movement, the advisor seemed invisible.

"Cruel, yes, and treacherous," Aldred agreed, his sneer returning. "For you knew I betrayed you a long time ago, did you not? You discovered the truth before you were even married to him. Let me ask you something, dear queen. Did you mean any word of your wedding vows?" At this I glanced at my wife, to see her gaze was resolutely on the palace floor.

"I meant every word," Evelyn answered in earnest, but her eyes still remained downcast. What had Aldred meant? Why was she unable to look me in the eye?

"Of what are you speaking?" I persisted, still looking at her. "What do you know, Evelyn?" Slowly my gaze moved to Aldred. Our eyes locked. His malicious grin was at its widest. Something again tugged at my mind, as suddenly I knew what had seemed impossible was true.

"You're the Wolf," I whispered hoarsely. At this, Aldred threw his head back and laughed again, like a maniac. In the next moment he wielded his blade and ran high towards Evelyn. All questions of his speech fled my mind as I darted forward and blocked him. He began chuckling again as our swords sliced once more though the air, metal clinking metal as we fought. His laughter was ever increasing, as though he was thoroughly enjoying himself.

"Finally, after all these years," Aldred mused, suddenly stepping back and lowering his sword a little. "Are you not taking pleasure in this moment also, my lady?" he mocked in an almost singsong voice. "Or are you preparing yourself that your marriage might be over?" I shot another glance at Evelyn, who I perceived could still not look at me directly.

"You're the Wolf," I whispered again, hoarsely. The simple yet nigh unbelievable fact was a thread, unravelling quickly in my mind. "You're the one who caused the watchmen to slumber, the night I could not sleep," I recalled. "You're—wait," I frowned, confused. "You're the one who told me of the Wolf's plan to murder Evelyn."

"A ruse for you to gain the Wolf's trust," he resumed. "There is more to me, though, than even that," he sighed almost lazily. "I was rather hurt," my foe added, "that you did not realise it was me when we first met. Though you did not recognise your dear late uncle, so why would you have recognised me?" He was almost whispering again, yet I heard him as loudly as if he had roared his question throughout the whole palace chamber.

This was the other inevitable conclusion, the one I realised my heart had desperately been avoiding. The thread my memory had been tugging suddenly unravelled. Abruptly I saw him, much younger, with that evil grin across his face. He was giggling as he ran towards me down the corridors of Klumeck—

"I do remember you," I whispered back, the revelation complete. "You are the Wolf. I saw you that night in Klumeck, after you murdered my parents and my uncle's wife and child. You ordered my uncle's death, didn't you?" Aldred grinned, clearly thrilled with this fact, rather than ashamed of it. "You've been destroying my family, piece by piece. The Wolf is unveiled at last," I concluded, stunned by the shock and anger of it all.

"Yes, boy, yes," he confirmed triumphantly, as though admitting to a victory, rather than a crime. He paused here, absently touching the tip of his blade with his finger. "Now, would you like to know the truth about your wife?" he added, eyes gleaming in delight.

"I should have killed you long ago," Evelyn finally uttered after her lengthy pause. Her countenance filled with anger as she now looked up at one of her foremost advisors. "I should have had you executed, the moment I knew your true nature."

"Ah, but you couldn't, could you? You couldn't disobey your father's orders, nor the wish of King Owain. He was so easy to manipulate," Aldred continued almost amiably. "It was almost too easy. At times I grew rather bored."

"How dare you?" Evelyn challenged with a shout. "How dare you stand there, so without mercy? You are the cause of so many deaths." Her eyes were fixed upon him, rage full in her features. "When I found out what you had done—"

"What, o great queen?" he laughed again. "You did nothing! I almost couldn't believe that the perfect, incorruptible daughter of Reghan could ever have agreed to something so foul and wicked." At this, I stepped forward once more.

"You lie," I declared at once. "You will not speak to your queen that way. My wife does not have a foul bone in her body," I affirmed, but this only made him laugh more. In fact, for a moment, he seemed as though he would dissolve into hysterics.

"Are you sure about that, Your Majesty?" Aldred laughed, but it was hollow as he raised his sword. "No doubt you thought you were done with life-changing secrets," he smirked.

"I thank you for your faith in me, my husband," Evelyn spoke quietly into this pause. At this, I looked at her to see she was finally meeting my gaze. The angriness was still flushed in her cheeks, but there was a glimmer of a smile and her eyes held so much sadness, it took my breath away. It was the pain I had oft seen her wearing when she thought I hadn't noticed. I had assumed her silent agony was due to infertility, but it seemed other issues were indeed at play.

"Your beloved wife knew it was me, all along, you see," Aldred said silkily. I glanced back to him. "Your queen even knew it was I who had murdered your parents. I would have completed my mission in killing you all, had your aunt not screamed," he added menacingly.

The mention of my aunt instantly made the anger and shock in my heart erupt. I charged forwards, with a cry of ire, but the Wolf immediately blocked it. I swung at him again, but he was fast: his blade came to defend him each time. He was strong, but I was quicker: I was beginning to wear him down. A moment later as I leapt out of the way of a blow, I brought my blade upon his arm. As the sharp metal kissed his wrist he groaned and dropped his sword. As my rage reached its climax, I took a step closer to slay him where he stood.

"Wait!" he suddenly shouted, leaping back. I came forwards, unrelenting. "Take one more step and your wife dies," he told me calmly. I halted, just in time to see an archer standing in the hall, an arrow pointed in his bow and aimed directly at Evelyn's heart. It was a soldier who I now realised had been standing at the back of the palace hall this whole time, with their helmet visor down, just as I had done when I had confronted King Reghan. With a heavy heart, I realised I already knew who the masked soldier was.

"Cara, lower your bow," I said wearily. Instead, she lifted her helmet, showing her conflicted gaze. "He is unarmed, Cara," I told her simply. "You are all that stops me from destroying him forever."

"I warned you last night this would happen, my king," my former recruit muttered back brokenly, "but you paid me no heed. You think Aldred has no one else? He will kill half of Rheged if you touch him."

"An empty threat," I said dismissively, but as I took a step towards her, Cara drew back the string of her bow ever tighter. One slip of her finger and the arrow would let fly. "You're an awful shot, Cara," I pointed out. At this the corner of her mouth turned.

"I have had almost a year of practice, my lord," she breathed. "Do you dare risk harm to the one you love?" I hesitated and finally stilled, for I knew I did not. "I'm sorry, sire," she added tensely. I sensed her remorse was genuine, at least in part.

"Well, this has been a most enjoyable afternoon," Aldred smirked in finality. He picked up his sword and sheathed it, in full confidence that I would not move whilst Cara pointed her arrow at my wife. He almost strolled past us. His frivolity was more than I could bear.

"Damn you!" I roared, cursing him as I took a step towards him. Cara pulled the string taut again. I was forced to be still, lest I risked my queen being murdered in front of me.

"I shall see you again, Aldred," was all I could say, as the Wolf opened one of the palace doors. He turned back to me as Cara lowered her helmet once more.

"I look forward to it," he replied brightly. "I bid you both a good day, Your Majesties," he added with a smile. He then left, leaving the palace door abruptly. Cara remained where she was, still aiming at my wife. Then abruptly she lowered her bow, to run out into the square

As soon as her bow was lowered I had raced forward, but as I entered the courtyard, there was no sign either of them. I realised Aldred had planned this well, for all the soldiers currently stood still in the square. Immediately I spotted John, standing at the head of Gaeson's army. In a moment they were about to lead another parade once more about the city. I had to stop them.

"Captain!" I shouted, as I spotted him. John and the soldiers immediately bowed as they saw me. "Did anyone see Aldred leaving the palace?" I asked, my voice shaking with rage. "Did anyone see an archer?"

"Lord Aldred?" John echoed in surprise. "No, Your Majesty." As he answered, I took in the formed lines of the regiment and the crowds watching the parade. I knew it would not be difficult for Aldred to lose himself in these people. As for Cara, with her helmet down, she could be in these lines. Or, by now, either of them could have left the square.

"Is the whole armour of Gaeson here?" I enquired quickly, my head turning back towards John. "Every single soldier?"

"Yes, my lord," John replied, "but what has happened?" he asked in a lower voice, but I could not find the words to tell him. Roughly I wiped my hand with the back of my mouth as I tried to think. "Sire?" John prompted. I became dimly aware that the whole army of Gaeson was watching me.

"Hear me!" I bellowed, as loudly as I could muster. The conversations of the citizens immediately ceased. "Has anyone seen Aldred, the counsellor? Has anyone seen an archer slip past, not in the regiment?" I shouted into the silence. The people looked to each other, confusion and apprehension on many faces, but nobody said a word. I frowned as I watched them all. I knew the Wolf's network was large. How many were working for him? I wondered. What if he had people protecting him, even now?

"Captain," I began quietly, "a word." My brother immediately stepped forwards. "John, Aldred is the Wolf," I whispered to him. Immediately my friend's dark eyes widened. "Not only that, but Cara was with him. She had an arrow pointed at Evelyn, so they could escape." As I spoke my wife's name, my heart plummeted. She had not been surprised. Was the Wolf right? Had she truly known of Aldred's true nature? That Aldred had murdered my kin?

"I understand, sire," John replied, snapping me out of these dark thoughts. "Are either of you hurt?" I shook my head. "What are your orders, my lord?" he whispered.

"Seal the portcullis to secure the kingdom. Have the soldiers search the square," I replied, still looking through the people to see if there was any extraordinary movement. "Take any you deem suspicious into the court. If you do not find Aldred, then you will search every home until he is found. Then," I continued, trying to think, "take those you have arrested to the banquet hall. You and Aife alone will question them. Trust no one," I emphasised, wondering again how deep Evelyn's deception might run.

"At once, Your Majesty," John replied with another bow. Since there was no reason to delay, I gave him a nod and headed straight back into the palace hall, my insides boiling.

Evelyn stood in the middle of the grand chamber. I saw she had retrieved her sword from behind her throne. She seemed to be waiting calmly for my return.

"Aldred has escaped," I informed her. My queen only nodded, seeming once again unsurprised. This made my anger rise up again. "He said you knew he was the Wolf," I said levelly. "Is that why you have been so apprehensive these last days?" I asked her pointedly. Evelyn did not speak for a moment. Her gaze slowly lowered, her shoulders slumped in resignation. "Well? Did you know, wife?" I asked her harshly.

"Yes." My queen's voice was a frail whisper, but I heard it. My insides reached boiling point. In my rage I could not even look at her. I turned to leave the palace hall.

"Daniel, wait," she called, hurrying after me. As I reached the door handle, I felt her hand on my shoulder. Immediately I swung round, so that our faces were inches apart.

"How could you?" I spat, in ire and disbelief. "You knew who he was the whole time and you kept it from me!" I shouted. I never would have believed I could be so furious with her. Currently, my regard for her was something akin to hatred. It continued to rise, threatening to consume my soul. "Why, Evelyn?" I roared ere long.

"Because it was my father's last command," she murmured brokenly. "King Owain ordered it, also," she added, her voice stronger. "Come with me to the library. I will show you."

"What? Go with you?" I echoed, laughing bitterly at the idea of trusting her. Then I stopped, reflecting with fresh horror at how similar I sounded to Aldred.

"Please," Evelyn implored, our eyes locking. It felt as though the entirety of our marriage hung in the balance of this moment. "Allow me this chance to explain my actions."

"Very well," I replied eventually. She looked a little relieved. "Lead on, wife of mine," I snarled, my voice rife with sarcasm. She flinched, but a moment later nodded. We walked outside. How different all seemed, to when we had last walked into the palace, but a few minutes ago! I perceived the soldiers were busy searching through the crowds. The sun was set low by now, gleaming gold onto the stone square. It would soon be dusk, but I barely noticed it.

Which members of my army could be traitors? I wondered, as John walked over to us. Which members of my people? Then, with some surprise at my dull, cold heart, I realised I hardly cared. Evelyn had already betrayed me, the most cruelly of all. It hardly mattered if those lesser known to me had done the same.

"Your Majesties," my captain greeted. "We have not found Aldred yet. It is possible he has escaped the courtyard," he explained. "The portcullis has been sealed," he reported in addition. Then quickly he glanced between us. I could tell my friend who knew me so well had probably perceived something else was terribly wrong. "Have you any further orders, sire?"

"No," I replied. "Queen Evelyn and I are going to the library," I told him. If my brother was confused by my latest statement, he did not show it, he only inclined his head in assent.

"John, I have another order." I frowned as Evelyn came to stand next to John, beginning to whisper in his ear. My friend frowned but said nothing, only nodding rapidly as his face grew more intense.

"I understand, my lady," John said eventually. His tone was quiet and even, but I sensed some anger underneath. "It will be done right away." He bowed again and left us.

"I'll explain that later," Evelyn added, looking around us. I supposed she was worried we might be overheard. "For now, the library." With that, she turned in its direction. Mostly because of my own curiosity, I followed her, despite her treachery.

It seemed the longest walk through the castle to the library, but I was glad of this, for it gave me time to digest the horrifying news about Aldred.

My advisor and friend was the Wolf. He had been the orchestrator of so many atrocities, including—I thought of my parents then and it was as if someone had stabbed me with a knife. I pictured Aldred again now, his younger features coming back to me. With a sick horror I recalled the words, spoken to me so friendlily when we had been formally introduced.

"Yes, Your Highness has a good memory," Aldred had said amiably. *"I did once briefly know your father while I was serving under King Reghan. I even met your mother once, but our meeting lasted only moments. I came to the house when you were a child".*

I stopped in the corridor, the palm of my right hand jerking out to lean against the stone wall beside me. With a staggering shock, I understood the real truth of his speech. At the time, I had simply assumed he had been speaking of my father who had raised me, but now I knew the real meaning. He had been speaking of his acquaintance with my parents in Klumeck. Their meeting had been brief, because he had murdered them where they slept.

"Daniel?" My wife's voice, as warm and concerned as it had always been, reached my ears. I jerked my head up to her, the terrible mixture of shock, anger, disbelief and heartache fixed entirely towards her. My queen, my wife, my love—my betrayer. Evelyn stood back and straightened, her expression unreadable.

"We are nearly there," was all my queen said, a little needlessly. She began walking again and as I followed numbly, I felt as though my legs had turned to lead. A minute or two later, we entered the library.

"Why are we here?" I asked roughly. Evelyn did not answer me. Instead she crossed the room, opened a drawer in a desk and retrieved a key from inside a book. I watched, frowning, as next she walked down an aisle of bookshelves and came to a cupboard at the other end. The key unlocked it and my wife pulled out a second book from within. She walked back to me as she turned its pages, presently pulling out what looked to be a letter and holding it out.

"What is in it, Evelyn?" I asked her quietly, making no move to take it. When she did not immediately reply, rage further consumed me as I grabbed her arm. Evelyn did not move, only stared back at me. "What is that letter's contents, that it could justify this evil?"

"Not justify," Evelyn returned swiftly. "Only to perhaps explain." Her eyes still bored into mine. True sadness was clear in her tone, but was this a lie also?

"What is in here could never atone for the wrong I have done you." My wife spoke low and brokenly, bitterness rife in her tone. "My only prayer is that by the time you have finished this account, you will understand a little better. Please..." she whispered.

"I..." I began, but I wasn't sure at all what to say, so my speech died in mid-air. My hand was still on her arm. Evelyn pushed the letter, so it just touched my free hand.

"I am so sorry, Daniel," she told me quietly. As soon as my fingers had taken the small bit of parchment, her hand moved to rest on top of my knuckles. "I want you to know, husband, my action is something I will always regret and be ashamed of." She spoke rapidly, her tone barely louder than a whisper. All the while she talked, our gazes were still joined.

"Also," she murmured, pausing, "I want you to know that I love you with all that I am." At this declaration, a single tear journeyed down her cheek. "You may not believe it, but this is the truth." Another tear fell, as suddenly she stepped back, breaking the spell between us. "I will go now to our chamber," she told me, a finality in her voice. "I will be waiting for you there, whenever you are ready."

Before I could say another word, my wife turned to leave the library, thus departing my company. I stood there, my eyes following her, my ears hearing her footsteps until she closed the library door quietly behind her, leaving only silence in her wake. I was left quite alone, with only the recent revelations for company. My right hand still clutched the letter my queen had given me, which I wanted to read and burn simultaneously.

I sat down at one of the tables, thrusting the foul document out of reach. I knew I could not read it yet, for my emotions were far too high. Indeed, the knowledge I had just come face to face with the Wolf, the assassin who had for so long tormented me, made me want to vomit. I swallowed the urge back down, but I was unable to choke back the angry hot tears, at last coming forth to spill down my cheeks.

It was here my rage exploded. Before I knew what I was doing, I stood up, picked up my chair and thrashed it against a bookshelf. The wooden chair broke and volumes fell to the floor, but I cared not. I thrashed the chair against the shelves again and again, cursing and shouting aloud. I did this until the waves of my emotions crested and my fresh anger began to dissipate. Ere long I slid down to sit on the floor, books splayed all around me. My ire had left the table untouched, however, where the document that would incriminate my wife remained unspoilt.

"Your Majesty!" John called as he abruptly entered the library, followed by two other soldiers. Their swords were all drawn: no doubt they thought there was an intruder here.

"You two, go and stand guard outside," my captain ordered his men. I was thankful for my brother's tact. Though most of my weeping had been done, thankfully, as I had poured out my rage on the library, the traces of my tears were probably still visible.

"Are you injured, my lord?" John enquired, sheathing his blade as he looked around. He glanced my way as I shook my head. "Where is the queen, sire? Is she safe?" In my anger I only snorted in derision. Then, I was again shocked at how much my scorn sounded like Aldred.

"Queen Evelyn is perfectly well," I said mechanically, after rubbing my face wearily. "She is in our chamber," I expanded. At this, John went to open the library door again. I heard him order the two soldiers to go at once and stand outside my chamber door.

"Report, John," I instructed with a sigh, as my friend came back into the room. He crossed the library slowly, taking care not to tread on the books. "Have you found Aldred?"

"No, my lord," John admitted wearily. I nodded inanely, for I had fully expected this. "We have soldiers positioned at all of the walls and we are going to every house in search of him," he added.

"He has probably already escaped," I reflected, sighing again. "He timed it perfectly, so he could hide amongst the crowd. No doubt Cara is with him. Half the army could be working for him." I knew I sounded despondent, for the height of my emotions had been replaced with pure weariness. I looked about the library, seeing the books strewn about the floor. Then, I caught sight of a window in the corner and wished I hadn't. Though the window was shut, I knew instantly it was the one that had the view of the stables. It was the one I had helped Evelyn climb through, when we were children.

The image, unbidden, came into my mind now, of Evelyn's dainty foot stepping into my hands as I lifted her up. The girl I would later vow to always love and protect. Was such a vow still even possible? This childhood memory of Evelyn had been one of my most precious, but the recalling it now repulsed me. I closed my eyes to try to shake the image away.

"Sire—Daniel," John said, gently. I opened my eyes, to see he had walked over to join me. He came to sit beside me but said nothing. I knew in his silence was deep compassion. I knew he understood full well, for I had told him Bredon's last words just after he had died. He knew the Wolf was also my parents' assassin.

"I'm so sorry, brother," he murmured ere long. I nodded mutely. He reached out then, placing a hand on my shoulder. I found his gesture a little comforting. "We will keep searching, Daniel," he told me earnestly. "We will find him." At this, a sardonic smile turned my mouth.

"I am not so sure," I returned. "He has operated in such stealth over this past year. You can keep up the search, but he has probably already gone," I murmured. My gaze now travelled to the letter on the table and the poison that was surely contained within.

"What was the command Evelyn gave you?" I asked John presently, remembering how she had spoken with him earnestly outside. Besides, I longed to distract myself, if only for a moment, from the scroll on that table and the secrets within. John dropped his hand at my speech, perhaps noting some formality in it. I found I missed my brother's comfort.

"Her Majesty ordered me to arrest several men we have been watching, my lord," John answered. I frowned as I glanced at him. "I thought you knew about it. The queen said they were part of the Wolf's network. I have arrested them and taken them to the banquet hall, as you ordered earlier, my lord."

"No, I did not know about it," I muttered ere long. "Leave me a while, John," I sighed. "I've some reading to do," was all I said. John frowned, following my gaze to the letter.

"Very well, sire," was all he said, standing again and bending his head in a quick bow. He then made his way to the library door but turned back to me as he neared it. "Aife and I are here for you, brother," was all he said, before I was alone once more.

With my heart now feeling like lead as well as my legs, I slowly lifted myself up, coming to sit at one of the other chairs at the table. I took the letter in my hands, abruptly regretting strongly that I had ever learnt to read. Many of our people, including the soldiers, were illiterate, but my father had also trained as a physician, after a few years of being a soldier. He had therefore learned this skill and taught it to me when I had been small. Now I almost wished he hadn't, for I yearned not to have the deceit of my wife revealed to me. It was no good, however, for the moment of inevitability had come and read it I must. With a resigned sigh, I began my weary task.

My dearest Evelyn,

If you are reading this, then no doubt I am already dead. King Urien will have decreed to have me executed and for that I cannot blame him. You know well enough what a fool I have been. In this letter I hope to disclose the truth, that will not atone for my sins but, perhaps, will lead to better understanding of my actions.

As I sit in this dank cell, I can see how much power has corrupted me. Daniel would have been well within his rights to kill me fully. It was only the thought of the pain it would cause you that stopped him. I believe he truly does love you. Now you know he is the Prince of Klumeck, he would make an eligible match.

I looked up from the letter. From the context, I could place the letter to be some time after the day I had nearly killed him in his cell, where he awaited his fate. Alas, out of curiosity, I read on.

My love, there is someone in my inner circle who I know now has always deceived me. It was on his counsel that I waged war against King Cedric, ordering the assassination of most of his kin. It is the assassin himself who I mistrusted. As he was a foremost soldier in my army, I ordered him to execute these commands himself.

This Bernician spy is Aldred, one of my foremost advisors, whom you have met several times. The chief interrogator told me all of this tauntingly in my dungeon cell. I have suspected Aldred is not my most faithful servant before now, but I had no idea his treachery ran this deep. The interrogator, that weasel of a man, said he wanted to reveal Aldred to me (the interrogator called him 'the Wolf') before I went to my grave. Ah, to think my foremost advisor is really my greatest foe. Aldred's exterior has been so flattering, so amiable, that he was able to delude me quite easily.

What the interrogator did not know was that I convinced another prison guard to permit me to write this note to you, for I knew not if we should ever meet again, my darling. Even if such a meeting were possible, I do not know if you would wish it, in light of my recent actions. Aye, the Wolf long tormented and used me, poisoning me by sowing distrustful seeds regarding King Urien who, so Aldred said, wished to wage war against me.

It was twenty-one years ago that the Wolf also told me King Cedric sought to overthrow me. Aldred convinced me the only way to defend Gaeson against his hands was to strike him first and kill his heirs, thus leaving the kingdom in ruins. In my folly and pride, I listened and sent Aldred off to do the evil deed.

I paused here again, for my hands were shaking with renewed rage. Evelyn had recently admitted she knew Aldred was the Wolf, but I was now realising she had known Aldred was the assassin of my kin. How much of our marriage had she known that the enemy who killed her husband's family was her advisor? How long had she seen him in the council chambers and done nothing?

I recalled Evelyn's anxiety of late, her strange manners of being withdrawn and distracted, then abruptly declaring affection with an urgency I had not been able to fathom. Was this why? I wondered, a deep frown creasing my features. Had she known the Wolf would reveal himself this day? Why had my wife, who claimed to love me with all that she was, kept such deception? Why had she entertained such a monster in her courts? Desperate for answers, I read on.

I write this to warn you, my daughter, because I now believe there is a plot to kill you. I will try to stop this myself if I have the opportunity but if I die first, then be on your guard. Aldred is following the orders of the Bernicians and the destruction of Gaeson would be for their gain. You must protect your kingdom at all costs. This I know you will do, for you have already done the hardest thing by taking my throne from me. I am sorry you were forced to resort to such actions. Now that it is done, however, you must continue to make hard choices for the sake of your people and Rheged itself. If you do not, all of Gaeson might be lost.

Here, then, is my last command: you must never tell Daniel the things of which I have just informed you. This will be even more difficult if you do marry him, but Aldred has no awareness that I know the truth. He must remain in your inner sanctum, for then you can feed him false information and seriously wound the Bernician campaign. His true character is arrogant, so it has not been impossible to get information from him. In doing so, I was able to foil a few of his schemes without him realising.

These orders are not just from me but come from King Urien himself. You can verify it with him. There are larger matters at work here than you, or me, or Daniel. The interrogator informed me that if Aldred is ever discovered, he is sure to unleash a far greater evil. He has a whole network of spies, enough to kill over half of our citizens. I also sincerely believe that Aldred's first action would be to complete the mission he began long ago and kill Daniel and his sister, as well as you. For the sake of their survival, my dear, you must keep your silence.

So, keep this secret, my love, I beg you. You must do this, for the good of all of Rheged and for the man whom I suspect you have come to love. Otherwise, you could doom everything we cherish. I shall end this letter to you now, for I do not have much time left. I am sincerely sorry to you and to Daniel, for all the harm I did you. I pray in this, some good will come out of evil. Rule with wisdom and put your trust in God, as I should have done long ago.

With fondest love,

Your father, Reghan.

I would never know how long I sat there on the table after finishing the letter, trying to digest what I had read. I was yet again incensed, for the former king had made himself appear so noble. He had admitted his guilt, aye, but it was confessed with an air of an innocent caught in a villain's schemes, when I knew how much blood his corruption had spilled.

When had Evelyn read this letter? This, again, was the most pressing enquiry. Had she known before we were even wed? Was it before or after we made our vows of faithfulness to one another that she had betrayed me so? My ire swelled further, considering how long I had spent in the palace alongside the Wolf. I had counted him as my friend, who had once saved Evelyn by foiling the plot to kill her, but that had been just another of his schemes.

Long had I suspected Melvyn to be the Wolf, who at the time of revelation had attempted so desperately to blend into the palace walls to avoid harm. No, it was Aldred who was this monster, who had crushed the life from my mother and my father, my aunt and the child that dwelt within her. He then had struck again in recent weeks, orchestrating my uncle's death.

Dimly, I became aware that I was crumpling the letter in my hand. As calmly as I could, I smoothed out the pages, carefully folded them and placed them within my clothes. I stood to depart the library then, uncaring about the scattered books and the broken chairs. I knew I only needed to speak with my wife. Whatever the consequences were, I needed the truth of her involvement. I needed to know how wet her hands were with the blood the Wolf had shed, not just of my family but countless others. With a heavy heart, I walked sombrely through the castle to my chambers where I would confront my queen, the woman I loved.

Chapter Eleven

As I reached the corridor of my chambers, I saw the two guards standing guard John had sent from the library. I dismissed them, for Aldred's damage was done and I assumed he was long gone from Gaeson. Besides, I suspected I would soon be shouting and I did not want anything to be overheard. As soon as I could no longer hear their footsteps, I thrust the door open.

Evelyn sat next to the fireplace, shawl around her shoulders, clearly waiting for me to return. Her countenance was carefully impassive, just like when she had waited for me in the palace hall. I banged the door shut loudly behind me.

"When did you first read this?" I asked her instantly, waving the letter. Evelyn looked up at me but did not answer. "How long have you known?" I prompted hotly.

"I first read it—" Evelyn began, then sighed resignedly. It was evident this was a question she had both anticipated and dreaded to answer. "I found it just after our engagement, before we left for Caer Ligualid, for King Owain's coronation," she now explained. My eyes had widened in horror. "I was searching through his things and I came across the letter in the book he always read to me as a child. When I saw it, I hid it, then—"

"Then you took it to Caer Ligualid, didn't you?" I challenged, guessing the ending of her speech. "Your father cited King Urien in his account. Of course, the great king was dead by then," I added, folding my arms. "You assumed King Owain would know."

"Aye, that was the logic of things," Evelyn replied quietly. "King Urien had told King Owain, shortly before that final battle. Maybe King Urien believed his days would be ending soon. King Owain confirmed the order to keep the contents a secret from you," Evelyn confirmed. "He too believed Aldred had a plan to destroy all of Rheged, should he be discovered. King Owain believed that as long as the Wolf remained in position, Gaeson and Rheged itself would be saved."

"An order you obeyed," I emphasised. My tone was quiet yet shook with disbelief and ire. "An order to keep the spy who murdered half my family close within your ranks, from before we were even married. A command not to tell me any of this." I crossed the chamber to the closed window, wanting space from her. Then I rounded back to her, glaring.

"So, you are your father's daughter after all," I said coldly. I saw her flinch in consequence of my speech, witnessed hurt take form in her features.

"Tell me you do not mean that," my wife implored. I said nothing further for a moment. I simply surveyed her with my arms still folded, regarding her conflicting emotions that seemed to mirror the battles of my own heart. How very far I was, I reflected, from the soldier who would have never imagined speaking to her in that way, but that was long before such rage filled my heart. How much had I really known her when we married, I wondered, that she could hide such deceit so easily?

"Our motives were different," Evelyn presently remarked. "My father deceived you for his own glory, selfish gain and corruption of power. I did it because King Owain ordered me—"

"Oh, well then!" I interrupted with a shout. "Obviously it was impossible for you to consider disobeying him! Have you forgotten I once had an order from King Urien, that I knew was wrong?" I challenged loudly. "He ordered me to ride with him against Gaeson, against you and your father," I pointed out. I tried lowering my voice to a more normal tone, but still it shook. "I disobeyed the uncle I had just discovered and risked the wrath of King Urien to come back to warn you. I endured torture, everyone regarding me as a traitor. All shunned me, including Bredon, my closest friends... you, whom I had loved from afar," I concluded, sadness suddenly winning in my tone. "All this, I did, disobeying orders."

"You did that to protect me and the rest of Gaeson," Evelyn returned, just as sadly. "I was trying to protect you, husband, and my people," she informed me, as if to remind me. "I believe, as King Owain does, that Aldred's first move would have been to kill you and Sarah. Then, he would have unleashed an evil scheme across Gaeson and Rheged herself."

"What evidence have you of such a plan?" I retorted hotly. "Your father said nothing to detail such a plot in his letter. I doubt King Owain gave such details, either, when you met with him. This very day when the Wolf is at last revealed, I do not see Gaeson falling around us, nor my life threatened," I ended dismissively.

"There were twenty men and women we were keeping watch over, whom we had seen talk with Aldred," Evelyn now declared. I straightened, lowering my arms as my eyes widened in further shock. "That's what my orders were to John earlier, to arrest them before any evil plot came to fruition. If I had told you of the Wolf's identity, he could have attempted further harm." My queen spoke with certainty, her eyes begging me to believe her.

"You do not know how many times I had longed to tell you, but I was afraid what Aldred would do," Evelyn emphasised now. "All these days I have been a queen I have lived in terror of that man! I have been trapped, but for the sake you and of Rheged—"

"Oh, of course, what a victim you are!" I snapped, then I saw her flinch again. "How noble and sacrificial, just like your father sounded in his letter," I continued, seething.

"What if I had told you, then?" Her own voice increased as she spoke. "What if I had told you and many in Gaeson, even those in Rheged had died? That was what I have been living in fear of, Daniel! He said if he was unveiled, he would kill you and countless others!"

"These are just excuses," I muttered, shaking my head to her last shouted speech. Deep down, I knew there would be truth to these fears, but I was far from ready to be reasonable. "You knew the man who murdered my parents, Evelyn," I reiterated hoarsely, as the whole full horror of her deception hit me again. "The whole time we have been wed. How could you?"

As I roared out this last bit of speech, my hand lashed through the air, punching the wooden door of the window. Immediately I felt my skin break, feeling blood beginning to run. Evelyn stood from her chair, starting towards me as if about to tend it.

"Leave it," I snapped, hardly able to register the cruelty in my voice. How could I be talking to her like this, this beautiful woman who was my wife? This queen, whom so long ago in the cold of the snow, I had promised to love. I felt my anger turning to inexorable sadness.

"So, this is who you really are," I murmured sadly. Evelyn's countenance looked as though her own heart was breaking too, but how could I trust it?

"You know I had to do it," she emphasised presently. Her tone conveyed both strength and brokenness simultaneously. "You always viewed me so highly," she resumed, her voice suddenly sounding so tender. "Almost as though I had no faults, that I could do no wrong."

"Are you saying I am to blame for this, because of my affection for you?" I challenged immediately, biting back at her despite her gentle tone. "Of course, I viewed you highly!" I shouted, enraged. "I loved you!"

Evelyn took a step back at this, her eyes widening in horror. I frowned, confused at her reaction, but then shock rippled through me, also, as I understood. For when had I began to speak of my love for her in the past tense?

Abruptly, I turned from her gaze to open the window, ignoring the splintered wood. A fresh cold breeze blew in, in contrast to the summer haze of the day. The chill in the evenings was growing, telling me the peak of the hot season had passed. It would not be too long before autumn was here. I sighed, unsure of why I was thinking so much upon the weather. Perhaps I was simply trying to distract myself from the horrors of this afternoon.

"Your hand is still bleeding," Evelyn said, breaking the silence. I turned back to her but said nothing in reply. I watched as she retrieved a piece of cloth and walked over to me. There was still some semblance of my soul that longed for her comfort, so I let her come close. I felt her gentle fingers on my skin as she wound the bandage round my cuts. "The last time it was anything like this was that day in the stables," Evelyn commented quietly, "when you had nearly killed my father after he was imprisoned."

"I remember," I replied quickly, an edge to my voice still. Did she think I would have forgotten? Then, I nodded. "That was the first time I ever thought my love for you could be complicated," I mused, presently passionless. Abruptly my emotions had dissipated, leaving me empty and drained. "Your father had risen up between us like a poison," I said. "For a moment I thought it could taint my regard for you forever."

"So, here we are again," my wife concluded sadly as she stepped back from me. She lowered her arms from my bandaged hand to rest listlessly at her sides. As well as sad, she sounded as drained, as hollow as I had done. I gave no further remark and the two of us stood together; my queen standing before me whilst I leaned against the window sill. Night was falling fast, with cool night air wafting on the back of my neck. For the longest time we remained thus positioned, with the only noise the quiet whistle of the breeze.

"Sometimes, I wonder whether it would have been better to not find out who I was," I admitted ere long. "Sometimes, I wonder whether it would have been better for me to have died when I fell from that cliff." As I spoke these words I despised myself, for I sounded so self-pitying. In truth, I had never felt weaker.

"Please, do not say that," Evelyn pleaded immediately. The sadness was strong in her eyes once again. "Think of all the happiness your uncle knew since he found you," she murmured. I felt a small stab of grief at the mention of his name. "Think of the joy you have known, since you discovered you were linked with Sarah by blood. As well as that..." Evelyn faltered. My gaze had lowered to the floor whilst she spoke, but now it rose up to her again. I thought I could guess her next speech and I was almost daring her to say it.

"It was when you came back from Caer Ligualid, when I saw you alive," she muttered, her eyes flickering over my face, "that's when I first realised—that's when I first began to love you," she ended.

"Indeed," I replied, my idea of her speech confirmed. "At least, that's what you told me, that day in the palace gardens when I asked for your hand in marriage." I heard the slight raising in my voice, the accusation of my tone. How cruel, how without feeling I sounded! A memory of our engagement swept through me, but it brought me no joy. Instead, all I felt was bitterness. "For if you lied about Aldred, what else have you lied about?" I challenged. "How do I know I can trust a single day in our marriage?" I ended scornfully.

"How can you say such things?" Evelyn returned harshly. It was her turn to express disbelief as she stepped back, shaking her head. "What about these last two years, Daniel?" she enquired intensely. "What about all the joy and heartache we have shared? Was that a lie also?" At the end of her sharp speech, she abruptly turned to sit down again.

"Shut the window, please," my wife instructed then, as she pulled her shawl about her. I hesitated a moment, before I reached out to pull the splintered frame closed again.

"You ask me how I can say those words, when such evidence is before me?" I posed quietly. "What has caused me to doubt, I wonder?" I too then shook my head in incredulity. "I thought the time for questioning the reality of things had gone," I murmured.

Evelyn did not reply to this. With a resigned sigh, I went to the table on the other side of our chamber to pour us both a generous measure of mead into the goblets. I crossed the room to hand her one, before promptly returning to the windowsill. I raised the goblet to my mouth, taking a long drink. She too brought the goblet to her own lips, but only had a small mouthful.

"Come, Daniel," she said after a moment, in the same quiet tone and then she paused. Again, I was surprised at her gentleness, especially after I had used such cruel words. Or was she simply trying to deceive me further?

"You know how much I love you," she declared, once again standing from her chair. "You know me better than any other," she murmured, crossing the chamber to me. "Anything else is surely folly." I understood then why she had spoken so gently, for had she spoken with anything else, I would have erupted in anger. However, this was almost impossible whilst her speech was kind. I took the time to taste the wine again, wondering if she could be trying to manipulate me this very moment.

"Is it, on the basis of the facts?" I questioned , lowering the goblet from my mouth. I knew I was saying more than I could ever retrieve, but still I went on. "Your father was so skilled in deceit and for the longest time I never knew any of his evil. I nearly gave my life for him, several times. I would have been glad to die in the service of my king," I pointed out, bitterly.

"Then, today, I learned the truth," I almost spat, roughly wiping my mouth with the back of my hand. "Then it was discovered that his daughter seems to have the same deceit running through her veins," I declared harshly. I saw objections rise to my wife's lips and then die there, for after everything that had transpired, how could my statement be inaccurate?

"I believed passionately that nothing of his foul character resided in you, that you were nothing like him." I went on. The wine seemed to have revitalised my anger and bitterness, the hollow feeling again disappearing. Still, my queen remained silent against my tirade.

"Do you remember why I almost killed your father?" I asked, my voice growing louder again. "Why I nearly slayed him where he stood, in chains as he was?" I pressed for an answer. Evelyn merely nodded. "He told me you were not so different from him," I resumed, though I knew she would not have forgotten. "That was what made my blood boil, wife," I told her quietly. "However, maybe he was right all along," I concluded, promptly draining my goblet.

"Aye, maybe," Evelyn murmured, her voice almost a whisper. "For I believe you speak wrongly about human nature, Daniel," she commented, folding her arms. "None of us are without evil," she continued, her gaze lifting to meet mine. "You yourself have just admitted to almost killing my father, when he was an unarmed prisoner in chains, unable to defend himself," she pointed out.

"He killed your kin, I know," she added rapidly, accurately guessing the objection that sprang to my lips. "I know you were also thinking of my honour," she went on. "This would not have cleaned the blood from your hands, however. I would have had every right to behead you," she concluded. Her countenance was sombre, but then she smiled wryly.

"For a time, I almost thought you might have," I murmured ere long. Her smile flickered a fraction wider. I felt the smallest tug of my own mouth in turn. There was a companionable silence between us then, so that for a moment, I could almost believe all would be well between us. But then the pain of her betrayal hit me again: it was as if someone had twisted a knife in my gut. Evelyn must have perceived this, for the slight humour in her countenance was replaced with sorrow.

"Are you really doubting everything?" My wife whispered, turning her goblet of wine around in her hands as she stood by our wardrobe, only a few feet away. "Can you really question each smile, each tear we have shared in our marriage?" she enquired painfully. The meaning of her speech

230

was clear: it had only been a month since the grief we had shared together. I could see the pain of it on her features. My queen took the final few steps towards me whilst I stood still, unmoving. I felt as though my heart was as hard as stone.

"Can you not trust this, my love?" my wife whispered, her body inches from mine. Before I could say anything else, she leant forward. Our mouths met fiercely, desperately. Underneath the wine was the familiar taste of her lips. Instinctively I then deepened the kiss, my arms snaking around her hungrily. But then, the knife twisted in my gut again. I pulled myself roughly away from her.

Was that not real, husband?" Evelyn implored, her eyes searching mine. In her gaze, I imagined I could see her heart breaking again.

"I do not know how I can trust you," I muttered back, my soul seeming broken also. "Do you not remember what I said to you, the day my uncle died? I asked you whether you knew anything about the Wolf," I pointed out. "You told me you knew nothing. You lied, so convincingly," I emphasised.

"I had to," she answered bitterly, her eyes lowering from mine. "Aldred had threatened to kill you and half of Gaeson. I could not bear to risk it," she pleaded sadly. "I know I have done wrong and I am sorry for it," I declared passionately, "but that does not mean there is no longer any truth in anything else." I said nothing to this and she sighed resignedly. "What do I have to do so that you believe me?" she murmured.

"I know not," I returned at last. With that, abruptly I moved away from her, running my hands through my russet hair. "I need some air," I informed her curtly, making to leave.

"Daniel," Evelyn implored, but I ignored this plea as I opened the door quickly. "Please…" she murmured. This time I turned back to her.

"There's something you've forgotten," I told my wife quietly. "I'm not the only one you have deceived. I have to tell Sarah the truth about this, too."

"Daniel, wait!" I just glimpsed the expression of pain upon her features before I closed the door, with my name still hanging in the air and with the taste of her lips, intermingled with wine, still to my mouth. I wiped my mouth again with my hand, feeling every quick footstep that took me further away.

I kept walking, hardly aware of my surroundings. I forgot all sense of time as I wandered about in circles about the castle, walking through corridor after corridor. Eventually, I recognised where I was going, as almost mechanically I came to Leigh's chamber. It was as though my footsteps had led me to the surgery, rather than my brain, similarly to when Evelyn had told me that she would be unlikely to bear a child. I resolutely pushed this memory away as it came to my mind, for even this shared pain was tainted by her betrayal. I sighed in frustration. Could I ever truly trust my wife again?

My conversation with Leigh was brief: he confirmed Ewan was recovering well. The other soldier was still alive but had sunk into the deep slumber of the wounded. The physician was unsure, at this point, whether he would wake again. I then left the surgery, continuing my aimless wanderings through the castle. My heavy limbs travelled up, rather than down, so that I emerged onto one of the higher ramparts of the castle.

As I stepped out into the night air, I realised I had come to the balcony where I had conversed with Captain Bredon, over two years ago. That evening, I had first learned King Cedric believed his heirs were still alive and that was why he waged war against us. It was also that night when Evelyn had been listening from the shadows, long before she had taken the throne from her father. I had not seen her since that day in the snow as children and though as an adult I looked familiar to her, she had not recognised me.

I cursed under my breath, that my unconscious mind had brought me here, where I could be reminded of her once again. Instead, I glanced up to the heavens. The sky that night had been full of stars, but now the canvas above me was covered in thick cloud, so that I could barely see in front of my face. The only light was from the nearest torch, flickering dimly in the distance.

The memory again surged through me of my first meeting with Evelyn, despite me trying to fight it. Almost before I realised it, I slipped a hand inside my tunic, retrieving the cloth Evelyn had given me as children. I still carried it with me everywhere and I turned the cloth over in my hands. I did not look at it, but my thumb moved familiarly over the pattern of lace, faintly tracing the seal of her name woven into the silky material.

This simple cloth had always been my treasured possession. It had often given me comfort over the years, for it reminded me of my vow to Evelyn and gave me motivation to continue fighting. Tonight, though, I found it offered no such consolation. Indeed, as the wind picked up again, I marvelled at how easy it would be to let this keepsake slip from my hands and be lost forever. It was only some sentiment, some desire deep within me to salvage my marriage that I folded it and stuffed it back into my inside pocket.

The chilly wind was helping to clear my head. For the first time I thought of God, but my emotions were so raw and the pain so deep in my chest that I felt hardly able to pray. Instead I simply groaned aloud, knowing that the one who made the stars, concealed as they were this night, would hear this unintelligible outpouring of my soul. I wished my thoughts would defog further, for I was already regretting the amount of wine consumed. It had seemed the best tonic at the time, but I saw now all it had done was exacerbate my emotions, the last thing I needed.

I realised anew it was also a mistake to have come out here, for exactly the same reason, for the memory of the night was still sweeping through me. In my mind's eye I saw Captain Bredon on the stone floor of the courtyard, covered in his own blood. I saw myself obey my master's order to take the woman I loved to Caer Ligualid. My mind relived the scene of fleeing with Evelyn to the forest, remembering again the talk we'd had in the woodland, where she had recognised me.

Presently, I bent my head against the wind. What would have happened, I wondered, had that secret Bernician force not breached the castle walls? I knew now the Wolf had been behind that, too—Aldred had been behind all of it. Would King Reghan still be on the throne, if I had not been recovered by my uncle and discovered the truth? Would I still be a soldier, content in my ignorance? Would Gaeson still be the same?

I knew if I had survived but not discovered my true identity, I would have remained as a soldier, loving Evelyn from afar. I would have continued in Reghan's service, completely unaware that he had ordered the deaths of my parents. I sighed aloud here, for it was with much tragic irony that the women I loved most in all the world was the daughter of such a man. I had ever clung to the belief that she was nothing like him, but as I had recently accused her, perhaps she was akin to his character after all.

Evelyn's actions had caused me to doubt the very heart of her. In truth, it was as if the very foundations of Gaeson's castle were shifting beneath my feet. As I had said to her, I had hoped the time for questioning the truth of things had passed, but this seemed all the crueller. Rather than questioning my own identity, I was forced to question hers. During those dark, uncertain days when I learnt of my true parentage, it was Evelyn who had remained steadfast. Now, however, with the scent of her lingering despite this cold, cloudy night, I feared I did not truly know her at all. Evelyn had strongly protested it would be absurd to question the whole of our marriage, but was it? Could I ever trust her again?

Fresh despair came upon me keenly, intermingling with remnants of sadness stemming from previous griefs. I thought of my uncle, who had died never knowing who the Wolf was. He had never known, either, that Evelyn had known Aldred's true identity. For the first time, part of me was glad he was dead, that he could be spared this agony.

Presently I lifted my head, quietly yielding my tears to the night. The roar of the wind cooled the tears and calmed my cheeks, no doubt turned ruddy from the wine and my anger. Here I did a quick survey of my heart, but my soul confirmed what I already knew: I loved her just as much as ever, even if it was pure folly. As I pondered this, I sensed the movements of another.

"What time is it, John?" I asked, already sensing who had come to join me on the balcony. I heard him come to a stop beside me.

"Two hours or so before midnight, my lord," John replied. I frowned: I must have been wandering around the castle far longer than I thought. "I'm sorry, sire," my brother said now. "I regret to report that Aldred and Cara seem to have escaped."

"It is no matter," I answered heavily. "It is as we already suspected." I rubbed my hands over my eyes, hoping to erase the signs of my weeping. "I suggest we go to your chambers," I informed him now, knowing I needed the company of my friends. "Bring Aife, also. I need your counsel," I concluded.

"I'm sure that can be arranged," he replied dryly. I was pleased he had dropped my titles. It would be good to speak to my brother and sister frankly again, away from all the pomp.

A few minutes later I was seated rather comfortably in a chair in John's main living chambers and accepting yet another goblet of wine from Aife. Was it my third, or my fourth? I could not recall. I had regretted drinking too much earlier, but the night had cleared my head too much for my liking and the tonic still seemed the best remedy for my warring heart. Thus convinced, I tilted the cup to my mouth, taking a swift gulp. John poured a goblet for himself and Aife before sitting down opposite.

"It seems a foolish question to ask how you are faring," John commented, as he took a sip of his own drink. I agreed to this with a simple nod.

"There's something else you don't know," I said eventually. Neither of them spoke, simply waiting. I knew I did not have to say any more than I wished.

"Evelyn knew," I disclosed flatly. "She knew all along that Aldred was the Wolf and the assassin that murdered most of my family."

"What?" John asked loudly, whilst Aife stared in shock. "How can this be true?" he challenged. I left his question hanging in the air a moment, taking in their horrified expressions. I was surprised at how satisfied I felt, that they saw our queen's actions as equally despicable. Somehow there was a justice in it.

"What happened, Daniel?" Aife then prompted quietly. Though I was still in great disbelief at many of the details, I took a deep breath and began to relate to them all that had happened this awful day.

By the time I had finished the account, a silence fell between us. In the interim, I poured myself yet another measure of the warming, deep red tonic and took a long drink. By now, any remnant of sobriety that had resurfaced outside had disappeared.

"I see," Aife said levelly, though from her countenance she didn't seem too certain. Indeed, I would have been impressed at her surety, for I could hardly understand it myself. "So, the queen's reason for not telling you," Aife reiterated slowly, "was that she believed Aldred would cause much damage to Gaeson and kill many citizens?"

"Aye, that is her defence," I answered, drained. "Evelyn was also convinced Aldred would kill Sarah and me if he discovered I knew the truth. She was also given this command by King Owain, when she spoke to him before his coronation to confirm her father's account," I concluded. I was lazily swirling round the small amount of wine in my goblet as I spoke.

"Her Majesty would have been in a very difficult position," John reflected now. My head jerked up at once to him. Surely, my friend was not taking her position? "I do not mean she is cleared of blame," he added quickly, seeing the sharp change in my temperament. "Only that it was an impossible situation."

"Was it?" I retorted sharply, before taking another glug of the wine. "She should have told me, John. I am her husband," I told him simply, bitterness rife in my tone.

"What would you have done, Daniel, had it been you?" Aife asked me. "Consider it," she added swiftly, before it could spill from my lips that of course, I would have told her at once. "Imagine you had been told by King Cedric and King Urien, that King Reghan had been murdered by this spy," she invented. "You know that as long as the assassin believes himself to be safe, all is well. You could even feed him false information, maybe even save lives."

"However," she continued, "you are also threatened that if you told Her Majesty, the Wolf could kill your wife and threaten to destroy Gaeson. Even Rheged herself could be at stake. What would you do, in such circumstances?" she ended her scenario.

"There could have been a way," I answered determinedly. "I even asked her, directly, because Sarah—" the truth hit me again that my sister had suspected Evelyn, but I had not paid her any heed. Rather, I had harshly refuted her speculations.

"Sarah believed Evelyn could have known something," I resumed, shaking my head. "I asked Evelyn if she knew anything and she directly lied to me." All at once I was tiring of their company. I stood, but then swayed lightly as I felt the effects of the wine. I rested my hand lightly against the wall to steady myself.

"She has committed an awful wrong against you," John emphasised now, as though to validate the betrayal I felt so keenly. "All we're saying is, perhaps measure it against her character," he added. His voice sounded far too reasonable to my unwilling ears.

"For knowing her as well as you do, which is more likely?" he continued in a carefully neutral tone. "First, that her deception is because she deliberately wished you harm. Therefore, your entire marriage is a lie and you can never trust her again," he outlined, holding up a finger.

"Or," he continued, as he held up a second finger, "that she has longed to tell you but has felt trapped by the Wolf's threat that if she tells you she risks losing you and the lives of her people." At once I tried to ignore him, but his rational arguments seeped into my brain despite my best intentions. Wearily, I rubbed my eyes with the hand that was not against the wall.

"I thank you both for your counsel," I told them ere long, my speech a little slurred because of the wine. "I have lots to think through," I added, a little tensely. I was appreciative of their wise counsel, but I was still too bitter to listen to reason. "John, would you be so kind…" I swallowed here, then sighed resignedly. "Would you please go to my chamber and tell Evelyn I won't be returning tonight?" I instructed.

"Of course," John replied, "but where are you going?" Instead of answering, I knocked back the dregs of my wine and placed it a little too loudly on the table before turning to leave.

"Daniel," Aife called earnestly as I crossed the chamber towards the door. I turned back as she put her hand on my shoulder. "We're so sorry, brother," she spoke with full compassion. "If there's any help we can offer you—"

"I thank you both," I repeated, nodding as I looked to both of them. "You have spoken with wisdom, even if I had not wished to hear it," I acknowledged wryly. "That is what true friendship is." With a final nod to both of them, I departed their company.

My next journey was far more deliberate, with one place in my mind that I hoped would give me some peace. Before long, I reached the stables. Almost as soon as the familiar, musty smell of hay reached my nostrils, I began to take comfort in it. Outside the house where I had grown up, this was the only place that ever truly felt home. Also, it evoked strong memories of my father who had raised me. As I lifted my head to look at the wooden beams above me, the soft murmurs of the horses comfortingly reached my ears. I bent my head again to glance around at these slender, magnificent creatures, feeling further tension begin to seep away.

Eventually, in this place, I felt the lurking anger in me start to lessen. I could even be considered relaxed, as I imagined the wine slowly lapping gently round my brain. I made my way through the narrow aisle down the middle of the stables slowly, for the wine was impairing my steps a little: I was not used to drinking so much. The horses' stalls stood high on either sides and as I passed them, a neighing reached my ears that I instantly recognised above all other sounds.

"Hello, old girl," I greeted her softly, a small smile touching my face as I reached my horse. My faithful companion ducked and darted her head in joyful agreement, as I rubbed her neck. "It's not been the best of days, my friend," I murmured to her softly. I gave her a few oats to nibble on, before continuing to the end of the stables.

Presently I reached the narrow, rickety ladder that would take me to the hayloft. The rungs creaked as I ascended it, as usual threatening to give way, before I emerged onto the higher platform. Then, I at last sank down onto the reassuring bed of golden grass. I had come here without hesitation, repeating the pattern I'd formed as a child. If ever my parents had lost sight of me, my father would know I had come up here. Once or twice I'd had the company of John or Sarah, but most times I was alone.

I had oft come here seeking comfort, especially during times of despair. I had hidden up here the night when my father had been unable to save the life of a horse who had died from fever. Instantly I pushed this memory away, for the next morning was when I met Evelyn for the first time. I had come here, too, at the age of fifteen. Sarah and John had found me in here, when I learned my father had died in battle. It was just a few months before John and I would enlist in the army ourselves.

I had been working in here a year later, during a week's leave, when Sarah had run in crying, to tell me her mother had died. I had held her quietly in the hayloft, seeking to comfort her whilst she grieved. Then, two years later, after her father had died in battle, I was the one who found Sarah up here, mourning once more. By that point we knew my mother's condition was almost without any hope of recovery. Unable to bear the thought of my oldest friend on the streets, I had employed Sarah to care for my mother and manage the affairs of my house.

In the days after returning to Caer Ligualid after discovering my true identity, I had also taken refuge in this place. During all the uncertainty, I had always found a security here that offered me serenity. It was as if here, no matter what happened or might change, I was simply myself. I felt this same comfort of the stables now, as I lay among the hay in the dark. As I did, I deliberately tried to imagine the parents who had borne me, whom I barely remembered.

With a certain amount of effort, I conjured them in my mind's eye, My father, with his storm-like eyes and strong jaw. My mother, with her vivid scarlet hair and laughter as sweet as honey. I felt sadness pull at my heart, but as I thought of them I began to feel a lightness I had not expected.

Presently I realised I had been so enraged at Aldred and my wife's betrayal, I had not appreciated the simple truth. The mystery was over. The Veiled Wolf, my kin's assassin, who had been eluding me for practically a year now, was finally unmasked. The one who had so brutally murdered my parents was finally revealed.

"It's over, Uncle," I whispered as I thought of him, imagining that he too had discovered the truth upon walking through heaven's gates. I imagined him, too, being reunited with the lost family that had been snatched away from me. This thought gave me some comfort, as this consolation enabled me to sink into slumber.

***

"Daniel?" My eyes opened wide into a sea of golden blades, as I jolted awake to Evelyn's voice. I sat up, the hay immediately cascading down my hair and clothes. "Don't get up," Evelyn called as slowly I moved towards the ladder. I looked to see the hint of a wry smile at the corner of her mouth, despite the troubled concern in her eyes.

"I'll come to you," she added now, as she made her way through the stables. I was glad of this suggestion, for I was acutely aware of the severe dull ache in my head. I knew this was entirely due to the amount of wine I had consumed the previous night. I sat up, thankful that at least I did not have the urge to vomit.

I watched as my wife walked down the aisle of the stables, as she looked more beautiful than ever. I noticed, though, the rings around her eyes: probably she had not slept at all this previous night. I tried to keep my face impassive, as my negative emotions began to dwell again at the sight of her. This was probably a futile exercise, for Evelyn had always been able to see through my military façade. Presently, Evelyn ascended into the hayloft, coming to sit beside me.

"Here," Evelyn said simply, holding a full skin of water. I took it gratefully, drinking thirstily as the refreshing liquid lessened the pain in my head a little. "John told me you wouldn't be returning last night," she continued, her tone carefully neutral. "He said you might be here."

"He spoke right," was all my reply, my tone evenly matching hers. "Did you send the messengers to Caer Ligualid?" I asked, guessing the next move would be to warn King Owain about Aldred and to recommend Sarah come back to Gaeson. I chose not to mention the short, angry note that I had given one of the messengers to take.

"Yes," Evelyn agreed quietly. "Though part of me wishes Sarah's return could be delayed," she admitted. I glanced at her sharply, but she was staring absently into the middle of the large barn. "I think I can know now, more than ever, the hurt you must have felt when we viewed you as a traitor," she reflected, sighing a little.

"You were expecting a different reaction?" Though my speech was nowhere near as hot and harsh as it had been the previous night, I still heard the edge to my voice.

"No, it is as I supposed," my wife replied quietly. "I just had not predicted it would hurt this much," she expanded. I gave a short nod, then stopped as the ache in my head worsened.

"Aye, well, that is the consequence of your decision," I told her flatly. Evelyn only nodded. This led to silence, the tension between us obvious.

"Daniel," Evelyn resumed somewhat abruptly, "I think we need to go to Caer Ligualid ourselves," she suggested, changing the subject. I looked up at her again. "The messengers won't be able to reveal the true nature of these events," Evelyn explained.

"No," I answered, uttering a short, humourless laugh. "I suppose you are right," I ventured. "Since Aldred is at large, we need to formulate a strategy of how we are to catch him." Here I lifted the water to my mouth again and drained it, taking some small comfort in that at least we could be united in desiring the Wolf's capture.

"I told John and Aife the truth of things last night," I told her next, as I tossed the empty skin beside us on the hay. Evelyn merely nodded again as she retrieved the empty skin and turned it over in her hands. No doubt she had anticipated I would tell them.

"Though they did not want to condone your deceit," I continued, "they did say it sounded as though you were in an impossible situation. That you would have been imprisoned by fear that if you told me the truth, both my life and all of Gaeson could be lost."

"Aye, that was exactly my circumstance," my queen answered, nodding her head emphatically. "You've no idea how many times I longed to tell you," she murmured, her hand inching across the hay to reach mine. Though I did not return the contact, I did not pull away, either. Evelyn looked at me, her gaze searching mine. "I did not want to lose you, husband," she ended passionately, her eyes begging for me to understand.

"I know," I replied heavily, after a moment. Sheer relief came into her features here, in my recognition that I understood, if not accepted, what she had done. "In doing this, though, you have paid a great cost," I added. At once, her countenance faded again. "Even if your motives were pure and you did it for the safety of Rheged—"

"I still did you a great wrong, I know," my wife cut in gently. "I still did not reveal that through the whole of our marriage, I entertained that man in my courts, listening to his advice. The truth is, you are no longer sure you can trust me." Her voice had never sounded so broken, as she looked down at her hands in her lap. "When we go to Caer Ligualid, if you wish to remain there with your people, rather than returning to Gaeson, I will not blame you.

"If you'll excuse me," Evelyn spoke abruptly before I could reply to this, "I have some duties to attend to." She moved onto the ladder, but stopped, catching my eye before she began her descent. "Know this, husband, whatever you do," she began adamantly, "I have loved you with

241

all of my heart, since the day you returned after falling from that cliff. Farewell," she added, sounding broken again as her head dipped out of sight.

It was on the tip of my tongue to reply to her, but any words seemed to freeze before leaving my lips. Instead, I only watched as my queen reached the bottom of the ladder. She walked back through the stables, the moment gone. Sighing, I rubbed my hands through my hair and reached for the ladder rungs myself. As I did so, my eye caught a flash of gold in the early morning light. It was my wedding ring I had seen. I lifted my left hand to examine it closer. The small band was a clear reminder of the oaths I had made to Evelyn before God. I had promised to love and care for her, as she had vowed to me also.

I did believe Evelyn's reasons and motives and though they explained her actions, she had admitted herself that she was still my betrayer. In a very tangible way, she had broken the trust of our marriage and therefore her vows. What for my vows, though? I wondered, casting my gaze to the stable roof. I felt suspended in time, with my right hand still holding the top of the ladder. Evelyn had given me the choice to end the covenant I had with her. I longed to remain wed to her, for I loved her as much as ever. Part of me yearned for nothing more than to forgive her, but the pain of her actions continued to bite deep into my bones. In truth, I did not know whether forgiveness was something I could give her. Therefore, a great barrier had formed between us, a wall I was not at all sure I could break.

Chapter Twelve

I looked up once again at the route before us, but still the steep incline continued, even as the curve in the hill opened up more land. This was frustrating, as I longed to reach the peak of the high ground, but this narrow, sharp path seemed to go on forever. I glanced down to Epos, but just as ever she was steadfast, unperturbed by the tough terrain. My hand lowered to pat her neck, instantly feeling how her thick coat was matted and covered with a damp sheen.

"It will not be long now," Evelyn murmured opposite me to her own horse. I looked to her and our eyes met. She tried to smile in greeting, but I found all I could do was nod. I saw the smile fade a little, saw the slight sadness enter her gaze before she looked away. I cursed inwardly, but I was finding any kind of talk difficult. Particularly if it was forced, which it always seemed to be now.

The chasm was still between us, ever tangible despite its invisibility. We had never before had this distance, this kind of tension between us, enforced by the barrier I still could not cross. The last three weeks we had seen very little of each other, such were our routines and duties. Any conversation between us in public was outwardly harmonious, so the rest of Gaeson believed all was still well. In private, our talk was quiet civility, almost as though we were strangers. In truth, part of me felt I would prefer blazing conflict, for I never believed I would not be able to talk openly with my own wife.

With this state of affairs, Evelyn still had not made the announcement to our people that we would soon be adopting. I imagined Leigh would be wondering at our delay, since Morwenna was due to give birth in only two months or so. My queen had once raised the subject with me: that day was the closest we had come to another altercation, for what child could we parent, I argued, whilst there was still this rift between us?

In truth I had tried hard to cross the chasm to forgive her, but each time I attempted this, the image of Aldred in that Klumeck corridor came to my mind, tormenting me painfully. His wicked, grinning face, with hot, fresh blood dripping from the knife he held, seemed never far away. Then, the notion that Evelyn had known him and had allowed his company in her midst—it was more than I could stomach.

Presently I shook my head animatedly, for it did not do to keep injecting myself with the same poison over and over. Instead, I focused on the task at hand. We were riding to Caer Ligualid to report the truth about Aldred, the fullness of which the messengers sent ahead of us would never be able to fully reveal. I had written a short, scathing note that the Wolf was Aldred and Evelyn had known of this, but had not gone into any further detail. Also, we had received no word from the Gaeson messengers, so we did not know whether this note had even arrived.

It was a relief at last, then, to be close to the great city once more, where we could discuss how to stop the poisonous Wolf. I hoped earnestly we would be able to stop his next strategy, whatever it was. I knew the villain well enough to know all of Rheged could be at stake. I glanced again at the armed guards accompanying us. Though John and Aife had wished to join our company, Evelyn and I had both agreed they should remain behind. My captain and my chief archer had stayed in Gaeson, lest Aldred chose to attack Gaeson in our absence.

It was Lord Melvyn who had suggested the delay in our travels, that faithful steward, whom I had so terribly misjudged when I thought him to be the Wolf. Melvyn had posed that Aldred would know our next move would be to ride for Caer Ligualid and could therefore be easily loitering nearby, waiting to ambush us. It was Melvyn who was ruling Gaeson in Evelyn's stead.

The lack of correspondence from King Owain seemed to confirm that Aldred may be waiting nearby, for it was likely they had been intercepted. I hoped this was not the case, but writing a warning to Caer Ligualid as soon as possible had simply been necessary. I had longed to go there in person at the first instance, but Evelyn had persuaded me to stay, threatening that if I left for Rheged's capital afore time, then so would she. To wait had been frustrating, but Evelyn was still my queen, as well as my wife. I would not break my vow to serve her and protect her from harm, even if I was no longer sure of our marriage vows.

This was also the first time we would see Sarah since the truth was revealed. I was looking forward to seeing my sister, but part of me also dreaded the reunion. We had no way of knowing whether she did know the truth, since we had not had word from King Owain, but we would not have a pleasant conversation about the Wolf's true identity, either way. I glanced at my wife again, who had gone back to staring grimly ahead, for even though I was still angry with her, I knew the emotional turmoil she must be going through, despite her external impassivity.

Since Evelyn and I married, Sarah and my wife had grown as close as any sisters could be. Both had often told me how much they valued the other's friendship and wise counsel. Alas, I knew that once Sarah found out about the Wolf, it could ruin their relationship forever. I knew it was Evelyn's doing, to hide the truth and betray us, but I knew well her reasons. It would be lying to say I was entirely without sympathy for her.

Presently, we reached the top of the hill and after we turned the path's final bend, the plains of the high ground evened out before us. Immediately I halted, pulling hard on the reins once I saw what was before us, for a little along the path in front of us stood a cloaked figure, wielding a sword. Dimly, I heard the rest of the riding party stop behind me.

"You," I uttered simply. My instinct told me it was the Wolf, long before Aldred removed his hood. That same scornful smile was on his countenance, as sardonic as ever. I dismounted from Epos and drew my blade: I sensed Evelyn do the same to my right.

"Your Majesties," my foe greeted us, his voice dripping with false pomposity as he bowed mockingly. "How goes your marriage?" I gritted my teeth in anger at his bristling tone. To think I had once called this villain my friend!

"I've been waiting for you, stable boy," he now said menacingly. "Did you think three weeks would be all it took to make yourself feel safe? Did you not think I had spies left anywhere in Gaeson, that could tell me of the moment of your arrival?"

"Enough of your poison," I commanded in return, taking a step forward. In response Aldred raised a hand, lazily. At this gesture, several Bernician soldiers leapt up from the brush beside us. My eyes darted to my left and right immediately, surveying them. It seemed these plains were not nearly as open as I had hoped.

"You're outnumbered, Bryce," Aldred stated obviously, glee clear in his tone. Indeed, he had spoken truly, for there were about twenty more than we had. I held my blade in front of us, breathing tensely. Though it might take long for the Wolf's goons would kill us all, we would still put up a valiant effort in this fight.

I glanced briefly at my wife and as our eyes met, I saw the same resigned determination in her gaze that I was sure was also in my own. At once I regretted the strained silence of late, longing to cross the chasm and tell her how much I still loved her. The moment was over far too quickly, however, as we looked away again to better focus on our foes.

"Charge!" Aldred shouted. Swiftly we launched into battle, whilst the villain himself remained further back from the fray. Instead he twirled his sword idly in his hands, making no move to join the fight. It seemed he was simply content to let his troops wage war for him.

"Leave their Majesties," Aldred now snarled. "Kill all the others." In that moment, I realised the Wolf would not allow us a quick, painless death, as he may have granted me when I was a toddler. My eyes hardened, as I grew ever more determined to kill this monster, even if it cost me my own life. If only I could get near—

My strategy to take my vengeance and kill Aldred must have been obvious, however, as his troops soon moved to block me at every turn. Three more of his goons withdrew a little, as if to guard him. The air was full of the sounds of battle, as I attempted to cut my opponents down to reach my enemy, but we were so vastly outnumbered it seemed a futile effort. The cries of the dead and wounded reached my ears, as many of my company fell to the floor. I gritted my teeth against more anger, for I knew many more would fall on my side than the Wolf's.

"Soldiers, halt!" Aldred called abruptly. A moment later his men straightened as they followed his command, their swords still pointed in our direction. I looked around to see over half my people dead: only eight of my soldiers remained. I saw Evelyn was bleeding a little from a cut above her left eyebrow, but other than that she was uninjured.

"I give you a proposal, my lord the king," Aldred said, the sarcasm for once absent from his slippery tongue. "If you surrender, I will spare the rest of your men. I will even allow them to return to Gaeson." His voice was loud and clear, now the fighting had ceased. "If you resist, however, I will cut down every last one of them," he warned. After his speech, all became as still as stone, the groans from the wounded the only sounds that pierced the air.

My gaze flickered to Evelyn: she nodded almost imperceptibly back to me. I hesitated only a moment, for yielding seemed so vile and cowardly. Yet, I knew it was folly to needlessly forfeit the lives of my people who still drew breath. I knew I could trust Aldred to keep his word as much as I could trust a snake not to bite me, but what other choice did we have?

"Agreed," I consented ere long. To my relief, the enemy soldiers retreated a step or two further, sheathing their swords

"Your weapons," Aldred instructed simply. Reluctantly, Evelyn and I removed our swords, handing them to one of my soldiers standing nearby. I also handed him my bow and quiver. Lastly, I stooped to remove the dagger I kept just above my boot.

"Leave, now!" Aldred directed loudly to my people, before I had the chance to say anything further to my troops. "Retrieve your wounded if you can, but do not bother with your dead." I swallowed hard, watching as those who could walk carefully retrieved three others who were still alive but had collapsed to the ground. I saw one of the injured bleeding profusely, at once knowing there would be very little chance of his survival. Those of my troops still standing secured the wounded as best they could upon the horses now without riders.

This done, they glanced towards Evelyn and me. We nodded at them once. Reluctantly, our people rode away then, guiding all of the horses away from us, including Epos. As the sound of hooves faded upon the earth, I turned back to Aldred, still stood on the path in front of us, which was now covered in blood. The Wolf's soldiers drew their swords once more, lest suddenly I tried to move towards my greatest enemy. Still, my gaze remained only on the villain, attempting to convey all the hatred I felt for him in a single glance. At once, I knew I had failed.

"Such contempt," Aldred commented with a smirk, as he saw my regard. "Such loathing of the one who has saved the lives of your men. Am I not merciful?" His smile faded. "Blindfold them!" he ordered abruptly, the humour gone again from his voice. My eyes remained on him, glaring at the man who had taken so much I loved, until thick, black material covered my face.

When the blindfold was removed, a dim light reached my eyes. I was lying on the ground, with my arms pulled behind my back. My wrists were restrained with a thick cord. I glanced up to see it was late afternoon, with black clouds stretched far across the canvas of the sky.

"Get him on his feet," the insidious voice of Aldred commanded. I heard footsteps and glimpsed legs clad in armour, then I was roughly pulled upwards. Immediately I glanced about to see Evelyn was still there. The small gash on her forehead had scabbed, but presently another captor held a blade against her throat. She was held similarly to when the interrogator had restrained her, after she had been captured following my return from Ynys Metcaut.

"Take your hands off my wife," I warned, trying to struggle against those who restrained me, but it was in vain, for the bonds which held me were too tight and each of my arms was powerfully held by one of the Wolf's men. "Let her go, Aldred!" I shouted to him, but my foe merely chuckled. I was utterly helpless, at the mercy of this monster. Even though I was a king, I had never felt more powerless.

"Oh, is that what you wish?" Aldred sneered. "After how she lied and betrayed you?" he challenged, clearly enjoying the difficulties he had caused in my marriage.

"Even if her actions were wrong," I replied, finally looking away from the Wolf to behold the woman I had loved for most of my life, "I understand why she did what she did. Besides, she is still my queen," I added, reiterating my earlier thoughts aloud, as I turned towards my captor again. "I want no harm to come to her." My eyes flickered back to her to glimpse a faint smile on her face, despite the severe danger we were both in.

"So, you still believe in her," Aldred reflected, shaking his head, scorn clear in his tone. "You are a sentimental fool, but it matters not. Your delusions of each other will only make my victory of all the sweeter. Today, you see," he expounded, "I will complete the mission I began twenty-four years ago, when I murdered your parents." A cruel snarl was in his voice now. With a renewed rage I fought against my bonds, but such was the grip of my restraints it was entirely useless.

"Let us be done with this," Aldred called to his men who held us captive. "After I have disposed of you and your wife," my foe directed to me, "then there will be only your sister left to eliminate. That weak fool, Melvyn, will not be able to hold Gaeson's walls. Your home will be destroyed, as was Klumeck over two years ago. Then, there will only be Caer Ligualid left for us to conquer." At the end of his speech, he grinned manically and triumphantly.

"No, you'll never win!" I retorted with a roar. I tried once more, desperately, to wrestle against my captors. With this concerted effort I managed to get an arm free, but Aldred merely raised his hand again. The blade near my love's throat grew ever closer. Instantly I stopped struggling, lest my actions caused her further pain.

"Let us proceed," Aldred commanded, sounding almost bored. He turned to mount his horse, whilst mercifully the enemy soldier removed his sword from Evelyn's neck. The Wolf sat lazily upon his horse, as the guards either side of me pushed me roughly forwards. One hand held his reins, whilst the other idly rubbed his neck, looking as though he had all the time in the world. I realised that in his moment of success, he rather did.

"What have you done with...?" I began to ask, but my last word died away as the subject of my question stepped forwards. As Cara came into view I watched her intensely, trying to ascertain her position in all of this. She appeared to be uninjured.

"I assume you refer to one of my best agents?" Aldred smirked. To my horror, Cara then smiled up to Aldred, with the same corner of her mouth turning, the same evil in her grin as the Wolf wore. "A masterful performance, was it not?"

"Aye," Cara turned back to face us. "I apologise, Your Majesties, for the charade. This has always been who I am," she declared, pointing her chin up to us. The words struck me cold and I would have believed her, but for a slight wavering in her voice and eyes. My former warrior was feigning strength, yet part of her had never been more vulnerable.

"How could you?" I challenged back as the guards continued to push Evelyn and I towards the cliff. "We trusted you, Cara. You gave your word to save us! You promised me you would tell all—"

"If you protected me from my Lord Aldred, yes," Cara returned, cutting me short, "but you did not. You failed to protect me, my liege. It is no matter, however, for that was deceit also," she added levelly. I frowned as I digested this.

"Ewan found out about you," I pointed out now. "He said you were a poor liar, he was able to discover your hand in this—"

"Only because I let him," she interrupted a second time, waving her hand dismissively. "You think my lord was not watching him? He was a useful tool to bait, that we might better find out what you knew of us. We need not have worried, though, for you knew little of our schemes. The Wolf had to tell you in the end, slowly, as though talking to a child." She sniggered.

"You speak without reason," I muttered, frowning, almost as though I was talking to myself, for as I stared at this sneering woman who professed to be in league with my foe, the Cara I had seen in the dungeon came to my mind, pleading desperately to be protected from Aldred. My senses told me she looked more like she was lying now, but I could not tell for sure.

"You do not have to understand, Bryce," Aldred remarked quietly. "The only thing you need to know is that all you hold dear is about to be over." With this speech concluded he turned around his horse, steering it straight ahead. With the guards pushing us forwards on either side, Evelyn and I had no choice but to follow.

We marched across the plain, a short distance. Then I could see nothing beyond and I presumed he was taking us to the edge of a cliff.

"I'm sorry I have failed you, my queen," I said to Evelyn in a low voice, as we were forced to walk this journey together. Perhaps today was the day I broke the vow I had made in the snow that day, to serve her faithfully and protect her from harm.

"The fault is not yours, my husband," Evelyn returned, a faint smile on her face. Abruptly I longed to hold her one last time, but the restraints would not allow us even that. I tried to think quickly, to claw up some attempt to escape, but all notions of freedom seemed equally futile. As we clambered along it began to rain, but only very finely, no more than a mere mist. Evelyn abruptly let out a cry. I jerked my head towards her to see she had stumbled and fallen to the floor.

"Up you get, Your Majesty," Cara instructed, as she walked over to my wife. She stooped over, grabbed Evelyn's arm and pulled her roughly upright.

"Get your hands off her," I commanded hotly. One of the guards holding me tugged my arm so sharply, I believed the limb might break. My eyes watered in pain, as Aldred turned back in his horse to see what was happening. His eyes twinkled with what appeared to be amusement.

"Onwards," he directed simply. Presently the march began again. I glanced at my wife, but she still appeared to be uninjured. My eyes flickered down her to make sure she bore no wounds and that was when I saw it. I risked a glance at my queen, but her gaze was still ahead of her, her countenance grimly determined. I quickly then looked away, before Aldred or one of his goons spotted it.

The movement had been almost imperceptible, but as I took another sidelong look at my wife's hands I knew I had been right. Evelyn held a sharp piece of metal in her hand, that appeared to be one of the pins she wore in her hair. One of her wrists flexed back and forth slightly, as she attempted to cut herself free.

Where had she got it from? I wondered. Then I remembered how Cara had helped Evelyn up. Could she be on our side after all? Could she simply be feigning allegiance to the Wolf, in order to survive? I knew not the answers, yet none of these questions held the most pressing thought. The most immediate notion was whether Evelyn would succeed, for it was all too obvious that our only hope of survival lay in her.

As we continued the journey, the high ground gave way and I saw I was right: we had come to a cliff. I did not have to wonder what would happen next. Evidently the Wolf planned to throw us from this precipice. I glanced again at my queen, who was still scraping the metal pin against her bonds. I had no way of knowing whether the rope was close to breaking, or whether this method even worked. I also knew one of the guards holding her could look down and see the pin at any moment. What my wife needed, urgently, was more time.

With this in mind, I abruptly launched myself forwards. The movement momentarily wrenched me free of my captors, as I sped towards the ground. Since my hands and feet were bound, I had no choice but to land squarely on my face. Instantly my cheek was torn. I winced inwardly, my teeth gritting with the pain.

"Come on, now, Bryce, you too?" the Wolf asked. "I would have expected a little more decorum from royalty," he sniggered, looking between us. "Not far now," he warned, tauntingly. I groaned aloud, making no movements to get up.

"Can you not stand? You are still a soldier at heart, aren't you? I thought I would have a little more dignity, at least. Get him on his feet," Aldred ordered. The guards came beside me again to hoist me up. As I was forced to stand, warm blood ran from my cheek to enter my mouth. I spat out its thick, salty taste.

"You're a weaker fool than I thought," Aldred said disdainfully, shaking his head as if truly disappointed. "Forward!" He shouted. I felt the rough hands of the guards push me forwards. I shot a look to Evelyn to see her watching me. Though she looked concerned, the slightest smile tugged at the corner of her mouth, as if she had known exactly what I was doing.

I risked another glance to her hands. To my encouragement, her wrist was moving much faster. I hoped she was about to succeed. The worry was that the closer she came to freedom, the more obvious her hand movements became. I turned to look at Cara, but she was staring ahead, her expression unreadable. Had she given Evelyn that pin?

"Almost there," Aldred called from the front, as the ground went downhill slightly. As we reached the cliff's edge, I took in the view. We towered above one of the narrow ends of a small, wide lake. It was not the great lake that I had oft glimpsed from Gaeson's ramparts. I looked right, however, at once recognising the sloped hills, where the path to home lay.

My surveying of the view was interrupted, as the guards abruptly pushed me closer to the edge. I peered over, quickly judging by the remaining daylight that we would survive the fall. The Wolf seemed to have planned this, however. Perhaps he simply wished to watch us drown. More than ever, I knew my survival depended upon my queen.

"Just tell me why, Aldred," I asked desperately, knowing all the while I kept him talking, it would buy Evelyn a few more precious seconds. I delayed a little, turning my head to spit out more blood onto the rocks. Only another instant more could decide whether we would live or die. "Why are you so determined to kill me?" I questioned. "Why did you murder my family?"

"Oh, Bryce," he answered patronisingly. "I always knew you had taken it too personally. I was simply following orders, my boy," he answered, whilst I turned my head to spit out more blood. Far less had gathered in my mouth this time: the bleeding was slowing. "I was tasked to infiltrate Rheged years ago, to turn you against each other. It was only too easy to befriend King Reghan and convince him Klumeck was his enemy, rather than his friend. When I advised him to murder King Cedric and his kin, he was only too happy to comply," he sniggered.

"Isn't that right, my dear?" he directed to Evelyn now. "No words of defence for your father? I suppose not," he added. "I suppose you're attempting to make your husband forget your father ordered the deaths of his kin and your chief advisor executed that order. Literally," he ordered with a grin.

"I understand you are following orders in this war, Wolf," I began. Aldred looked back towards me. Out of the corner of my eye, I saw Evelyn's hands start moving again. "It does not explain, however, that you take such sadistic pleasure in it. Why do you love violence so much? Why do you take life with such relish? What made you so cruel?" At this, Aldred chuckled again. For the first time I was not entirely displeased to hear his laugh. Every moment he delayed the order to kill us gave my wife a moment more time.

"Perhaps you would relish every victory as I do, had you been in this war as long as I have," Aldred returned. "Every Briton I kill makes the Angles grow stronger." As he spoke, the dark clouds gathered above us suddenly burst forth. The rain fell thick and fast.

"You think you are the only one to have lost someone, boy?" Aldred roared. "You think your people have never taken innocent lives? I have lost everything in this fight!" His shouting reached my ears above the sound of the storm, whilst my eyes blinked hard and fast to deter the water that fell into them. The sarcastic veneer had gone from his voice, a thread of pain now to his voice.

"Who did you lose, Aldred?" I asked, no longer just to delay him but because I was curious. What had made him into such a monster of hate? The Wolf glared at me.

"My wife," he admitted ere long, deciding to tell me. "Also, my daughter, just eight years old." The thread of pain grew stronger. "Never forget this, Bryce," Aldred called. I frowned, wanting to ask how his family had died, but the moment seemed gone. "Whilst I was the one who murdered your parents," he continued, "the order came from your father-in-law, that king you once served. Do you think he only gave such a command because I manipulated him to? The seed of corruption was in him already. All actions are permissible in war, it seems," he said. At this, he raised a hand to run through his thick, black hair, now sopping wet.

"Enough of this. Restrain his feet!" Aldred commanded loudly. My stomach tightened, for it seemed the time for delaying was done. The guards either side of me pushed me roughly to the ground. Rope was hastily yet firmly tied round my ankles and tightened, giving me no hope that I could wriggle out of it. I glanced up towards my wife, but the rain was so thick and fast I could barely see her. As the guards took hold of my shoulders, I shook my head to get rid of more rainfall that had gathered in my eyes. I blinked hard, at last getting a brief respite from the elements. What I saw gave me hope, for whilst Evelyn's hands remained behind her back, one fist was now curled. I presumed it concealed the pin.

The relief flared further, as I saw that the cord around her wrists was now gone. Then the rain obscured my vision again. As the guards roughly raised to me to my feet, I blinked hard again to clear my vision. Then, my eyes locked with my wife's. In that moment, complete understanding passed between us. It was the best communication we had shared in weeks, for if Evelyn jumped off the cliff unbound as she was, then perhaps she would be able to save both of us.

"Any last words?" Aldred snarled from beside me and I knew this was it. My gaze lingered upon my wife, before I turned back to him. His countenance was once more sneering with glee, at the thought of our imminent deaths. I straightened, in the face of the killer of my kin. I knew that if I was to die here, I would die with dignity.

"Long live the Kingdom of Rheged," I declared. Aldred's mouth tugged as he smirked. That was the last of his malicious smiles I saw, before he nodded to the guards. The ones either side of me lifted me off my feet, my view of the world turning horizontal. The thugs swayed me back and forth then finally threw me off, with all the ease of tossing a bale of hay over a fence.

"No!" I heard Aldred roar as I thundered down, but as I rushed towards the body of water I barely heard him. I inhaled as deeply as I could, before I crashed into the lake, the water smacking me painfully upon impact.

Then the next thing that hit me was the cold of the water, enough to almost shock me into paralysis. In the next moment, the instinct to survive kicked in. I squirmed and wriggled, trying to break free of my restraints. I found neither my hands nor my feet, could move at all. Any attempt to use my energy upon them was futile. I had filled my lungs with as much air as they could hold, but even so, in a minute or two I knew I would drown.

I knew Evelyn was my only hope. I forced myself to grow calm, for panicking would only make me drown faster. I thought of her, having faith she would save me. Even if I were to drown, despite our recent conflict I knew I wanted my last thought to be of her. I recalled Aldred's last defiant shout. Had she jumped from the cliff? I knew not.

Soon my lungs threatened to burst from lack of air. I feared I was to die here, in this cold and dark abyss. A moment later, however, I felt a strong hand thrust underneath my arm to pull me upwards. My wife was my saviour and though it was a tough battle, for both of us still wore armour that weighed us down, soon she broke us both through the surface of the water.

At once, I began to gasp in the warm night air. It was the sweetest stuff I had ever breathed. My wife's hand weaved round my arm, using her other arm to propel us through the water.

"Evelyn," I called, my voice raspy from the lack of oxygen and the continual spray of rain. I began to kick my legs to free the ropes, but they were as tight as ever.

"Daniel!" My wife cried, as my rash action against my restraints caused me to submerge again. A moment later she had dragged me above the water again. "Stay still," she cautioned at once. I heeded this instruction, as she pulled me through the lake. It was evident, though, that my armour made me far too heavy, for I kept sinking back under the water.

"Listen," she murmured eventually, "I need you to take a deep breath." Her speech was paused as a wave swept over us, swaying us to the right. "I still have the pin, I'm going to try to cut the cords underwater. Are you ready?" she shouted. I nodded, inhaling deeply again.

"Now!" she called, then we both submerged under the water again. She reached for my hands. I stayed as still as a stone whilst she used the pin. Now that she was not under the threat of detection and had the angle right, she could move the pin much faster. I felt the cords weaken, but as moments passed by the cords did not break. My wife grabbed hold of me and pulled me upright. Immediately I exhaled.

"Another breath," she ordered simply. I obeyed. Once more we plunged under the surface for her to hack away at my bonds again. At last on this second attempt, the rope broke. It was such liberation to use my arms! I could not use my feet, but I could now partially swim, much to her relief. Immediately, we both headed for the surface.

The rain still battered down upon us and the current swayed us about with the wind, but both of us were strong swimmers and we simply moved with the current, manoeuvring as little as possible to conserve our strength. After a few moments, both of us ducked under the water again to remove pieces of armour. I was loath to part with it, especially if Aldred's men would be pursuing us. If we could not make it across the lake, however, then we were doomed before we began. It was with an extraordinary lightness of feeling that each metal plate was shed, at once sinking to the depths of the lake.

"The pin," I requested directly, when this was done. Finally, it was with great exhilaration that I was able dive under once more and use the sharp pin to break the restraints around my ankles. True freedom at last! I was so giddy with relief at our escape from death that immediately I longed to embrace my wife. I swam a few inches towards her.

"Bryce!" I stopped still in the water, my heart filling with dread and anger anew at the voice of the Wolf. How his taunting words reached me through the storm I knew not, but I heard him clearly enough. "This is not over, my boy! I will find you! We will finish what we started!" he roared.

"Hurry," was all I said to Evelyn. We both swam swiftly to the shore. It seemed to take forever, for such was the darkness and the rain that we had lost all bearings. Still we sped through the water, my only thought to get as far as humanly possible from our tormenter.

"There!" the Wolf cried, as a bolt of lightning flashed through the sky. The light had proved invaluable, for it had shown where the edge of the lake was. Evelyn seemed to have spotted it, also, for we both had turned in the same direction. The only danger was that, from my enemy's palpable shout, he had also seen our exact location.

Sure enough, there was a soft splash nearby. I felt the tip of an arrow brush past my arm as it floated past me. On impulse to have any kind of weapon, I seized the arrow, holding it tight.

"Swim!" I called to my wife urgently. There was little need, however, as Evelyn was racing through the water. I quickly followed, having to go a little slower because of holding the arrow, but I was not about to let go of my only weapon.

Eventually, after an eternity had seemed to pass by us, I was aware of the lake's edge nearing, for my feet soon began to touch lightly upon the lake floor. Soon we were wading and half running, then a few seconds later we collapsed upon the shore floor, spent. We both lay there for a few moments, as the rain beat down upon us.

"Thank you," I managed ere long, as I glanced at her. "You saved my life," I stated obviously. Evelyn opened her mouth to respond, but then somehow through the storm I again heard shouting. I guessed Aldred had probably raced his horse across land to us, whilst we had been forced to swim. I quickly stood, slipping the arrow from the lake into my belt.

"Come on," I called to her, the instinct to survive causing fresh adrenaline to fill my body as I held out my hand. I pulled her to her feet and there was one instant where our eyes locked before we ran out into the night, our wet clothes clinging to us. As much as I hated running away, I was desperate to escape the Wolf's claws, for the monster would not risk leaving nature to kill us again. If he had the chance, he would surely slay us with his own blade.

As Evelyn and I ran, the storm began to lessen a little. My body temperature began to rise, though the rain still fell. I hoped my queen's body was warming, too. The hot, summer air helped, enveloping me like a warm blanket. I strained to hear my pursuers, but all I could hear was the continual fall of rain and the blood pounding in my ears. I could not even hear my wife, even though she only ran a little ahead of me.

Presently, the rain thickened again and as my vision was momentarily blurred, abruptly I tripped. I flew into the air before landing hard upon the sodden ground. With a stab of pain, I felt something sharp scrape my cheek again and knew the wound had been reopened.

"Evelyn," I called out loudly for her to stop, but I didn't know whether she had heard me. I stood a little clumsily, for the stumble had disoriented me. I looked about me but all I could see was the thick, driving rain.

"Evelyn!" I shouted again, but there was nothing. I began to feel vulnerable in the dark, so my hand went for the reassuring tip of the arrow, the only weapon I held. I could not hear anything above the sounds of the storm. Quickly I began running again, hoping I was going roughly in the right direction. I swiftly lifted up a prayer to God as I sprinted, petitioning that my wife was safe from harm, that I would find her again. Another few minutes passed by, as I ran across the even plains. Soon the rain began to lessen again.

"Evelyn!" I cried repeatedly, hoping that the diminishing storm meant I would be able to hear her. I was uncaring for my own safety, for I just wanted to know my queen was still alive.

"Daniel?" It was her voice, fragile, uncertain, but it was hers. I turned on the spot, desperately searching for where the voice had come from. "Daniel!" Her voice, louder now, came from somewhere to my left. I ran towards the voice, fresh hope revitalising me.

"Where are you?" I bellowed back stupidly. I cried her name again, but there was silence. Had I lost her once more? The storm, that had convinced me it was passing, abruptly amplified. I tried not to blink as I scrutinised the grey blanket around me. Soon my eyes were so full of water I could barely see anything. I was full of desperate anguish, but then I saw a flicker of movement, almost imperceptible. Cautiously, I took a few steps towards the figure.

"Daniel!" I heard her passionate refrain suddenly, somehow above the noise of the storm. The figure moved — it was her! I broke into a run, this time not to escape the Wolf but to race towards her. I realised she was running too. A moment before I reached her, I opened my arms and she flew into them.

At once the feel of her, tangible and physical in the rain, was all the comfort I had ever yearned for. I embraced her tightly, my good cheek coming to rest against hers. I was almost glad of the rain, then, for in all the fatigue from nearly drowning and in the sheer despair of thinking I might never see her again, I had begun to weep.

For a minute or two we remained thus positioned, clutching each other tightly as if we were the other's anchor. It was as if the storm ever threatened to sweep us away, as if holding each other fast was the only way we would survive. Eventually, I became aware the storm had finally passed. Soon, it seemed nothing more than a mere drizzle.

"Let us take refuge," I suggested presently, for I knew we could not remain here forever. Evelyn sniffed and nodded. Together, we began walking through the dark greyness.

We had not been travelling far, when suddenly the ground beneath us gave way. We both gave grunts of surprise as we ended up rolling down a steep mud bank. The earth ever softened as we fell, akin to a thick, slippery blanket as we finally landed.

"Daniel?" My heart sang in relief at hearing her questioning voice. I sat up in the mud, miraculously uninjured.

"Aye, I'm here," I called back, scanning for her in the darkness. "Are you hurt?" I asked, spotting her sitting a few feet below me.

"No," she answered simply as I then half scrambled, half slid towards her. "We cannot stay here," she muttered, as I pushed a hand through my mud-clogged hair. I nodded, for I knew well how exhausted I was, as my adrenaline continued to drain away. Evelyn could be all the more fatigued, for she had dragged me, restrained and clad in armour, for so long, through that freezing lake.

As I got to my feet I could feel my body getting colder, but there was a current of warm air returning and I clung to it like a lifeline, as I rubbed some of the mud from my face. My clothes seemed a dead weight on me. Gingerly I inspected my cheek, which was sore but seemed to have stop bleeding. I looked about, thankful that now the rain had turned to drizzle, the day was lightening, if only slightly. Soon we could make out tall, looming shapes that revealed themselves to be trees.

"Look." I pointed, as I made out something in the distance. Evelyn followed my gaze, as in the last few remnants of daylight, we saw the mouth of a cave. We walked towards it as swiftly as our weary bodies would allow, using the constant drizzle to try to wipe the clinging mud away.

The water was running down in rivulets from the cave mouth. For a few moments we stood by the entrance, faces pointed towards the sky as we quenched our thirst. The stream of collected rain was so cold it made my teeth chatter, but the fresh purity of it was deeply exhilarating. Next, I moved fully under it, rubbing away more of the mud and dirt. The water also offered a cool balm to my cheek, which was now rather swollen.

This done, we went further into the cave and sank down to the floor, leaning our backs against the stone wall. It was a relief indeed to finally stop. We sat a few minutes quietly together, neither of us speaking, as the temperature cooled. Abruptly, I realised the danger of our wet garments.

"Here," I said as I turned to my wife, as I began to pull at the laces of her clothes with numb fingers. "We have to take our clothes off," I explained to her frown.

"This is hardly the time," she murmured, a faint smile flickering across her face and despite the severity of our circumstances, I felt the same expression tugging at my own mouth.

"Hush," I whispered, gently teasing. I admired her humour in this dire situation. "We have to get you out of these things, otherwise you might die." My queen seemed to have very little strength left, so I went onto undo her battle dress and disrobe her. I left her in her shift, for I reasoned that would dry quickly and perhaps she would warm quicker with a little clothing left. I instructed her quietly to sit with her knees drawn up and her arms around them.

Whilst she was thus reposed, I squeezed, shook and wrung all the water I could from each piece of her clothing, before stretching them out flat on the cave floor. I then hurriedly undressed also, only keeping my underwear. When I had laid my garments upon the floor, too, I moved to sit beside her, winding an arm round her.

"Daniel," Evelyn whispered hoarsely, leaning into my embrace at once. As she spoke, my free hand moved to clasp her joined ones. "I want you to know, if we die here—"

"Hush," I repeated, my voice a little louder. "We're not going to die," I told her firmly. "Can't you feel the warm air?" I asked. After a moment, she nodded slowly. Indeed, now we were mostly out of wet clothes, the close summer air was beginning to warm us. Though it had rained, the weather was hot and humid. Presently, Evelyn moved her left hand to interlink it with mine. I felt the gold of our wedding bands clink softly together, reminding me once again of the promises we had made to each other before our Creator.

"I wanted you to know," she whispered again, haltingly. This time I did not interrupt, for I sensed the importance of what she was about to say. "I love you, Daniel," she said at last.

"I know," I replied, my hand squeezing the one that still held hers. I leant my head against the wall of the cave as I held my wife in my arms. I had been so consumed with hatred and rage, I reflected. Was I such a fool, I reflected, that it had taken her pulling me from my near-watery grave for me to trust her once more?

"I love you," I declared to her, turning towards her. I regretted how long it had been since I had spoken the words. "I always have, I always will," I said, almost urgently. I heard Evelyn sigh in relief, felt her body relax more against mine.

"My boy from the snow," she muttered roughly, voice thick with emotion. At that, I turned and bent my head towards her. I kissed her deeply, revelling in this simple intimacy, for we had been starved of almost all touch for so long. I was full of feeling, too, that the chasm had been crossed at last.

"I'm so sorry, Daniel," she murmured, moving her head to my chest now. I moved my arms tighter about her, enjoying the feel of her head on my chest and her damp, raven curls upon my bare skin. "I feared I had lost you," she admitted.

"Never, my darling," I whispered, kissing the top of her beautiful head. "I forgive you," I murmured to her, resolute to let no more of Aldred's poison ruin our marriage. My queen made a small choked noise as she held back a sob.

"Try not to weep, love," I cautioned her teasingly. "We're both dehydrated enough." My wife half sobbed, half laughed in response, as her emotions were further unleashed. As I held her, I thought that if we were to die this night, at last we were to do so reconciled.

As time passed, though, it seemed we would not die. Though I was still damp from the mixture of sweat and rain, I was no longer cold. Evelyn, too, felt warm beside me. For a long while we remained huddled together in our dark shelter, saying little. Presently, my wife slept. It seemed a particularly deep slumber, as though she hadn't slept properly for weeks. Most probably she hadn't since the Wolf had poured forth his poison upon us. Despite my own exhaustion, I tried to remain awake. My free hand clutched my arrow, the only hope of defence if Aldred found us.

When was the last time I held her like this, I wondered? It seemed such a long time ago, even though it had been but three weeks since the Wolf had been unveiled. It was a joy to at last forgive Evelyn fully. How could I not, after she had just saved my life? In truth, right from the beginning I knew she would be speaking the truth about her part in it all. That she had feared she would lose me and her kingdom. Indeed, as Aife had pointed out, who was I to say I would not have done the same given such dire circumstances?

In the quietness of the cave, I was more aware than ever of a monarch's difficulty of ruling. Yes, they were recipients of much luxury and resplendence away from many hardships, but the throne was also a curse as well as a great privilege. The curse was being the one to make such choices, with potentially disastrous consequences. It could mean either saving or killing those who ruled. Even though I did not directly command Klumeck's citizens the way Evelyn had to reign over Gaeson, the burden of the crown had never been heavier. Indeed, my admiration for my wife grew even more at the thought of how she ruled our people. It gave me great comfort to know I could trust in the love of this woman I held, not only for our home but also for me. The notion was like a warm blanket. Though I had tried so hard to remain alert, the exhaustion of the day and the balm of my wife's regard sent me off to sleep.

Part Four

Chapter Thirteen

The following morning, I woke gradually, with remnants of sleep still pressing heavily against my eyelids. In the half slumber I was aware of Evelyn curled up against me, her head resting gently upon my bare chest. Her sleep was contented, like that of a child as we reposed together, safe and warm in our chamber in Gaeson. Except we weren't in Gaeson...

My eyes snapped open as I awoke fully, coming to stare at the charcoal of the cave walls. The events of the previous day rushed through my mind: being captured by Aldred; almost drowning; running through the rain. I tried to sit up without waking Evelyn, inwardly cursing myself for yielding to slumber. I looked about me, my free hand grasping the thin rod of the arrow beside me, but nothing seemed out of place. Carefully I disentangled myself from my dreaming wife and stood, mentally checking my state. There was a dull throb in my cheek, my muscles groaned in tiredness and there were still flecks of mud upon my skin, but apart from that I seemed to be well.

After stretching, I proceeded to the mouth of the cave, peering. The only movement, however, was that of a raven, swooping grandly into view. It landed squarely a few feet away, in my direct line of sight. Abruptly its dark beak and feathers darted in my direction, as if staring directly at me. The bird then ducked its beak down, ostentatiously pecking the rocky floor. A moment later and it leapt forth from the earth once more. I followed it with my eyes, until it blended with the ashen canvas beyond and disappeared.

The raven was the only sign of life, much to my relief. I was elated at our escape, but a shadow of anger threatened to fill me at how my wife and I had been forced to hide in this dark cave, where we might be shielded from his villainy. I felt like an insect, trying to escape its prey. How I longed to confront him and be free of him, one way or the other! I made a vow then that when I next saw the Wolf, it would be either his life or mine.

"Daniel?" Evelyn's sleepy voice reached my ears. I turned to see her rubbing her eyes, still dressed only in her shift. "Are you all right?" she asked. At her question I realised that my fists were clenched. I took a moment to deliberately relax and uncurl my fingers.

"Yes, thanks to you," I told her quietly. I made my way back over to her, sliding back down beside her. My hand reached out, my thumb caressing her cheek softly. My queen gave a little smile, closing her eyes briefly as she leant into the contact.

"I've been such a fool," I murmured, for her reaction to my simple touch made me realise anew how vast a chasm there had been between us. At once Evelyn shook her head.

"No, you haven't," she emphasised quietly. "Had our positions been reversed, I would have felt just as betrayed and rightly so." I saw sorrow once more begin to take shape in her eyes. "I longed to tell you so many times—"

"I know," I interrupted her murmur softly, my hand moving now to run once through her loose curls, still damp from the night before. "I think we've let Aldred poison our marriage long enough," I reflected presently.

"You're completely forgiven, my love," I reiterated now. "You're my girl from the snow." It was the first time I had ever used the phrase about her. "How could I have ever believed your intention was to cause me harm?" Evelyn smiled widely at this, a beam of joy illuminating her countenance and reaching her eyes. She came forward and we embraced tightly. I pressed a brief kiss on the top of her damp curls.

"Come on," I murmured as we broke apart. We got to our feet, turning our attention to our clothes. Due to the humid weather our vestments had dried a little, but they were still fairly damp. I was glad for the hotter temperature, for there was still a little chill in my bones from the lake and running so long in the rain. Our clothes were ragged and caked in mud, with our boots still soaked, but they would do.

"Your cheek looks a little better this morning," Evelyn remarked from beside me. Her speech was slightly muffled from a hairpin in her mouth as she wound her hair atop her head.

"The pin," I said, remembering suddenly. "The pin we used to break our cords," I added, at her confused expression. "Did Cara give it to you?"

"Aye," Evelyn replied, taking the pin from her mouth to place it intricately into her woven curls. This done, her hands dropped a little listlessly to her sides. "After I fell, she pushed it into my hands as she pulled me up again. I owe her my life," she concluded.

"Mine too," I affirmed, as I buckled my belt and stooped to lace my boots. "Perhaps she has a little loyalty for Rheged left after all," I reflected, straightening and moving to the cave's entrance. I looked out again, but all still seemed safe.

"What do you propose, my husband?" Evelyn murmured from beside me, her hand slipping into mine. I squeezed her fingers back gently.

"Well, our first task will be to discover where we are. Caer Ligualid will not be far," I reasoned. My wife nodded beside me. "Beyond that, our next strategy will be to stop Aldred. We must destroy him once and for all," I added and paused to glance back at her. "If we are indeed to adopt Morwenna's child."

"Oh, Daniel," my queen murmured back. There it was, that vast smile again, a look of happiness I had not seen in her for so long. As I looked upon her countenance, I could not help but return the expression broadly, despite the severity of our circumstances. "Let us depart, then. We'll head uphill," my love suggested.

"Aye," I agreed, squeezing her hand a final time. We left our refuge, only delaying to drink from the water running off the cave's mouth, now as a trickle rather than a stream. We looked about, already able to see where the terrain climbed. We set off in that direction, soon only speaking little as the incline grew steeper. Even though it was quiet between us, it was comfortable, worlds away from the strained civility we had endured of late.

Presently, as we clambered higher, the grey blanket of the sky lightened as the sun began to poke through. At first I was glad, for it did well to remove the last remnants of chill in my bones. Soon, though, the humidity grew too much to bear as we climbed further still. Indeed, it was with great relief that we reached the crest of the hill. The landscape before us then evened out into several long fields of tall grass.

"Look!" Evelyn raised an arm to point. To my delight, as I followed her gaze, I saw one of the fields had a large patch of dandelions. We almost ran towards it out of our hunger. We sank down and thrust our hands into

269

the soft earth to scoop up the flowers. They were still damp but had been warmed considerably by the heat of the day. Part of me yearned for nothing more than to collapse on the gentle grass, to do nothing but slumber and eat dandelions. I was ever aware, however, that the Wolf could be on our trail.

Therefore, we made do with feasting on the dandelions as we walked, savouring the sweet, delicate flowers and the nutty, bitter leaves. There wasn't enough to fill either of us by any means, but it was good to have something in our stomachs. We journeyed on, walking to the edge of the fields, where hopefully we would have a better chance of catching sight of the Wolf if he should be following us. As we followed the course of the higher ground, a drop to our right suddenly emerged. I stepped forwards a few paces across the grassy knoll, to see the small lake was beneath us. From this vantage point, the whole of the mere could be seen.

"We must have fallen into the lake there, around halfway up the east side," Evelyn presently remarked, just as I came to the same conclusion as her. My wife turned to look beside her. "That mountain in the distance seems to stretch on forever," she observed. I raised my head up to see the mountain top disappearing, as it blended with the canvas of the sky.

"Aye," I agreed, reflecting. "I think it is the same peak my father talked about, the one he could see from the great lake when standing on the west side and looking to the east."

"That would make Gaeson lie to the south-east," Evelyn deduced, "which means that Caer Ligualid is to the north-east." I nodded again, turning my head to gaze around us.

"The city cannot be far," she murmured as we looked in that direction. "If so, on the other side of these hills there should be villages soon. They cannot be more than a few miles." She paused here. "We must be careful, Daniel. If that is the nearest civilisation, it is likely Aldred will be waiting for us there."

"I know," I agreed in a murmur. Though her voice had been as strong as ever, I imagined the apprehension behind it and wrapped my arm around her. Evelyn took a step closer and pressed her head against my shoulder. How good a simple embrace like this felt, I reflected. Such warmth, after weeks of coldness.

"It is probably still our safest endeavour," I said now. "Far better than standing here when anyone can see us," I added abruptly, with a sudden sense of urgency that we should leave.

"Agreed," Evelyn muttered swiftly. With that, we began walking away at a march, all the more determined now we had a destination in mind. As we journeyed, we kept looking around us. For though nothing seemed out of place, we knew Aldred and his guards could be lurking behind any rock, ready to ambush us at any moment, as they had done the previous day.

The morning ascent to survey our location had taken away most of our energy. That, coupled with only a few hours' sleep in the cave plus the physical exhaustion of escaping Aldred, meant it did not take long for any remaining strength to ebb away. The sky continued to clear, until the soft grey was replaced with azure blue. Soon, the sun was beating down on us with all intensity, in sharp contrast to yesterday's storms.

Our clothes were damp again, this time with sweat. We were greatly relieved to come across a stream, which helped greatly to slay our thirst. We scooped up armfuls of the clear water, spattering it across our faces and limbs. Still, even with this idyllic, refreshing source babbling away, we could not let ourselves rest longer than we had to. At last as the terrain turned downhill, we saw a valley emerging and part of the way up the other side of it stood a village. We almost giggled at it, at the mere notion of houses and people and civilisation.

"We should wait for the night," Evelyn commented from beside me. It struck me anew how similar we were in mind, for I had also spotted how the path before us was through open fields and low ground, making us far too easy a target.

"Aye," I agreed, as I looked up again to the sky. "The day has become clear, so we should have the light of the moon and stars."

"Also, the light of the oil lamps in the village will help us keep our course," Evelyn affirmed. This decided, we climbed a little to the east, to a rocky crag we could hide in until dark. I sat down on a low rock and my wife joined me. Despite the warmth of the day my wife leaned into me. I wound my arm around her as my body relaxed a little, grateful for the chance to rest.

There, as we waited until nightfall, we began to talk in low, quiet voices. Evelyn spoke first, her voice still clearly laced with guilt and regret. Though it was tempting to quickly assure her of forgiveness, I made myself simply listen, for it had been far too long since we had simply talked openly like this. My queen reiterated her rue for her deception and how imprisoned she had felt by the Wolf's poison.

Next, my queen spoke of her father. She had not mentioned King Reghan in a long time and did so now haltingly, with her hands folded in her lap. Evelyn related how although he could never be fully vindicated for his crimes, the letter had gone some way to help her understand his actions. Though there was a tremor of emotion as she spoke of his last actions on this earth, her eyes were dry; my wife did not weep.

We remained thus positioned as the sun slowly continued to descend. At one point, my hands joined hers, as they still lay on her lap. After Evelyn had finished her speech, I too began to talk. I apologised for how hatred and thirst for vengeance had consumed me these last few weeks. I could see now how I had simply allowed Aldred's venom to seep into my very bones, rather than fighting against it. As we sat with our hands clasped together in front of us, I knew I tasted the sweet liberation of forgiveness, rather than the shackled bitterness that had been my diet of late.

Lastly, as the sky darkened, with deep hues of lavender and coral creeping across the horizon, we quietly declared our love to one another, reaffirming the covenant of marriage we had made to one another before God. By the time we had finished this much needed conversation, twilight had quickly transformed into night. As we had hoped, the sky remained clear and the moon and stars were bright sentinels to guide our way.

Under the cover of darkness, Evelyn and I made our way across the long grass, attempting to strike a balance between speed and care so that we did not fall on the uneven ground. As we had thought, the village would be lit. The soft amber glow of the lamps in the distance filled me with hope. The closer we got, the more I imagined the food that would await us, for we had eaten nothing all day save the dandelions we had been able to scrounge.

Ere long, after perhaps an hour or so of walking through the dark, we reached the outskirts of the village. A few houses lay scattered across the dimly lit landscape, where most prominently there was a farmhouse with a barn attached. Arbitrarily we chose the farmhouse, knocking on the door loudly. We both knew it could easily be Aldred waiting on the other side, but what else could we do? I was so fatigued I hardly cared, but one hand tightened on the arrow behind my back as the door opened, lest the Wolf be lurking.

"Aye?" a voice snapped. Despite the stern voice I instantly relaxed, my grip on the arrow slackening slightly, for though the voice was angry, I knew at once it did not belong to the Wolf. I slipped the arrow back under my belt as the door opened wider, enough for a lamp to illuminate a rather annoyed but ordinary-looking farmer.

"I am sorry to intrude upon your hospitality at this late hour, sire," I greeted him formally, "but we come seeking refuge and—"

"Oh, are you the ones the soldiers were asking about earlier?" The farmer interrupted, his eyes shifting between us. "They said there were two criminals, a man and a woman, who would probably look a bit battered." I tensed inwardly, for this meant Aldred and his thugs had been in the village earlier, searching for us. It was just as well we had waited until nightfall.

"We are not criminals," Evelyn stated now in a firm tone. "I am Evelyn, Queen of Gaeson and this is my husband, King Bryce of Klumeck," she introduced us regally. She reached inside her ragged vestments to bring out a letter she was planning to give to King Owain when we arrived, to send back to Gaeson. Most importantly, the cover contained her royal seal. How the writing remained legible through the lake and the rain I knew not, but miraculously the seal was clear enough.

"Your Majesties!" the farmer gasped, jerking as he recognised us and the seal. He then bowed so abruptly it nearly sent his lantern crashing to the floor.

"Quiet, man," I whispered harshly, for I ardently did not wish for us to be discovered. "Our foes are pursuing us unjustly and we need your help," I explained rapidly.

"Sorry, sire, my lady," the farmer whispered, regaining his composure quickly as he stepped back to admit us. We gratefully entered his home, instantly feeling the warmth of a roaring fire as it began to heat us.

"My name is Seoras, Your Majesties," he said, speaking much quieter now. He set the lantern carefully on a table, before bowing low to us once more. "Please see all of this house as yours."

"Thank you, Seoras," Evelyn replied to him with a courteous nod. "We must ask you for some food, water and a place to sleep. Also, we need a messenger to go directly back to Gaeson to tell the others we are alive. We were kidnapped by our enemy, but we were able to escape," she added in a brief explanation.

"Of course," Seoras replied, nodding hastily. "We have somewhere you can rest undetected and we will send someone at first light," he added. "Please, follow me."

We gratefully followed the farmer through his house, finding comfort in the quiet and the dark. On the way we passed two maids and we paused briefly as he gave them hushed instructions. We then continued up to the second floor of the house and along a dark corridor. It was considerably colder up here, seeming far away from the crackling hearth in the kitchen below.

Seoras admitted us into a small bedchamber and closed the door behind us. I frowned, wondering how this room could be considered hidden, when Seoras moved a small table where it leant against the far wall. Then, with a quick flourish, he moved his hand to slide the wall effortlessly out of sight, revealing a hidden chamber.

"Perfect," I marvelled, impressed. "Why do you have a secret chamber such as this?" I asked as we went into this hidden compartment. It was even sparsely furnished, with a table and two chairs, a bed and a large tub for bathing.

"It used to be an extra part of the barn roof, my lord," the farmer answered. "My father built this when war broke out between us and the Bernicians. Many soldiers have used it on their way back from battles, for it is one of the first outposts for those who have managed to traverse the mountains to return to Caer Ligualid."

"How far away is the city?" I asked him. As I spoke, the two maids came in behind him. One had brought a tray laden with a pie and green leaves, a few slices of fresh bread and a small jug with two goblets. I immediately reasoned this had been the farmer's own dinner, with bread added to stretch it to two people.

"Your generosity is to be commended," Evelyn told him, as the other maid, bearing a large jug, now poured the contents into the tub. Fresh, hot water filled the wooden basin, obviously having been just made for his own use.

"It is no trouble, my lady," Seoras answered her. "My view is that all that is mine is yours. In answer to your question, sire," the farmer added, "it is about a day's ride away." As he finished this statement, the maid who had taken out the empty jug presently returned with clean, dry clothes and I was further impressed with his efficiency. "I'm sorry these are not as fine as you are used to," the farmer apologised, for they were the clothes of servants.

"Not at all," I said as I held them up to inspect them. "The plainer the better. You have our thanks," I reiterated. "They look as though they will fit well," I remarked.

"Very good, sire. Do let me know if you need anything. I pray God keeps you safe this night." He had crossed the chamber to the panel door and now glanced back. "The door can be locked from the inside. I bid you turn it after I leave," he added in a quiet instruction. "Then even if those pursuing you happened to touch the door, it would not move but only look like a wall." With that, Seoras gave a final bow. "Goodnight, Your Majesties."

"Goodnight," we bade him in return. The moment we were alone I crossed the chamber and slid the metal bar across, securely locking the wall. We then only had the restraint to wash our hands and faces briefly before diving into the food. I took huge bites, almost scalding myself with the heat. I knew any food would have tasted good given our hunger, but Seoras definitely had a good cook. The meat was succulent and strong without being overwhelming and the pastry was thick without being laden with fat.

The pie was gone within minutes, as were the refreshing green leaves and the crusty white bread accompanying it. Replete at last, I sat back and poured us another goblet of wine each. Whilst we sipped at the fortifying drink, my wife at last removed our grimy, tattered clothing. I was careful to remove Evelyn's cloth from the inside pocket, which brought a wry smile to her face.

It was then pure joy to wash ourselves in the hot water. My queen attacked her hair first whilst the water was the cleanest, then I gathered my old tunic in my hands, scrubbing myself with it to get the worst of the dirt off. After all the dirt was finally gone, we dressed in the simple nightclothes Seoras had given us. At once we retired to bed, at last able to yield to exhaustion. My last coherent thought was of putting my arm around Evelyn before we fell asleep.

I was sharply awoken a few hours later by a loud thudding sound in the near distance. I sat up in bed, rubbing the remnants of sleep from my eyes.

"The front door," Evelyn whispered, who had risen to sit beside me. I nodded mutely, as I caught the dim light flickering through a hole low in the wall. Silently I climbed out of bed, crossed to the end of the chamber and lay flat on my stomach. In front of me was a gap in the wall about four inches wide and an inch high off the ground. The light was from the torches that soldiers were carrying with them. I immediately recognised the armour of Caer Ligualid, apart from one figure who was disguised in a large cloak.

"Is it Aldred?" Evelyn whispered, coming down to lie beside me. I moved a little to the left and we discovered that with our foreheads touching both of us could look through the hole with one eye each. I was about to reply, when the figure in the cloak removed his outer garment, handing it to a nearby guard. My wife's sombre question was thus answered, for the man who had removed his outer garment was the Wolf himself. His ornate garments were pristine as always, his dark pepper hair slicked back with immaculate precision.

"I think it is the same party that forced us off that cliff," I whispered, as I surveyed the scene below. Evelyn's head moved against mine as she nodded in accord. "I do not see Cara," I murmured, for the warrior was nowhere in sight. A few moments later the heavy door of the farmhouse creaked open, but from our view we could not see the farmer.

"Oh," came the voice of Seoras gruffly, his tone clearly irritated. "I saw you around in the village earlier. You're the soldiers looking for someone, aye?"

"That's correct, sire," Aldred answered him grandly, sounding as amiable and noble as he had ever done before his treachery had been revealed. "We are looking for two fugitives, a man and a woman, who have violated his majesty King Owain's laws. We must search your property. Here is the warrant." My eyes widened at this, in surprise that he should have such a legal aid in his possession. However, we had long suspected the Wolf had spies in the legendary city itself. Perhaps he had friends in high places who had produced the document, or perhaps he had simply forged it himself.

"Well, if you must, but could you not have done this whilst it was still day?" the farmer complained as Aldred and his company began to enter the farmhouse. "No doubt you've woken up half the village." The front door was shut before Aldred could reply. Despite the tension and danger of the situation, I had to smile slightly at Seoras' good acting.

"Aldred has no reason to suspect that this chamber is even here," I whispered to Evelyn, sitting up from the hole. I strained to listen to the mumbled voices downstairs. At one point a door creaked open and the voices became much louder. I suspected they were in the barn, almost directly below us. Neither of us dared move as one person in particular spoke louder. I imagined him to be in the hayloft, ensuring we were not hiding amongst the golden grass.

Ere long the noises faded as they had left the barn. We stood and moved quickly, knowing the Wolf would now be investigating the rest of the house. I silently crossed the room to pour the remaining mouthfuls of wine from the large metal jug into a goblet before handing the jug to Evelyn. She quickly wielded it, holding the handle high in her hand so that she might strike with its pointed lip. My wife had already removed the small metal plate that sat on top of the metal candlestick Seoras had given us, so now it ended as a sharp metal stick.

I swiftly took a quick gulp of the wine remaining in the goblet, before setting it back down and arming myself with the arrow. In my other hand was the heavier jug that the hot water had been in. None of these were the most formidable weapons, but it was better than facing the Wolf empty-handed. My queen and I moved strategically to face the wall, a little way either side, so that we could pounce with the element of surprise.

I held my makeshift weapons firmly in my hands, knowing there was nothing to do but wait. I swiftly worked out a plan of combat. I would bring the jug down hard to incapacitate my first opponent, for it would be logical to use the blunter weapon whilst we had the element of surprise. I would then try to plunge my arrow into the next foe. As Aldred continued his search, I wondered briefly whether Seoras had any skills in combat.

Louder creaking on the floorboards told me they were now on the second floor of the farmhouse. I imagined them making their way towards us. With some surprise, I realised a large part of me was hoping we would be discovered. The core of my heart still longed for vengeance, to slay Aldred where he stood. This thirst for justice raged within me, as I secretly willed the Wolf to discover the false wall, that I might see his blood spilled across the floor in the same way he had shed the blood of my kin.

Presently, as the anticipation grew so close I could almost pierce it with my arrow, the door to the main chamber opened. Very dim light began to softly filter through the specks in the wall.

"We definitely believe the outlaws are still in the area, probably hidden somewhere in this village," Aldred said, his treacherous silky tones filled the air. Anger swelled further at his voice and the temptation to thrust back the false wall and slay him where he stood grew. I could do it, I thought wistfully. I could unbolt the lock, slide the wall, vault over the table and plunge the arrow into his neck. If I had the aim right, I could deliver the fatal blow—

Suddenly, through the dim light of Seoras' lantern, I caught Evelyn's eye. Her countenance was full of sad understanding, as my wife slowly shook her head. I knew she guessed my thoughts perfectly. At once the rage within me lessened, despite my greatest enemy being mere feet away. I could not risk the lives of my queen or the farmer just to satisfy my vengeance. Indeed, if I failed to kill him, it was not outside the realms of possibility for the monster to burn the whole village down, given his previous threats. Therefore, I gave my wife the smallest of nods, to tell her I would not do anything so reckless. A sad smile flickered across her features.

"Well, this was the last chamber in the house, my lord," Seoras grumbled now. "As you can plainly see with your own eyes, my lord, they aren't here. Why don't you go search another village and let the rest of us sleep?" the farmer asked impatiently.

"Ah well, there are other houses we have not searched yet," we heard Aldred concede at length. "Very well, sire, we shall disturb you no longer. But you will tell us, won't you, if they should appear?" His voice was still full of courtesy, with only the faintest trace of a threat.

"Of course, you'll be the first to know," the farmer answered. This time there was only a slight hint of sarcasm. "Well, I'm up with the dawn, so if that will be all, I'll show you out."

"Lead the way," Aldred agreed. We then heard the sound of the door to the other chamber opening, footsteps retreating. Despite him going further and further away, neither of us risked any movement or speech, lest somehow we should be detected. In silence we stood still as stones and waited. Ere long, finally, we then heard the thud of the front door and I felt like I could breathe again.

Immediately and still without speaking a word, Evelyn and I crossed to the gap and lay down again, angling our heads so that both of us could partially survey the scene as before. Aldred was standing out there, slicking his dark hair back with one hand as he spoke. The Wolf instructed in an urgent tone that Seoras should contact him if he saw anything suspicious. Then Aldred pulled up the hood of his cloak, turning around decidedly. His small band followed him, no doubt to search the other houses in the village.

I kept my eye fixed on my enemy until he disappeared from view. Then at last I sat up, sighing audibly in relief.

"Thanks be to God," Evelyn murmured from beside me, sitting up also. Then she glanced at me. "For a moment, I almost thought you were going to reveal us," she added quietly.

"I know. I'm sorry," I muttered back, reaching for her hand. Presently we heard Seoras making his way back through his house and heard the creaking once more on the stairs. As I stood, the door to the other chamber opened and once more tiny specks of amber light filtered through from his lamp.

"Your Majesties?" Seoras called low through the door, even though Aldred had long gone. Perhaps the farmer thought we were still slumbering, but it was hardly possible we should have slept through such a near encounter.

"We heard everything, Seoras," I replied quietly. "We are fine," I added a little unnecessarily, for in the end harm had been avoided. "I thank you for your protection. You played your role quite convincingly," I added. In the near-darkness I saw Evelyn smile faintly.

"You are most welcome, my lord," the farmer replied. I got the strange impression that he was bowing, even though we could not see him. "I have another light for you, my lord," he added, as he moved the table away. I unlocked the door and slid the wall back a little, enough for Seoras to pass through the lantern. "It should be safe now, sire," I heard him add, although he sounded still slightly uncertain.

"Aye," I replied as I took the light from him. "They're likely to believe we are hidden elsewhere and not return. We'll say goodnight, then, till the morning," I added decisively.

"Of course, Your Majesties. I pray you get some rest, we are still three hours or so from dawn." The farmer bowed to me once more, as I smiled slightly and nodded. Purely for precaution, I slid the lock shut again as Seoras moved the table back against the wall.

As the door to the other chamber shut once more and the sounds of his walking again faded into silence, I sighed again in relief. I realised then we were safe inside this chamber, even if Aldred was watching us and could capture us as soon as we left. The night was ours and the elation of it made me feel giddy. Due to the few hours' sleep, I also no longer felt tired. Indeed, Aldred coming so close to discovering us had left adrenaline coursing through me.

I turned to Evelyn, to see she was just as alert as I was. I did not break my eye contact with her, as I placed the arrow and the lantern on the table. Our eyes remained locked, as I reflected how long it had been since we had lain together. It was long before the Wolf had poured his venom on us and the near unbreakable chasm had formed. It was also before we had discovered the truth about our infertility. By God's grace, I felt that at last all the barriers were broken between us. As we gazed at each other, I felt the adrenaline fuelling a fresh rush of desire.

"Evelyn, my love," I whispered to her tenderly. A moment later, the spell was broken as we almost ran into each other's arms, to meet together in a passionate embrace.

When I woke the next morning, I opened my eyes to see daylight filtering through the same crack in the wall Evelyn and I had peered through the previous night. I rolled to my other side, to see my wife sleeping contentedly. Her long raven locks covered most of the right side of her face, so I could not resist but reach to brush them away gently. I had used the softest touch, but it still caused her to stir. My queen yawned a little as she opened her eyes sleepily.

"Morning," Evelyn mumbled. I smiled, moving my mouth to hers in response, feeling her lips yield to me at once. In this simple embrace I felt almost giddy again, at the weight that had been lifted from us. My wife shifted a little closer to me and I wrapped my arms around her. Just as I pressed a gentle kiss to her forehead, there was a loud knock on the wall.

"Your Majesties?" Seoras called in a loud voice. "Your Majesties, are you awake? It is a little after dawn," he added.

"Aye, a moment," I called ere long, for I was reluctant to leave my wife's side. Still clad only in my nightshirt, I climbed out of bed and walked to the wall. I could already hear the farmer, moving the table on the other side again.

"A messenger has already left at dawn to go to Gaeson, as per your instructions, sire," Seoras reported presently. "I do not think anyone followed him, for that official is still here."

"Very well," I murmured, knowing he referred to Aldred. I ran a hand once through my auburn hair before opening the wall a little to better talk to him. "What are they doing, the men who followed us?" I enquired quickly.

"They are standing guard at certain points of the village, my lord," he replied swiftly. "Another two seem to have joined their party. There is one who has a full view of the farmhouse," he added. Whilst he spoke, Evelyn lay down on the floor to look through the hole.

"Aye, I can see him from here," my queen called, after looking through the gap to survey the scene outside. "How can we leave here without being detected?"

"Do not fear, my lady," Seoras called from the outside of the door. "I have a plan. If it please you, sire," he added to me, "I suggest you dress and I can bring you both a simple breakfast and inform you of my strategy." I nodded back to him, the farmer's heroic resolve made me smile slightly.

"Very good," I replied. He bowed once more before departing. I then shut the wall completely and turned to see Evelyn had gone straight for the clothes Seoras had given us.

"There is probably not one inch of this village that is safe from Aldred's scrutiny," Evelyn pointed out, as she handed me a fresh tunic. "What on earth can his plan be?"

"I know not," I admitted, as I hurriedly began to dress. "However, we did not fathom there would be a secret chamber in this barn roof, either," I reflected, as I pushed my feet into still wet boots and began to lace them. "His ingenuity has impressed me," I murmured.

"Aye, he seems to have helped Rheged soldiers before, from what he said last night," my wife muttered, as she deftly finished pulling on the maid's garments. I sensed, though, that she was not fully convinced.

"Whatever happens," I said, catching her arm as she reached for a plain-looking shawl, "I'm so glad we reconciled," I told her solemnly. My queen smiled, her hand now touching mine.

"As am I, my husband," she replied in earnest. Just then, there was another knock on the wall. "Well, he certainly is efficient, I'll grant him that," Evelyn added, as she pulled the shawl closer about her shoulders. I sent her a quick smile, before turning back towards the wall.

"Enter, it is unlocked," I called. A moment later Seoras slid back the wall, followed by a maid who bore a tray. On it looked to be two bowls of boiled wheat, each with a puddle of honey on the top. "Thank you," I directed to the maid, as we took our breakfast gratefully. "What is your proposal?" I added to the farmer, as I fetched a small, wooden spoon.

"It is a simple plan, Your Majesties, if you will allow me to expand upon the details," he replied, with another swift bow of his head. I nodded as I hid a little irritation, for the man before me oft seemed to use twelve words instead of three. "In a few minutes, my hand at the farm and I will set off in my cart, bearing goods to the next town, several miles from here. If it pleases you to be swift, my lord and lady, then we might stow you in the cart. Then, when you arrive at your destination, you are welcome to take one of the horses, or both, if so be required," he finished and bowed. I longed to tell him he didn't have to bow after his every sentence.

"That sounds like a tremendous plan indeed," Evelyn declared graciously at this, whilst I was still busy scooping the warm, sustaining wheat into my mouth. Seoras smiled, looking delighted that she approved his strategy. "However, I can think of only one flaw," she added. I wondered secretly if she could think of several. "How is it that we should get into such a vessel, with every door being guarded?"

"Ah, an excellent point, Your Majesty," Seoras replied. "Allow me to show you the solution to that problem." He then crossed to the middle of the chamber, where by the dim light the night before I had hardly noticed the small rug on the floor. My eyes widened as he now swiftly tossed the scarlet fabric aside to reveal a trap door.

"Marvellous!" I exclaimed, as the farmer opened it. I perceived it led to the hayloft. "Alas, the guard outside also has a clear view of the barn," I reminded him.

"Aye, sire, but the cart is always loaded inside the barn, as hay is also traded," Seoras explained. "Your Majesties could jump down into the hayloft," he continued. "The barn was securely checked by the official last night and has since been guarded, so they would have no reason to check again," the farmer pointed out.

"The cart itself will probably be checked as it's brought into the barn, to ensure nothing is concealed," he continued. "Then, one need only distract him for a moment whilst, if it pleases my lord and lady, you could both climb inside. There should be no reason for them to suspect anything is out of order," he concluded with a final incline of his head.

"That is very good," I emphasised. "This really is not the first time you have done this, is it?" I added with a frown, folding my arms.

"It is not, sire," Seoras affirmed. "As I said last night, we've often had those fleeing the Bernicians hiding here. Though," he added with a frown, "it is the first anyone has had to hide from Caer Ligualid."

"They are not from Caer Ligualid," Evelyn answered him decidedly. "Their leader is a worm of a man, an imposter. He is a Bernician spy," she informed him.

"Of course, my lady," the farmer answered hastily, bowing quickly. "I meant no offence, I assure you," he added, slightly flustered.

"None taken. These are certainly strange times," Evelyn answered, again with all graciousness. "Might I suggest we move quickly with your plan. If you were to distract the guard, we would be most grateful. We will await your signal," she ended.

"Oh," I added before he could make a reply, "When we are in the cart, of course you should not give us any royal titles or bowing. It would not do to be discovered because of needless formality," I concluded.

"Of course not, sire," he replied, giving a faint laugh. "I shall take the opportunity to bid you a formal farewell once my hand and I have arrived at our destination. For now, I hope it will suffice for me to say what an honour it has been to serve Your Majesties," he added with a final flourishing bow. Thence he departed, leaving us once again alone.

"That man can talk for all of Rheged," I muttered. I gave a small sigh, for listening to the pomp of the farmer was becoming quite draining.

"I quite agree," Evelyn agreed with a small chuckle, "but you were right to trust him. What providence we knocked on his door!" she remarked.

"Indeed," I nodded. Then, as I thought of our situation, my countenance hardened. "Aldred was so close to us last night. Once more I have to run away from that villain," I muttered in frustration.

"I know, but what choice do we have, Daniel?" Evelyn returned. "I saw even more of his men out there. There now look to be at least ten in Caer Ligualid armour. We have no proper weapons," she added.

"Aye," I murmured, reaching for my arrow, still the only proper hope we had of defending ourselves. As I did, we heard the noise of the cart reversing into the barn. "Come, let us be quick," I whispered as we got to our knees. I opened the hatch, shifting near it so that the barn below was just visible. If all worked well, I thought, then our escape might just be possible.

"Is that cart loaded yet, boy?" the farmer called to his hand loudly, his tone rife with grumpiness. "You must be swifter if we expect to make the deliveries on time! Can't you see you're in the way?" he complained to the guard.

"Sorry, sire, but precautions must be taken," the guard replied as he made his way to inspect the cart, turning his back to the hayloft.

"Go!" I hissed to Evelyn, seeing the moment of opportunity. My queen jumped swiftly down through the trap door to land softly in the hay. In the next instant I followed, landing almost silently beside her. Immediately, both of us burrowed into the thick, musty golden strands as we attempted to rustle as little as possible. I moved the hay a little out of my eyes. The guard was back looking in our direction, but to my relief he had not spotted us.

"It's all very well, these accounts of fugitives hiding mysteriously in the village," Seoras was saying, "but this is our livelihood! Who's going to trade with us, whilst you're on the lookout for thieves and murderers?" As he spoke, there was a small thud above us.

"I truly am sorry for this inconvenience," the guard sighed presently, yet with an edge to his voice. I could tell his patience was wearing thin.

"Must be one of the maids," Evelyn whispered, glancing instead up to where the hatch had been closed above us. It was becoming all the more evident that the only way out of this village was in that cart.

"Daniel," my queen hissed. I looked back to see Seoras and the guard now stood near the entrance to the barn, having just turned their backs to us.

Without another word, whilst the farmer continued his grumbling distraction, we crawled the last few inches through the hay. Swiftly Evelyn began climbing down the ladder. When she got halfway down, I placed my feet on the first rung, quickly beginning to descend also. We were in full view of the hired hand, who did well preparing his goods and completely ignoring us.

"Hurry!" Evelyn whispered as she touched the ground, racing a couple of steps towards the canvas door of the cart. "He's coming back!" she hissed to me, peering a moment around the cart's frame. I glanced around to see she was right.

I leapt from halfway down the ladder, somehow managing to land almost silently. In the next moment we were pressed against the canvas wall of the cart. Then, with a casualness that was almost too convincing, the hired hand strolled over with another forkful of hay. His sauntering demeanour was in complete contradiction to the immediate danger we were all in. As soon as he moved the canvas flap, Evelyn and I slipped into the cart.

"I bid you lie down in the corner, Your Majesties," the hired hand murmured quietly. We obeyed his instructions, Evelyn lying down first with her face pressed against the far wall of the cart. I quickly tucked myself behind her, reposing like spoons to take up as little space as possible. Quickly, the hired hand covered us with a large cloth, casting us into darkness. I felt light objects landing on top of us: it felt like it was bundles of hay and an empty crate.

"I'll have to inspect the cart again, of course," the fraudulent soldier said. My breath halted. At a glance all things would look well, but if the guard investigated further...

"What? Now this is ridiculous!" the farmer retorted. "You already checked it when it was empty. You've been on guard outside since before dawn," he pointed out angrily. "How do you imagine that my servant has suddenly loaded two criminals in with the hay, when your master woke me in the middle of the night to check every chamber?" There was a pause in the speech. I imagined the soldier deliberating.

"Very well," Aldred's goon replied ere length. Slowly I released the tense air I had been holding. "You would do well to remember we're here on official orders from His Majesty King Owain himself," he then added tightly. I heard the irritation clear in his voice. "He would not take too kindly to your un-cooperation."

"I haven't stopped you, have I?" Seoras replied, still grumbling a little. "Come on lad, that'll do," he added to his hired hand. "Finish your task, before I dock your pay." The guard said nothing further. For a few minutes, the only sound was the hired hand loading the cart.

"All ready to go, sire," the lad called presently, from the front of the cart. "Forward!" he called, as the carriage began to rock us forward.

"This might well work," I dared to whisper to Evelyn a few seconds later. I gently pressed a kiss to the back of her neck. In response, Evelyn moved her hand to one of mine.

I felt every movement the cart made keenly. I imagined Seoras and his horses taking us through the village, no doubt on a well-worn route, then along the road to Caer Ligualid. We both stayed as motionless as possible, lest somehow we would be discovered. The seconds ticked by and all the while we remained undiscovered. Soon relief turned again to anger, for each clop of the horses' hooves reminded me how we were forced to flee, rather than to stand and fight the Wolf.

"We are a few miles away from the town, Your Majesties," at last Seoras called from the front of the cart. "I expect it is safe to come out of hiding." Grateful at last to move, I rolled over, pushing aside the cloth, hay and crates as I did so. We both stood, stretching cramped limbs. I judged it had been an hour since we had left the barn, but had no idea whether my timing was accurate. Presently, I took a step to the edge of the cart, lifting up the canvas flap.

"If it pleases you, sire," the farmer said, as he turned back to glance at me, "presently we will be arriving at the town where we are to trade. If you wish me to take you further—"

"That won't be necessary," I interjected at once. Seoras had already risked his life to help us escape from Aldred's clutches. I did not want to endanger him, nor his servant, any further than was needed. "How far is the town from Caer Ligualid?" I asked next.

"Perhaps three hours on horseback from the village, my lord," our helper answered, his eyes now fixed on the road ahead. "When we reach the town, you are welcome to take one of our horses to continue on your journey." I nodded, giving a small smile to the back of his head.

"I thank you both," I returned sincerely. "You have saved our lives." With that, I closed the tent flap again. I was certain the farmer would warn us if Aldred suddenly arrived. Evelyn was now sitting on one of the bales of hay, her hands poised on the golden grass for balance as the cart rocked. I sat down across from her on an empty crate, thankful we had escaped unscathed.

We spoke little to each other for the rest of the journey. Seoras' timings proved accurate, for only a few minutes later we arrived in the town. The farmer gave us a hasty, simple meal of some bread and cheese before we prepared for our departure. It would be good to be on horseback again, but it meant we would no longer be hidden under blankets and hay.

"Our journey to Caer Ligualid should be safe," I assured Evelyn as I made the final adjustments to our steed, "for Aldred should have in his mind that we were simply hiding in one of the other villages."

"Aye," she agreed quietly. I paused in preparing the horse to look her way, for there was something sombre about her tone. Her countenance was apprehensive, but suddenly I knew her anxiety was not about Aldred. She was worried for what would happen once we arrived at Caer Ligualid. I reached across the horse's thick, hazel coat to take her hand briefly.

"All will be well in the end, love," I murmured to her, hoping beyond hope I was right. "We will explain things to Sarah and she will understand and forgive you, just as I have done."

"I pray you are right," was all she replied, still sounding a little sad. "Come, there's no reason for further delay," she added, breaking the contact as her features stiffened determinedly.

"Very well," I answered, before turning to mount our horse. Evelyn rose up to sit behind me as I took the reins. "Ready?" I asked, already knowing the answer.

"Let us depart," Evelyn agreed. "Thank you so much, Seoras," she added to the farmer. "Your kindness will not be soon forgotten."

"A pleasure to serve you both, Your Majesties. May God grant you a safe journey," Seoras replied, bowing grandly. The hired hand also bowed beside him, a little more clumsily.

"Farewell," I uttered simply, with a nod at both of them. With that, we set off for Caer Ligualid at a swift canter. Soon we had left Seoras and the town he had stowed us too far behind. At last, as we rode back on the road to the legendary city, I uttered a quick prayer that Sarah would indeed be as forgiving as I hoped.

Chapter Fourteen

I was greatly relieved when, finally, I caught my first glimpse of Caer Ligualid. The grand castle towered over the plains in the distance. It was providence indeed that we had been able to slip through the Wolf's grasp. In truth, it gave me some satisfaction to imagine Aldred searching village after village for us.

Then, though, my hands tightened on the reins considerably, as I imagined the terror of the Wolf. I saw him unleashing his wrath on the innocent citizens of Rheged, burning down homes and land without a care. The horrifying truth was that such carnage was not implausible for such a monster. Quickly, I uttered a swift prayer that no lives would be forfeit because we had escaped him. I prayed, too, that Aldred would never suspect Seoras and his hired hand.

I felt Evelyn tense, too, as we neared the city. She was still sat behind me, but I could well imagine the grim determination setting upon her countenance. We did not yet know if the messengers had reached Caer Ligualid with our warning about Aldred, but if they had, then the note I had written to Sarah would also have arrived. If the message had gotten to her, then Evelyn could be sure of a frosty reception from my sister. I reminded myself that Sarah's anger would be far easier to face than the Wolf's wrath.

At last we entered Caer Ligualid, being promptly admitted through the gates. We walked our horse up the path through the city to the castle, as a crowd began to gather. People were excitedly pointing and cheering, making me wonder if our arrival had been hoped for and expected. We came to the large courtyard, far grander than the one in Gaeson. We dismounted the farmer's horse as a stable boy ran out to take our steed from us. In a quick murmur, I told the lad to inform his master that the horse should be returned to Seoras as soon as possible.

Beside me Evelyn stiffened, so slightly it was almost imperceptible. As I turned back, I saw why, for across the courtyard stood my sister.

"Sarah," I said warmly. I took a step instinctively towards her, as if to run to embrace her. In the next instant, I stopped short, as I saw the cool demeanour of her walking. It was immediately obvious the messengers had indeed reached Caer Ligualid's gates. This meant she had received my note, hinting at Evelyn's involvement with all the fullness of my rage.

"It is good to see you alive and well, Daniel," my sister murmured, but she did not embrace me. "I got your message," she added, confirming what I already suspected. Her eyes shifted coldly to my wife as she spoke.

"I'm so sorry, Sarah," Evelyn began, at once holding out her hands in reconciliation. Sarah's eyes only narrowed further. "Truly," she emphasised. "If I could but explain—"

"King Owain wants to see us in the palace hall," my sister interrupted harshly. "It would not do well to keep His Majesty waiting." With that, she abruptly turned away from us.

"Let her go," I said, as Evelyn opened her mouth again. "Let me talk to her," I suggested. "She'll understand," I added. "We'll make her." With a last touch to my wife's arm, I sped off in my sister's direction.

"Sarah, wait!" I called, but she kept on walking. As I neared her and reached out to take her arm, she whirled around to face me, almost violently.

"I do not want to discuss it," she hissed angrily, her cheeks flushed with rage. "She had so many chances to tell us, Daniel," she said, shaking her head. "When you first told us about the spy, Evelyn was just as shocked as we were. Did I not warn you of this, brother?" Sarah emphasised bitterly, her tone harsh. "Whilst we were walking on this very path?" She gestured wildly around in front of us as she spoke.

"I am sorry," I replied, realising anew that she was right. When my sister and I had last conversed together on the way to see King Owain, Sarah had tentatively voiced her suspicions that Evelyn might know who the spy was. In response I had rudely dismissed her, finding the prospect outrageous. Our uncle had been alive then, I reflected sadly. We had both ceased in the journey to the palace hall and for a moment neither of us spoke. Sarah looked in the direction of the mountains, whilst a quiet breeze rifled past us.

"Come," Sarah said eventually, her voice suddenly sounding dull and tired. The two of us began walking again, as I glanced back to see my queen trailing a way behind us. "What happened to you?" she enquired abruptly, irritation still clear in her face and tone. "We expected you here three days ago. Also, why are you dressed in servants' clothes?"

"We were kidnapped along the road to Caer Ligualid, by Aldred and his goons," I began. Sarah's eyes widened in surprise. "He took us to a small lake, to the west of the great one." Swiftly, I related to her all that had transpired after our capture.

"She may have retained some elements of her previous good character, then," my sister replied cynically. She folded her arms as I finished the account. "So, you know not Cara's true character," Sarah guessed.

"Aye," I replied heavily. "She claimed to have been lying when I spoke to her in the dungeon, but then she gave Evelyn the pin that saved both our lives. I suppose only the passing of days will tell us where she stands," I concluded.

"I am glad you are safe, Daniel, truly," Sarah said now. Although she did not fully embrace me, she touched my arm briefly. Then, with her hand still on my arm, her eyes narrowed as she searched my face. "You have forgiven her, haven't you?" she challenged, her voice a little louder. "You've already forgiven what she has done."

"Yes," I admitted directly. At once Sarah dropped her hand from my arm, as the bitterness came back to her features. "There were reasons, Sarah," I was keen to explain. "There is so much more to tell you than in my note. When I wrote it, emotions had displaced all my clear thinking on the matter," I ended, desperate for her to understand.

"So, I am not being reasoned?" Sarah retorted, the sharp note of accusation clear in her voice. Her eyes sparked with anger once more. "Brother, you wrote that note when you felt her betrayal the fullest, when it still cut you to the heart." Her gaze narrowed again.

"Did it only take a month for you to forgive what wrong she did you?" she enquired quietly. A slow, heavy sadness had filled her tone. "Did it only take your jumping off a cliff for you to forget what kind of a man she knowingly entertained in her court and council?"

"No!" I said passionately. "I did not forget. I will never forget Aldred or what he did, for as long as I live," I added tightly. We had come to a stop near the palace doors, but before I could say more the guard outside the door stepped towards us. The soldier bowed low and opened the door to let us in. By this point Evelyn had caught up with us, but Sarah still did not look her way. Instead, she marched directly into the hall, eyes straight ahead.

"Your Supreme Majesty," we all chorused, as Evelyn and I followed Sarah into the throne room. I bowed low, whilst my sister and my wife curtseyed to him.

"Welcome, King Bryce, Queen Evelyn, Princess Lynette," King Owain returned formally, as he stood. "I am glad you have arrived at last. What delayed you?" he asked at once. The great monarch sat back down upon his throne, as Evelyn swiftly reported to him our conflict with the Wolf and our escape, aided by Seoras.

"We do not know Aldred's current whereabouts, my lord the king," I said, as my queen finished the account. "His treachery seems to know no bounds," I continued. I could not help but stare directly at him as I said this, for he had also known of the Wolf's identity all along. Indeed, it was he who had encouraged Evelyn to keep this truth from me, as his father had also.

"Indeed," King Owain reflected dryly. He now stood, taking a mouthful of wine. The Supreme Ruler of Rheged then lowered his goblet before descending the shallow steps towards us, moving with all royal pomp and finery.

"The deceit upon you, your sister and King Cedric was most unfortunate," he admitted as he came to a stop. "It was done, however, for the sake of yourselves and the whole of Rheged. It could not have been avoided," he finished flatly.

"So it would seem, sire," I responded to his speech meaningfully. My gaze was still locked with this mighty king, only fifteen years or so my senior. "It seems more unfortunate still that my uncle died before the mystery could be revealed to him. He never knew who murdered his kin, so brutally and so without reason," I added, my passion rising.

"Aye," King Owain frowned. He took another swig from his burgundy tonic. "It is also a shame that your wife's own father was the one who ordered such violence," he concluded hotly. "I did all that could be done, so let that be an end to it."

"You expect us to take such injustice, Your Majesty?" Sarah spoke now, bursting her speech out as if she could not contain it any longer. King Owain broke my gaze to glance at her. "To endure such deceit and wickedness, done by those we most love?" My sister glared in challenge at Evelyn as she spoke, who at once averted her eyes.

"I do," the great king responded evenly. "You must have a little more perspective, Princess Lynette," he continued, "for there is more involved here than you and your brother realise, sad though it was. Aldred would have done far more evil had his truth been known. Or have you forgotten that he ranks high within the fold of Bernician spies?" He paused here to hand his goblet to a servant, then wiped his mouth with the back of his hand.

"This is no time to have a family feud," our chief monarch declared pointedly, "not when the Angles are moving against Rheged as we speak. The latest word is that King Morgant has made a deal with King Hussa, the chief Bernician King. No doubt Aldred has joined them."

"King Morgant?" I repeated in dismay and in disbelief, as though I had not heard him right. "That makes little sense, my lord," I added hastily, as King Owain fixed his piercing gaze back upon me. Under his cold scrutiny I was again reminded he was his father's son. "After all, his own kingdom used to be Bernicia, until the enemy dispossessed him of it. He should desire vengeance on the Anglian scourge more than any other," I pointed out.

"Of that I am aware," King Owain replied shortly. "It is our belief that King Morgant has made the deal in the foolish notion of reclaiming some of his former power and land. This is why, we reason, he ordered the assassination of my father on the battlefield," he declared sombrely. "He is trying to fracture Rheged as an act of good faith towards the enemy," he said now as he folded his arms, looking at each one of us in turn.

"It is good to see you are here without harm," the great monarch added, in a concluding tone. "My scouts are currently trying to ascertain Aldred's whereabouts. I will inform you when his location his known." He nodded to us. Duly dismissed, we left King Owain's presence.

The three of us barely spoke as we went to one of the smaller reception rooms in the caste. I had barely shut the door behind us, however, before my sister whirled on her feet to glare at Evelyn.

"Daniel tells me you have already been acquitted of your crimes," she snapped. "It did not take him long. Unfortunately for you, I still see your actions objectively. I do not possess the blindness of being in love with you," she added scornfully.

"Peace, sister," I said, stepping forwards towards her. Sarah shot a glare my way but said nothing further. I had expected Sarah to be angry, but not this level of ferocity. Then I remembered she did not fully know these events. "Sarah, there are reasons for why she did what she did," I told her again, reiterating my words from earlier.

"Aye, reasons I know full well," my sister replied as she looked between us. "King Owain told me King Urien had ordered King Reghan to keep Aldred in position, without telling us. A tradition you decided to carry on," she directed to Evelyn, her eyes still blazing.

"Did he also tell you why I did this?" Evelyn spoke so softly, it seemed to dispel some of Sarah's fury. My sister merely regarded my wife, her mouth drawn tight in anger. "I found a letter, just after Daniel and I were betrothed. A letter he has also read," she said. "It was from my father, explaining why he had kept silent about Aldred. That villain had threatened to do unspeakable harm to Gaeson and the rest of Rheged. He also told me that Aldred would certainly kill Daniel and you as well."

"Oh, so it was really your noble sacrifice to not tell us?" Sarah bit back. It was exactly the same reaction as I'd had, a few weeks earlier. "What a victim you have been! Evelyn, he is directly responsible for why I have no memory of my true parents!" she exclaimed bitterly.

"I am not saying I chose what was right," Evelyn replied, her tone still quiet in sharp contrast to Sarah's loud anger. "There was no right decision," my wife murmured sadly. "It was either lie and keep you alive or tell the truth and risk what Aldred would do to you and Rheged. I longed to tell both of you so many times," she added, her speech a little quicker as she looked between us, "but I feared I would lose those I loved most if I did."

"I will not be persuaded by this," Sarah responded. "If he was as powerful as you suppose, why not just have him killed before he could enact his awful schemes?" she snapped.

"It was not that simple," my wife answered her calmly. "You saw the documents about the Wolf that Daniel found in King Urien's tomb. You know how vast a network he yields. He claimed that any time, others could unleash his contingency; a ferocity that could destroy not only Gaeson but half of Rheged itself."

"I see," Sarah sighed heavily, folding her arms. Though her voice was still hot, some of the bitterness in her speech had gone. "Well, brother?" My sister continued abruptly, looking to me. "What is next?" I swallowed as I looked between them, these two women I dearly loved.

"We have to find the Wolf," I stated the obvious, "before he commits whatever evil he is planning. We must stop the storm he is brewing, lest all he has ever threatened comes true," I emphasised. "For that to happen, though, we must work together," I added, pausing as I looked directly at Sarah. "We must trust each other."

"Trust?" Sarah cut back scornfully. "Tell me you are in jest," she muttered, shaking her head. I frowned, for she knew full well I was being serious. Presently my sister sighed. "I can work with her, Daniel, but I fear I may never trust her again. Her father ordered this man to kill our parents," she added bluntly. "Let me know when you have a plan," she concluded decisively.

"Wait, Sarah," Evelyn called as my sister turned to leave, but Sarah kept walking away. "Please..." my wife added, starting to go after her.

"Leave her, Evelyn," I murmured, touching her arm as she went in pursuit of my sister. "It took me three weeks to be able to listen to you. Allow some time to digest what we have told her. Forgiveness is not often quick," I reminded her gently.

"Aye, I know," she agreed at length, emitting a small sigh of resignation. "Daniel, what if she never forgives me?" My wife enquired now, as I wrapped an arm around her. "You were angry," Evelyn shook her head a little as she spoke. "I thought I might never see you smile again." Her voice was quiet, low and a little broken. "This, though... her hatred seems even stronger. I have never known anything like it, except perhaps the loathing I've had for myself in all this." I knew my wife well enough to know she was not being dramatic. It struck me anew that the person Evelyn had been harshest with was probably herself.

"It is the Wolf who deserves our rage, not you," I told her soothingly. "She is angry and grieves her parents. I think she finds it harder, too, that whilst I have some memories of Klumeck, she has none," I continued. "She will forgive you in time, just as I have," I concluded, bending my head to kiss the top of hers as it rested on my neck.

"I pray you are right," Evelyn murmured before stepping back from me. "Do you have a plan for catching him?" she asked me quietly. "Presumably he will have joined King Morgant's ranks, as King Owain said. I do not think we have such an army to mount against him, even with the aid of Caer Ligualid."

"Aye," I agreed, stepping backwards to lean against the table as I thought. "Besides, there is little we can do whilst we do not know where the party are. Hopefully the scouts will be able to find out where he is."

"Even if they do, what then?" Evelyn asked a little sadly. She came to lean against the table, placing her head on my shoulder. "How are we ever going to stop him?"

"I know not," I murmured thoughtfully. "For if we cannot kill him by taking on his king's forces, then…" I paused, standing straight, away from the table as a plan came to mind. "I do not believe the Bernicians will be happy to learn of how many times Aldred has crossed them," I pointed out. "I must request to speak to King Hussa, King Morgant, or whichever Bernician lord he is moving with. If I tell them of his treachery, they may allow me to confront him—"

"They will not believe you, Daniel," Evelyn pointed out, shaking her head. "The Wolf is a Bernician spy. He will simply claim all his actions were to advance his people's cause."

"Aye, but remember the documents my uncle and I discovered in King Urien's tomb," I recalled, folding my arms. "They said that Aldred persuaded King Urien to join with the Coalition Kings to take Ynys Metcaut. Even if he claims this was for their campaign, they will not thank Aldred for wiping out most of the Bernician Army."

"The evidence you speak of was taken," Evelyn pointed out gently. "They will only have the word of a Briton king against a high ranking Bernician official and war legend." I ceased here momentarily, for I knew this was right. Surely such a meeting would result in my instant death.

"It does not matter," I muttered ere long. "I must go and stop Aldred, before he uses his venom to bring another war to our door. King Owain said they are moving against Rheged, but perhaps if Aldred was revealed to them it might stay their blades. If any peace is possible, then it must be attained. I have to try," I declared to her. Evelyn was still shaking her head.

"Why must it be you, husband?" she asked now, looking up at me. "King Owain, for example, would yield much more authority."

"The mutual hatred between King Owain and King Hussa is well known," I pointed out. "If Aldred is with King Morgant then it will be even worse, for the last time King Owain saw that traitor, he had just ordered the assassination of his father. King Owain cannot confront either Bernician King without risking bloodshed, right then and there." Evelyn sighed here.

"Besides, it is deeper than that," I continued, stepping forwards to take her hands. "I believe God has bound our destinies together. He has killed so many of my kin, pouring his venom since I was a child. I think it has to be me who finally stops him," I admitted.

"Daniel, you cannot," Evelyn implored again. "Without the evidence of those documents, they will simply kill you on sight, no matter you they tell him."

"Is it evidence you require?" A new, silky voice came into the chamber. I turned swiftly, a hand already on the hilt of my sword. "There is no need to be so defensive, my lord," came the voice of Taliesin as he walked into the chamber. One hand was behind his back as he bent his head to us in a brief bow. "After all," he resumed, "we are all on the same side."

"Are we?" I questioned him with a frown. "What is it that you want, bard? How much did you overhear?" Taliesin gave a small smile as he came to a stop in front of us.

"Enough to know that you plan to confront Aldred," Taliesin replied. "A bold move, Your Majesty, but Her Majesty is right," he added, his eyes flicking to Evelyn as he spoke. "Without any evidence, neither of his lords would have any reason not to kill you on sight. With the documents you seek, however—" as he spoke, he abruptly showed his other hand. He held a wad of pages I instantly recognised.

"The records!" I gasped, almost snatching them as he handed them back to me. I did not look at them but kept my eyes on the bard. "You were the one who stole them from my uncle's drawer," I realised slowly. At the time, I had simply assumed it had been the Wolf, or one of his spies, who had taken them.

"Indeed, my lord," Taliesin freely admitted with another bow. "I only did it to protect them, however. I had to take them, before Aldred did and destroyed the evidence."

"You knew," I stated heavily, as further realisation struck. I slapped the precious evidence heavily to the table, before clenching my fists at my sides. "You knew it was Aldred, when you sent me on that ridiculous quest?" I ground out.

"I only suspected, sire," the poet replied quickly. "You see, you might not have realised that it was I who made the records," he admitted. My eyes flew wide in further surprise. "The Wolf was always very careful, however, that I never saw his face. At every meeting, he wore his thick cloak to disguise his identity. I only observed those few conversations," he said.

"Then, the last time you came to Caer Ligualid, when Aldred came with you—as soon as I heard his voice, I knew," he declared. "He even had the gall to look me directly in the eyes and sneer. It was clear he knew I had recognised him, but he did not care."

"Yet you said nothing," Evelyn pointed out, folding her arms. "You knew what he was capable of and you kept your silence."

"Indeed I did, my lady. I kept my silence because I knew well his power and villainy, from those conversations I witnessed. I feared things could be much worse if I spoke out. I understand that was your motive as well, Your Majesty," Taliesin directed to Evelyn. The bard's point was clear, for he was not the only one to hide the truth about Aldred.

"Aye," my wife muttered softly, her gaze flickering away from him. A moment later, however, she looked back. "Why did you tell King Bryce about the records?" she asked.

"I always wished for the Wolf to come to the end, my lady, knowing his true character," Taliesin answered with a short bow of his head again.

"When I knew you were coming here with the purpose of discovering his identity, I reasoned I could tell you of the documents that might well one day be the weapon to stop him," he concluded.

"I knew that was why you spoke in such a riddle that day," I said now, folding my arms as I leant against the table again. "You knew Aldred might be listening."

"Aye, sire," Taliesin affirmed with another nod. "I saw the Wolf only minutes later, walking about the castle. Though his movements seemed innocent enough, I decided to follow him. He stopped to wait, not far from the path to the tomb," the bard continued, "so it seems he overheard me after all. After you passed him by, he followed you back to King Cedric's chamber until the horn sounded for battle."

"I assumed the Wolf had stolen the documents, or one of his associates," I reiterated, as the bard finished his account. "How did you steal them from under his grasp?" I asked next, as Evelyn looked my way.

"Aldred quickly left the corridor when the horn sounded, knowing you would make your way immediately to the battle ground," Taliesin responded. "However, I remained hidden along the corridor, still unseen. A fairly easy manoeuvre for me, Your Majesties, given my stature," he quipped wryly. "Then, once you had departed, I entered King Cedric's chamber and found the documents easily. I hid them away somewhere else in the castle, waiting for the day when they would be needed. That time seems to have come," he concluded, looking to the documents.

"I understand," I said here, straightening from the table again and turning to pick up the documents more carefully. "Thank you, Taliesin," I directed, glancing back to the bard as I spoke. "I believe I have misjudged you," I added, "but in this, you have proved your character and your loyalty to Rheged." Taliesin gave small smile.

"I live to serve, Your Majesties," he responded, before bowing grandly. "If that is all, sire," the bard added. I nodded at him and Taliesin then left our company, almost as abruptly as he had appeared. As he departed the reception chamber, my gaze went straight back to the documents I held in my hand, opening the only evidence of Aldred's treachery.

"It is all here, as the bard says," I murmured, as I scanned through the records quickly. "I can confront him with this, Evelyn," I added, looking up to her. "This contains enough proof for me to beg an audience with whichever Bernician King Aldred is travelling with. I shall speak to His Majesty King Owain, now," I declared, taking a step away from the table.

"Wait," my wife said, her hand quick on my arm. I glanced back to her. "Would you risk your life so easily, my love?" she murmured, her concerned gaze meeting mine.

"Aye," I told her simply. My free hand went to the one of hers on top of my arm. "You know as well as I do that he must be stopped," I told her quietly, "before he has the chance to enact his evil schemes."

Evelyn said nothing more to object, but instead her gaze lowered from me to the floor. Knowing this was likely all the agreement I was to receive, I pressed a swift kiss to her forehead and thence departed from her, heading back to the palace hall. I kept hold of the documents carefully, clutching tightly at perhaps the best weapon I had against my greatest enemy.

***

"I thought I might find you up here," I said, as I saw Sarah standing on one of the higher ramparts of the castle a week later. I had come to join my sister at one of the best viewing spots in all of Rheged. To our east stood the legendary spires of the castle and below, spreading out from the ancient keep, was its city. Beyond Caer Ligualid itself stretched the magnificent terrain of mountains in the distance, with sparse lakes gleaming in the broad daylight.

"Aye," was all she murmured and then glanced at me, her expression sombre. "I wish you did not have to go tomorrow, brother," she said abruptly, reaching out to take my hand. I returned the contact immediately, glad she no longer had any residual bitterness towards me.

"So do I," I admitted, "but I believe it is the only way to confront Aldred without risking open war." It was six days since King Owain had agreed to my proposal and we had spent the rest of this week waiting for the scouts to return. They had come back yesterday, to report that Aldred was in the company of King Hussa and they were near Klumeck. I was therefore leaving with a small force of Caer Ligualid soldiers to confront them.

"We cannot risk that," I told her adamantly. "Rheged has not recovered yet. It is not yet three months since the last battle," I reflected. A little sadness entered her features, no doubt at the thought of our uncle.

"As much as I wished there was another way, I think you are right," she admitted presently. Her gaze flickered back to the view as she spoke. "He will hurt us and the rest of Rheged for as long as he lives," she declared quietly.

"That is true," I agreed. For a moment the two of us stood there in silence, admiring the spires whilst the sun dipped lazily lower into the sky. "Evelyn is not our enemy, sister," I pointed out quietly. Sarah did not speak for a moment. I wondered if she had chosen not to answer.

"I know," she agreed ere long, with a soft sigh. My heart leapt at her words, hoping a little time had softened her regard for my wife. "It was a terrible situation," Sarah admitted, "but that does not make her treachery right."

"Aye," I answered at once, turning to look at her. "As Evelyn said, she was in a position where there was no right answer. She believed she was either betraying us, or risk the destruction of half of Rheged," I concluded.

"I know," she repeated softly, as we both looked out to the afternoon sun again, casting its golden hues on everything it touched. "I can't imagine what I would have done, in her situation," Sarah conceded with a murmur. I nodded beside her and all fell quiet momentarily.

"Sister," I began hesitantly now, "there's something else I've been meaning to tell you. Nothing to do with Aldred," I clarified swiftly. "We discovered it only three days after parting your company and returning to Gaeson." I paused to swallow. "Evelyn and I planned to come to Caer Ligualid to tell you, after the parade, but that was when Aldred was revealed..." my voice trailed away as I faltered.

"What, Daniel?" she asked, the frown deepening. I found myself hesitating again and despised my weakness. It was over two months since Evelyn had told me, so why did the words stick in my throat still? "Tell me what's happened," Sarah implored, a little louder.

"I wanted to tell you earlier, but because of everything that's happened..." I knew this was an excuse, though. Although her regard had cooled considerably, I had still seen her several times this week. Each time I had almost told her, but the timing had never seemed right.

"Evelyn was examined by Leigh," I at last informed her gently. "She discovered she is unable to bear a child." At once, I saw sad surprise shape her countenance. Her brows creased as they knitted together in sympathy.

"Oh, my brother," Sarah murmured sorrowfully. Without another word, she stepped forward towards me. "I'm so sorry," she whispered, putting her arms around me. I returned the gesture immediately. It was our first full embrace and I revelled in its warmth, making all earlier contact seem even more perfunctory and distant.

"It is the road God has chosen for us to walk," I muttered to her, reiterating the phrase Aife had once told me, a few days after discovering the sad truth. Sarah pulled back from me and nodded slowly. I saw her eyes had filled a little with tears, but they soon receded: my sister was not to weep.

"It is not all sadness, though," I was now quick to relate. "There is a maid in Gaeson, named Morwenna, who is soon to give birth." Very soon, I realised, as I said this. I had not realised how fast time had progressed, after the Wolf's unveiling. It was two months till the child was to be born, sooner if the child came before time. "The child will be ours," I concluded presently. Sarah smiled instantly, a full smile that reached her eyes. It was the first time I had seen her properly smile since our arrival in Caer Ligualid.

"Well, that is wonderful news indeed," she replied happily. Then her countenance changed abruptly, as her eyes widened. "Then surely you cannot confront Aldred, Daniel! Not if you have a child soon to be born to you!" she exclaimed.

"I have to, Sarah," I told her quietly, taking her hand again. "It is for the sake of the child that I must go. Evelyn knows this, also," I continued emphatically. "Neither my wife, nor this baby, will be safe as long as Aldred lives," I pointed out.

"That is why," I now said passionately, "you must make your peace with Evelyn. If I should die—listen!" I almost hissed, as she automatically began shaking her head. "If I should die," I repeated quietly, "then I do not know whether Evelyn will choose to adopt the child on her own. Either way, she will need you as friend and kin more than ever. You would become Queen of Klumeck, but even if your duties threaten to keep you away from Gaeson, you must promise me you will be there for her when the time comes. Promise me," I repeated imploringly. Sarah held my eyes a moment longer before nodding.

"Aye, Daniel. I promise," she said. I smiled at this, in relief that Sarah would reconcile to my wife and support her, should the worst happen.

"Your Majesty, Your Royal Highness." Both of us turned from each other's gaze, one hand still joined, to see a guard suddenly to come to a halt before us. "I apologise for the disturbance, but…"

"What is it?" I asked, for the guard, having noticed he had interrupted a conversation, seemed to falter. "Has something happened?" I enquired, as Sarah's hand dropped from mine.

"No, my lord king," he replied, giving a small, hasty cough. "Sire, Queen Evelyn bid me send for you," he continued, in a much clearer tone as he straightened. "A small contingent from Gaeson has arrived," he added in brief explanation.

"Very good," I said, giving him a formal nod of dismissal. We followed on his heels as he quickly descended the spiral steps from the rampart. Our steps matched his as we returned to the Caer Ligualid courtyard.

"Captain," I greeted with pleasant surprise, to see John talking to Evelyn. It was with further joy I witnessed Aife also standing there.

"Your Majesty, Your Royal Highness," the troop from Gaeson chorused, as they sank to bended knee towards us.

"Lord Melvyn sends you greetings, my lord king," John added as they straightened once more. "We prayed we would see you safe and well. We also came to report to His Majesty King Owain," he added, but did not specify more. I gathered from this there was more for him to say that he could not relate so publicly.

"Of course. You and Aife can come through, the rest of you go and rest," I dismissed and the rest of us began to cross back to the palace hall, but then a loud neigh reached my ears.

"Epos," I greeted with enthusiasm. Her ears had pricked, as her head darted left to right in excited recognition. "Hello again, old friend," I murmured as I stroked her mane softly. "Go and rest, girl," I murmured then, giving her coat a final pat before a stable hand took her away. I then re-joined Evelyn, John, Sarah and Aife and the five of us walked to the palace hall.

"It is good to see you, my friends," I told John and Aife, as we walked a little away from the throng of people who had gathered. Caer Ligualid's citizens always seemed interested in anyone who came through their gates. Now we were a little more in private, I greeted them more informally and I clasped their arms warmly in turn.

"We are glad to see you alive, brother. The soldiers brought Epos back when you were taken by Aldred. We also brought you this," he added. He then removed another sword from his belt that I hadn't noticed.

"Wonderful!" I exclaimed, seeing it was my old blade, the weapon my father had given me not long before he died. As I drew it from its sheath and held it closer, I perceived it had been recently cleaned. "No other sword has felt as fine," I commented, as I admired the newly polished metal.

"It is good to see it back in your hands," John replied with a grin, as I slid my sword back into its sheath. I replaced it on my belt, taking off the plainer blade I had used since coming to Caer Ligualid.

"What happened to you, brother?" John asked, as he took the other sword from me. In swift tones, whilst we walked the outer corridor, I related at once the account of how Aldred had kidnapped us and how we had escaped.

"Your timing is most fortunate," I told them presently. "We have discovered that Aldred is near Klumeck, travelling with King Hussa himself." In still-rapid speech, I explained to them how I was to present the records from King Urien's tomb to reveal the Wolf's true nature.

Before I could ask them what they were to report to King Owain, we had arrived at the palace hall, so our talk ceased as we walked through the grand doors. I then found out the nature of the discourse, however, as my captain reported to the Supreme King of Rheged that there was a Bernician force on the march against Gaeson, led by King Morgant himself. John had led his small troops, therefore, not only to see if Evelyn and I were safe, but to request Evelyn return to Gaeson, as well as asking for any additional troops Caer Ligualid might have to spare.

***

"I was going to come with you, my love," Evelyn murmured sombrely, as my wife and I prepared for bed that evening. "Are you sure you have to do this?" she then asked. "In just eight weeks, a baby will be born to us in Gaeson. I do not want to raise a child alone," she reflected sadly, raising a hand to lay it gently across my cheek.

"You know it is because of the child I have to go," I replied quietly, reiterating what I had told Sarah earlier today. "I do not want to have this child born in a world where that villain roams free. He is determined to destroy us: you know he will never cease. We cannot be truly safe until the Wolf stops drawing breath," I concluded. Indeed, I had never been more convinced of this truth. Evelyn looked down, looking as resignedly accepting of the strategy as when we had first planned it a week earlier.

"I know, I just—" she whispered, then stopped. A few tears began to form in her eyes and one proceeded to roll down her cheek. "I don't want to lose you, Daniel," she blurted. "Not after all we've been through."

I caught the rough, pained edge to her voice. It threatened to break my heart, for we both knew I could die at the hand of the Wolf. Or, I could survive the confrontation, only to come home to see Gaeson devastated, my wife and friends dead along with it. Therefore, I did not reply to her with words. Instead I stepped forwards, my hands framing her face as I met her mouth urgently. I kissed my love soundly and my queen at once yielded to it, wrapping her arms about my waist. Ere long I ended our passionate embrace, my hands rising to move my thumbs gently over her face to remove the traces of her tears.

"I want you to know," she spoke haltingly, "I'm so glad we were able to reconcile and understand—" she hesitated only for a moment, "before…" her words trailed away, but I felt I knew her sentiments exactly. I was just as glad we had been able to forgive one another, in case this was the last night we would ever spend in each other's company.

"As am I, my love," I told her tenderly, my hand coming to brush one of her raven curls softly. "As am I." I paused a moment to regard her then, this strong, wise woman that I cherished most in all the earth. My free hand

305

came to join hers and as I did, I saw the gold band on my finger, a sign of the covenant I had made with her before God.

"I will always love you," I declared to her now, in that same quiet, impassioned tone. "You who are dearest to my soul." My wife smiled faintly. Here I bent my head to kiss her again, revelling in her scent as we came together passionately. Afterwards we slipped into slumber still embracing, curled into one another, as though to defy the hell that threatened to tear us apart.

I woke shortly after dawn the next morning, as the sunlight of early autumn filtered through the open window, warming my closed eyelids. I then opened them to find my wife watching me. As I saw her observing me, she gave a small smile. She leant into me, then her head came to rest in the usual place against my neck.

"How long have you been awake?" I mumbled drowsily, my arm naturally winding around her shoulder. Partially, I wondered how long she had been observing my slumber.

"Only a few minutes," came her reply. I nodded, my chin rubbing against her tousled hair. I closed my eyes again, feeling the warmth of the sun on them. I revelled in the simple peace of this moment, intending to dwell in this sleepy embrace for as long as my conscience would allow.

"A little longer," she protested sadly as only a minute longer I sat up, causing Evelyn's head to slip off my shoulder and back onto the pillow.

"I would if we could, my love," I replied, "but others will be waiting, we cannot tarry. You need to be ready too, to ride for Gaeson," I added tightly. My wife sat up reluctantly.

"I wish you could ride home with me, that we could face the perils together," she murmured as her head rested briefly on my shoulder.

"As do I," was all I responded, taking hold of her hand tightly for a moment. "Come then, love," I added decisively, with a resigned sigh. We both dressed, preparing for the road to war with equal reluctance. My heart was heavy indeed that we were heading for different battles: I for Aldred; Evelyn for King Morgant's band against Gaeson. John had told us that they estimated the force to be small and easily conquerable. I knew Evelyn would go to the caves, but still I wished our destinies were not separating so at this moment.

Ere long we left the chamber together, making our way through Caer Ligualid's grand corridors and halls. This morning I had never felt more the strangeness of my uncle's absence, for I knew King Cedric would have joined the extra force to defend Gaeson immediately.

As we entered the grand courtyard of the city, I was keenly reminded of the time when I had left Gaeson to ride for Ynys Metcaut, where the Coalition Kings had fought against the Bernicians. That was when King Morgant had been revealed as the traitor he was. There was the same kind of slowness to the day, yet a speeding up of time. This was common only to those waiting the arrival of the inevitable. From this, I feared inevitability had come at last. The crowds were ready to meet us, as they always were whenever royalty came and went. King Owain was there himself, coming to wish us farewell. I exchanged a formal greeting with him before turning to my sister.

"Remember your promise, sister," I whispered in her ear as we embraced. I took comfort from the warmth of our contact. She nodded against my shoulder. "All my love goes with you," I added, my tone slightly louder as I stepped back.

"As does mine with you, brother," Sarah returned a little tightly, her hands still clutching mine. Besides me, Aife and three other archers had climbed atop their horses, as well as four foot-soldiers from Caer Ligualid who were also accompanying me.

"We prepare to ride for home," Evelyn called to those who were returning to Gaeson, her words more formal because of the crowds. Then she turned to me and took my hand. Across her countenance was a little smile, unshed tears welled in her eyes. "Come back to me, my boy from the snow," she directed to me quietly. "Come back home and meet me there." I squeezed her hand in turn. It touched my heart she was reiterating the instruction she had given me over a year and a half ago, the day I had ridden for Ynys Metcaut.

"I will do all I can to come back to you," I murmured, repeating the promise I had made to her that day in turn. Abruptly I no longer cared about formality, or the fact the crowds were watching. I closed the gap between us to kiss her desperately, our mouths meeting for what might be the last time. "I love you," I whispered fiercely, after we broke apart.

"I love you, also," she instantly repeated. My hand rested but a moment longer upon her cheek before I turned to mount Epos, patting her neck briefly. Evelyn then swung up onto her own horse and gathered her reins. I saw Sarah nudge her horse alongside my wife. My sister was also riding back to Gaeson, ready to give whatever aid was needed. I was relieved at this, that Sarah was following what she had promised. If Evelyn were to survive and I was not, our queen would not be left alone.

"We march," Evelyn commanded, with John beside her. I had told my captain to go and aid Gaeson in the battle. I had however retained Aife in my company, knowing how her sharp eyes would easily be able to spot the Wolf at a distance. So it was that we then set off from the beautiful citadel, knowing that with each hoof Epos struck upon the ground, it brought me one step closer to the greatest enemy I had ever known.

Chapter Fifteen

Three days later, Aife and I came to a slow stop as we emerged from a tree line, reaching the crest of a hill. I scanned our surroundings, perceiving the gradual downward slope of the hill. Halfway down, a stream gleamed in the afternoon sunshine. As the hill ended another slope ascended, rising to form a parallel hill opposite us.

"I think this is the valley," I murmured ere long. We had spent the last day circling around my former inheritance, trying to find the exact location of King Hussa and Aldred. King Owain had sent a messenger to King Hussa, begging my audience with him. The Anglian King had been very precise with the meeting point and I was glad we had given ourselves so much time to find this specific location.

To the northeast I could just make out the Kingdom of Klumeck, the first home I had ever known but could now barely remember. Every time I glimpsed it on the bleak horizon, it brought back a sharp memory of the last time I had traversed its gates. The failed recapture, a year or so ago, was still freshly imprinted on my mind, as though it was yesterday. I did not even have to close my eyes before the memory came, of King Owain and my uncle fighting off the sudden ambush. I saw the Bernician soldiers rushing over the top of the cliff again, spilling down towards us in a rapid descent. I saw us retreating, having no other choice but to flee across the darkened plains. Only the bravery of the decoy soldiers had allowed our escape.

"Is all well, sire?" Aife murmured, as she slowed her horse to a stop beside me. I nodded mutely, exhaling deeply to dispel the memory. I pulled myself slowly back to the present, my breath lingering in a puff before disappearing into the chill air. In our travels to find King Hussa, it seemed autumn had fully arrived. There was a thick ashen blanket over the land, with fine rain moistening the air and the earth. Presently I lifted one hand to run through my russet hair, a little surprised at quite how wet it was.

"There is movement, my lord," Aife muttered now, raising a hand to point. I dropped my hand from my head to follow my friend's gaze, to see a troop of perhaps thirty emerging from a woodland at the valley's bottom. I swallowed, tightening my grip on the reins again.

"Archers, prepare for His Majesty's descent," Aife ordered next. Despite the severity of the danger we were about to be in, the corner of my mouth twitched, for I was pleased to see how well Aife commanded her warriors. Aife had been chief archer for a little over a year and she ordered them with ease. When I turned in my saddle, I saw they had already dismounted and were setting up positions just inside the edge of the wood.

"Well, we know why King Hussa proposed this location," Aife muttered to me in a low voice, as her horse bent his long neck to sniff the grass.

"Aye," I agreed, smiling a little at her words, for I could be sure that there would be enemy archers looking down at me from the opposite hill. "It is good to know your arrows are near. I am glad you are with me, sister," I told her quietly.

"It is my honour to serve, sire," she answered with a formal bend of her head. "God be with you and keep you safe, Daniel," she whispered, so that only I could hear her.

"With you also," I murmured back swiftly. "I am hoping to engage Aldred in one-to-one combat," I informed Aife in a louder voice. "Do not engage, even if I am on the brink of death. Only shoot if you perceive the foot soldiers have begun fighting first. I do not want to start a war here, unless we have to," I reminded her.

"I understand, my lord," she murmured back. With that, the four foot-soldiers and I began to descend the hill, heading towards the valley. It began to rain thicker as we trotted down the slope. We had ridden about half a mile when we reached the party, then abruptly stopping. All of their eyes were on us. Rage swelled within me at the sight of Aldred, but I forced myself to remain impassive.

"Peace be with you, Your Majesty King Hussa," I greeted formally, dismounting Epos. My feet squelched into muddy, wet earth long softened by rain. The mud slid more as I sank to bended knee. I longed to touch the hilt of my blade, but I resisted the urge. Instead I made myself instead hold both hands out, palms turned towards the enemy king in a symbol of peace.

"King Bryce, you may rise," King Hussa declared grandly. I stood. The four soldiers behind me remained where they were, a few feet away, their postures still bent. "King Owain said you have come to speak to me on a matter of urgency. This had better be worth my time," he added, his eyes narrowing as I met his. His face was solemn, gaze sparked with anger about to be lit. His hair was sandy, but for the edges that were beginning to turn grey.

"Aye, my lord," I returned presently, after bending once more to him. "I mean to tell you that you have a traitor in your midst, one who has as much of your side's blood on his hands as of mine. He calls himself Aldred," I declared evenly.

King Hussa threw his head back and laughed at this, a sound that seemed to reverberate longer than normal in his mouth. My gaze darted towards the Wolf, to see his hardened countenance gazing back to mine. Then, even in the face of accusation, his usual sneer was tugging at his mouth.

"What nonsense is this?" the Bernician King asked, still a tremor of laughter in his voice. "Aldred is one of my most loyal subjects and a high-ranking official within our army. It is only you he has betrayed, in service to me," he continued with a dismissive wave of his hand.

"He has long been a spy within Gaeson's walls and has served you there faithfully, outwitting all who stand opposed to him, my lord the king," I partially affirmed his speech. "However—" I added gently. At this, King Hussa's hand moved to hold the hilt of his blade, eyes flashing dangerously. I swallowed, knowing I would have to tread very carefully. Even though I was a king myself, to dare to contradict the ruler in front of me could easily mean my death, before I had the chance to offer the proof of the documents.

"I believe His Majesty may not be aware of all the facts surrounding his character," I concluded ere long. King Hussa's scrutiny hardened further, brow creasing as he frowned.

"Is that so?" King Hussa sneered and I held my breath. "Very well then, do tell me what I am so obviously missing." My breath evenly escaped my lips again. He had spoken with scorn, but my life was not ended. My foe had given me an opportunity tell him the truth.

"Aldred has not been as loyal to you as he suggests, Your Majesty," I began. In my peripheral vision, I saw the Wolf's sneer widen. It took every ounce of my will to not seize my blade, charge at him and draw his blood, no matter what the consequences.

"Oh, it is you," Aldred said then, as if he had only just recognised me, his silky tones as airy as a gentle breeze. My hatred of him blossomed further. To think I once considered his character so amiable and loyal! That I thought of this monster as my ally, my friend!

"This boy is the nephew of the late King Cedric, my lord the king," my greatest foe addressed to his king smoothly. "I murdered his parents when he was an infant," he added brazenly. "It was on the orders of King Reghan, but also it was the wish of our forces, sire, to further sow seeds of distrust between the Britons. It was very successful," Aldred concluded casually, "for the Kingdoms of Gaeson and Klumeck warred needlessly for two decades." He gave a hollow laugh here, as I fought to remain impassive. Aldred had been the seed of such a war, of such violence between peoples that should have been united. How many citizens were lost, when truly they were brothers and sisters?

"I see," King Hussa replied, then clicked his tongue. "So, this is petty vengeance, is it?" He shook his head. "That is a foolish reason to talk to me, boy," he added dangerously.

"I suspect there might be another reason, my lord king," Aldred continued. "He is further enraged because his wife, Queen Evelyn of Gaeson, daughter of King Reghan, knew that I was a spy and yet said nothing to him. It seems I may have caused a little marital discord," he added, his smile broadening.

"It was much more than that," I returned angrily, unable to keep my silence any longer. "He caused me to distrust my wife's character, sire," I added to King Hussa. "It turned out she had been forced to keep silent because of his threats to kill me and half of the rest of Rheged. This man also kidnapped Queen Evelyn and me and tried to have us thrown off a cliff to drown in a lake," I pointed out. Here King Hussa gave a quick glance at Aldred.

"I grant you his methods are a little unorthodox," the king granted reasonably, as his gaze returned to me again, "but that does not amount to disloyalty to me."

"Aye, my lord king, I quite agree," I responded, "but it was not this matter I came to speak about, sire." I was managing to hold my composure, whilst my insides boiled with fury. "I came to reveal to you, sire, that it was Aldred who convinced King Urien to attack you at Ynys Metcaut, with the aid of the Coalition Kings," I explained. I saw King Hussa's eyes widen in surprise, as my verbal arrow hit its target. He turned sharply back to Aldred.

"Many Bernicians were lost that day," King Hussa said now. His voice had gone deadly quiet. With the rain and wind picking up, I strained my ears to hear him. "We had no word of their marching against us. Our people were almost wiped out. If there is any truth to this—"

"There is not, my lord, I assure you," Aldred replied calmly. "They are heatless accusations, sire, only meant to sow distrust between us. It is a pitiful shot," he added to me. "You have lost, Bryce. Do not make it worse for yourself by inventing such fabrications."

"Oh, indeed?" King Hussa replied softly. Abruptly the wind and rain died down as quickly as it arisen, so that all could hear him. The gentlest breeze rifled through my hair, whilst we waited for this Bernician King to continue. He turned his gaze back to me. "Do you have any evidence, King Bryce, to support your claims?" he asked evenly.

"Aye, Your Majesty," I returned, fighting to keep any triumph out of my tone. "If you'll allow me—" I added, gesturing to Epos. King Hussa gave one short nod, regarding me impassively whilst I retrieved the leather case. As I turned back to him, the great king raised one hand to beckon me to his presence.

"I bring you documents that were sealed in King Urien's tomb, my lord," I began. "They were retrieved only months ago, just before your people reached Caer Ligualid's gates," I began. At this, I saw the sneer begin to vanish from Aldred's face. Though otherwise the Wolf remained impassive, I hoped he was squirming with panic inside. "They detail conversations Aldred has had between both King Reghan and King Urien on separate occasions, recorded by King Owain's bard, Taliesin. This paragraph in particular…"

My voice died away, as King Hussa held up a finger to demand my silence. I waited with bated breath. The king hastily turned the pages, scanning the evidence against my enemy. Then at length he straightened, staring hard at Aldred as the pages crumpled slightly in his hand.

"What say you, Aldred?" King Hussa breathed dangerously, the air hissing from his lips. "For if this is false, how is it so accurate about you? Your reports of your meetings with King Urien are almost identical to these," he continued, waving the wad of paper in his hand. "Except, you failed to mention it was your scheme to encourage King Urien to align himself with other Briton kingdoms to march against us." His tone was harsh. The Wolf opened his mouth to reply, but his lord raised his hand to stop his speech. It was good indeed to see Aldred's poison curtailed.

"What is it you want, King Bryce?" King Hussa asked, as he turned back to me and thrust the papers back in my direction. I stepped closer from where he still sat upon his horse, taking the documents from him with a swift bow of my head.

"I wish for justice to be done, Your Majesty," I answered him calmly. "This evidence not only points to the evil he has done in Rheged, but also of his direct betrayal of you, sire, when he persuaded King Urien to march upon you at Ynys Metcaut," I concluded.

"This is folly, sire," Aldred said rapidly, daring to speak after King Hussa had commanded his silence. "Do not forget, sire, it was I who persuaded King Morgant to join our ranks, including his agreement to assassinate King Urien."

"Remember also, my lord the king," I resumed quickly, "that even with the assassination of King Urien, much Bernician blood was spilled. There would have been a way to kill him without waging war, like he did with most of my kin," I pointed out.

"Your Majesty King Hussa," I continued swiftly, "I ask your permission to make this villain pay for his crimes. He must be called to justice. I know my wife and I will never be safe while he walks this earth," I implored him. "Sire, he must be brought to account for the great betrayal he has committed against your people, as well as mine."

I ended my speech here, waiting with bated breath. The one who held our lives in the balance surveyed me, weighing up my word against

Aldred's. I bent my head slightly out of respect, my view focused on the landscape beyond his shoulder. Absently, I noticed the sheen of moisture on a crow's wing, gleaming as it flew across the sky.

"Very well, King Bryce," King Hussa interjected at last. My gaze darted back to him. "You have my permission," he declared. I nodded as Aldred's eyes widened. Clearly, he had not expected my request to be granted.

"Your Majesty," Aldred protested, but he faltered under King Hussa's stare. It gave me some satisfaction to see one who had power over him. "Sire," the Wolf attempted, "surely you do not believe his account? The word of a stable boy?"

"He is also a king, Aldred," King Hussa answered him shortly. "The evidence against you is compelling," he concluded. Anger began to fill the monarch's features. "Though you have served me well in recent years, the thought that you have instigated our failure at Ynys Metcaut is most troubling. Therefore," he continued, his eyes flashing dangerously at the Wolf, in the same way they had done at me, "I believe justice will prevail in the face of combat. If you put him to the sword, I will know your loyalty."

"Thank you, my lord," I directed to King Hussa. He turned back to me, giving another curt nod. I then smiled, as I finally took the hilt of my blade.

"Come then, Aldred," I challenged him hotly, drawing my sword. "If I am just a stable boy, then how am I a threat? I have been searching for you for almost a year, Wolf," I muttered angrily. "Let us see who we truly are, now you are veiled no longer. You began a mission to murder all my kin, over twenty years ago. Why not attempt to complete it?" I taunted. For a moment Aldred remained silent, his angry countenance surveying mine.

"Very well, then," Aldred agreed, then easily dismounted his horse. He removed his thick cloak, throwing it absently onto his horse. The Wolf's dark hair blew a little in the wind, in contrast to his pale, angular features. King Hussa and his troops manoeuvred backwards a few paces, presently forming a circle around us.

"I have been trained with a sword since before you were born," he threatened, as he drew his own blade. I raised my shield, the two of us surveying each other.

"Age does not guarantee success," I retorted loudly. The two of us began to circle around one another. "I am not a boy, nor a fool," I declared presently, "I am a king, the heir of King Cedric." I hoped my uncle would have been proud. "One way or the other, this ends today," I promised him. Rage still threatened to consume me: I used all my self-control not to simply charge at him.

"You were the one who wished to fight, Daniel," Aldred taunted after a moment, as we continued to move around the outside of the circle. "Sooner or later, I will kill you. Then, I will come after your wife and your sister. Soon, everything you love will be gone," he concluded.

His taunt succeeded. Hardly aware of what my feet were doing, I sped towards my foe, my blade raised high. Aldred, of course, was expecting this attack and easily blocked it. I jumped backwards and leapt forwards again, thrashing towards him, but once more he parried me.

"This is where your journey ends, boy," the Wolf sneered, as he dodged my next attack. He then lunged forwards and I leapt back to avoid a blow. I gripped the hilt of my sword tighter, as I jumped to the left. Metal crashed against fast metal. He parried me and I him. Then our dance of blade and blood momentarily ceased as we broke apart. Slowly, we began circling each other again.

"This ends with your death," I declared to him. I knew I had been waiting for this my entire life, ever since I had glimpsed him in that corridor in Klumeck, with his dagger glistening with my parents' blood. Facing this monster was my destiny. At last, I could avenge my kin.

"No, Bryce, it ends with yours," Aldred contradicted. "You look just as weak and helpless as you did that night in Klumeck," he sneered, as if he could read my thoughts.

I gritted my teeth in fury at his poison, letting out a loud cry as I rushed towards him. I wished dearly to break his mouth, so that no more venom could be unleashed. My foe was ready, jumping to the side as I neared him. He brought his sword down, just as I lifted my shield. Both of us staggered back in the mud with the impact of it.

Both of us were locked in this move, of my butting my shield against blade. We were both trapped by the other's defence. I watched his angry eyes, the sweat trickling down his forehead. In that moment, I realised this was not going to be a quick fight, for we seemed equally matched. With all the strength I could muster, abruptly I pushed back against him. I broke us both free, as he skidded back in the mud a little but then righted himself. The Wolf was almost snarling.

We began to circle one another again. I caught a glimpse of King Hussa. Was he bored? My eyes went back to Aldred. I bit back on my frustration, telling myself to be patient. I had to wait for him to show a weakness. Presently he moved around the space between us again. My feet copied his. The concentration on his countenance told me he had the same strategy of waiting. I wondered if we would be locked in this battle forever, trapped and propelled by mutual hate.

Abruptly, both our patience seemed to give out simultaneously. Suddenly we charged once more at each other. Metal clashed and scraped, as he brought his blade down against mine. I raised my sword as he brought his down. Again, we were both locked. Our blades remained almost still, as we forced equal pressure upon them. It was another moment of calm in this hell of a storm. My eyes bore into his again, with undiluted rage. I continued pressing down on my sword. Once more, I was close enough to see the bead of sweat trickle slowly from his temple. My hand gripped the hilt of my sword ever tighter, as if I was glued to it.

"I have to give you some credit, boy," Aldred ground out through gritted teeth. I swallowed hard, breathing loud with the exertion of holding my blade against him. Each time he called me 'boy' it was a small dagger, burrowing deeper into my throat. "You're lasting much longer than your parents did." His voice was suddenly deadly soft. "At night, sometimes, I imagine I can still hear her scream," he whispered softly.

"Ah!" I cried out again, as the rage in my throat exploded. I leapt to the side, disentangling our blades. Swiftly I pirouetted before bringing my sword down again, but as ever, the Wolf was ready as my blade once more crashed against his.

"You dare even mention them!" I shouted in fury and my enemy's sneer returned. At once I knew he was trying to get me to display weakness in my anger. As he proceeded to strike, I leapt back. His blade sliced through the air cleanly. I took a few more paces back, forcing myself to grow calm.

317

"I can hear her scream in my dreams, too," I told Aldred evenly, "but she is about to be avenged." I wondered if my parents were watching with my uncle, if they would be proud too. Wait, I told myself. Evelyn flashed through my mind's eye, as did my imagining of the child that was soon to become ours. I would not falter, now I was this close to victory. This was a mental battle, as well as a physical one. I forced myself to become still, to let go of my hatred.

"Does the King of Klumeck need a rest?" Aldred sneered. "Not that Klumeck exists any longer. I have destroyed it, just as I destroyed your family," he declared. He was viewing me as though I was an insect he had found on the bottom of his boot. In a moment of clarity, I realised why he despised me so. It was my resilience that angered him, for each time I evaded him, his original contempt and dismissal further bore fruit into intense hatred.

"You must need the rest far more than I, Aldred," I began, choosing my words with care. He was not the only one able to goad. If this battle was psychological, then I could bite back just as hard. "After all, I started this battle with you in recent months, but you started it decades ago," I continued, as we traversed the edge of the circle.

"When we first met, it would have been like trampling an insect underfoot," I continued, articulating the imagery I had recently thought of. "How embarrassing to be battling this stable boy you could not kill," I taunted, "in front of your wise and great king, no less. You must be nothing less than humiliated."

"You will not win this battle with words, boy," Aldred sneered, but the tightening of his brows and the hardening of his eyes told me my words had hit their mark.

"Oh?" I challenged softly. I deliberately lowered my blade to the ground, so that the sharp end gently punctured the soft, wet earth as I provoked him. "How shameful still, when you even tried to throw me from a cliff, yet still I evaded you. You tried to poison me against my own wife, but my marriage is stronger than ever. I am a constant reminder of the time you failed," I concluded, speaking louder.

"You will be my failure no longer!" he erupted, his face contorting with rage. He glared at me with all the fullness of fury, as he sped towards me. I was ready for him and as he rose his blade, I jumped to the right, crashing my sword against his armour. The force of it made him stagger backwards, clutching at his side.

"You'll have to do more than that, boy," he groaned, but his words told me how pained he was. My instinct told me the battle was nearing its end. I pointed my sword at him calmly.

"What's the matter, Wolf? Is your prey beginning to conquer you?" I taunted him. My jibe worked, for with a grunt he raised his sword, leaping forwards to me. As I evaded him, in the flash of a single moment I saw his weakness. He thrust his blade, but I ducked. Before he could block it, I sliced my blade across his abdomen underneath his chainmail.

"No!" he cried out with agony, as blood began to flow down his armoured legs. It turned his silver armour to deep, vivid crimson. With an effort he pulled himself to stand, his breathing laboured as one hand clutched his injury. "You will not defeat me," he rasped.

"You are the one who does not know you have already lost," I told him, my calmness returning at the sight of him staggering. I knew King Hussa and his soldiers were still watching, but I was barely aware of them. It was though the entire world had reduced to just the two of us.

"Your failure is complete, Wolf," I told him, the anticipation of his death sending a shiver down my spine as I neared him. "This is for my kin and to protect my sister and my wife. I shall finally be free of you," I concluded loudly. I gripped ever tighter the hilt of my blade.

"You will never be rid of me!" he roared. With a cry of his own, he leapt a final time with his blade. It was his last attempt to destroy me. I saw his move coming and easily parried him. A moment later my sword knocked his blade out of his hand.

Aldred glared up at me, yet there was something solemn in his eyes also. It was almost a sadness there, as he resigned himself to his fate. I witnessed this only in the moment before my sword reached him. My blade sliced into his abdomen, where I had already pierced him. Further blood flowed forth. I pushed forward with my sword, until it came through the other side. Aldred grunted in pain. Blood spewed from his mouth as well as his body. I let go of my sword and stood back from him.

"Justice has been done, Aldred. You can hurt me no longer," I told him evenly, as I watched the villain's demise. With a strangled cry, he collapsed onto his side. His angry countenance bore into me, until the Wolf breathed his last.

"The victory is yours, King Bryce," King Hussa declared. With this sudden speech, reality abruptly extended beyond myself and my foe who lay dead. "It seems you were telling the truth," the king continued flatly. "For that, you have my thanks. You may collect your sword," he added, keenly reminding me that I was at his mercy.

"Your Majesty," I said, bowing low, "I thank you for your audience: for letting justice be done this day." With that, I then bent to Aldred's corpse, grabbing the hilt of my blade with two hands. I pressed my foot down on his chest. With a large tug, my sword became free. It loosened, with the remnants of his body still on it. I took a moment to wipe it roughly on the wet earth, smearing his blood on the ground where our destinies had finally separated. I then straightened, sheathing my sword. Finally, I turned to face King Hussa again.

"You have proven yourself a great king and warrior, King Bryce," the King of Bernicia told me. His countenance was serious, yet there was a gleam of humour in his eyes. "I look forward perhaps fighting you in battle myself one day," he added thoughtfully, with a wry smile.

"It would be an honour to face you, my lord the king," I returned, unsure of what else to say. "With your permission, sire, I shall now return home." King Hussa gave a curt nod. I began retreating, still facing him, until I reached Epos. I mounted my horse and gathered my reins.

"Your Majesty," I added, with a final bow. Then I turned Epos around, giving her a gentle kick into a gallop. I knew King Hussa could easily give the order to kill me, but I had no other choice but to trust he would keep his word. With each clop of hooves my breathing eased. Finally, I reached the crest of the hill where I joined Aife again.

"They are not following you, my lord," she reported, as I came to a stop. "We saw the whole fight, brother. You did well," she murmured. I tried to smile, as the reality sank in that my greatest foe was dead.

"Thank you," I managed to rasp, as the adrenaline had suddenly left my system. I breathed deeply, suddenly feeling weak. I swallowed, steering

Epos around. I ignored my slightly shaking hands. I perceived King Hussa and his troops also leaving. "It looks as though the King of Bernicia is to keep his word," I reflected, as they reached the opposite wood.

"My lord, your arm," she said suddenly. I glanced down to my forearm, to see it was bleeding. I remembered Aldred had pierced me early on in the battle. I had entirely forgotten about it, but then agony jolted through me, as though the wound was only just inflicted.

"We can tend to it later, for it will not kill me," I decided quickly. I spoke through gritted teeth, for it hurt like the blazes. "Come," I added quickly, turning Epos back around. "Let us depart before he changes his mind." Aife and the others voiced their obedience. We left the hill and entered the woodland at an easy canter. I was immensely thankful that not only was Aldred dead, but all other lives were spared.

After we had put a good few miles between ourselves and King Hussa, we came down yet another hill in the lake area of Rheged. At last, I allowed myself to breathe. I ordered our party to come to a stop near a river. I needed to wash, to free myself of Aldred's poison. After tending to my arm and carefully dressing it Aife stood guard at the top of a ridge, an arrow already poised to fire should any of the enemy come into view. I ran down the bank to the water, clutching a set of spare clothes.

The river turned a light shade of red momentarily, as I plunged my face and hair into it. The shock of the chilly water was exhilarating, making my teeth chatter. I rose my hands to scrub my hair clean, rubbing fingers that were already growing numb. My hands and head were now unmarked by his blood, but my armour was still stained with his gore. I removed each piece of metal. As I did, I felt my soul lightening along with my body.

I stripped to my underclothes as quickly as I could, mentally checking my condition as I did so. My head was bruised, one cheek stiff and sore from where he had hit me. Then there was the blazing wound to my arm, that Aife had carefully dressed. Miraculously, there seemed to be no other injuries.

The gore from Aldred had seeped through to my underclothes, so I peeled off my long shirt. Even my chest was a little stained with the Wolf's blood. I therefore bent further into the water, scooping armfuls of the clear liquid onto my chest and stomach. Ere long, my upper body was clean of his foul stench.

Next, I kicked off my boots and pulled down my trousers, also sprayed with his blood. Though it had not transferred onto my bare legs, I washed these also. This done, I began to change into the fresh clothes. I left off my tunic, whilst I used moss and water to clean my sword and armour. Eventually, after much scrubbing, these were clean too. When at last all seemed free from Aldred's blood, I pulled on my tunic and strapped my armour on again.

With these tasks done, there was nothing else to distract me from what had just happened. I sat down, in shock that the Wolf was dead. I found my hands were shaking again and clenched them into fists. The relief he was dead conflicted with weakness, an uncertainty I hadn't expected.

"Sire?" The voice of Aife reached me, as perceptive as always. She came to stand next to me, putting her hand on my shoulder. "Are you all right?"

"Aye," I answered, a little wearily. I felt drained and empty. "It's just..." I searched for the words. "He's finally gone," I vocalised my thoughts. "That must sound foolish," I muttered.

"Not at all," she replied at once. "You've spent so much time and energy chasing him, Daniel," she said. "Over a year you've sought to discover him, to bring him to justice. Today, this you have done," she concluded. I nodded as her hand came upon my shoulder again. "Come, brother, it is time to focus your energy on other things. I bid you think upon home. Think upon your wife and the child that is soon to be born," she encouraged. As I did this, my heart lightened considerably.

"Thank you, Aife," I responded. I was relieved my voice sounded stronger, more normal. "Yes, let's go home," I concluded.

"My lord," she agreed, with a nod and a small smile. The two of us trudged up the bank towards our party. "No enemy seems to be in sight, sire," Aife reported, as we reached them.

"Good," I answered, mounting Epos once more. "Let's pray it stays that way. Come on, girl," I murmured softly, patting my faithful mare's neck. "Home," I murmured, as we set off.

After a day's riding, we parted ways with the Caer Ligualid soldiers. They bowed farewell, departing for the great city. The rest of us continued our journey to Gaeson. All of us surveyed the landscape with scrutiny, but it seemed King Hussa was to keep his word and not pursue us. Presently, secure in the knowledge we were not followed, I even afforded myself the luxury of removing my helmet. Some remnant of the summer's warmth seemed to have returned, in contrast to the chilly air yesterday. Here I smiled, at last beginning to feel a little relaxed.

Over the course of the last day I had done as my wise friend had suggested. I had tried to think of Evelyn and the child to be born to us, in a little under a month's time. I prayed that Gaeson and all within her walls was safe. I imagined my babe's first cry, when it would first look into my eyes. Such ponderings strengthened my soul, as potent as any healing tonic could be.

I continued such pleasant thinking, whilst we made good progress on our journey back to Gaeson. Until at last, four days after we had set off from the valley where I had confronted Aldred, I gave the order to make camp a final time.

"It will be good to reach home tomorrow," Aife said, leaning comfortably back against the trunk of a tree, turning a single long blade of grass in her mouth. I smiled in agreement as I rested against another trunk. A small fire was lit a little way off: currently some kind of stew was being prepared. "Her Majesty will be pleased to see you," she presently added, causing a faint smile to touch my features.

"Aye," I murmured softly in agreement, "I hope all in Gaeson are safe," I added. We still did not know whether King Morgant had indeed marched against our home, or whether our army had been able to ward off our enemy. I then glanced at my companion to see she was staring straight ahead. Her face was impassive, her features having tensed slightly.

"I pray John is safe, also," I murmured. At this she sighed a little, letting me know I had been right. She had indeed been thinking of his welfare. "He will be happy to see you return?" I continued lightly. It was a statement, but I had phrased it as a question. A wry smile appeared upon her features, as she continued to gaze ahead. She seemed to look at nothing in particular.

"I imagine so," she replied evasively, before at last glancing at me. "I have not spoken to him," she revealed at last, as a hint of melancholy took form in her expression. "I think we have mutually decided to stay as we are," she concluded.

"You say this is mutual," I replied with a frown, "but you have not spoken to each other, have you?" I asked. "How do you know, therefore, if he has made the same decision? Why not at least find out again?" Here, the same wry smile appeared on her countenance.

"We are both warriors, my lord," she sighed. "I do not think it is the same kind of love that others share. It is a bond without words," she explained. "It is some kindred understanding, allowing us to truly partner in service to you and to Queen Evelyn. I am content with this," she added, before I could protest that I would not want them to remain apart on my account.

"You see, the connection I have with him..." she continued, before faltering. She seemed to be searching for the right words. "I cherish the way things are," she went on. "Even if there was room for that kind of love, and I am not even certain I desire that..." Again, she paused. "I would not want to take the chance and ruin what we have," she finished, her head leaning further back against the tree. I frowned as I digested her meaning.

"I think I understand," I murmured, for I knew that love was not necessarily the same. I loved Aife too in my own way, for her friendship, her wisdom, her skill in battle. I had witnessed, too, the connection she had with John in battle. As Aife described, they seemed to operate perfectly together, without a single word. After all, I reminded myself, choosing to remain unmarried certainly was not a sin. Rather, it brought its own advantages.

"I admire your decision greatly, my friend," I told her now, "as long as you know I would not be against it if you did desire something more. In fact, I would encourage it, if it was what you both wished," I concluded, reaching for her hand.

"I know," Aife answered, squeezing my hand back briefly, "I thank you, brother. I'll let you know if anything changes," she added, with a final smile. We let go of the contact, then, just as a soldier came towards us, bearing two bowls of steaming stew.

Though we spoke no more of the subject, the conversation stayed in my thoughts that night. It remained in my mind, too, as we made the final journey back to Gaeson. I marvelled at the strength she had to make her decision: at her wish not to jeopardise friendship or duty. Surely, that had to be as much a gift from God as marriage itself. I smiled as I thought of my friend, who had learnt to be content in all situations. It reminded me of trying to be content as a soldier, loving Evelyn from afar, thinking I could never even tell her how I felt. Still, though, I thought Aife had learnt the art of contentment far better than I.

At last, my thinking on this theme was diverted as we climbed Gaeson's hill. I was greatly relieved to see the castle intact. None of the fire that had burned Klumeck had touched it. I lifted my eyes to the glorious sunshine and praised God, that He had granted us safety and freedom from Aldred's tyranny. We cantered past the exterior barricades, entering under the portcullis. My heart threatened to explode with euphoria to see Evelyn waiting outside the palace hall, looking safe and well.

"King Bryce," my wife greeted joyfully, as I swung my feet down onto the smooth stone of Gaeson's courtyard. I felt much gladness of heart to be home. Sarah and John also stood there, smiling broadly.

"My queen," I gave short bow to her. To my delight, she then rather abandoned royal decorum, coming forward to embrace me. I slipped an arm around her, my other hand lifting to frame her face. Abruptly, then, I bent my head to kiss her soundly. The crowd cheered almost hysterically. It was only days since I last saw her, but I felt the joy of our reunion so keenly that it could have been years.

"I am glad you kept your word and came back to me," my wife said a moment later as we both broke apart. Evelyn wore a relieved smile. "Is it done?" she asked urgently.

"Aye," I answered solemnly. "The Wolf is dead." Sarah had stepped forward, relief evident in her features also as we greeted one another warmly.

"Thank you, sister, for keeping your word," I murmured. As I said this, out of the corner of my eye I saw John and Aife embracing. I reflected that they did appear to be quite content. "It is good to see you, brother," I turned to address John, clasping arms with him.

"My lord," John replied with a grin. The crowd's cheers had died down a little, but they soon grew loud again as Evelyn stepped forward to me again.

"You are just in time, my husband," she murmured in my ear. At this, I caught her wrists to hold her in place. Delight began to fill me, at what she could possibly be suggesting.

"For what?" I whispered back, seeing for the first time that her joy might signal something else other than my homecoming. I stepped back, unable to ask further. Already, though, I could see the answer on her face, as my hands still clutched her.

"Come, husband," was all Evelyn said, her eyes shining with happiness. With that she led me through the palace doors and through to the rest of the castle, as the cheers from the crowd faded from my ears. As we walked swiftly down the corridors, my wife rapidly explained that the child was not yet born, but that Morwenna's waters had broken a few hours ago. Leigh had confirmed she had gone into labour, a month before time. Leigh and the midwife were currently treating her in the chamber where she had been concealed after her pregnancy began to show.

"I gave a royal announcement yesterday," Evelyn explained, now looking to me. "My speech explained our troubles," she continued vaguely. I nodded, understanding her meaning at once. We had meant to inform our people earlier, but then the Wolf had been revealed.

"Gaeson looked sad indeed," she reflected, coming to sit in a small hall along the way from Morwenna whilst we waited. "Then when I announced we were about to adopt a child, the crowd's cheer was deafening," she grinned. "I trusted God would bring you back to me, but even if you did not, I could not delay it any longer, even if Aldred still lived," she continued. "This was still my best chance of securing an heir," she concluded.

"You did right, my love," I murmured. From here, I could hear the cries of Morwenna in the throes of labour, reaching our ears only faintly. Swiftly, I ran to our chamber to wash. Whilst there I prayed quickly to God, lifting up the child and Morwenna in petition to Him. My heart filled with joy and apprehension at the thought of the new birth. I then ran back to the hall, pausing only to thrust my armour into the hands of a nearby guard to take it back into the armoury for me.

"There's been no change," Evelyn answered my unspoken question, as I joined her back in the small hall. My queen was sat calmly, but I found I could not sit still. Instead, I needlessly walked from one end of the chamber to the other, again and again.

"Sit down, before you wear the floor out," my wife ere long instructed with a sigh. I glanced to her, smiling ruefully.

"It is made of stone," I pointed out. She smiled as I sat down beside her. One hand came to clutch hers tightly, whilst the other absently patted my knee.

The minutes turned to hours, with each one seeming to last until eternity whilst we waited. Presently I got up again, standing frequently by the open window. If Evelyn found this as annoying as my pacing, she did not object. Whilst we were waiting, I enquired of my wife how Ewan fared. She told me Ewan had almost recovered. Indeed, he had almost begged John to let him be in the party that came to join us at Caer Ligualid.

I could understand why, for I guessed the young lad would have then tried to join Aife and me to confront Aldred, if only for a chance to glimpse Cara.

"Cara was not there," I presently told Evelyn, my arms folded. I knew this would comfort Ewan, that he had not missed a vital opportunity to see again the woman he loved, but it would also discourage him. Where was she? I wondered. Which side was she on? Her loyalty seemed indeed to be a mystery.

"I told Ewan she gave me the hairpin that saved our lives," my wife said now, as I nodded. I knew that hairpin was the only clue that she might still stand with us after all. Only time would tell whether she would ever return home. I glanced back at the window for the countless time. The orange glow of the sun was sinking just below the horizon, so that everything it touched gleamed. As I watched the last moments of daylight ebb away, the hall doors burst open and I whirled around.

"It is done," Leigh reported with a smile. Though his hands and face were clean, it was slightly alarming to see his tunic stained with blood. Unfortunately, it reminded me of the way my armour had been, right after

I had killed the Wolf. The surgeon bore a beaming grin, which was very reassuring. As the physician wiped his mouth with the back of his hand, I reminded myself that the Wolf's blood could not be more different from this. This was the sign of new life.

"Your baby is quite healthy," Leigh smiled, looking between us as we stood on tenterhooks. "A girl," he supplied. At once a grin spread across my countenance, stretching from ear to ear as if my face was about to split open. "Morwenna is also healthy," my friend added, as I reached for Evelyn's hand.

"She is sure to recover and in time, she will resume her services at the castle," he said now. I was pleased indeed Morwenna would be well. "She left it for Your Majesties to name the child," Leigh continued. My heart warmed further at this extra gift, then I shot a glance to Evelyn to see her looking back at me. In all that had happened, we had not even considered this. "Would you like to meet her?" Leigh prompted gently.

"Aye," I rasped softly, suddenly hardly able to speak. "We would like that very much indeed." Leigh smiled, gesturing that we should follow him. The three of us began walking down the corridor. I felt that though I was going at their normal pace, this mundane route was both a blur and yet that every moment stood out at once. Abruptly, then, we came to a different chamber than the one Morwenna had been in, for she had been taken to rest in another area of the castle. Leigh opened the door softly.

"My lord, my lady," the midwife greeted with a bow. I gave her a small nod, my throat still too dry to speak. Then, my gaze went right from her happy countenance to the wriggling bundle of cloths held securely in her arms. The cloths were arranged so that I could not see my daughter yet. I longed to behold her.

"Thank you," Evelyn replied, for both of us. The midwife stepped towards us with the bundle, whilst all I could do was stare.

"It is a pleasure to serve Your Majesties," Leigh answered formally from beside us. As the midwife further neared us, the physician clasped my arm. "The service has never brought me more joy, Daniel. Congratulations," he offered simply. At once, I felt the impulse to weep.

"Thank you, my friend," I whispered back sincerely, at last able to utter something. Then, as he departed, the midwife took one step closer to us, at last moving the babe to place her into Evelyn's arms. Abruptly, I could see the face of our child. I felt the impulse to weep again. The midwife said something about waiting outside, but in the joy of this moment I barely heard her.

"Oh, Daniel," was all Evelyn whispered. "She's perfect." Our gazes met briefly then, to see her eyes were shining with unshed tears. My wife unwrapped the bundle of cloths further, to look at the child fully. As I stepped closer, Evelyn shifted and carefully handed our daughter to me.

The moment my daughter finally came into my arms, after waiting and wanting so long, my heart erupted into a million tiny shards. It was enough to stop my very breath. At once a love for this tiny, helpless creature I held in my arms came over me, intense, powerful and exquisite. Right then, I knew I could not love this child any more than if she had come from our own bodies.

As I abruptly came to embrace fatherhood, my eyes misted with tears. I blinked them furiously away, so they could not obscure my vision of her. My daughter was — my daughter, I realised abruptly, revelling anew in this new title of relationship — she really was lovely. Her eyes were only slightly open. The child was not crying, but only making stirring noises as one upon the point of waking. In truth, I hardly found the words to describe her. There was the small curve and point of her nose, the slight bulge to her cheeks, the little dimple of her chin. Her skin was reddened due to labour, but this was already beginning to fade.

I perceived, then, that her skin would be pale. There were no lashes around her eyes, but her head already had a few sparse strands of dark hair. She had minute arms and legs, complete with the bent lines of elbows and knees. As I stared further, her tiny hands wriggled out of the cloths. The sight of her almost transparent fingernails, fully formed despite her size, made me gasp at nature's complexity.

"Welcome to the world, my darling," Evelyn whispered beside me, but again I found I could not speak. My child's eyes opened further: my wife gasped at the sight of them. The tiny orbs moved about, taking everything in, yet at the same time still too young to register anything. Her eyes were dark blue, almost black in colour. It was like the hue of the deepest ocean, right at the very edge of the world.

"Are you all right, love?" my wife asked me quietly, taking our daughter back into her arms. I nodded as the child whimpered, emitting a single cry before settling down again. "You are crying more than she is," Evelyn quipped. I gave a short laugh at this, venting some of my emotion at the sheer joy of it all. "What shall we call her?" Evelyn asked, as I swallowed.

"I had one thought," I told her haltingly at last. It was my first words since Leigh and the midwife left the chamber. My gaze was still lingering over our daughter. I drank in the pure sight of her, until my heart felt it would burst apart all over again. I then raised my head back up to look at Evelyn, whose eyes were sparkling in delight whilst she waited. "We could call her Imogen, after my mother," I suggested hoarsely. Evelyn's smile broadened.

"Imogen," she repeated gently as she looked at our daughter, testing the name out for the first time. "Immy, for short?" she considered.

"Aye," I murmured in a whisper. "Little Immy," I murmured. Evelyn smiled further, bending her head to press a kiss to our daughter's forehead.

"It's perfect," she whispered. My heart nearly burst then, as I wound one arm around my wife. My other hand reached to grasp one of Imogen's tiny fingers. I prayed silently, then, thanking God for this precious gift.

"Can we enter?" Abruptly, I heard Sarah's slightly impatient voice. I chuckled slightly, as I straightened once more.

"Aye," I called back. The door opened instantly, revealing Sarah, John and Aife. I smiled at my sister as she came forward. "This is your niece, Imogen," I introduced them. I perceived she, too, was about to weep.

"Oh, brother," Sarah murmured, taking the child into her arms. I knew she understood the reason why we had chosen that name in particular. "Our mother and father would be so proud," she said now.

"As would our uncle have been," I responded, my voice taking on a hint of sadness. My smile then returned, as I saw the baby gradually make her way to John and then to Aife. Presently, my daughter began to whimper. In a moment Imogen would have to go back to Morwenna to have her first feed, who had agreed to nurse her. My heart then took on more joy at the thought of Imogen meeting Enid, my mother. I imagined standing on the royal balcony beside Evelyn, introducing our child formally to the rest of Gaeson.

Imogen was also a symbol, I reflected now, of the further union between Gaeson and Klumeck. She would, one day, inherit both kingdoms. As Sarah again took our daughter into her arms, I prayed our child would have the grace and wisdom for such a task. For now, though, I simply took in the joy of this moment, of becoming a father. As Sarah passed Immy back to Evelyn, my heart soared. It truly was a joy to see this wondrous change that my wife had now become a mother. It was something she had longed for almost as soon as we had wed.

The five of us merely stood there for a few more moments, simply watching Imogen wriggle. As we reflected upon the beauty of this child, I knew that though my parents and my uncle were gone, I still had the truest family I had ever known. My wife, my sister, my closest friends were all here. I gave a small smile then at this family, ever thankful that Aldred's poison had not divided us all, despite the Wolf making the rest of us question Evelyn's identity and trust.

I knew now, though, that this family did not exist only as individuals. There was a corporate nature to us, a kinship and trust that was unsurmountable. I knew that as long as we lived, we would love Imogen well, until we no longer drew breath. Indeed, the birth of my daughter sparked a hope for our people and our lands, a flame that even the strongest Bernician onslaught could not put out. That fire was the hope of peace, that I prayed would continue to spread. I hoped it would burn until at last Rheged was safe, as secure and tangible as the bond here between my closest kin. That, I concluded, was a fire worth celebrating and nurturing for as long as we lived.